Assumed Obligation

By Kara Louise

© 2001 by Kara Louise
© 2007 by Kara Louise

Cover image by Kara Louise
ISBN 978-1-4357-3283-4

Published by Heartworks Publication

Printed in the United States of America

Library of Congress Cataloging-in-Publication Data

Kara Louise
Assumed Obligation

Note from the author~

"Assumed Obligation" is the sequel to "Assumed Engagement,
a variation of Jane Austen's *Pride and Prejudice*.

I have taken the liberty of moving the time of this story to 1815,
when the Napoleonic Wars were over. It was imperative to the story
that Darcy and Elizabeth travel to France to visit the deaf school
in Paris, and they could not have travelled there as freely
when England and France were at war.

Again I must thank Mary Ann for her excellent editing skills.
I thank her immensely. She does a great job!

I owe all my inspiration to Jane Austen,
whose story and characters
continue to touch the hearts of people today.

As with my other stories, I hope you find this enjoyable.

Chapter 1

The waters from the great sea of the English Channel lapped up repeatedly against the shore. The sun had begun its ascent higher in the sky, but there was a persistent breeze that whipped at the strings of Elizabeth Darcy's bonnet. She held it down with one hand and had her other arm in that of her husband's, as they stretched their legs after their long carriage ride. It had been two days since they were pronounced husband and wife, and much of that time had been employed in travelling. It was good to be able to stroll about in the fresh outdoors.

Fitzwilliam and Elizabeth Darcy walked leisurely along the shore, gazing up at the massive stark white cliffs protruding out of the blue sea. Small white caps hurled themselves mercilessly at the sheer wall. And there, rigged to the dock, was the ship that would take them across the sea to the continent, where they would spend ten days in France.

Darcy's coachman, Winston, had delivered them by carriage to Dover, on the eastern coast of England, where they now walked and were delighting in the White Cliffs and the Dover Castle, which loomed high above them. Elizabeth repeatedly voiced her delight in viewing this picturesque prospect. The ship, which was to take them across the English Channel to France for their wedding journey, was not to leave for another hour, so they leisurely took in the sights around this eastern port.

Elizabeth enjoyed breathing in the distinctive salty air that permeated the coast. She felt that she could not be happier; with her husband on her arm and the anticipation of spending the next ten days with him in Paris. She dug her arm more deeply into her husband's at the mere thought of it.

A bit of a fog teased them, seemingly content to remain off shore, but occasionally stretching out one of its fingers to the mainland. The cool coastal breeze combined with the early morning chill brought a shiver to Elizabeth.

"Are you cold, my love?" asked Darcy, noticing her actions and pulling his arm out from hers and bringing it around her shoulder. "Would you care for my coat?"

"No, it actually feels quite refreshing," laughed Elizabeth, "compared to what it has been like at home." Back in Hertfordshire they had had some of the hottest days, especially on Jane and Charles' wedding day. This was unquestionably an improvement.

"Would you care for something to eat before we board the ship?"

"I should like that very much," answered Elizabeth.

They had stayed the night before in Darcy's London townhome, and a small basket filled with foods was sent along with them. They found a bench to sit upon and Darcy looked in the basket, announcing to Elizabeth what had been provided for them to eat.

"It appears that we have some apples, breads and cheeses, and some sort of cake. Does anything sound to your liking?"

"I think I shall have some bread and an apple."

Darcy pulled out two linen napkins, placing one on Elizabeth's lap and one on his. He handed Elizabeth her requested bread and fruit. Nestling her head against her husband's large frame, and taking small bites of the food in front of her, she thought back to their wedding night.

~~*

Darcy had made arrangements for them to stay at a bungalow in the far south of Hertfordshire their first night as husband and wife. He would not yield to Bingley's insistence that they stay at Netherfield. He politely but firmly declined. He did not wish to be anywhere near Netherfield or Longbourn! He wanted to be alone with his precious bride without any chance of being bothered.

They departed Netherfield in the late afternoon and arrived a little after dusk at a charming bungalow that Darcy had earlier secured for them. It was one of several which spread around the grounds that surrounded an inn. The bungalow had been meticulously prepared for their arrival with lit candles, flowers arranged around the room, (of course most of them were gardenias) and a plate of hors d'oeuvres and a selection of wines set out for them.

As their trunks were being carried in by Winston and Durnham, Elizabeth understandably felt a nervousness that compelled her to distract herself, and walked over to the plate of food that had been set out on a table. Without thought, she picked up one large, ripe strawberry from upon the plate. She found herself simply looking at it in her fingers, as she was really not very hungry. She could not determine whether it was lack of hunger or plain nerves that caused her hesitancy to eat. Darcy happened to glance over at her and noticed her hesitancy as she brought the fruit up, and he continued to watch in stirring amusement as she toyed with it around her lips. Unaware that she was the object of his distraction, she began to take only small nibbles on it. When she raised her eyes up, she met Darcy's amused stare. In a moment he was hastily walking toward her. Upon reaching her, he gently took hold of her wrist.

"If you do not wish to eat this, my dearest," bringing up her hand that held the food, "I shall oblige and eat it for you. But if you do wish to consume it yourself, please do so quickly. I do not think I can endure watching you a moment longer."

Elizabeth's heart had pounded as she slowly brought the strawberry up to his lips, and he took it in one bite. His eyes did not leave Elizabeth's face, until he abruptly remembered Winston and Durnham.

He turned to see that Winston had returned from taking their things into the bed chamber and was patiently awaiting further directions from him. Durnham remained in the room setting things out for the next day. Darcy quickly urged them both on. "That is good enough Winston. Durnham, I think that is all for the night. Thank you."

"Shall I put...?" began the manservant.

"No, no that is all, thank you."

Elizabeth nervously smiled at his apparent impatience. Darcy left Elizabeth's side to walk the two men to the door, and her eyes were brought down to his hand. She smiled when she noticed it. His right hand was tightened into a fist and he was furiously rubbing his thumb and finger together. She had often noticed him doing that when he appeared nervous or impatient. Certainly *he* would not be nervous tonight; that was *her* role!

Winston and Durnham excused themselves, wishing them a good night and confirming that they would see them in the morning. Then the two men set off for the room inside the inn that Darcy had procured for them.

~~*

Now, looking out at the great blue sea, a brisk gust of wind whipped at them both, bringing her back to the present. They both finished their small snack, and stood up to begin walking again.

They had departed the townhouse very early that morning to arrive in plenty of time for the ship's departure. As the sun had not even appeared when they had boarded the carriage hours earlier, Elizabeth had been content to quickly fall asleep in her husband's arms once they were settled in and on their way.

Now, as they continued their walk along the coast, watching the luggage being loaded, Elizabeth let out a big yawn. She leaned her head more deeply against her husband and sighed. Her thoughts continued to return to the two previous nights. How many times was it, she wondered, that one of them awakened and effectively managed to awaken the other? She smiled. She was not sure if every night would be like the last two nights. If they were, she was sure they would both suffer greatly from lack of sleep.

"Are you fatigued my dear? Is there anything you need?" asked Darcy.

"Nothing that a nice comfortable bed will not remedy."

Darcy raised his eyebrows in surprise and turned to look at her, noticing her already coloured cheeks. He lowered his lips to her ear and whispered, "Is that sleep you desire, my love, or could it be something else?" The teasing look in his eyes was mixed with an earnest passion.

"Sleep does actually sound quite appealing as I am quite tired. I think I shall attempt to get a little rest once on board the ship." Now she met his eyes with an enticing look. "Consequently, by this evening I will most likely no longer be tired and I think I shall have to find some diversion to occupy my..., I mean, our… time."

"I believe, according to the itinerary I have, that this evening does hold some free time available for… uh… such a diversion."

Elizabeth shivered again, but most likely not from the cool air that was surrounding her. They continued to walk along the coast at Dover with his arm securely around her and she felt the same unmistakable assurance and unfathomable comprehension that Darcy loved her very deeply and unselfishly. That she was the object of his affection never ceased to amaze her. Recollecting that she almost threw his love away grieved her. But what had happened between them brought about for her a deeper regard for this man who had continued to pursue her, even when she had given him every indication that she wanted nothing to do with him.

At length it was time for the passengers to embark the ship. Darcy and Elizabeth walked back over to Winston to bid him farewell. "Goodbye, Winston. I trust you will take good care of Georgiana as you return to Pemberley."

"I most certainly will. Goodbye, Sir. Goodbye, Mrs. Darcy. A pleasant journey to you both."

"Goodbye, Mr. Winston. Thank you so much for everything."

"We shall see you in ten days, then." Darcy turned, and taking his wife's arm, walked alongside her toward the ship.

As the two departed, Winston could not but feel that this was a good thing for his master. From the moment he met Elizabeth, not more than four months ago, he had been convinced of her sweet, pleasant, and lively character. He could tell she was a woman of integrity and compassion, especially noticed in the interaction between herself and his master's sister. When she had first come to Pemberley, Darcy was unconscious from a carriage accident. The engaging way in which she handled herself had been noticed by all the household staff. They knew there was some sort of history between Darcy and this young lady, but they knew not what. Little did they know that in a few months' time she would become the Mistress of Pemberley. They had given their hearty approval when it was announced.

Once on board the ship, Elizabeth and Darcy stood together at the rail, as it slowly sailed away from the dock. They took in the sights and watched as it sailed past the white cliffs. The breeze over the open waters was brisker and therefore it was cooler out here.

"If the winds continue in our favour, we shall be in France by dusk. Because of the fog, we most likely will not see the coast of France for some time. Shall we go inside where it is warmer, Lizbeth?"

"Oh, Will, let us stay outside as long as we can. The cliffs are too majestic a sight to not view from the deck." Suddenly there was a great sound from up above them as all the sails were unfurled and immediately the wind caught in them. The ship responded by picking up some speed. Elizabeth watched with great excitement. "Did you see that? Look at how beautiful those sails are!"

Darcy glanced up at the sails, but returned his gaze to his wife, as he felt she was more beautiful to look upon than any sail. He especially loved it when something delighted her. She found great pleasure and enjoyment in many things, even the simplest things, and he had come to delight in her more so because of that.

The wind, beating against them, increased in intensity as the ship picked up speed. It somehow caught Darcy's neckcloth, loosening its knot. Elizabeth turned to him and began to repair it, pulling out the pin, and reinserting it back in its intricate fold so it would hold. When she finished, she slowly brought her fingers down, pausing ever so slightly as she touched the buttons of his waistcoat.

Darcy had been watching Elizabeth, and as she peered up to him through her lashes, her thoughts returned again to two nights ago. The smile that came across her face in remembrance matched that of her husband's and she somehow knew that he was thinking back to that night as she was.

~~*

After Winston and Durnham left that night, Elizabeth changed in the dressing room into her silk gown. When she finished, she came out to meet her husband. He had removed his overcoat, vest, and neck cloth; the top two buttons on his shirt unbuttoned. He was sitting, in the process of removing his boots, when she stepped into the room to join him.

He immediately stood up and gazed upon her with complete abandon. As he took two large strides to meet her in the middle of the room, Elizabeth's eyes remained transfixed on his chest. Her mind went back to the night at Pemberley when she had clumsily struggled to unbutton his nightshirt because of his fever. Her attempts to do a simple task as unbuttoning a button had caused her much consternation.

Darcy had put his finger under her chin and lifted her face up so she would look at him. He assumed she was feeling rather shy and that was why she was unable to meet his eyes. But when her eyes came up, they were filled with much amusement. Darcy furrowed his brows in an attempt to discern what was causing this.

"What is going on inside that little head of yours, Lizbeth?"

She looked back down to his chest and timidly brought her fingers up to the next button of his shirt, which he had not yet undone. "Just a memory."

"Pray tell, of what?"

"Of the first time I did this," she answered as she nimbly took the button in her fingers and unbuttoned it.

Elizabeth noticed the abrupt change in his breathing as he struggled to say, "Sorry? You did *what*?"

She very softly answered, "Unbuttoned your shirt."

Darcy drew in a sharp breath as Elizabeth proceeded down to the next. "My dearest Lizbeth." He paused, making a vain attempt at self-control. "If you had ever engaged in this type of activity with me, be assured I would have a vivid memory of it."

Her fingers went to the next button, coyly meeting his gaze. "I fear you were not in any condition to recollect." She looked up at him and smiled. "It was when you had a fever and I had to open your nightshirt so I could wipe down your chest with cool cloths."

He slowly shook his head and closed his eyes. "Lizbeth, it is perhaps best that I never knew this until tonight, as it would have been one more thought of you that would have incessantly tormented me."

Elizabeth returned her focus to the next stubborn button, which upon release caused his shirt to fold down at the collar and revealed a pleasantly sculpted chest. Now it was Elizabeth's turn to take a deep breath. "I hope you will not think me imprudent when I tell you how often *I* have thought back to that night."

He pulled her close and suddenly her face was brushing up against him. She closed her eyes and could feel his heart pounding deep within. After a few moments he was able to whisper the words, "No, indeed I do not, Lizbeth. Indeed I do not."

~~*

Elizabeth eyed the neckcloth, bringing her back to the present and was only partially satisfied with her attempt at salvaging its knot. Her abilities in this arena would not compare to the exquisite aptness of his manservant Durnham. Darcy had decided that for the time they were to stay in France, he could do without him. And he knew that at the inns they were to visit, they could avail themselves of menservants and maids as needed. So Durnham had stayed behind in London.

When they had sailed quite a distance from the England shore, the newlyweds went down below to the small sitting room that Darcy had secured for them. The room was simply furnished with only a small sofa and chair. The two chose to sit together on the sofa, Elizabeth leaning her head in the crux of her husband's arm. The gentle rocking of the ship had increased some as they reached more open waters, but fortunately neither of them seemed unduly affected by it. And as the gentle rocking of the ship continued, Elizabeth and Darcy both succumbed to the relaxing movement and soon they both were fast asleep.

The two slept very soundly, waking only when some bells were rung above them. Upon waking, both required a few moments to realize where they were. Darcy stretched out his legs and one free arm in front of him.

Elizabeth stood with him and reached up to straighten her bonnet, only to discover that it had slid off and was lying against her back, held only by the ribbon around her chin. She reached back to pull it back up, but Darcy put his hand up to stop her.

"No, no, leave it down."

"Down?"

"Yes, I like it better this way." He cocked his head to one side, admiring her beauty.

Elizabeth reluctantly agreed, and looked in the small mirror that hung on the wall to check her hair. She repositioned some pins that had pulled loose and pulled up some errant strands of hair that had tried to sneak down.

They freshened up and ate a light snack that had been provided before going up. As they made their way back up the stairs to the deck, Elizabeth noticed a buzz of excitement coming from the crowd of people at the railing of the ship. When the Darcys made their way over to join the group, they could see land.

"Look, Will. There is France! I cannot believe it! This is so exciting!"

"Yes, I daresay I am all flutterings myself!" he said drolly.

Elizabeth laughed at his attempt at humour. "I shall not let you dampen my excitement about seeing France for the first time. I know you have been here before and it is all a common, everyday experience for you." She turned from him to the land they were approaching. "But this is brand new to me and I shall shout with glee at seeing the Notre Dame, taking a boat ride on the Seine River, and viewing Luxembourg Gardens and the Louvre."

"Lizbeth, it does not matter to me where I am, as long you are by my side. I could be lost in the sands of the Sahara desert or the frozen wastelands of the north, but as long as I had you by my side, I would be happy."

"Well, I am certainly glad, then, that Paris is where we are headed. You shall not have any doubt that I will enjoy every moment we are here!"

"*Every* moment? For that I am most pleasantly grateful!" He pulled her close, but did not look at her and see the askance glance she gave him. But he was indeed smiling.

As the ship approached land, the sun was making its descent toward the western horizon, shining its gold and red rays out across the sea like little fingers below it and a watercolour picture above it. Elizabeth had never seen such a beautiful sight - the sun setting on the ocean. She folded her arms on the rail, intently watching and enjoying this memorable scene.

Darcy again took notice of her pleasure in the setting of the sun. "I hope you are pleased with the sunset. I ordered it especially for you tonight, my love."

Elizabeth chuckled, "Yes, I like it very much! Did you order one for every night of our wedding journey?"

"Ahh, that I will not say. In that I will leave you to be surprised. We shall have to make sure we venture out at dusk each night to check, shall we not?"

Elizabeth took his large hand in hers and squeezed it. He leaned over and nuzzled his nose into her hair, enjoying the freedom from its bonnet and her scent that was more pleasing to him than the salty air. He put his other arm lightly around her back and coarsely whispered, "What would you do if I pulled you into my arms right now and kissed you in front of all these people?"

Elizabeth felt a tingling down her spine, and forced herself to not lean in to her husband, but to straighten up. "Will, you would not truly do such a thing!" Her mock indignation amused him. Under her breath she added, "You may save it for later! When we are alone!"

With a smile tugging at his mouth, without her knowledge, he placed his lips on the top of her head and kissed her.

The ship came into port at Calais, and as everyone left the ship, Elizabeth held tightly onto Darcy's arm. There was something both exciting, yet frightening about being in a foreign country. Suddenly almost everyone around them was speaking a foreign language. Elizabeth could speak a little French, but understood even less, especially when spoken by a native Frenchman. She suddenly realized how terrifying it would be to be here and not know the language. She was grateful that her husband was most proficient at speaking and understanding it.

They walked up to a line of waiting carriages, their drivers calling out in French and broken English that they were for hire. Darcy eyed the drivers and singled one out, a young man, and walked over to him. He spoke to him and introduced himself. It appeared to Elizabeth that her husband was making arrangements with him.

Darcy and the driver walked over to where they were unloading the passenger's luggage and Darcy pointed theirs out to them. He brought it over and the young man loaded it on the carriage.

Darcy introduced the coachman to Elizabeth. "Elizabeth, this is Jacques. Jacques, this is my wife, Mrs. Darcy."

Jacques smiled and uttered some words in French. Elizabeth understood him to say *pleasant… beautiful…* and *wife*. Elizabeth returned his smile, knowing that whatever he had said, it would have sounded most lovely to her ears. The French words seem to pour like honey from his lips.

Elizabeth tried her hand at French in returning thanks for the apparent compliment. "Merci beaucoup."

Jacques smiled and helped the two on board. He seemed impressed with his patron's choice of accommodations and knew that if he handled things right, he would get a big tip. And possibly an extended hire.

Before he closed the door, he spoke. "If you go on to Paris tomorrow, I would be most happy to oblige you with trip. If you tell me what time to be at hotel, I be there. I know Paris well and could tell you all best places to see. You probably know most famous places to go, but I know places that most tourists not aware of," he said in his broken English. "I have aunt there I can stay with so you not need worry about where I stay."

He did not wait for an answer, but closed the door, hoping to give the gentleman a chance to consider his offer.

Jacques drove very carefully through the streets of Calais. He concentrated on getting his patrons to the hotel without any discomfort or difficulty so they might think favourably on his offer. Inside the carriage, Darcy and Elizabeth had quite forgotten the young man's request, as Darcy had pulled Elizabeth close to him, wrapped his arms around her and lost himself in the scent of her hair. He began to slowly pull out the pins that had been holding it up. She was mindful that he was playing with her hair, but was not aware, until suddenly some of it came cascading down, what he had done.

"William!" She grabbed at her hair that had come loose. "Look what you have done! What will everyone think?"

"My dear, here in France *they* do not worry about what others think and neither should *you.* They enjoy life. They will look at you and see a beautiful lady who is with her husband who admires her." And with that he continued to pull out the pins until her hair was loose around her shoulders. When it was completely down, he took his fingers and ran them through her hair, loosening it from the hold that the pins had on it. Elizabeth silently admitted to herself that it felt much better down, but was not sure she was ready to go out in public with it like this, even if it was France.

The carriage travelled across the small city of Calais; the sights and sounds of this bustling port town going unnoticed by Jacque's patrons.

The carriage pulled up in front of a large inn, the Calais Magnifique. Jacques reined in the horses, and brought them and the carriage to a stop, instantly hopping down to open the door. He inwardly berated himself for his promptness as he discovered the couple in a very fervent embrace, completely oblivious to the fact that they had stopped and the door had opened.

He discreetly cleared his throat, but Elizabeth had already become aware of the carriage stopping and the subsequent opening of the door, and she was prudently trying to disengage herself from her husband's arms.

Jacques stood off to the side, politely averting his eyes, as Darcy sighed and slowly pulled himself away. When Darcy emerged from the carriage, he straightened himself up and smoothed out his clothes. He reached in for Elizabeth's hand and helped her out. Jacques looked at her and smiled, noting her change in hairstyle but being discreet enough not to mention it.

Jacques went around to the back to remove the luggage and carried it inside the inn. They walked toward the front desk, admiring the elegant room with its ornamental gilding and fine polished brass. Jacques followed them with their luggage. When Darcy procured the key, they made their way to their room.

Upon reaching the room, Darcy opened the door, and Jacques brought the luggage in and set it down. "Is there anything else you need, Sir?"

"Jacques," Darcy began. "If you would be so kind as to remain down at your carriage while we get settled. Then, would you take us to the very best restaurant in town? We are quite hungry and would like to eat some place that has the finest food and a pleasant atmosphere."

"Sir," Jacques replied. "I be most happy to convey you in my carriage to best restaurant. But as it is located across street, I must decline. I believe you can walk across easily." With that he bowed.

Darcy pulled out some money and handed it to the young man. "Thank you. Now, can you be here at eight in the morning?"

"Sir?"

"You said you would be willing to take us to Paris and remain there as our driver?"

"Oui! Yes!"

"Then be here at eight in the morning."

"Merci, Sir, thank you very much! And may I wish you and your beautiful wife to have wonderful night!"

Darcy looked from him to Elizabeth and then back. "Thank you, Jacques. And perhaps you should make it nine."

Jacques politely bowed, and with a lighter gait exited the room and closed the door.

Elizabeth looked at her husband. "What was that all about?"

"I knew that the best place to eat here was at LeMieux, and it is situated across the street. I was giving him a little test to see what he would do. Since he did not insist in driving us somewhere else, I figured he was good and honest, and we could hire him and his carriage to convey us to Paris and take us around while we are there."

Darcy brought his arms around Elizabeth. "Now, my dear, as much as I would like to continue where we left off in the carriage, I fear my stomach is making some very loud demands. Are you hungry?"

"Yes, very."

"Then let us go eat." He reached down and gently kissed her, bringing both his hands up and letting his fingers saunter through her long hair. "But then again…"

Elizabeth gently pushed him away. "First I think we must eat."

Darcy slipped his hand around Elizabeth's arm and they walked out. As they passed once more through the entryway, Elizabeth marvelled again at the grandeur of it. A huge chandelier hung from the centre, its hundreds of candles flickering their light around the room. The wooden floors throughout the lobby were graced with area rugs that looked as though they had come from Asia, with very intricate woven patterns. Chairs and sofas had been placed around upon which guests could lounge.

Darcy turned to her. Noticing the look of admiration on her face, he asked, "Are you pleased with it?"

"Yes, very much. I am not quite sure I will want to leave this place tomorrow morning."

"I am quite certain, my dear, that you will be as happy with our accommodations in Paris. Besides, we shall come back here and stay one night before our return to England."

Darcy and Elizabeth then proceeded across the street to eat. The little restaurant was dimly lit with dark furnishings and fine linens gracing each table. A trio of men played romantic melodies on violins as the diners ate. The air was filled with the aromas of different foods, causing the two of them to realize how hungry they were. The menus were brought to both of them and Darcy conversed with the waiter in French. He then returned the menus.

"What did you order us? I only understood the word potato."

Darcy laughed. "That is exactly what I ordered for you -- a potato." He shrugged his shoulders.

Elizabeth smiled at her husband's attempt at humour. For most of the months that she had been acquainted with this man, he had seemed aloof, sombre and acutely arrogant. To now see him tease, smile, and laugh warmed her heart. She could not help but return his smile.

He took her hand in his, and wrapped his other hand around them both, inattentively rubbing the back of her hand with his thumb. She smiled softly, as she thought back to Jane's wedding, and how this little nervous action of his drove her to distraction.

"What do you find so amusing, Lizbeth?"

"I am enjoying being with you, my dear, and enjoying all your idiosyncrasies."

"Sorry? What idiosyncrasies would you be referring to?"

"Why that you always rub your thumb and fingers together when you are anxious about something. But, if my hand happens to be in the way…" Elizabeth glanced down at it, "…as it is now, your thumb rubs my hand. I believe you are not even aware of it!"

Darcy looked down at his hand and shook his head in disagreement. "I do no such thing! Perhaps I like the touch of your hand."

Now it was Elizabeth's turn to laugh. "I have been watching you do it all evening, but I will give you the benefit of the doubt tonight. I shall let you think whatever you like about why you do it."

"Thank you." Darcy looked at Elizabeth and smiled, making a mental note that she was a most observant and precise studier of persons and she knew him, oh too well. He had to admit to himself that she was right. He *was* anxious. Although it was an eager anxiousness, he did not know how long it would be before he did not feel the butterflies and anxious anticipation of their nights together. But then, he hoped he would never get to the point of feeling impassive about it.

Chapter 2

Netherfield

Georgiana Darcy opened her eyes slowly and quickly snapped them back closed as the bright sun coming through the window assailed them. She waited momentarily, this time burying her head into her pillow before opening them again. Rubbing her eyes with her hands, she slowly lifted her head to look at the room about her. She was in one of the rooms at Netherfield, a guest of Charles and Jane, and as her mind wandered back to the previous day, she smiled, as she recollected her brother's and Elizabeth's wedding. To this young sixteen-year-old girl who idolized her older brother, it had seemed the most perfect wedding. She could not be happier with his choice for a wife and the woman who would henceforth be her sister.

It had been a busy day and a late night, and she wondered if anyone else would have yet arisen. She glanced over to the small clock on the mantel above the hearth and saw that it was eight thirty. Certainly someone would be up. She sat her tall, but slender form up, dislodging herself from the light blanket that covered her this warm summer morning. She knew she could call for a maid to help her dress, but wanted some time alone, so she went to the chair that was placed in front of a small dresser and mirror, and sat down in front of it. She picked up her brush and began brushing her straight, blond hair, then proceeded to put it up with a few strategically placed pins.

She poured water from a blue porcelain pitcher into its matching bowl and rinsed her face and hands. It felt refreshing and soothing and helped her shake off the effects of sleep. She went into the dressing room, selected a canary yellow polished cotton dress, and made herself ready to present herself downstairs.

Quietly making her way down the long, wooden staircase, she turned toward the dining room. She passed the large ballroom; empty now, save for remnants of ribbons and flowers that had decorated the room the day prior. She took in a deep breath as she saw the gardenias, savouring the scent of those flowers so special to her, her brother, his wife, and, as she recently found out, her late mother.

The newlyweds departed in the evening and it was decided that Georgiana would remain on at Netherfield for a few additional days. The young lady eagerly looked forward to remaining here a few additional days, hoping to form a better acquaintance with Elizabeth's three younger sisters, with whom she had spent very little time since arriving in Hertfordshire a month earlier.

She tiptoed across the hall downstairs, crossing over toward the closed door to the dining room. She thought she heard voices coming from inside and hoped that it was Charles or Jane. As she drew closer, she realized most likely that neither were there, due to the direction the discourse was going.

"Louisa, I cannot bear to remain here any longer! Now that these tedious weddings are over, I must be on my way! We must consider leaving this very morning!"

"Caroline, it would appear so sudden. What would Charles think?"

"I really do not care! I have remained here long enough! I do not think I can bear this insipid country village any longer. I am in need of some pleasant distractions, which the society of Hertfordshire cannot satisfy. We can go to your townhome in London until I decide what to do."

"You are more than welcome to travel with us to our home, Caroline. But are you sure you wish to leave Netherfield today?"

"The sooner the better! Charles has his little wife to help him out with the place here. All the guests here now are inconsequential to me, being solely *Mr. Darcy's* family and acquaintances. Most of them are staying another day or two. We must take our leave today!"

Georgiana easily heard Miss Bingley's sarcastic tone as her brother's name was mentioned.

"If you are certain, we can make every effort to leave some time today. Do you think we could somehow manage that, dear?"

Georgiana stood outside the door and continued to listen, but did not hear the reply. She believed she only heard a grunt.

"Good!" was Caroline's reply. "There is nothing left for me to do here! I only wish… Oh, why do things never turn out like you wish them to?"

Georgiana heard the forceful meeting of a piece of silverware against a plate. The sudden sound of a chair being abruptly pushed back startled her and she stepped away from the door a few steps. As the sound of angry footsteps drew closer, she began walking toward the door, as if she had just come down.

"Why dear Georgiana," cried Caroline with an artificial smile. "If you will please excuse me, I am sorry but I shall not be able to dine with you this morning. You see, the Hursts have invited me to stay with them at their townhome for a while and I must get ready as we are to leave this very day."

Caroline quickly moved past her and Georgiana thought back to all the times Caroline would simply hover about her, unduly praising her, trying to flatter her, and incessantly referring to herself as her close friend. It was interesting that all that now seemed to have changed. She smiled to herself, with an inaudible *Thank goodness!*

Walking into the dining room, Georgiana found the Hursts still dining. Mr. Hurst was devouring what was still left on his plate in a most ungentlemanlike manner. Mrs. Hurst seemed to be picking at her food.

"Good morning," Georgiana said politely.

"Oh, good morning, Georgiana. How are you this fine morning?" Mrs. Hurst at least seemed civil towards her.

"I am well. And you?"

Mr. Hurst grunted in between bites and Louisa Hurst replied to her that they were both well. Georgiana took a seat at the end of the table and hoped that Charles and Jane would come down soon. As much as she admired Charles and Jane, it was the company of his sisters that heightened her reserve. Whereas she flourished in the presence of Elizabeth, she floundered in the presence of Caroline and Louisa.

"Miss Bingley informs me that you all are leaving," she spoke quietly and with great effort.

"Yes, my dear. We will be leaving as soon as everything is readied. We do not want to overextend our welcome here. We believe Charles and Jane would wish a little peace and quiet and some privacy. They have had little of either since returning from their wedding journey."

"Yes." It was true that Charles and Jane, having married three weeks prior, left on a ten day journey, only to return in the midst of final arrangements for Darcy's and Elizabeth's wedding. There was little Charles and Jane had to do, as most of the details were already taken care of, but as the wedding breakfast was at Netherfield, and most of Darcy's guests invited to stay there, it had been unusually hectic.

Georgiana looked at the selection of foods in front of her on the table and decided she would enjoy eating right now more than conversing. She helped herself to some fruit and bread.

After a few minutes of eating in silence, Charles and Jane came down and joined Georgiana and the Hursts. Georgiana's face lit up as they entered the room. She had greatly enjoyed getting to know her new sister-in-law and was grateful that she also felt very comfortable in her presence. She discovered that Jane's quiet demeanour was very complementary to her own.

"Good morning, Georgiana!" beamed a smiling Charles. "Good morning Louisa, good morning, Hurst."

He was rewarded with another grunt from Hurst, and a good morning from Louisa.

Jane came to Georgiana, putting her arms around her. "Good morning, Georgiana. Did you sleep well?"

"Yes, thank you."

Charles and Jane took their seats at the table. Charles looked at the young girl and said to her, "Jane tells me that you are going to be visiting Longbourn today to spend some time with your other new sisters."

"Yes, I am looking forward to being with Mary, Kitty, and Lydia. Since coming here, I have had little opportunity to spend time alone with them."

"Now, Georgiana, remember that they are nothing like my angel, Jane, nor are they like Elizabeth." He laughed as he gave her this admonition and brought his arm around his wife, patting her on the shoulder.

Jane took the young girl's hand in hers and smiled. "Do not pay any attention to my husband. He likes to tease so. They are all very sweet girls."

"I shall enjoy my time with them, I am quite sure."

Louisa had finished all she was eating and set down her fork. "Charles, Caroline and I have talked, and we shall all be leaving this morning. She would like to go back to town for a while, so she will be staying with us. She is upstairs getting ready to leave, as we speak."

"I hope you do not feel as though you have to leave. You are welcome to remain here as long as you wish." Bingley assured her.

"Charles, you are too kind, but I fear country life is beginning to wear on Caroline. I do not believe she is suited to life here."

"But…" Charles began.

Jane put her hand out and placed it on Charles' hand, patting it gently. "Charles, not everyone enjoys being so removed from city life. I can understand her wanting a change."

"So, you are all leaving this morning?"

"Yes, we talked about it last night and then again this morning. It is settled."

"I shall inform Metcalf, then, that you are leaving and to make the proper arrangements."

As soon as Georgiana heard this, she breathed a sigh of relief. She was hoping Charles would not talk them out of leaving. She would feel much more comfortable here without Caroline's presence looming over the place.

The Hursts and Caroline were quickly packed and had left Netherfield by eleven that morning. Georgiana spent that time talking with Jane and Mrs. Annesley, her governess. In the afternoon, she was taken, along with Jane, by carriage to Longbourn, where she was to spend the rest of the day in companionship with her new sisters.

As she and Jane entered the modest Bennet home, she was greeted effusively by Mrs. Bennet.

"Come in, dear Jane. Come in dearest Georgiana. Was that not the most beautiful wedding yesterday? I dare say that I have not seen a finer one, excepting of course, yours and Charles', Jane. But the flowers yesterday, were not the gardenias most heavenly? They had the most beautiful scent! And Mr. Darcy, is he not the finest husband for our Lizzy?"

Georgiana was grateful that Mrs. Bennet did not allow enough time between all her questions to require an answer. She simply nodded as Jane gently took her mother's arm. "Mamma, I believe Georgiana would like to spend some time with the girls. Do you know where they are?"

"Of course! They are all in the sitting room. Hill, will you show Miss Darcy the way."

"Thank you," replied Georgiana.

Georgiana was grateful for this opportunity to talk with her new sisters and was hoping she would find a bonding friendship with one of the younger girls more her age. Georgiana came to the sitting room where Mary was reading and

Lydia was working with some ribbons and flowers to decorate a bonnet. Kitty was sitting forlornly at one of the windows looking out.

"Georgiana!" cried Lydia, even before she was announced.

Georgiana smiled timidly as the youngest of the sisters came running up to her. "Good afternoon Lydia." She looked to the others sisters and greeted them also. By the expression on their faces, it appeared to Georgiana that Mary was inwardly berating Lydia, and that Kitty was upset about something. Obviously, something had transpired before she arrived that elated Lydia but was not as agreeable to the other two girls.

She soon found out what it was.

"Georgiana, I have the most exciting news to tell you!" Lydia grabbed Georgiana's hand and pulled her over to a chair where she motioned for her to sit. "I am to go to Brighton!" She looked over to Kitty as if in triumph. "As the particular guest of the Forsters!"

Georgiana looked a little puzzled. "Brighton?"

"Yes, where the ____ militia went to! They had been here in Meryton, and we got to know so many of the officers. I was so distressed when they left! But now I shall see all those handsome officers again! Denny! Wickham! Chamberlayne!"

Georgiana's heart began pounding and she reactively brought her hands up to her now warm face, covering her mouth. She recalled Lydia's outburst the evening they dined at Longbourn about how handsome Wickham was, and realized the youngest Bennet sister had no inclination of his true character.

Mary, seeing Georgiana's reaction, began to comment. "I can see from Miss Darcy's response, that she, too, must be appalled at this very impolitic course of action. A woman must be very careful with…"

"Oh, Mary! Georgiana is just envious! As Kitty is!" interrupted Lydia.

Kitty looked at her in anger. "Lydia, I am not envious. I would not be interested in going with you even if they had asked me." Tears came to her eyes and she looked away.

"Ah ha! I hardly believe that!" Lydia beamed at her and turned back to Georgiana. "I shall be leaving on the morrow! Mamma is so happy for me as well!"

Georgiana felt a dread rise up in her and she knew, as distressing as this was going to be to her, she needed to talk to Lydia -- alone!

Georgiana did not want to draw attention to her going off alone with Lydia, so she searched for a way to secure some time by herself with her. She quickly came up with an idea.

"I only have a little bit of time today to spend with the three of you, and I would take much pleasure in getting to know each of you a little better. Do you suppose that I could have some time alone with each of you, and then we can all visit together after that?"

Lydia squealed that it seemed like a fine idea. She was so looking forward to telling her all about her plans and was more than happy to do it without the sermonic platitudes of Mary, nor the whining objections of Kitty. She wrapped her arm around Georgiana's and looked to the other girls and announced, "I am first!"

The two decided to walk outside, and Georgiana prayed for the words to say and the courage to say them. Georgiana's heart was pounding as she knew what she had to say would not make Lydia happy and would cause herself much shame. She remembered Elizabeth's words to her that she should not worry about what others thought when she had something to say. And she knew that this was something she *had* to say for Lydia's own good.

Georgiana did not want to appear that this was the only thing she wanted to talk to Lydia about, so at first they discussed Lydia's interests and accomplishments. Lydia had never learned to play an instrument; only Jane, Elizabeth and Mary had been given lessons. By the time Kitty and Lydia came along, things had become somewhat lax around the Bennet household and they were never encouraged, nor expected, to take any musical lessons.

Georgiana did find out that she enjoyed decorating bonnets, embellishing them, as well as embellishing the dresses that were bought or made for her, or handed down from one of her elder sisters. No, she did not sew herself. She did a small bit of needlework and read even less. Georgiana was soon under the impression that Lydia's main interests were officers. As much as she tried to steer her away from talking about them, Lydia always found a way to go back to the subject of handsome men in redcoats.

"Oh, I have been so bored these past few months with the militia gone. To be sure the weddings were nice and all, but they would have been so much better if the men in their redcoats were there. Do you not think they would have been precisely what was needed to liven things up a bit?"

Georgiana weakly smiled, not even knowing how to begin to break into her exuberance.

Lydia tightened her grip on Georgiana's arm. "I think those men in the militia can dance so much better than anyone else here, everything would have been so much more fun!"

"I…uh…" Georgiana stopped walking and turned to look at Lydia. "Lydia, there is something I need to tell you before you leave for Brighton."

Lydia cocked her head at the seriousness of Georgiana's tone and noticed that her face grew flushed. She felt a wave of fear course through her, wondering whether Georgiana would be of the same mind and disposition as Mary and would begin giving her sermonic platitudes against it.

"What is it?" Lydia asked cautiously.

"I must tell you…warn you…about one particular officer." She looked down, but then forced herself to look back up. "Mr. Wickham."

"Mr. Wickham! What is there to warn me about *him?*"

Georgiana swallowed, her mouth turning very dry. "He is not what you think. He is not what he appears."

"But we all know Wickham is friendly, and fun, and…"

"Lydia, I have known him all my life. He grew up with our family." She turned her eyes to the ground again, as she tried to summon the strength to continue. "Last year, he deceived me and tried to talk me into eloping with him. I am ashamed to admit that I agreed. I was only fifteen. If my brother had not come when he did, I would have made a terrible mistake. He only wanted to marry me so he could inherit my fortune and have revenge on my brother." Here she looked back up at Lydia. "If he had married me at all."

Lydia, for one time in her life, stood speechless. "I cannot believe it!"

"Oh, please do believe it! He is not to be trusted! He says one thing but does another. He is only looking for an easy way to make a fortune. He lives his life by gambling and building up debts. And he has spent his adult life looking for some young, wealthy girl to marry, solely for her fortune."

Lydia laughed. "Well, I guess that would certainly leave me out, then!"

Georgiana took her hand. "Except for the fact that you are now my brother's sister. Mr. Wickham may try something deceitful through you to extort money from him. There are many reasons he may still seek revenge against my brother. Please be careful Lydia. Do not trust him. No matter what he says."

Lydia saw the earnestness in her eyes and promised she would. They walked back to the house, and talked of other things. Before they walked in, Georgiana stopped her. "Lydia, I know you will have a good time with your friends. But please, do not share with anyone what I have shared with you unless you really need to. As you can imagine, I am quite ashamed of what I almost did. I only shared it with you because I felt it was so important for you to realize what Mr. Wickham is really like."

Lydia promised that her secret was safe with her.

They went inside and Georgiana asked Mary to join her next. Instead of going for a walk with her, they went up to her room. Mary showed Georgiana her library of sermon books, philosophy books, and doctrinal commentaries. She had a miniature library in her own room! Georgiana now understood a little bit more about her by looking at the books she surrounded herself with.

"Mary, have you read all these books?" asked Georgiana.

"Not all of them all the way through. But I have made it a practice to read something from one of these books every day and make a practical application of it to my life."

"That is quite an achievement."

"Thank you." Mary smiled. "I do not believe one can go through life without basing it on some fundamental principle of truth. Do you not agree?"

Georgiana smiled as she knew she could agree with her on that point, but was hoping she would not engage her in a conversation that was so philosophically deep that she would be lost. Georgiana answered her. "I think it is very prudent to know what truths guide your life, the decisions you make, and the actions you take. Yes I do agree."

"I thought so." Mary said triumphantly. "I see so little of that these days. People say and do things on the whim of the moment. That is why there is so much inconstancy."

"Mary, do you like to do anything else besides read?" Georgiana tried to change the subject.

"I love my music. I love to play the piano and sing."

Georgiana nodded as she recalled hearing of her less than proficient musical abilities. "Someday you must play and sing for me."

"I would be most happy to."

They talked for some time on their preferences of music. They actually both liked similar music, mostly classical, although Mary's favourites extended more toward the intense and melancholy tunes. Georgiana encouraged her to faithfully practice and discovered that one of the reasons Mary was not proficient on the pianoforte was that she was always trying a new piece of music out before she had mastered the ones she should have been practicing.

At length, Georgiana thanked Mary for the time spent with her. Mary stood up with her and they proceeded back to the sitting room where Kitty was still in a deep despondency. When Kitty saw them walk in, her face brightened, and she asked if she could take her time with Georgiana outside.

Georgiana heartily agreed.

They walked deep into the yard and sat down together on a bench. There was silence between the two. Georgiana was at a loss as to what to say. Kitty did not speak as she was still quite despondent over the matter of Lydia leaving.

Finally Georgiana broke the silence. "Are you particularly unhappy about not being able to go to Brighton, Kitty?"

"It is not merely that." Kitty took in a deep breath and shook her head. "So much has happened this past month. Both my elder sisters are married and gone. Lydia will be away most likely for the remainder of the summer. That will leave me with Mary. I am dreadfully anticipating being here and being very lonely."

Georgiana looked up at her and smiled. "I believe I know a little how you feel. You have been very fortunate to have four sisters. What fun you must have had growing up. For most of my life I have only had my brother, and he is so much older, and was often gone, so I know what it is to feel lonely." Georgiana turned her eyes off to the distance as she continued. "As much as I love your sister Elizabeth, and look forward to her being my sister, I know that things will be different from now on between my brother and myself. I know that the two of them will need their time alone, and I wonder if I might at times feel somewhat in the way." She turned back to look at her. "Kitty, I should very much like it if you and I could correspond with each other. I believe we could help each other get through these next few weeks."

Kitty allowed a smile to grace her face. "Oh, Georgiana. I think that is a wonderful idea! I should enjoy that very much! Lydia has told me that she would write, but I really doubt that she will take the time to do it."

"I shall make every effort to be faithful in writing you, Kitty."

Georgiana was pleased with Kitty's eagerness and willingness to be her friend. She had sensed in the days since arriving in Hertfordshire that she and Kitty were very compatible. She noticed that Kitty often followed Lydia, but in her heart felt that she needed some gentle prodding in the right direction. She wanted to be a friend who could do that.

They sat and talked of other things for quite a while. Kitty was drawn by her quiet, but caring nature. There was something about her that touched her, and although Georgiana was not as lively as Lydia, Kitty felt they could be good friends. She looked forward to writing to her.

As they were about to join the others, Georgiana made the hopeful suggestion that Kitty might possibly be able to come to Pemberley some time and visit. She would have to wait to talk to her brother and Elizabeth about it, but hoped they would agree to her scheme. This pleased Kitty to no end, and she was actually pleasant for the rest of the day.

When their visit was over, and Jane and Georgiana returned to Netherfield, the young girl shared with Jane about her talk with Lydia.

"Oh, Georgiana, I was so concerned when Mamma told me what Lydia was doing. I know it was not easy for you to do, but I trust that knowing the truth about Mr. Wickham will hopefully keep Lydia out of trouble."

"I hope so, Jane. I truly hope so."

Chapter 3

France

Darcy and Elizabeth promptly came down from their room at quarter before nine and found Jacques waiting for them.

"Good morning, Sir."

"Good morning, Jacques. If you will go for our luggage, we can be on our way."

Jacques went immediately to retrieve their luggage.

Darcy and Elizabeth had eaten a filling meal before leaving their room in search of Jacques. Darcy was anxious to see how prompt this young coachman would be. He happily found him waiting for them at least fifteen minutes before the time he had been asked to come.

The Darcys walked around outside the carriage, enjoying the fresh morning air, and giving their legs one last opportunity to stretch before they were confined in the carriage for the full day's journey to Paris. They were grateful for the blue sky that promised a most pleasant day's travel.

Now in the daylight, Elizabeth noticed with fascination the detail on Jacques carriage. There was an emblem of some sort on the door. It was quite large; a pair of crossed swords and in between the two blades, a flame. The wood of the carriage was a highly polished dark wood with polished brass railings and racks along the sides, top and back. Elizabeth made a mental note to ask Jacques about his carriage when she had the opportunity.

The area around the inn was bustling with people, either preparing to leave for Paris, as Elizabeth and Darcy were, or preparing to embark on a ship that would take them back across the channel to England, as they would in a little over a week. Carriages, such as Jacques, were being loaded and people milled around waiting.

Darcy made little attempt to hide his affections for Elizabeth, winding his fingers through one lock of hair she let fall freely. When she made no attempt to discourage him, he turned to her, and raised his hand to the back of her neck, reaching his fingers into the nape of her neck and into her hair. He looked into her eyes, waiting for some objection, and when there was none, he leaned over and gently kissed her on the lips.

He took her a little by surprise, and she blushed, but she forced herself not to look around at the people walking past them to see if anyone was watching. Whereas she enjoyed the attention and affection of her husband, she was still not certain whether such a public display was acceptable, even here in France.

"Will, what am I to do with you?" Elizabeth laughed nervously.

"What is this? I always thought you were the impetuous one!" He smiled, underscoring his statement by bringing his arms around her and locking them behind her back. "Do you dislike my attentions?"

"May I remind you, Sir, that while I am extremely fond of your attentions, I have not had considerable experience in this area while in the midst of a crowd of people!"

Darcy only shrugged. "Wait until we get to Paris. I believe you shall feel differently about it there!"

Elizabeth tried to hide the smile that was forming on her face. "Yes, well Paris is quite a distance from here so for now, we have a long ride ahead of us."

Darcy's eyes lit up. "Yes, it should be a *very* long ride. And with only the two of us in the carriage!" He raised one of his eyebrows as he said this.

Elizabeth reacted with feigned shock at his statement. "Fitzwilliam!"

"What did I say? I was only stating a fact! I cannot help it if *you* misconstrue what I say!"

"Yes, well, this time it was in the way you said it as well as the accompanying look on your face!"

"Oh, I see. And what, exactly, did you surmise me to mean, then?" He asked, now his words accompanied by a smirk.

Elizabeth was grateful Jacques had returned with their luggage and prevented her from having to answer. Darcy went back and helped the young man load and secure their bags. "Merci, Mr. Darcy, but I think I can do it."

"It is no trouble at all," Darcy answered as he handed Jacques one of the bags.

When they walked toward the front, Elizabeth stopped Jacques. "Tell me, Jacques. What is the meaning of your emblem?"

"Oh, that. It was family crest that I designed for myself and had it made for my carriage."

"You say you designed it?"

"Yes, I always wanted a family crest, but I did not really have a family."

"What? No family?" Elizabeth was flabbergasted.

"I was orphaned as a child and was raised in an orphanage."

Elizabeth was amazed at how matter of fact he stated this. How could one be so casual about not having any family? But suddenly she thought of something.

"But Jacques, you told us you have an aunt living in Paris."

"Oh, *oui,* she is much older and could not raise me on her own. She is the only known family I have."

Darcy then interjected. "So you said you designed the family crest?"

"*Oui.* I wanted swords to represent power. In my case, power to overcome circumstances I born into, and flames represent moving ahead with my life."

"It is beautiful, Jacques, and a wonderful tenet to guide your life," Elizabeth told him.

Jacques opened the door, helping Elizabeth in and then Darcy. "I thought we stop in Amiens, which is about half way there. If you have need for anything, just tap on front of carriage or holler out at me."

"*Merci,* Jacques. Thank you."

The carriage pulled away from the hotel at precisely nine o'clock. They both had brought books along to read, but Elizabeth enjoyed watching the scenery pass by through the window. She was not sure when she would have the opportunity to come back and wanted to see and enjoy every bit of France that she could. It also gave her a chance to think about what Jacques had told them. He certainly seemed to have overcome his circumstances in life. He did not appear bitter, had a very good outlook on life, and seemed to be a most conscientious worker.

As Darcy read, he kept one hand on his book and the other combing through Elizabeth's locks of hair, and occasionally reaching over to her in their solitude, displaying his affections to his lovely wife.

~~*

Their short stop in Amiens allowed them to stretch their legs, and have an enjoyable meal at an inn that Jacques recommended. They were ushered into a well lit room that boasted red checked tablecloths and fresh flowers on the tables. The servings for the day were hand written on a board that they passed as they walked in.

A woman came by and asked what they would like to order. Darcy knew they would be travelling until dark, so they decided to eat heartily. They began their meal with fresh fruit in heavy syrup, then had a plate of sliced pork roast, potatoes and beans. They ended with pudding. When they finished, Darcy ordered a box of food to be sent along with them that they could eat in the carriage later.

Jacques spent the time changing out horses for the carriage and ate some food he had packed for himself back in Calais. He was ready and waiting for the Darcys when they returned from eating. Jacques had them settled in quickly, and they were soon off again to Paris, travelling as expeditiously as possible.

They arrived in Paris well after eight o'clock in the evening. Elizabeth had fallen asleep late in the afternoon, but as soon as they reached the city limits she was wide awake and watching the sights as they drove through town. She was delighted with the new sights, sounds, and even the smells of this city. Darcy only smiled at her obvious pleasure.

It took them nearly another hour to reach the hotel where they were to stay the next week while in Paris. It was larger than the inn in Calais and Elizabeth was quite awed by its stately presence. It appeared to be three floors high and the length of the whole block.

Jacques unloaded their luggage and they walked inside. The lobby of the hotel was open all the way to the ceiling of the third floor. Railings on each of the two levels above allowed guests to look out over the lobby from the second and third floor. A chandelier, grander than the one in Calais, lit the room. Little prisms hung from every candle that was lit.

Darcy went up to the desk and talked to the manager while Elizabeth took it all in. A plush, red carpet covered the floors, except in the centre, where there was a square of beautiful marble. The wallpaper covering the walls and the velvet coverings on the furniture gave an overall warmth and grandeur to this room.

They were to be on the third floor. Darcy took his wife's arm and led her to the stairs, Jacques following with the luggage. They came to the room and Darcy opened the door. Elizabeth could barely contain herself when she saw it. It was, she was quite certain, almost the size of four rooms at Longbourn.

"Thank you, Jacques. I will not keep you, as I am sure you are tired. Does your aunt live close by?"

"It would be about a twenty minute carriage ride. What time should I come tomorrow?"

Darcy looked at Elizabeth. "What do you think, dear? We can do whatever you like tomorrow."

"Is there anything within walking distance from the hotel?"

"*Oui,* yes, Madame Darcy. The River Seine is beyond the hotel, you can walk along it, visit shops, and there are a couple of museums."

Darcy then interjected. "Why do you not come back in the afternoon around three. We shall do some sightseeing on foot in the morning and then use the carriage into the evening."

"*Merci,* Monsieur." Jacques quickly left. "Good evening."

"Oh, Will. This is too beautiful!" She walked over to a chair and brushed her hands across its back. "Everything is so elegant!"

"And if it were still daylight outside, I would show you the most beautiful view. I am sure you will like that, too. But we shall have to wait for morning to feast our eyes on it."

He walked up to Elizabeth and cupped her face with his hands. "And now, dearest Lizbeth, you are the only thing I would like to feast my eyes on."

~~*

The heavy drapes in the room kept out almost all of the natural sunlight the next morning. Darcy and Elizabeth, both naturally early risers, were surprised when they each awoke and found it to be close to eight o'clock. Darcy was up first and slipped on his robe and slippers. He opened the drapes slightly to let a little bit of light in and began reading, not wanting to awaken his wife. He turned the chair he was sitting in so it was facing her and he could easily look up and admire her beauty.

Her long hair was splayed out across the pillows and she had the most content look on her face. It almost seemed to him that she was on the verge of a smile all the while asleep. She eventually began to move and slowly reached out to stretch. When she opened her eyes, it took her a moment to get her bearings.

"Good morning, darling," Darcy whispered. He walked over to her and sat beside her on the bed.

"Good morning. Did I oversleep?"

"We both did. I have actually been up about a half hour. The drapes in this room keep it exceptionally dark in here. I think neither of us realized it was morning."

"It also did not help that we had a late night last night."

"Is that a complaint I hear?" He took his finger and trailed it down her neck and shoulder.

"No, I was only stating a fact." Elizabeth repeated his words from yesterday morning.

Darcy pulled back the covers and handed her robe to her. Now, if you get yourself up, I want to show you the view our room affords."

Elizabeth slipped on her robe and walked with him over to the window. Darcy opened the drapes the rest of the way and the two of them were afforded a beautiful view of the Seine River. A bridge below them crossed across it. The sun glistened on the water and reflected back up to them. Elizabeth looked out to the left and noticed a small flower garden, and off to the right, across the river, was a street filled with small shops.

She sighed. "I think I shall like it here very much!"

"There is one more thing you need to see and I think we still may have some time. But you need to hurry and get dressed."

Elizabeth eagerly accommodated his request and he was pleased when she promptly returned from the dressing room with part of her hair pulled up and twisted, but even more of it loose and falling gracefully down her back. He did not say anything but reached over and as a token of affection, entwined her hair with his fingers and pulled them through all the way to the end. The two stepped out of their room, but instead of walking toward the stairs, Darcy brought them over to the railing that looked over the lobby. Elizabeth gasped when she saw the lobby. The rising sun was hitting the chandelier with all of its prisms, and little rainbows were reflected all over the walls.

Elizabeth gasped, "Oh, my!"

"This only happens in the morning when the sun shines through that front window. The sun, hitting each prism, and each facet in it, is bent, and elicits a beautiful band of colours, like a rainbow. Once the sun goes up beyond that window, these will all disappear."

"I have never seen anything so beautiful in my life! Can we make sure we come out every morning and see it?"

"Not only that, but we can have our breakfast brought to us right here and eat it at this table if you like." He pointed to several tables placed along the rail.

"I think that would be a delightful idea!" Elizabeth wholeheartedly agreed.

This morning, however, they decided to find some small place to eat away from the inn. They stepped outside and began their walking tour of Paris. Darcy had never stayed in this part of the city before, but had visited it. He had, a few years earlier, stepped inside the hotel and knew immediately back then that this was a special place to which he would one day have to bring a very special lady.

They walked to the river and crossed over the bridge, stopping in the middle to look down at it. The morning breeze was ruffling up the water with tiny white caps. It gently brushed Elizabeth's and Darcy's faces and sent errant strands from Elizabeth's hair flying.

"Now I know why I usually wear *all* my hair up!" she laughed.

Darcy took his hand and smoothed it down. "And I appreciate you wearing some of it down today. You look enchanting. Besides," he suddenly changed from serious to teasing. "I have to put up with the wind completely wreaking havoc with my hair, so you can too."

"I will be glad to smooth it down if it gets too out of hand."

Darcy shook his head in an action of shock. "In public? You would not do that in public, would you?"

Elizabeth pursed her lips. She gingerly brought her hand up and ran them through his hair.

He quickly reached up and grabbed her wrist, pulling it down and behind him, drawing her closer to him. "And what do you think of doing *this* in public?"

He leaned over and gave her a light kiss that lingered quite a bit longer than yesterday morning's kiss.

"Do I detect that you are getting bolder, my dear?" teased Elizabeth.

"And am I correct in that you are a bit more accepting Elizabeth?"

Elizabeth shook her head. "Only by virtue of the fact that no one else is on the bridge with us."

Darcy chuckled. "And what about yesterday?"

"You caught me off guard."

Darcy smiled and looked as if he was about to say something, but changed his mind. He took her arm and began walking with her the rest of the way across the bridge.

A smile tugged at Elizabeth's lips. Her husband appeared to have no uneasiness in his display of affection in public, or so it seemed at least here in France. It was something quite out of character for her husband.

They crossed over the bridge and walked along the small street that was filled with little shops. Each one seemed inviting and soon they came to a bakery. The aroma wafted through the doors as someone walked out as they strolled by, and without a word spoken to each other, both turned and walked in.

They walked up and down the glass display, which had every sort of baked good one could imagine. There were fruit filled, cheese filled, plain, heavy, light, dark. They could come here for every meal each day they were here and each order something different, and would not have sampled even half of the choices offered.

Elizabeth finally selected a light, sweet bread, while Darcy preferred heavy dark bread. They each ordered tea and took their selections to a table that was set outside the bakery. Darcy brought out some butter, which they both liberally applied to their bread.

As they enjoyed their first Parisian meal, the sun shone deeply on them and

Darcy noticed the glow on Elizabeth's face. He reached out with his hand and took Elizabeth's, bringing it to his lips. He lightly kissed her palm several times and then trailed kisses up past her wrist. Elizabeth enjoyed the gesture, but instinctively looked to see if anyone was watching. People were briskly walking past them, but no one seemed to pay them any attention.

The rest of the day was spent visiting an art museum, strolling through a beautiful garden, and then sitting in it while watching children frolic in a water fountain. They both enjoyed the myriad of artists who had placed themselves in strategic locations as they were painting pictures of this beautiful city. Elizabeth found herself drawn to one particular artist's watercolour paintings and Darcy, upon inquiring which one of his finished paintings she liked particularly, promptly picked it up and purchased it. Elizabeth felt an initial rise of protest within her, never having had the privilege of buying something without giving it a second thought. Fortunately she realized there was no need for concern before she said anything to stop her husband.

"Thank you, Will. It is simply lovely! How I wish I had learned to draw and paint. It is something I have never been able to do."

"Perhaps when we are back at Pemberley, we can hire someone to teach you."

"Oh I am quite sure I am beyond the teachable years."

"Nonsense!" insisted Darcy. "But in the meantime, we shall have to settle for these Parisian artists' works."

They were back at the hotel a little after two, and went up to their room and freshened up. Jacques was waiting for them when they walked out of the hotel at three o'clock.

"Good afternoon, Mr. and Mrs. Darcy. Have you enjoyed your day in Paris?"

"It has been quite enjoyable, Jacques. Thank you." Elizabeth said, giving him a warm smile.

"You look very nice, Mrs. Darcy. I believe Paris agrees with you."

Elizabeth laughed. "I have seen very little so far, but what I have seen is very delightful!"

Darcy came up and put his arm around her shoulder. "I beg to disagree with you Jacques. She has been married to me longer than she has been in Paris. I must deduce that it is being married to *me* that agrees with her!"

Elizabeth and Jacques looked at each other and shook their heads.

Darcy had Jacques drive them to the Arch de Triumph and Champs Elysee, where they rode around the circled road quite a few times per Elizabeth's request. Then they got out of the carriage and walked. Darcy knew of a fine eating establishment nearby and they went there for a meal.

When they had finished eating, the sun had set, and darkness was beginning to settle over the city. The streetlamps had already been lit and an ethereal glow radiated out from them. Jacques was waiting and Darcy asked him to take them down to the river. As they rode through the streets, Elizabeth was amazed at how many people were out enjoying this beautiful city.

When they approached the river, the sight that greeted the couple was breathtaking. Lamplights from the sides of the river reflected into the waters below. Couples walked along the banks of the river, enjoying the music being played from boats floating by.

Elizabeth turned eagerly to Darcy. "Do you think we can go out on one of those boats? It looks like it would be so much fun!"

"Your wish is my command," he asserted and made a quick bow. "I believe we can pick up one of these boats down here, but let me tell Jacques." He knocked on the front of the carriage, and Jacques quickly pulled over. As he did, he explained to Elizabeth what they could do. "We can take a boat all the way down to one of the docks by our hotel and walk back to it from there, if that sounds reasonable to you."

"That sounds delightful!" exclaimed Elizabeth.

Darcy dismissed Jacques for the evening, letting him know that tomorrow they would be going to the School for the Deaf, gave him the directions to it, and told him they needed to leave by nine.

They had to wait about a half-hour before the next boat came, but once they boarded it, they felt it was well worth the wait. A small string orchestra was set up inside and played music as the boat slowly drifted across the water. Darcy and Elizabeth stood at the railings, watching the city pass by. Elizabeth watched, as couples in love seemed completely oblivious to others around them. She had to admit that this boat ride down the Seine was very romantic and most everyone on it was caught up in that atmosphere as well.

She was watching the lights from the banks of the river reflecting on the water between them, but was more acutely aware that her husband had turned to face her and was standing very close. She could almost feel his warm breath on her.

"Elizabeth."

He did not need to say another word. Elizabeth turned to him and looked up. That was all the encouragement he needed and he slowly leaned down and kissed her. This time, though, he brought his arms up and behind her, and held her close to him for the duration of the kiss.

When he drew his lips from hers, he continued to hold her tightly. He raised an eyebrow at her and breathed in deeply. "Do you forgive me for this fault of mine, Lizbeth, that I am so inclined to kiss and hold you even in public?"

Elizabeth could barely speak. She had to admit that in these last few moments she did not give one thought to the people around her. She did not give one thought as to whether anyone was looking at them or what they would think if they had been. She did not care that her husband kissed her in public. She reasoned that it was only because it was dark, they were on a most romantic boat ride, and...yes, because they were in Paris.

"I would hardly be wise to call that a fault, my love. If that be your only fault, I am the luckiest of wives!"

He kept his arms tightly around her and pulled her to him again.

The boat leisurely drifted through the city of Paris, a cool breeze playfully ruffling both Darcy's and Elizabeth's hair. They soon began to stroll around the boat, enjoying both the sights of the city going past them and the music as it continued to play. They walked around couples that seemed as much in love as the two of them were, and very indifferent to the watchful eyes of others as loving affection was displayed without reserve.

When they disembarked from the boat and began walking back to the hotel, Elizabeth closely held on to Darcy. They walked back to the hotel in silence, almost afraid of breaking the spell that seemed to have come over them. Neither of them could have imagined a more perfect day nor a more perfect person with whom to spend it.

They finally reached the hotel and went straight up to their room. Elizabeth was ready to retire, and pulling the covers back from the bed, she lavishly expressed to her husband her delight in their first full day in Paris. "Today has been the most perfect day," she exclaimed. "I do not think I could have dreamed of a finer day."

Darcy, who was blowing out the candles in the room, turned to her with a look of disappointment written across his face. "I am sorry to hear that."

Elizabeth looked up at him with her mouth dropping open. "But why should you be sorry to hear that?"

"I would have thought…uh…hoped, that one more thing was needed to have made it perfect." He walked over to the last candle that was lit, looked at Elizabeth, smiled, and abruptly turned from it and crawled into the bed next to his wife.

"Will, did you not forget to snuff out the last candle?"

He looked at her through the dim flicker of the last candle's light, admiring her beauty. "I think not, my dear. I think not."

Chapter 4

Pemberley

During the past few days, news had spread quickly throughout Derbyshire and even to some of the neighbouring counties regarding the recent marriage of Fitzwilliam Darcy, Derbyshire's most prominent land owner, to a mere country girl from a modest family, albeit a gentleman's daughter. The article that appeared in the paper took many by surprise - and disappointment. They were surprised that he had finally married *and* that he married someone quite unknown in the ranks of society. Many a mother and daughter were disappointed that he had selected someone else.

The folk of neighbouring villages, having seen the change in him and the accommodating nature he had of late displayed toward them, were not as surprised as some. They had come to know and appreciate this man whom they had always held in high esteem, but who only recently began to keep company with ones, such as themselves, from a class very much beneath his own.

Those who enjoyed the same superior society as the man himself were not jst astonished; they questioned his good judgment, to say the least. For him to marry a lady with little or no wealth and of the poorest connections, they reasoned she must be a tantalizing beauty or had used her artsy wiles to entrap him. They figured Darcy too intelligent to be taken in by the latter, so they trusted their reasoning to the former.

This was the atmosphere that Georgiana and the Pemberley staff returned to after the wedding. The staff that had remained behind had been the ones who had to try and refute any and all rampant rumours when they first began to circulate. It was an easy task, however, as they had grown to admire Elizabeth for the person she was. When she had been a guest there while their master was unconscious from his accident, they had seen nothing in her demeanour that would have given any concern about what her intentions were. She was not one who was trying to seek out Mr. Darcy's fortune; in fact, it seemed to be of very little enticement to her. She had appeared to be a caring and unassuming young lady and they were additionally pleased that she and the master's sister had developed a fond attachment toward each other.

When Georgiana's carriage finally pulled up after a full day of travel, Miss Darcy and Mrs. Annesley were eagerly greeted by the small staff that had stayed behind. Shouts of "Welcome home!" "How was the wedding?" and "Is the Master happy?" rang out to them. Georgiana felt a little overwhelmed. As much as she would have liked to answer everyone, she simply nodded to everything that was asked of her and stated that everything had been perfect.

Her belongings were brought in and as she walked through the heavy wooden doors, she sighed deeply with a grateful sentiment that signalled she was glad to be home; glad to be back at Pemberley. She knew this stay at Pemberley would be different for her. She usually was only here when her brother was present. When he was absent, often as he was, she would normally spend that time in London. Now she was here at their great estate alone, but for the servants and Mrs. Annesley.

Mrs. Reynolds, the housekeeper who had returned a few days earlier, greeted them, and presented Mrs. Annesley with a letter. "This arrived while you were away, Mrs. Annesley."

"Thank you, Mrs. Reynolds." She turned to Georgiana. "It appears to be a letter from my son and his wife. If you will excuse me, I shall go up to my room and read it."

Georgiana excused herself as well, saying she was fatigued. She went directly to her room and flung herself across her bed. She pulled out her journal -- a journal that Elizabeth had wisely encouraged her to start -- and opened it. She looked down and began to reread her very first entry:

Today Misses Jane and Elizabeth Bennet departed Pemberley. These last few days have been laden with emotional ups and downs. When Miss Elizabeth arrived, Fitzwilliam was unconscious, as he had been for days, and we were most concerned for his condition. At that time, I believed she and William to be engaged and I was most happy to have made her acquaintance and to have found her to be so amiable. When I found out I had been mistaken about them being engaged, I was terribly grieved. I still do not fully understand the whole situation between them, but I know she is very different from any other woman who has been in his life, and I hope and pray they can work things out between them.

It had not been an easy road for any of them, including Georgiana herself, in trying to sort things out between them. Her brother had apparently done and said some foolish, heartless things to her. It had taken some clever manoeuvring on Georgiana's part to help speed the process along.

She ruffled past all the pages on which she had written since those first days, finding the next blank one. She began to write.

Today I am back at Pemberley. I am very happy, knowing that Elizabeth is finally my sister-in -law. And I do not believe I have ever seen William happier. I do not think he could have chosen a more perfect wife for him; nor I, if I had been trying. But it is good to be back at Pemberley, in my own home, in my own room, to be able to sleep in my own bed. Here I can be alone when I wish and need not worry about entertaining anyone. At least for the moment. I hope that nothing changes for a very long time. I like things just the way they are.

She closed the book and lay down, feeling all the contentment of a young girl with neither a care nor a worry in the world. Soon she was fast asleep.

~~*

Georgiana was awakened by a dinner bell. She had been in such a deep sleep that she felt she had been asleep forever. She pulled herself up and stretched. How she would love to curl back up and climb under the covers and stay there for the night. But she knew that could not be, so she pulled herself up off the bed and went to her dressing table, looking quickly in the mirror to repair any damage to her hair.

With that done, she proceeded to the dining room. Mrs. Annesley was there and Mrs. Reynolds came out and joined them. She suddenly realized how large and ominously empty this house felt without her brother, even with all the help that roamed about. She also realized how much better she would like it when Elizabeth would be here, too. Right now she was grateful for the two ladies who were present with her instead of the two ladies who had been a constant irritation to her in Netherfield, namely Bingley's sisters. She had enjoyed Jane's company, but the disconcerting presence of Caroline and Louisa always cast a pall upon the atmosphere there and caused Georgiana more grief than comfort.

After the evening supper, Georgiana took a book into the sitting room and read for quite a while. Mrs. Annesley sat across from her working on a needlework sampler.

"Georgiana, dear," she said after a while. "You are aware that I received a letter from my son and his wife today." She took a deep breath, as Georgiana looked up and met her eyes. "They wrote me to inform me that they are expecting their first child, due in March. They would very much like for me to come up north and live with them."

Georgiana looked at her and saw in her a mixture of joy and sorrow. "Mrs. Annesley, does that mean you will be leaving as my companion?"

"Yes, Georgiana, I think I must. I cannot help but think the timing is right for me to leave."

"I am terribly sorry to hear that. I have learned considerably under your instruction this past year."

"Yes, my dear, but there is so much more that I have not been able to do." She rose and walked over to Georgiana, taking her hand. "Once your brother returns, I will talk with him about my leaving and will only remain until he finds someone to replace me. That is, if he even *wishes* to find a new companion for you. He may feel you do not need one anymore."

Georgiana squeezed her hand, and felt her eyes well up with tears. "I shall miss you, you know that."

"That is sweet of you to say, Georgiana. I shall miss you also. But I also am very anxious to live close to my son and his wife as my first grandchild is born." As a single tear escaped and ran down her face, she stood up and excused herself. "I think I shall retire now, Georgiana. Good night."

"Good night, Mrs. Annesley." Georgiana sat in the large room, her brows furrowing as she contemplated the news. She would indeed miss Mrs. Annesley. She had been her companion for a little over a year. She felt as though she had finally begun to feel comfortable enough around her to easily converse with her.

She knew that if her brother insisted on employing someone else, it would be difficult for her, as it always took her time to warm up to new people. *Oh how I hope he does not insist on hiring someone else,* she thought to herself. She curled up in her chair, contemplating what she could tell her brother to convince him she did not need another companion. Most of her studies were completed, and if there was anything else she needed to learn, he might allow her to learn from Elizabeth. Certainly he would agree to that!

At length, Georgiana retired to her room. After readying herself, she crawled in her own bed. How nice it felt! She was glad to be home, but in her mind knew she would be counting the days until her brother and his wife returned. She blew out the candle on the table next to her bed and was soon fast asleep.

~~*

Georgiana slept well that night and she spent the next morning going over some studies with Mrs. Annesley. Both felt the weight of the awareness that there would be but a few more times they would spend like this. Neither seemed really able to concentrate, and finally Mrs. Annesley made a suggestion.

"It is such a fine day, Georgiana. What do you say we have Lawson take us in the carriage to Lambton?"

"I should like that very much!" Georgiana exclaimed enthusiastically. "What shall we do there?"

"There are a few things I need to purchase. We could also stop by and see how the Franks are doing."

"That is a wonderful idea! It has been over a month since we have seen them. Let us do that!"

Mrs. Annesley smiled. How grateful she was for Georgiana's tender, compassionate heart.

After eating a light meal, they set out in the carriage. Mrs. Annesley seemed to appreciate today's drive through the grounds, realizing she would not have the enjoyment of seeing them for but a few more weeks. How many times, she wondered, had she driven through them recently and not really noticed them anymore? She had been most impressed with them on her very first visit here. Now she knew she would most certainly miss them.

They came into Lambton and Mrs. Annesley purchased some itmes that she needed. Georgiana simply looked at the merchandise on the shelves, not really interested in buying anything for herself. She did, however, find a small doll and thought it would be a nice gift to bring to Eleanor, the four year old daughter of Mr. and Mrs. Frank, who was deaf.

Georgiana had them wrap it in a simple paper and bow, one that she would easily be able to open. Mrs. Annesley took great delight in this act of thoughtfulness on Georgiana's part.

They made the short trip to the Franks, where they were greeted most warmly. Mr. Frank was still at Pemberley. He was the head stableman there. Mrs. Frank invited them in, and offered them some tea.

They came into the small front room, where Eleanor usually played. As she did not hear them come in, she was startled when Georgiana reached down and touched her shoulder. A huge smile came across her face.

Georgiana took the girl's hand and waved for her to come over with her to a chair. Georgiana sat down and handed her the wrapped gift. Eleanor took it eagerly, obviously knowing that a wrapped gift contains some precious treasure inside and that the paper and bow are there only to tear through quickly.

"Miss Darcy, you need not have brought her anything."

"Oh, but I am so fond of her. I saw this and had get it for her."

Eleanor pulled out the doll and instantly brought it up to her and hugged it. She had such a smile on her face that the three ladies in the room smiled back at her and one another.

"Miss Darcy, Mrs. Annesley, I must show you something." Mrs. Frank got down on the floor and brought Eleanor's face to look toward her. She began making some movements with her hands and the two guests watched in amazement as Eleanor responded by making some signs herself. She suddenly put her doll down and ran out of the room.

"Mrs. Frank, what happened?"

"I asked her to bring in the plate of cookies…in sign language. She answered that she would."

Georgiana's eyes widened in amazement. "You and Eleanor have been learning to talk with signs?"

"Yes, the information Mr. Darcy brought us has some very basic instruction. We have somewhat adapted it for our use and Eleanor seems to come up with some signs on her own. I believe she is a quick learner."

Eleanor came back with the plate of cookies, a proud look across her face. She handed the plate to Georgiana and immediately picked up her new doll.

"How do you say 'thank you'?" asked Georgiana.

Mrs. Frank signed out the words.

Georgiana then looked down to Eleanor and repeated the gesture. Eleanor grinned and Georgiana pulled her close and hugged her. She looked up to Mrs. Frank whose eyes were becoming glassy with tears. "This whole idea of communicating to her with signs has made such a difference in our lives. Our whole family is learning together and Eleanor seems so much more a part of us."

"I am sure most families with deaf children would feel the same way," put in Mrs. Annesley. "I think the idea of a school where people can learn to communicate with their deaf family members and friends is wonderful. And to think one shall be right here in Derbyshire! It is simply wonderful!"

"We could not agree more."

Georgiana and Mrs. Annesley visited with Mrs. Frank for about an hour, telling her all about the wedding and of all the news that had happened in Lambton and the surrounding county of Derbyshire the past few weeks. When they left, Georgiana felt that she could not have spent the day in any other way that would have been more enjoyable.

Once they had left Lambton, before they drew again into the extensive grounds and lush woods of Pemberley, the road took them through a few other smaller private farms and property. At one such particular farm, Lawson, their coachman, noticed a young man stooped down on the side of the road, his tethered horse off to the side. He slowed the horses down and brought the carriage to a stop. He saw that the young man was struggling with a lamb that had apparently attempted to sneak out through a hole in a fence and had entangled itself.

Lawson jumped down to see if he could help and Georgiana and Mrs. Annesley looked out to see what the delay was. Georgiana could not see what was going on and curiosity prompted her to open the door to the carriage and step down. Mrs. Annesley followed.

Lawson was at the side of the young man and was giving some kind of assistance. The two ladies walked over and noticed the lamb. Georgiana gasped, as she watched the young man carefully untangle a bleeding lamb from the fence. They finally freed the lamb and the young man stood up slowly, cradling it in his arms. Georgiana's eyes widened as she recognized David Bostwick, an under gardener from Pemberley. In his full stature, he towered above the three.

"Mr. Bostwick!" exclaimed Georgiana.

"Hello, Mr. Bostwick," Miss Annesley said. "What happened?"

"Good day, Miss Darcy, Mrs. Annesley. I suppose this little fellow tried to escape through the hole in the fence and was caught. It looks like some makeshift wire was put here at some point to temporarily repair it. That is what cut up the lamb. I would not be surprised if some other sheep got out and he tried to follow. You know how dumb sheep can be, always following where they should not go."

He continued to hold him and pulled out a handkerchief, pressing it against the one small laceration on the side of the lamb's leg. He spoke soothingly to it, trying to calm it down. The lamb was squirming, but he held on to it firmly.

"You seem to have a way with him, Mr. Bostwick," Mrs. Annesley commented.

A thought suddenly came to Georgiana and she declared it aloud before she realized what she was saying. "Like David!" When everyone looked to her, she blushed and looked down.

"What was that, Miss Darcy?" David asked.

"I am sorry, I…you… are like David."

He shook his head and looked at her in a puzzled way. "I *am* David. David Bostwick."

"No," Georgiana softly replied. "David, in the Bible. David the Shepherd!"

"Ahhh, yes. My namesake, actually."

"Is that so?" asked Lawson.

"My parents have often told me I am named for David in the Bible. I do not know whether my parents had meagre ambitions for me to become a shepherd or lofty ones for me to become a king." He looked directly at Georgiana. "Do not forget that he was not a shepherd, he was the shepherd who would become a king!"

Georgiana forced herself to up look into his face. He was smiling at her and Georgiana felt her face warm. *Why does this always happen around him?* she asked herself.

He continued, "I do not claim to be a shepherd even now, but do you think if I pursue this line of work that maybe in the future I should become a king?"

Mrs. Annesley then added, "Most likely not of England, Mr. Bostwick, but perhaps you could find some small country in need of a good king."

Everyone laughed at their remarks and Georgiana blushed even more. David looked at Georgiana, as if expecting her to make an appropriate response, but she could not think of one thing to say. The smile he gave her only caused her to look down at her feet, wishing she could disappear.

She was relieved when everyone's attention was drawn away from her and to Lawson. "Do you think the lamb is well enough to put back in the pasture? Has the bleeding stopped?"

"Yes, I think this is all pretty much stopped now. I will ride up to the Prestons' house, though, and let them know what happened with their lamb and the fence."

Georgiana took this opportunity to excuse herself and returned to the carriage. Mrs. Annesley remained out for a while and this gave Georgiana time to calm her nerves. The last time she had seen David Bostwick, they had taken a short walk together around Pemberley as he told her stories of her mother. She had enjoyed his company that day, but was not sure how to interpret these new feelings that she was experiencing when she found herself around him now that they were both grown up.

Being the son of the head gardener, he had often come to Pemberley as a young boy and he and his brother had played together with Georgiana around the grounds. But after seeing him when he returned from spending several years at trade school, she realized he had grown into quite a pleasing young man. Now she struggled with even the simplest conversation and feeling distress as a wave of colour would invariably wash over her every time she saw him.

Mrs. Annesley finally returned and joined her in the carriage. "Fine young man, that Mr. Bostwick." She looked obscurely at Georgiana.

"Yes," was Georgiana's only reply.

Georgiana wondered if Mrs. Annesley had been aware that she blushed at her mere attempt to talk to him. She hoped not. She did not want to have to discuss it with her. Feeling a pang of guilt, she knew she would easily be able to talk about it with Elizabeth and wished at that moment that she was here with her.

Lawson returned and took his post in the driver's seat. David came over, after putting the lamb back inside the fenced pasture. "I thank you, Lawson, for stopping to help. That little lamb thanks you, too. Good day."

He walked to the window of the carriage and looked in. "Good afternoon, ladies. Have a pleasant day."

The carriage moved away, and there was a silence inside that seemed to hang heavy. Georgiana felt as though Mrs. Annesley wanted to say something. She was grateful for the silence, however, as it gave her time to give full reign to her thoughts. What did it mean that she felt so disconcerted around him? And why did it have to happen when others were around to notice it? Why could things not be as they were when they were younger and were simply friends?

Finally, after a few moments, Mrs. Annesley spoke. "Georgiana, there is much I have tried to teach you this past year. And you have been an exemplary student, a most compassionate friend. I have attempted to give you an outlook in this world that goes beyond the family you were born in, the fortune that is your portion. You have a natural gift and ability to reach out to those less fortunate than yourself. You have a most caring, selfless demeanour."

"It is because *you* have been a wonderful teacher and example to me, Mrs. Annesley. I could not have learned as much without you."

"Yes, but I fear I may have let you down in one area. And I still am not quite sure how to address it."

Georgiana looked at her, her heart beginning to pound nervously.

"When I came into your life a year ago, I was told only minimally what had transpired in your life while at Ramsgate."

Georgiana responded by dropping her head, feeling the disgrace begin to rise up inside her again.

"Georgiana," she began, reaching out her hand and taking Georgiana's. "I do not mean to cause you shame by mentioning this. As a result of what I was told, I have spent this last year being content to keep you focused on other things, such as reaching out to the needs of others. When Mr. Darcy seemed disinclined to present you at court and bring you out for your first season, I happily concurred. I felt it would be best for you to postpone that a year or two. But now, I fear I may have done you a disservice."

Georgiana looked up, finding it hard, though, to meet her eyes. "What do you mean by disservice?"

She turned and looked intently at Georgiana. "You are a very pretty, kind, and compassionate young lady, who also happens to have a great amount of money coming to you when you marry."

She paused and Georgiana inwardly flinched.

"Dear Georgiana, you must make careful consideration of the young men for whom you develop a regard. You have an obligation to your family, to their name, and the wealth into which you were born. I am not sure if I am saying this in a way you will understand. While Mr. Bostwick is one of the nicest young men from around here, you must remember who he is and who you are."

Her words brought Georgiana's face up to meet her. Those were Elizabeth's exact words to her when she had shared with her the confusion she felt whenever she encountered Mr. Bostwick. She made an attempt to smile. "I understand you completely, Mrs. Annesley. In fact, Elizabeth said to me the same thing."

"Georgiana, it may not be easy, but there are some things that have to be. I cannot say that I agree with all the rules of society by which we are bound, especially those unwritten rules, but I do know that sometimes it is for the best, especially in a situation such as yours. I am glad Mrs. Darcy shared that with you. I have much esteem for her."

Georgiana could only nod and look down.

"I would imagine, then, that when you begin attending all the balls once you have been brought out, especially in London, and begin meeting the eligible young men who are more your equal in society, you will find that special someone from among them. I am quite certain of it."

Georgiana contemplated her words. She knew most young girls her age would look forward to all the balls and all the young men out there to meet. But meeting new people was so difficult for her and if she felt unsettled around Mr. Bostwick, whom she had known most of her life, how would she ever handle introductions to other young men.

But she knew it was something that had to be. She reasoned that all her years of instruction had been to prepare her to be the wife of a well-bred man of excellent connections and equal fortune.

Yes, she had to remember who Mr. Bostwick was - simply a hired hand at Pemberley, the son - younger son at that - of Pemberley's head gardener. Her mind, however, would not let it end there. He was kind, handsome, and tall, although not as tall as her brother. He had fair features and deep set blue eyes that matched her own. When he gave her one of his smiles, she would feel weak. She had to remember who *she* was - a young lady born into a wealthy family with a fortune that would entice any man. She knew she had an obligation to her family and her wealth to marry someone of equal standing.

Why was she suddenly wishing she were anyone other than Georgiana Anne Darcy of Pemberley?

Chapter 5

Pemberley

Georgiana pondered the reaction that invaded her normally gracious demeanour when she encountered the young Mr. Bostwick again and again. Could she even begin to sort out how she felt about him -- why she reacted to him the way she did? She knew how unsettled she was whenever he came near, but what, indeed, were her *feelings* toward him? She absently shook her head. Not that it mattered; an attachment toward him would without doubt be discouraged, even forbidden, due to his lower station in life.

As she crawled into bed that night, she grabbed her journal and thought ahead to this coming season. She anticipated being presented at court before the Queen. That would initiate her into performing her endless societal duties and attend balls. There would be lavish ones in London in addition to the smaller ones here in Derbyshire. She would be required to meet an infinite number of young men, each looking for that certain someone who would meet his every need; at least his need to be raised up one notch in society or to augment his already extensive fortune.

She comprehended that she would be ushered into the higher ranks of society merely by being Fitzwilliam Darcy's sister. She would not have to do anything to earn it. Just as her brother had never sought to be elevated to a superior rank, so she would not. His acceptance into the upper echelons of society in London had been literally handed to him because of his large fortune, his education, and his previously very eligible status as a handsome bachelor.

During her time spent in London, Georgiana had watched and listened to the goings on of those well steeped in the affairs of society. Much of what she learned came indirectly from the staff in their London townhouse. Gossip was prevalent as to who was seen with whom, who was admitted to Almacks, and who was presented at St. James' court. Mrs. Annesley had attempted to shield the young girl from any sort of active interest in the trappings of society, but Georgiana had conveniently found that by doing her studies in the dining room, she could overhear any and all the gossip that the kitchen help repeated amongst themselves. She had learned much, but one thing she realized -- she did not like what she heard.

From the standpoint of the servants, most of those people who were recognized in the higher ranks of society had little concern for anyone but themselves. Many were driven by avarice and self-indulgence, motivated only to increase their status, and determined at all costs to be included in society's who's who. The last thing Georgiana wanted was to enter this world of self-adulation and contempt for anyone unequal in consequence.

Georgiana knew Mrs. Annesley helped form this perspective she had on life, although part of it was, indeed, due to her own temperament. She had a very quiet and unassuming nature, a giving and wholesome spirit, and very altruistic ideals. She could not see herself living an indulgent life that was solely concerned with her position in society and how others viewed her.

While she did entertain expectant thoughts about the coming season and being presented to society, she also had much apprehension in that regard. As much as she knew this would be required because of her position, she wondered of its relevance to her. She had come to enjoy the freedom that her time at Pemberley presented her as well as the opportunity to visit the common folk in the nearby villages and small towns. She felt as though she was more like these people than their acquaintances in London.

As these thoughts whirled inside her head, she thought again of Mr. Bostwick. She could not come to any conclusion concerning how she felt about him. There had only been a few encounters with him recently and she could only say for certain that when around him, she felt and acted nervously. That in itself was certainly not an indication of any regard she had developed toward him.

She took up her writing pen and dipped it in the ink. Elizabeth had told her to write down her thoughts and feelings, so she began to write.

Today I suddenly feel extremely anxious about growing up. I know in some ways I already feel grown up, yet in other ways I am not quite certain. There is a great deal ahead that alarms me; there is much in my position as Georgiana Darcy that will require me to behave in a certain manner and make choices of a certain leaning. I question whether I have it in me to live up to my name.

She closed her journal and put out the last candle that lit the room. In the darkness of the room she thought of Elizabeth. How grateful she was for her new sister. She was unlike any woman in their close acquaintances either in London or in all of Derbyshire. She was not certain whether her brother realized it or not, but it was the very fact that she cared not whether she was one of society's chosen elite that made her exceedingly superior over the others.

As she slept that night, her thoughts took the form of bizarre dreams in which she roamed the streets of London scared and alone, yet in the midst of a throng of people. It was dark and cold, and everyone either ignored her or angrily cast her away. She wanted to go home, but could not seem to find her way. When she finally found her way back to their townhouse, it was her brother himself who shut the door on her and locked her out.

The next morning she felt lethargic, unable to shake the longing to crawl back into bed for the rest of the day. She was also unable to shake the teasing in her mind that she had been anxious about something in her dreams, but could not summon up exactly what it was. She remained in bed a short while longer, trying to recall what had caused her such distress in her dream, but it would not come to her. Being unable to draw it to the surface, she finally decided to shake herself of this uneasiness and get up out of bed.

She dutifully performed her studies with Mrs. Annesley, both of them aware that as each day passed, it brought her closer to the day she would depart. Georgiana liberally expressed her appreciation to her companion for all she had done for her, and Mrs. Annesley, in turn, expressed to Georgiana that she was indeed turning into quite a remarkable young woman.

After her lesson, Georgiana practiced for several hours on the pianoforte and found herself with a little free time in the afternoon. Being another warm, pleasant summer day, she decided to take a stroll about the grounds.

She had learned to appreciate walking around the grounds of Pemberley when Elizabeth had been there. Although Georgiana was not the avid walker that Elizabeth was, she found a new enjoyment in meandering around the paths -- even *off* the paths -- that surrounded her home. She opened the large door that took her out to the front.

Stepping out onto the large porch that graced Pemberley's entrance, she looked in both directions, trying to decide which way she would venture off today. She settled that she would go around to the south, past the courtyard, and off toward the lake. As she walked down the massive steps, she looked over at the gardenia bushes that had been planted months before. The gardenias were finishing their blooming season, but the scent from them still spilled out into the air. She leaned over and breathed in the fresh, floral scent.

The scent and its associations put a livelier gait in Georgiana's step, as she recalled bumping into David Bostwick those few months back. On the first occasion she had almost not recognized him, as she had not seen him in several years. He had been helping plant the gardenia bushes and she stopped and talked with him about them.

The next time she encountered him, they strolled about the gardens as he shared with her his memories of her mother. Georgiana recalled her joy in hearing about her, as her memories of her mother were few and faded. How special and enlightening that day was. A faint smile spread across her face, but only for a short moment. She reprimanded herself with, *That was no reason to think more particularly of Mr. Bostwick or to view him as anything but a friend.*

As she came to the far edge of the manor, her eyes were drawn to the large tree that shaded the south part of the house in the warm summer months. A swing that had been there for many years was somewhat shielded by the foliage and hung on a thick branch. It had been there for many years. She walked over to it, drawn by the comfort that it had afforded her through the years.

As a young girl, there had been other childhood amusements out here such as a teeter-totter and a sandbox. But they were long gone; time and forces of nature taking their toll on them. The swing remained, Georgiana was quite certain, because an observant groundskeeper now and then would repair one of the ropes or replace the wooden board that comprised the swing.

Throughout her life, she had taken refuge on this swing for different reasons. In the most recent years it was to sort out her feelings and her dilemmas.

She walked over to the swing and sat down upon it, taking one rope in hand and letting her feet drag along the ground, which caused her to sway at a crooked angle. She smiled as she noticed that it had again been raised, as it often had been over the years, to allow for her growing stature.

Her thoughts went back to a year and a half ago, after she nearly eloped with Wickham. When her brother removed her from Mr. Wickham's clutches and Mrs. Younge's schemes, and returned her to Pemberley, she spent many an hour sitting on this swing berating herself for her naïveté, wondering of her sensibility, and despairing of her worth in the eyes of her brother.

The swing had become her constant companion. It always welcomed her, never condemned her, and always lifted her spirits. She found the back and forth swaying to be soothing, whatever disposition she was in. And it welcomed her again today.

Today her thoughts went further back, to the summer when she was seven. David Bostwick was nine and his elder brother Samuel was ten. The two boys had often joined their father on the grounds when he came to work that particular summer, basically to get out of their mother's way as she had twin babies at home. Much of the time the boys spent exploring, pretending to be soldiers or some such silly thing.

Georgiana would come out to the play area and it was David who took the time to talk with her. Samuel wanted nothing to do with this little 'skinny sort of quiet thing' as he called her. But David always took the time to give her a push in the swing, sit on the other side of the teeter-totter, or help her build castles in the sand. He was always so kind, never compelling her to say anything, but encouraging her to do so when he could, and always listening when she did.

She recalled that as the years passed, she saw the boys less and less. They both began working on the Pemberley grounds in their early teen years and Georgiana only saw them occasionally when she happened upon them. Eventually both went off to some school; she was not sure where. When Georgiana had seen David a few months back by the gardenia bushes, the young boy David and grown into a handsome young man.

It is merely because we are both now grown up, and I had never related to him before as an adult. That is why I feel so nervous around him. That is all, nothing more. Georgiana suddenly took the other rope in her hand and raised her feet from underneath her. Pulling on the ropes and leaning back, she let the swing take her higher.

She enjoyed the wind beating against her face as she found a nice moderate pace, closing her eyes against all that was around her. She thought about how simple things were as a child and how complex they became when you got older. Sometimes she wished she could go back.

Unexpectedly, she felt a push on the bench beneath her from behind. She grabbed the ropes tighter as she sailed higher. She tried look behind her, but she could not turn her head back far enough for fear she would catapult off the swing.

It was but an instant later that David Bostwick walked around to the front of the swing, facing her. A big grin appeared as he watched a nervous smile spread across Georgiana's face. He sat down on the grass a few feet in front of her and waited for the swing to come to a stop.

Georgiana's heart pounded; her mind frantically searching for something to say. He seemed so calm and sure of himself, and here she was, as nervous as a lamb facing its shearers for the first time.

When the swing stopped, she began dragging her feet again, giving her something to do to help distract her.

"Hello, Miss Darcy. Are you well?" he asked, tilting his head, and causing the sun to bounce off his curly blond hair.

She looked down at her lap, then forced herself to look up again. "I am well... thank you. And yourself?"

"I could not be better, thank you! But I fear I was negligent yesterday and did not inquire about your brother's wedding. Was it as grand as everyone says?"

"Yes. It was very nice...very beautiful, thank you." She was grateful for at least some direction of this conversation and that it was a subject she was comfortable talking about. "I believe that he and Elizabeth shall be very happy. They... they have a great love and admiration for each other."

"I am so pleased to hear that. Do you find her agreeable? Are you fond of Mrs. Darcy?"

"Oh, yes, very much! She is wonderful and I cannot wait for them to return."

He smiled at her sudden burst of animation. "That is fortunate. I often hoped, for your sake, that Mr. Darcy would marry someone who would be to your liking, as well."

Georgiana wrinkled up her nose, not sure how to respond to this, but felt a warmth radiate inside her. "Thank you," was all she could politely say.

After a strained silence, Georgiana remembered David's newly married brother. "Mr. Bostwick, how are your brother and *his* new wife doing?"

"I believe they are doing very well, thank you. A small addition was added to our house for them and a future growing family. As the house and land will go to him someday, they are very eager to make it suitable. Samuel and Deborah have great plans for it, although I must say their plans exceed their income at present. He does not have much patience for things and I fear that might some day get him in trouble."

Georgiana smiled, thinking back to their childhood, and how meticulous she and David used to be in building a magnificent sand castle, whereas Samuel would give up after a few minutes, impatiently crushing it and usually David's and hers along with his. There was many a time that she would end up in tears because of Samuel's actions.

"I hope he has more patience building his home... than he did building his sand castles." She said this very quietly and slowly and almost stopped in mid-sentence, her heart suddenly pounding as she recalled this youthful pastime.

He continued to look down at the grass, picking up a few blades and twirling them between his fingers. Georgiana continued to absently sway on the swing, barely able to look up at him. She held onto one of the ropes with both hands, wishing he would say something.

He looked up at her on the swing and seemed to begin to say something, but then hesitated. He took in a deep breath, looked at her as if some sort of debate was going on in his mind, and then let it out slowly. Finally he said, "So you remember those times we played out here together?"

Of course I remember! Georgiana thought. *It is what I was thinking about before you came by!* A tinge of colour spread across her face and she instinctively looked down, trying to attain a semblance of composure on her reaction to his question. As she timidly peered back up at him through her lashes, she noticed that he had also looked down.

He spoke again before she was able to formulate an answer. "I did not intend to make you uncomfortable, Miss Darcy."

"I do remember," she quickly replied, suddenly determined not to let him think her uncomfortable around him. Georgiana timidly laughed. "I recall your brother certainly used to love to torment me."

"Hah ha!" David laughed. "I do not think there was one day that you did not run off in tears because of him, but I do recall the day you stood up to him!"

Georgiana raised her eyebrows at this; unsure of what incident he recalled. "When did I do that?"

"He grabbed a new doll you had just received and he threatened to bury it in the sandbox. You were so angry. You did not want the doll to get dirty and when he bent over to begin digging in the sand, you jumped on his back and began pounding him with your fists. He was so startled, he dropped the doll and you promptly retrieved it. I do believe he looked at you differently afterwards!"

Georgiana laughed with little restraint, remembering the incident. "But that did not stop him from tormenting me."

"No, maybe not completely, but I think he came away with a little more respect for you that day."

Georgiana looked down at him and his eyes looked up and met hers. She willed herself not to look away.

David pulled himself up off the grass. "I best be getting back."

"I must return, as well."

David reached out his hand toward her to help her out of the swing. Georgiana looked at it and her heart faltered in its beating. She slowly reached out her hand and he took it, gently pulling her to her feet. Suddenly a feeling swept over her that her hand felt so right in his, and just as suddenly, she reprimanded herself for such feelings.

"Let me walk with you back to your house."

Georgiana kept her gaze upon each foot as she walked forward. He strode along side of her, keeping a proper distance away, but she still felt his close presence ever so acutely.

They walked along in silence for a short while and then David spoke. "I shall not be able to come by Pemberley as frequently anymore. I have been able to secure some occasional work with Mr. Lochlin, as his land holdings have recently increased and he needs some additional help managing them. Although the work I will be doing for him shall be somewhat sparse, it will suffice for now. I eventually hope to find something else. I have a desire to go on to university someday, but at present it does not look possible."

Georgiana cast a shy glance up to him as he spoke of his plans. He stared straight ahead, as if seeing in his mind's eye exactly what he wanted to do with his future. She felt admiration for him and the noble goals he had. But it was that, she reminded herself, which presented the greatest barrier to them; at least any sort of attachment between them. He would be a good, hard working man someday, who would eke out a steady, but hardly illustrious income. She would be obliged to marry a man with the noblest connections and comparable fortune.

He continued with his dreams as she continued with her arguments. "It is my greatest desire that I might be able to attend Oxford or Cambridge, although realistically I cannot get my hopes up. It would afford me better opportunities if I graduated from such a place." Suddenly he seemed self-conscious talking to her about this. "I am sorry; I tend to get a trifle bit carried away sometimes."

Georgiana admired him for wanting to improve himself and his station in life as best he could. His father, as head gardener at Pemberley, oversaw all the gardening staff. He would have been considered a little above a hired hand. He was most certainly a young man of excellent manners, but the family, having two sons and three daughters, would certainly not have the means to support their younger son at the university. He had the desire but not necessarily the means to make it happen.

David continued, "I hope to be able to come by when your brother returns and talk with him. I also look forward to meeting his wife. I must say that I have only heard good things about her from the staff that had the privilege to meet her when she was here before. I was not fortunate enough to make her acquaintance. I do hope to as soon as they return."

Georgiana turned her gaze upon him as she spoke. "They should be returning in about two weeks, I would imagine."

They walked in silence to the front steps and David gave a slight bow before he turned to go, "Good day, Miss Darcy. I have enjoyed our time together."

Georgiana immediately took the steps up to the front door. She turned back when she reached the top, only to see that he had not yet departed. She swallowed hard and whispered back, "Thank you, Mr. Bostwick. Good day."

David Bostwick watched as she entered the house. He slowly turned and walked away. He knew he was playing with fire. When he saw her walk to the swing earlier, he should have ignored that impelling force that drove him toward her and should have listened instead to the inner voice telling him to stay away. He should never have yielded to his longing to spend some time with her. He was no longer a little boy. She was no longer a little girl. He knew for a certainty that there could never be an accepted attachment between them, so why even fool himself into thinking it. Even if she returned his regard there was her brother. He, or anyone else who regarded equal rank to be first and foremost in a marriage, would never condone it.

Chapter 6

Paris

"**A**re you quite certain this is where you want to go, Sir?" asked Jacques as he looked at the address.

"*Oui*, Jacques. Do you know how to get there?"

"*Oui,* Sir. But it is not in best part of town."

"That is fine, Jacques," Darcy told him. "Take us there."

Darcy pressed his hand against Elizabeth's back and nudged her toward the carriage. They had an appointment at ten o'clock and hopefully he had allowed enough time to get them there on schedule.

Sure enough, as Jacques had declared, this was not the best part of town. Darcy and Elizabeth looked through the window of the carriage as they passed homes that were run down, in disarray, or even boarded up, yet still lived in. There was squalor in the streets and children playing outside wore tattered and ill fitted clothes.

They came upon a large building and the carriage stopped in front of it. Jacques hopped out and opened the door. "We are here."

"Thank you, Jacques." Darcy stepped down from the carriage and he and Jacques helped Elizabeth out. There was a great iron gate surrounding the brick building, but it was not locked. A large lawn encircled the school and a play area was situated off to the side. Elizabeth thought it might once have been a grand home.

"I shall wait for you here, Mr. Darcy."

"Thank you, Jacques. We should be several hours, if you wish to go someplace and then return for us around two o'clock, that would be fine."

"*Merci.*"

Darcy and Elizabeth entered through the unlocked gate and made their way to the front door. A small sign on the door indicated that they could walk in. Upon opening the door, they found themselves in a large hallway. Some voices drew their attention, and they followed them. They found themselves in what looked like offices.

Darcy walked up to one of the women, and in French, told the woman who they were, that they were here to see Monsieur Bonne, and tour the grounds. She nodded, and walked to a door towards the back. She returned with a short, balding man who had a contagious smile.

"Good day, Monsieur Darcy, Madame Darcy. How good it is to meet you. Will you not come this way?"

Elizabeth was grateful he was able to speak English.

They were ushered into his office and Monsieur Bonne handed them a packet. "This is all the information you should need, Monsieur Darcy, to know what is involved in starting a school for the deaf such as this one. I have planned for us today to visit some of the classes and to introduce you to Monsieur Fleming. He is an Englishman who has been here for three years. He and his family came over with his daughter who was born deaf. They came to learn to sign and he ended up staying on as a teacher. He would like to return to England, and if it is acceptable to you, would very much like to teach in the school you wish to start."

"I should certainly like to meet him," Darcy replied.

"Before we go, let me tell you one thing. Not all of us here are deaf, but many are. Once we leave this room, everything I say to you will be both spoken and signed. That is the way of it here. Those who are deaf will sign, those who are not will speak and sign. That way all communication is understood. Since you do not sign, if it is needed, I will interpret."

"I fully understand."

"Good. Shall we go then?"

The two walked down the hall and Elizabeth noticed immediately the effects of his words. He said something in French to the ladies in the office while at the same time signing to them. She wondered if any of these ladies were deaf, being fairly sure the one her husband spoke to at first was not.

"Were either of those ladies deaf?" asked Elizabeth.

"Only one. The one who came and told me you were here."

Elizabeth's mouth dropped open. "But how…"

Monsieur Bonne looked at her. "Signing is only one way to communicate with the deaf. For years deaf people have learned to read the lips of those speaking to them. Mademoiselle Chapelle learned to read lips and communicated that way for years before learning to sign. She can actually speak, although it is sometimes difficult to understand her."

Elizabeth was amazed. She had never been around anyone who was deaf and had really never thought about the great chasm that would exist in trying to communicate with others. It was remarkable to her the resourcefulness of people who set their minds to something.

As they walked the hall, those they passed either signed and verbally offered a greeting, or simply signed it. They finally came to a room and stopped.

"This is the classroom of Monsieur Fleming. He is presently teaching young children. His daughter is in here and she is five years old. She is the one with the unruly blond hair." He smiled and opened the door for them.

Darcy and Elizabeth quietly came in and sat down. Mr. Fleming looked up only temporarily, smiled, and returned to his work. Elizabeth was amazed that he spoke as he signed, knowing full well that the children all had to be deaf. Since he spoke in French, she was able to understand but a few words.

Each child, ranging in age from about four or five up to fifteen or sixteen, signed every word, phrase, or sentence that was presented to them. Elizabeth mimicked the signs along with the students and by the end of the session could sign a few words herself.

Before he dismissed the class, Mr. Fleming had the Darcys come forward and he introduced them to the class. When the students were told that they came all the way over from England, their eyes widened. One boy anxiously raised his hand for a question. When he began speaking, Elizabeth was stunned. He obviously was not deaf, although she could not understand him for his French.

Mr. Fleming laughed, along with Darcy. "No, no," said Mr. Fleming as he signed. Elizabeth could only wonder what transpired.

The class was dismissed and Elizabeth had many questions. First, "That last little boy was not deaf?"

"No, his parents are. He has had to learn to sign, along with his parents, so he can communicate with them. There are others who have taken classes who have brothers or sisters, occasionally a friend, who is deaf and they want to learn to talk to them."

"What did he ask that was so funny?"

"He asked me that since you were from England as I was, whether we were acquaintances." Mr. Fleming began picking up around his desk. "He probably thinks it is a very small country. I must correct him of that assumption, and soon!" He laughed and pointed to the door. "The children are going to their play time now. If you wish, we can go observe." He directed them down the hall.

They came outside and watched the children play. Elizabeth noticed immediately the difference in this play area as there was no squealing or yelling. It was all very quiet, but the children seemed to be having as much fun. Not being able to take her eyes off the children, Elizabeth walked over to a bench and sat down, while Darcy and Fleming continued to talk.

A small girl with dark hair and eyes shyly came up to her and signed something. Elizabeth reached out her hand and the girl took it in hers. Elizabeth felt a great desire to introduce herself to the little girl, but she had no idea how to even begin. The girl stood off to the side, holding her hand in hers, but turned to watch the others play. Elizabeth tapped her on the shoulder, and patted her lap, hoping the little girl would know she was welcome to sit upon it.

The little girl slowly walked toward her and Elizabeth picked her up, placing her upon her lap. She stroked the girl's dark brown curls and the child leaned back and snuggled against her. Elizabeth looked at her husband and Mr. Fleming, who had noticed this interaction. Darcy smiled at her and Mr. Fleming nodded, all the while continuing to converse.

Elizabeth gently stroked the child's hair and rocked her back and forth while humming to her. It suddenly occurred to her that the little girl would not hear her, so she stopped. But instantly the little girl turned around, as if she noticed it. Elizabeth began humming again, the girl smiled, and turned back around.

When the two gentlemen came back, Elizabeth inquired about the little girl.

"Her name is Michelle," Mr. Fleming said. "She was abandoned at the doorstep here when she was barely two. She is now about four."

"But if she is deaf, how did she know I stopped singing?"

"The vibrations. Deaf people are very acute to their other senses. She felt the vibrations and to her it is very soothing. When you stopped, she noticed."

"How do you sign her name?"

"You do it by spelling it, like this." Fleming signed out each letter of Michelle's name, and Elizabeth watched with great joy as little Michelle's face lit up when she saw him spell it out.

Elizabeth tried to mimic him and soon Michelle was helping.

The sight of this little girl and his wife getting along so well moved Darcy. He knew that leaving in a few hours was not going to be easy. "Lizbeth, would you excuse me for a moment?"

Darcy left, and Elizabeth continued to practice signing Michelle's name. The little girl then pointed to her and signed something.

Elizabeth looked at Fleming and asked what it was she wanted. "She wants to know what your name is."

"And how do you sign Elizabeth?" she asked.

Fleming signed her name, one letter at a time. Michelle picked it up immediately and Elizabeth laughed. "She is so quick!"

"Well, it also helps that we have another Elizabeth here, so she is familiar with the name."

"Oh," laughed Elizabeth. She looked out to the other children playing and then turned to Fleming. "Why does she not want to play with the other children?"

"She is a bit younger than most of them. She keeps her distance, as it has been extremely difficult for her to bond with anyone, being left as she was. She is terribly hungry for affection and no matter how much we give her, sometimes she accepts it and sometimes she does not. Apparently now she wants it."

"With whom does she live?"

"Michelle lives with my family, as we are in the process of trying to adopt her. It is not that easy, with us being from England. It is almost finalized; I hope they do not see a problem with us wanting to return to England with her." He smiled at the child's rapport with Elizabeth. "It appears, Mrs. Darcy, that Michelle has really taken to you."

Elizabeth sighed. *Such a sweet girl to have been abandoned.* She could not imagine such a thing.

After an allotted amount of time, Mr. Fleming rounded up the children and led them back inside. "The children will now be resting. If you would like, you could take a look around the school. I shall try and find you after a while." With that he nodded, and the Darcys were left to look around.

"This is quite a remarkable place," Darcy stated.

"Yes. Mr. Fleming seems quite committed to it."

"He greatly desires coming back to England, though, to teach in our school."

"Oh, Will, I think that would be wonderful!"

"The problem is we have no school yet. But I should like to have him there as soon as possible just the same."

"Could we not have the school in a temporary location while it is being built? I am sure the Franks would love to have their daughter instructed as soon as possible."

"I should like that, as well, but where?"

Suddenly an idea came to Elizabeth. "Why not the church? It gets used only on Sundays and occasionally on a weekday. Do you think the reverend might allow it?"

"I believe that it would be worth looking into. I shall check with Pastor Kenton when we return." Darcy put his arm around Elizabeth's shoulders and pulled her tightly to himself. "I went out and told Jacques that we would probably be later than two o'clock. I told him to return at five, if that is acceptable to you."

"Oh, Will. You know it is! I should love to spend more time with each of these children!"

"Not just little Michelle?"

"Well, she is adorable. I wish I could sneak her into my travel bag and take her home with me."

"Lizbeth, I fear that if I were to allow you to do that, every little child and creature that wound its way into your heart would end up at Pemberley by your doing and before long, we would soon require a larger home!"

Elizabeth smiled at the thought of needing a larger home than Pemberley. "Mr. Fleming and his wife are in the process of trying to adopt her."

"Yes, he told me."

They continued to walk through the halls, quietly stepping into a class and observing here and there. They sat down in the back of an adult class and were amazed at the extent of their signing. This class was obviously an advanced class, as most of the students were as active in signing as the teacher.

Soon Mr. Fleming joined them again and escorted them to the dining room. "The children will be coming in to eat in a few minutes. Is there anything else you would like to know before they come in?"

Darcy asked how long it took for one to become proficient enough to carry on conversations.

"It is like learning to speak as a child. One must start with the basics and continually add. We use a combination of signing whole words and spelling out words. Since the children cannot attend a regular school, we also teach them reading and writing and spelling. That way, they can at least spell out a word if they do not know the sign for it."

Elizabeth eagerly informed him, "I should like to learn to sign the alphabet."

"You should have the complete alphabet and its signs in that packet Monsieur Bonne gave you."

Darcy decided it was best to get down to business with Fleming. "Is it acceptable with Monsieur Bonne that you return to England to teach?"

"Yes, I have been open with him since I became aware of your intent to begin a school. I believe he knew, from the moment you contacted him, that he would most likely lose me. I have been waiting for an opportunity to return to England so we could be closer to our other family members there."

"We have not even begun building the school, but my wife suggested we see if the church will allow us to use it temporarily for classes. If for some reason that does not work, there is always Pemberley, our home. I am sure we can work out the location. When do you think you would be able to come?"

"I should imagine it would be six weeks to two months before I could come."

"Good," Darcy replied. "I shall be in contact with you. Plan for your family to stay at Pemberley when you arrive and at length we shall help you find permanent accommodations."

It seemed as though the children were waiting for the two of them to finalize their discussions, as the doors suddenly burst open and they rushed in. Again, Elizabeth was amazed at how quiet all these children were, although the energy level was as normal as any group of children.

They all seemed to know exactly what to do, where to go, and hands were flying everywhere as they signed to one another. Elizabeth's eyes were on the children, searching out one little girl in particular, when she felt a tug at the back of her dress. She turned, and found herself looking into Michelle's big eyes.

Michelle took a seat next to Elizabeth and soon plates of food were brought out. As they enjoyed their meal, how she wished she could talk to this precious little girl! The only thing she could think to do was to smile at her and keep her hand upon her shoulder.

Mr. Fleming turned to Elizabeth. "It does not hurt, Mrs. Darcy, to speak to Michelle. Although she does not yet read lips, and she most certainly would not understand English, it will mean something to her that you are paying attention to her. Try not to treat her any differently than you would any other child."

Elizabeth took his words to heart and began talking with her, telling her what each of the foods on her plate was in English. When Elizabeth smiled and laughed, Michelle returned the gestures. Soon Elizabeth forgot all about her deafness and simply enjoyed her presence.

After the meal had been eaten, the children all took their plates and utensils to the kitchen area. Some children remained to clean them, while others went their separate ways.

"Now it is chore time. Some of the children work in the kitchen. The others work elsewhere. The little ones, like Michelle here, go to one of the play rooms where we encourage them to rest."

"All the children seem so well behaved and have such good manners!" commented Elizabeth.

"That is one thing we strive for. These children are taught not to expect special treatment because they are deaf. They must learn to live life as it is in the real world."

Elizabeth was so impressed her heart ached. She wished she could snatch up this whole school and take every teacher and every child with her back to England. But she knew that with Mr. Fleming coming, the school in Derbyshire should be as excellent as this one.

Darcy and Elizabeth spent the afternoon visiting different classes. At one point, Darcy returned to the offices to make some final arrangements with Monsieur Bonne, and Elizabeth settled herself in one of the classes with the children again. She sat with Michelle on her lap and enjoyed repeating the signs herself that the children were learning. She saw on one of the walls a large chart with the alphabet and the different signs for each letter. She moved her hands into the position of each letter, trying to memorize them as she did.

Before she knew it, the day was over. She did not look forward to leaving. Michelle had been her faithful companion for most of the day. She glanced up at the clock in the room where they spent their last few hours. It was almost five o'clock. School had been over for several hours, but many children had remained because they lived there during the school year.

Elizabeth continued to hold on to Michelle tightly, putting her head down against the girl's hair. Michelle had a wide grin on her face and Elizabeth tried to bring one to hers, but could not. She suddenly felt herself shaking, and was determined not to let Michelle see her cry. She closed her eyes, fighting off the tears.

Darcy and Fleming continued to talk, and she watched, with great dread, as her husband stood up and walked toward her, holding out his hand. "I think we must leave now, Lizbeth."

She took in a deep breath, as if it would steady her and prepare her for the difficult task she now faced. She leaned over and kissed the top of Michelle's head, very gently lifting her off her lap. The young girl turned around and reached back up with both hands. Elizabeth solemnly smiled and shook her head no.

Elizabeth watched as tears began forming in the child's eyes and she felt as if they were mirroring her own. She pulled her close one last time, hugging her tightly. Darcy came up and took Elizabeth by the arm as Fleming came to Michelle and picked her up. "Goodbye," whispered Elizabeth, waving at the child.

Michelle abruptly turned her head and buried it into Fleming's chest. "She will be fine after a while. She does tend to attach herself to some people for one reason or another."

"I do hope you will be able to get the adoption finalized so you can bring her when you leave."

"Thank you, Mrs. Darcy. We are doing everything we can to speed up the process."

"Thank you, Fleming for all you have done." Darcy held shook the other man's extended hand. "We shall see you in a few months, then?"

"Yes, and I shall be in contact with you."

Darcy and Elizabeth turned and walked away, his arm around her shoulders. He felt them rise and fall as her tears gave way to sobs. When they stepped out of the front doors, Elizabeth turned to him and collapsed into his chest. He wrapped his arms tightly around her, not sure what he should do.

"Elizabeth…"

Elizabeth brought her hands up to his chest and pushed herself away from him. "Will, I am so sorry. There was something about that little girl that has deeply affected me." She looked up at him with tears glistening. "I do not know what came over me. I shall be all right.

"It is your caring, nurturing nature, my sweet Lizbeth. That is one of the many reasons why I married you. You have a caring heart."

She tried to smile as they walked to their waiting carriage.

Jacques had seen what had transpired and when he saw Elizabeth as they approached, he asked if they were well.

"We are, Jacques. It has been an emotional day. Take us back to the hotel, please."

Inside the carriage, Elizabeth rested against Darcy. Michelle had certainly found her way to Elizabeth's heart, and the thought that her adoption was still questionable concerned her. She had spent but only a portion of the day with her and found it difficult to leave her. How would the Flemings feel if the adoption was denied them?

Her thoughts went to the school that would be starting in the vicinity around Pemberley and she realized she wanted to have some involvement in it.

"Will," she said softly.

"Yes," he answered as his fingers played with the loose curls along her neck.

"What would you think of my being involved in the deaf school in Derbyshire?"

Darcy took a deep breath. "I had a feeling you would ask that." He paused, carefully choosing what he would say to her. "I would imagine you can be involved as much as you would like, as long as you do not overdo it, and that you do not take on things that will interfere with your being my wife, the mistress of Pemberley, and someday, a mother to our children."

Chapter 7

Darcy and Elizabeth fervently enjoyed their remaining days in Paris. Each morning they awakened early enough to step out of their room and see the magical display of colour and lights as the sun hit the hundreds of prisms that hung from the huge chandelier. They enjoyed a leisurely start of their day as they took in its beauty and enjoyed a delicious meal.

A few days after going to the school, Darcy and Elizabeth took an early walk through the neighbourhood. They strolled down small streets near the Seine, not really caring about where they would end up. Elizabeth walked with her hand wrapped snugly in her husband's arm. It was down one of these small side streets that something caught Elizabeth's attention.

"Will. Look over there! Is that not Jacques' carriage?"

Darcy turned his head in the direction of the carriage. It was parked off the main road, the horses unhitched; most likely boarded at a nearby livery stable. "If not his, it certainly looks very similar."

They walked over to it and Elizabeth immediately recognized the emblem on the side.

She whispered, "What do you suppose it is doing here? He said his aunt lived about twenty minutes away."

"Of that I am not certain. Wait here a moment." With curiosity propelling him, he walked over and carefully peered into the window. Sure enough, as he suspected, Jacques was fast asleep inside, covered with a blanket.

He turned to Elizabeth, put his finger up to his lips so as to keep her quiet, and drew her away. When he was a good distance from it, he said, "Jacques is asleep in the carriage."

"But why? Last night we did not get in late. He would have had plenty of time to return to his aunt's."

"If indeed he even has an aunt here in Paris."

Elizabeth looked at her husband with a startled and confused look. "But why would he conceal something like this from us?"

"I would suspect this concealment was due in part to him not wanting any of the wages I am paying him to go toward room and board. If we put him up somewhere, that would take away from the amount I offered to pay him. Since he most likely knew I would not look highly on his sleeping in the carriage, he made up the story of having an aunt."

Suddenly the truth of the situation hit Elizabeth. "Will! He told us that his aunt was the only family he had, when he told us he was orphaned. Do you suppose that means he actually has no family?"

"That could very well be."

"Oh, how sad! What shall we do?"

"Well, for one, I am going to secure him a room. I shall get one for him by the livery inn. That will allow him to easily park the carriage, stable the horses, and walk to his room. I shall tell him that it is his to use when we have a late evening or an early morning. That way, he can use it as he pleases, and he should not get suspicious that we know."

"But should we tell him we know?"

"Not yet, Lizbeth. I think we best wait and see if he decides to inform us himself."

When Jacques came by later that day to pick them up, Elizabeth could not help but ache for this young boy. Not having any known family must be the most difficult thing in life to face, and in the past week, Elizabeth had encountered two children who had been orphaned. She truly appreciated his "family crest" and what it meant to him.

Jacques was a most efficient driver and he took them to places very few knew about, giving Darcy and Elizabeth a rare, enjoyable, and comprehensive view of Paris. By their last full day, he still had not said anything to the Darcys about not having an aunt in Paris, but they were aware that he was using the room and they were grateful for it.

On their last day in Paris, Darcy and Elizabeth spent the morning wandering around on foot. They had formed an attachment to certain places along the Seine, parks and gardens scattered throughout the city, and historical places of interest that they wanted to visit one last time before leaving on the morrow.

They stepped outside, enjoying the cool morning air. Their intent was to walk to a park they had discovered a few days earlier. It had been the day after they had visited the deaf school and Elizabeth was still feeling a tug on her heart for little Michelle. Darcy had debated trying to take her mind off of the little girl by either engulfing her in the midst of a crowd of people and sights, or allowing her to enjoy one of her favourite pastimes -- walking.

They had wandered aimlessly, working their way up and down the side streets, enjoying the small shops and homes that lined them. Many had beautiful flower boxes hung beneath their windows, as their yards were too small for gardens. It was at the end of one of these streets that they found this park.

It was not exceptional, compared to the likes of the gardens at Luxembourg or Versailles, but it had an atmosphere that drew one in. It made one want to stop and rest, simply to breathe in the scent of the flowers that were still in bloom, and to enjoy the colour they dispensed. Benches were placed in strategic places, allowing the best view of the park and its surroundings.

Darcy and Elizabeth returned to the same bench in the park that they had occupied on their previous visit. They watched as people hurried through the park. They conjectured where they might be off to, whether to work, shop, or simply out enjoying the morning as the two of them were.

As they sat quietly and watched the people stroll by, Elizabeth turned to her husband and gently combed back some loose curls from his forehead with her fingers. But instead of bringing her hand back down when she had finished, she cupped his face with her hand and turned it toward her. He raised his eyebrows at her, expecting her to say something to him. Instead, she very slowly leaned toward him, and much to Darcy's astonishment pressed her lips against his. His surprise was quickly suspended as he gave in to the delight that her spontaneous display of affection brought.

When she finally pulled away, Darcy smiled. "Elizabeth! What am I to make of your behaviour! I cannot believe that you would do such a thing in public with no apparent consideration for propriety!"

Elizabeth teased him back. "I would imagine it is solely because we are in Paris, my dear."

Darcy's face suddenly turned downcast. "Are you telling me that once we return to England, I cannot expect to receive such outward display of affection?"

Elizabeth continued to stroke his face. "Let me assure you, Fitzwilliam Darcy, if you are so inclined to do away with the dictates of society when we return, then I shall be likewise."

Darcy smiled. He knew that back in England, he would, by his very nature, be inclined towards a more reserved behaviour and conduct -- at least in public. Things were slightly different there than they were in Paris, and, he had to admit that reserve was ingrained in him. He was fairly certain Elizabeth knew that as well.

Here in Paris he had felt a freedom with Elizabeth that had surprised even him. He wondered if it was she that brought it out in him, the ambiance of Paris, or a combination of the two. He could not speculate now, but in the meantime, as long as they were in Paris… He pulled Elizabeth toward him again and kissed her deeply, wrapping his arms tightly around her. And neither of them gave a second thought to those passing by who were marvelling at the evident love these two shared.

~~*

When Jacques came by in the afternoon as they requested, they decided to invite him to share a meal with them as their guest. They had, throughout the course of the week, only been able to visit sporadically with him. He was reluctant to take them up on their offer to join them, but Darcy insisted and would not take no for an answer.

As they inquired of Jacques for a place to eat, he recommended a small café that was nestled on a side street near the Place de la Concorde. They walked along the gardens, enjoying the fountains and statues that were within it. Darcy and Elizabeth attempted to draw the young man into conversation, desiring to learn more about him. Finally Darcy decided to inquire directly about his aunt.

"Tell me about your aunt, Jacques. Are you and she very close?"

"Uh, no, not very."

Darcy gave a quick glance over to Elizabeth. She pleaded with him using her eyes to proceed cautiously.

"You said she is the only family you have?"

"That is correct, Sir."

"And what of other family on her side? Does she have anyone else?"

Jacques suddenly stopped and turned his head off to the side, taking in a deep breath. "I am sorry, Monsieur Darcy, Madame Darcy. I am afraid I did not speak the truth when I told you of my aunt. I do not have one."

Darcy and Elizabeth were quiet for a time. Elizabeth resisted the urge to reach over and hug the boy, to let him know they were not angry with him.

"I am sorry that I was not truthful. Pardon me if I have angered you by this. I shall wait for you at the carriage until you finish eating."

"No! No, Jacques." Darcy held up his hand. "We are not angry with you. We would still like you to join us. We have actually known for a few days that you were not staying with your aunt."

"You knew?"

"Yes Jacques," Elizabeth told him. "We found you asleep in the carriage a few days ago. That is why we secured the room for you."

Jacques suddenly looked down at his feet, unsure of how to respond. He could not think of one other time in his life where someone, especially complete strangers, bestowed upon him such an act of kindness.

"I... I... do not know what to say. You, the two of you, are so very kind and generous. I do not deserve it. I will, of course, expect you to deduct my room from my wages."

"Nonsense!" Darcy declared. "Now, let us see if this café has the good food you promised it would!"

When Darcy, Elizabeth, and Jacques were seated at their table, Jacques continued to feel ill at ease. He had never been in a situation before where he was being treated as an equal by someone who was far superior to him. He could not believe the Darcys, who were of such superior consequence, were concerned for him.

They learned he had been orphaned at three, so he never really knew his parents. He apparently had no brothers and sisters and there was no other family known to take care of him. It had been a difficult life in the orphanage, but he learned how to work hard and much of what he knew now was a result of a great deal of studying on his own. He learned to speak English from one of his teachers who was married to an English woman. When he was sixteen he was allowed to leave the orphanage.

He had found work with a blacksmith and had worked long and hard hours while living in a small room above the blacksmith's house. He had scrimped and saved until he had enough to buy a carriage and began his own meagre business four months ago. He worked the dock at Calais, knowing people would require the use of a carriage on a regular basis as ships came in. His normal fare, however, was merely a short distance from the dock to their lodgings.

"Where do you live now, Jacques, when you are in Calais?" asked Darcy.

Jacques took in a deep breath and grimaced. "At the moment I live in my carriage. I keep it parked by an inn that lets me use their facilities for a small fee. I could not afford to keep up payments on the room since I no longer worked for the blacksmith. It is not bad. It will do for now."

Elizabeth leaned in to him and asked, "What are your plans, Jacques? Is this what you want to do all your life?"

"I know I am excellent carriage driver. I know my strengths -- I am prompt, honest, and can find my way around anywhere. I only need that one opportunity to get myself consistent work."

Elizabeth turned sharply to look at Darcy. He did not miss for one minute that look in her eyes that said, *Surely we can help him out!* Darcy fought back a smirk as he thought to himself, *Here is my wife, again, getting involved in the lives of the needy and downtrodden! We have been married but a little over a week, I cannot imagine what years of this will bring!*

"Jacques, if you need any sort of recommendation, I shall gladly give it!" Darcy offered.

"Thank you, Sir. *Merci.*"

They continued to eat, and Elizabeth could not help but enjoy the engaging personality of this young boy. All the while they talked, her mind turned over every possibility, attempting to figure out some way they could help him. When a solution finally did come to her, she suddenly sat back in her chair and smiled.

Darcy readily noticed the change in her demeanour and had a strong suspicion that she had come up with some notion about how she was going to take care of Jacques and get him all situated in life so he would never have another care in the world. He smiled to himself as he reasoned it probably had something to do with Jacques coming over with Michelle and the Flemings, and moving them all in to Pemberley, and they would all be one happy family. As Jacques continued to talk, Darcy and Elizabeth talked between themselves with their eyes, silently commenting, and inwardly deciphering what the other had on their mind.

After the meal, Jacques drove them around Paris for one last evening ride. They enjoyed watching the brightness of the city as it began to pale at dusk, and soon, as the lamps were lit, the magical atmosphere again reappeared. In the solitude of the carriage they began to discuss the events about which Jacques had told them and what, if anything, they could do about it.

Elizabeth began, and in over a week's time of marriage, she had learnt exactly how to affect her husband for her benefit. She turned in the seat to face him directly. With one hand she began stroking her husband's arm. She brought her other hand up behind him and began to massage his neck slightly; moving her fingers up into his curls, and then down towards his firm shoulders. He relaxed his head, leaning back against her hand; he smiled, and closed his eyes, content to enjoy her priming of him, while waiting for her impassioned petition.

"Will…"

Darcy opened one eye for a moment, lifting his brow to look at her. "Hmm?"

When she began to talk again, without thinking she pulled her hand away from his neck. He quickly retrieved it with his, and replaced it where it had been. He knew if she was going to use her alluring powers to get her way, he wanted to enjoy her soothing ministrations as long as he could.

She resumed the kneading of the tense muscles in his neck and he smiled. "Now, what were you going to say?"

"When the deaf school is completed, do you not think it will require a carriage driver?"

"For what purpose?"

"Pick up students, drop them off. Mr. Fleming himself, most likely, will need to avail himself of a carriage on a regular basis."

"And you are thinking of Jacques for this position?"

"Of course! Jacques could be most useful to the school."

"I shall have to think on it." With his eyes still closed, he let his head lean back as he enjoyed Elizabeth's fingers rubbing little circles around his neck and shoulders. "If you rub a little harder on the sides, I believe I could begin to see the merit in your suggestion."

~~*

The next day Darcy and Elizabeth packed and left the hotel early. The sun had not yet appeared in the sky, although the horizon anticipated its ascent with bright oranges and pinks streaming out from the centre. Jacques was waiting for them when they came out of the hotel and quickly retrieved their luggage.

The morning was cool and a shawl was wrapped around Elizabeth's shoulders to help take away the chill. She looked about her, taking in for one last time the sights around the hotel. The city was awakening and fairly empty. She knew in a few hours it would be bustling with people.

They settled themselves in the carriage, ready for another full day of travel. Elizabeth watched through the window as Paris drifted past. She sighed to herself as she knew this may be the last she would see it. She wondered if they would ever return to this magical place.

Darcy noticed her ever so soft sigh. "Did you enjoy your time here, Lizbeth?"

"Oh, yes, it was wonderful." She turned from looking out the window, to him. "I do not think I could have had a more wonderful time."

"I am glad." Darcy brought his hand up, and with the back of his hand, gently stroked Elizabeth's cheek.

"I shall miss our breakfasts each morning surrounded by a sea of rainbows!"

"Did you enjoy that?"

"Yes, I did."

Darcy leaned over and pulled a box out from under his coat that was lying on the end of the seat. "Here then, my sweet, this is for you."

Elizabeth's eyes lit up. "What is it?"

"I believe you must open it to find out."

Elizabeth took the parcel and began to lift the lid, occasionally lifting her eyes to her husband's.

"Now be careful," he warned her.

When she opened the lid, she encountered a lot of crumpled paper. After carefully pulling it away, to her great delight she found a small crystal candelabrum, with eight miniature prisms suspended around it.

"Oh, Will, this is beautiful! When did you ever buy this?"

"I saw it in a store window and sent Jacques back for it. Do you like it?"

"I love it! And you must help me decide in which window to place it so it gets the most direct sun in the morning!"

"I believe, Mrs. Darcy, that it would be our bedroom window. We shall awaken every sunny morning to a roomful of rainbows!"

"Thank you, so much. This is not only the most delightful gift, but it was very thoughtful on your part." Elizabeth leaned over and kissed him.

~~*

When they arrived at Calais, Darcy and Elizabeth stayed at the same inn as they had their first night in France. Darcy talked with Jacques, inquiring whether he had any inclination to come to England and work for them. He agreed with Elizabeth's suggestion that the school would benefit from and most likely could use a carriage and driver on a regular basis.

When Jacques expressed interest, Darcy gave him Mr. Fleming's name and told him to contact him back at the school in Paris. He could find out from him approximately when he would be coming over and could plan to do so at the same time. He left with him directions to Pemberley and his London home and encouraged him to write in about a month to confirm his plans. Darcy again arranged to put him up in a small inn by the livery stables. The boy tried to talk him out of it, but Darcy would hear nothing of it.

After getting their belongings up to their room, they bade goodnight to the young man. Elizabeth turned to Darcy, with much gratitude in her eyes.

"You know, Mr. Darcy," she began coyly. "I do believe that you have a heart of gold inside you."

Darcy looked down, seemingly feeling uneasy at her words. He walked toward her, bringing his face up to look at her, and putting two fingers under her chin, slowly lifted it up. "Mrs. Darcy, whatever you see in me must be attributed to *you*." He leaned toward her, anxious to place a kiss on her lips.

She halted him in the object of his intentions. "You were very kind to him."

He took in a deep breath. "I have no difficulty helping someone who has proven to me that he will be faithful to the task. Jacques has proven that, and besides, I like the young man. Now, my dear, enough talk of Jacques. We leave tomorrow early for England, and this is our last night in France."

When she again began to speak, he moved his hand which still cradled her chin and covered her mouth with his fingers. "Shhh, Lizbeth. We could talk about this all night, but now I have something other than conversation that is foremost on my mind." As he lowered his lips toward hers, he kept his hand over her mouth until his lips were about on hers, then he released his hand and the kiss that he placed on her lips removed from her all thought of any further discourse.

Chapter 8

Upon finally setting foot back on English soil, Darcy and Elizabeth were met by Winston when the ship arrived in Dover. He conveyed them by carriage back to their London townhouse, where they spent two nights, allowing themselves a bit of a rest and refreshment from the travels that preceded and would follow. Darcy himself took the opportunity to catch up on some business while there, as Elizabeth continued to acquaint herself with the home, its servants, and its surroundings.

Elizabeth took great delight in her stay at their London residence on this their second visit. When they previously stayed there the night after they were married, their arrival had been in the evening. Elizabeth had not been able to familiarize herself with it as well as she would have liked. She had only been able to determine that it was elegant and spacious, was located in a most fashionable part of town, and she enjoyed meeting the handful of people who kept the home running in both Darcy's presence and absence.

On her first visit, she could not help but feel as though she were a guest in a grand hotel, as there was not yet a sense of ownership for her in the home. It had all been new and different to her. Her husband had given her a quick tour to familiarize her with the house and she saw many of the rooms only briefly. She was unmistakably pleased with it, although took note of areas that were needful of some updating and a loving woman's touch. But she did not have time to dwell on that during that stay, nor was there time to relax and enjoy it.

Now, having arrived earlier in the afternoon and having the opportunity to spend two days there, she could wander through the rooms of the house and give them more careful scrutiny. She enjoyed studying all the little accessories that were meticulously arranged on tables, on shelves, decoratively on the walls, and behind glass doors of cabinets. She wondered of their background, their meaning, how old they were, and who purchased them.

The staff was genuinely interested in and excessively cordial to her. On their first visit, being as short as it was, few had the opportunity to meet her. There had been much speculative communication between the staff in London and the staff at Pemberley, when one or the other would make a trip to the other home. The Pemberley staff had the privilege of getting to know her when she visited there, so they were questioned excessively about this lady who had finally won their master's heart. Now, they were able to judge for themselves whether their master had done well for himself. They were most pleasantly surprised that they felt an instant camaraderie with her.

Darcy and Elizabeth enjoyed a brief, but very enjoyable visit with her Aunt and Uncle Gardiner the evening before they departed. Elizabeth was grateful it was these family members of hers that they were first to see on their return. Elizabeth could relax in the presence of her aunt and uncle and she and Darcy had a wonderful visit. It was much too short, however, and Elizabeth knew that the very next day she and her husband would be travelling back to Longbourn.

They left the London town home early the next morning. From the moment they set out, Elizabeth began having misgivings about coming back into the presence of her family. The dread of whether they would behave with want of propriety, in even the short visit they had planned to make, grew more and more formidable the closer they drew. She had had her husband all to herself since their marriage, and now he would be forced to try his hand at civility again as he entered the society of her most dubious family. She noticed that Darcy seemed unusually quiet. She wondered if he, too, was dreading or mentally preparing himself for the encounter.

She was grateful that they would be staying only one night and it would be with the Bingleys at Netherfield. How much she looked forward to seeing Jane again! That thought alone instilled great anticipation in returning home and she could almost push back the nagging worry about her family in the joy of seeing her sister. By late afternoon, after a leisurely carriage ride, they arrived at Longbourn. Winston immediately brought himself down from his driving post after bringing the horses to a halt. He opened the carriage door for the Darcys and helped them both out.

As he performed his duty, Mr. Bennet emerged from the house. "Darcy, my dearest Lizzy, it is so good to see you both! Did you have a pleasant journey?" He reached out and took his son-in-law's hand, then turned to his daughter.

"Yes, Papa, we enjoyed it immensely." She brought her arms up around him and gave him a hug. "Paris was wonderful. I kept thinking how much you would enjoy visiting there. We saw so many historical sites, and every time we did, I wished you could have been there with us, to see them also."

"Now that, my dear, I find hard to believe! But I appreciate the thought!" He slapped Darcy on the back. "Sir, it appears to me you are taking good care of my daughter."

"I certainly am doing my best, Sir."

"Well, do not just stand there, let us go on in, shall we?"

As he said this, Mrs. Bennet was heard from inside the house approaching the door. "Oh my Lizzy! You are home! Did you not have a grand time in Paris? Was it not everything you could have imagined?"

"Hello, Mama. We did have a wonderful time." Elizabeth walked up to greet her and gave her a kiss.

"Good day, Mrs. Bennet." Darcy walked up to her and slightly hesitated, but followed Elizabeth's example and leaned over and in like fashion also gave her a kiss.

"Ohhh," exclaimed Mrs. Bennet, apparently rendered speechless by his accommodating gesture and nervously waved them towards the house.

Elizabeth could not help but smile at him. She took his arm and gave it a tight squeeze as they began to walk, letting him know how much she appreciated it. She stopped when Mary and Kitty came out to join them and momentarily removed herself from her husband's arm while she greeted them both and gave them a hug. She turned to look at Darcy, noting the look of uneasiness that was spreading across his face. She gave him a heartening smile, not to demand, but to encourage a similar response. Again, he followed suit, giving the sisters a hug.

Mary was quite taken back by his hug; Kitty was awed by it. This gentleman had always appeared to both girls to be so formidable and aloof, that it was quite disconcerting to have him display such actions toward them. Mary was reticent to acknowledge to herself that she was indeed rather flattered he would take notice of her. Kitty could not help but feel admiration for this man in the fact that he had married her elder sister. She also felt privileged that she had a new friendship with his sister, from whom she had just received a letter.

As they walked in, Elizabeth inquired after Lydia. Mrs. Bennet was most willing to provide them with all the details of Lydia going to Brighton. "Why Lizzy, you remember that Lydia was invited to join Colonel Forster and his wife in Brighton?"

Elizabeth felt fear and trepidation seize her heart as she gripped tighter to Darcy's arm. "Yes, Mama."

"We had agreed that she should be allowed to go after you were married. She left two days after your wedding."

Elizabeth's eyes grew wide with anxiety. "But Mama, Papa," she turned from one to the other, "surely you did not believe it was in her best interest to journey there unescorted, all alone?"

"Lydia is not going to be alone. The Forsters assured us, most emphatically, that they would take good care of her."

Elizabeth looked up at Darcy and saw the look of concerned resignation on his face. He knew there was nothing that could be done about it now, save pray that she not behave improperly. Elizabeth looked over to her father, who was standing off to the side in silence. "But Papa…"

"Now Lizzy," her father began, "this is a wonderful opportunity for our youngest. Let her have a good time, and at very little expense or inconvenience to her family!"

As they proceeded inside and to the sitting room, Mary came up behind Elizabeth and whispered, "I can see that you are as appalled as I am. Certainly you see the impropriety in this that I do. If only you had been here to talk some sense into Father, he might not have allowed her to go!"

"Yes, Mary, well it is done! We shall have to hope for the best!" Elizabeth felt more anger at the situation than at Mary and realized how she appeared. "I am sorry, Mary. It does concern me, but there is nothing we can do about it now." She also felt her anger directed toward herself in not disclosing Wickham's character.

This revelation caused Elizabeth and Darcy to feel somewhat strained for the remainder of their visit. She no longer had to worry solely about the behaviour of her family; she was now unwittingly forced to worry about Lydia, the officers, and Wickham, all together in Brighton.

Elizabeth greatly desired to get away and talk with her husband about the situation. She was concerned enough that they allowed Lydia to leave home and be amongst all the officers. But knowing that Wickham was there and how much Lydia favoured him caused her greater consternation.

They spent several hours visiting with the Bennet family and then embarked for the short ride to Netherfield, bidding farewell to her family. As soon as they were alone in the confines of the carriage, Elizabeth could suppress her thoughts and feelings no longer. "William! What are we to do? Lydia in Brighton with those officers! And Wickham being there! She is not even aware of his true character! How I wish I had said something to her. Warned her!"

"Lizbeth, you had no idea this was going to happen."

"Oh, but I should have seen it coming. I knew the Forsters had invited her. I only hoped that Papa would have had the prudence and conviction to forbid it!"

"Perhaps we are worrying for nothing." He said this feeling even less assured of its truth than his tone of voice suggested.

"Oh, Will. You do not know Lydia. I fear that she may do something we shall all regret! She acts in such impulsive, imprudent ways."

"Perhaps you are not giving her enough credit. She may surprise everyone and act fittingly."

"Not likely, indeed! I fear that would be an impossibility on her part. I only hope the Forsters will take their responsibility of her seriously."

Darcy turned to her, pain now was written across his face. "I hope so. When you put a young girl in someone's trust, you do expect them to live up to their responsibility."

Elizabeth took Darcy's hand and gave it a slight squeeze. "You are thinking of Mrs. Younge, are you not?"

Darcy took in a slow breath and began speaking as if he had been transported back a little over a year ago. "She had come to us with many references when she applied to be Georgiana's governess. She had the position for about three months when she asked permission to take her to Ramsgate to visit some of her family. I had no reason to have any concern. What I did not know, however, was that somehow she was acquainted with Wickham and the two had conspired to get Georgiana away from home; away from me. That allowed Wickham to pour on his disgusting charm and deceive Georgiana into thinking he loved her and persuaded her to believe she loved him. He was only hoping to secure her fortune for himself." He almost spat out the words as he spoke. "I believe Wickham offered Mrs. Younge some sort of payment in exchange for her being an accessory to his scheme."

"How did you come to find out about the elopement?"

Darcy's eyes narrowed as he continued. "Someone must have seen what was going on and recognized that it was wrong." Darcy brought his hand up to his chin, rubbing it in contemplation. "I received an anonymous letter, telling me that I had best get to Ramsgate quickly as Mrs. Younge was putting Georgiana in some very inappropriate situations with Mr. Wickham."

"Anonymous? You do not know who wrote it?"

"No, I did not know then and I have never found out. I assume it was some acquaintance of Mrs. Younge, possibly even some family member that learnt what she was doing and saw the impropriety in it. Thankfully they wrote me informing me of the situation. I would have never gone if it were not for the letter. Needless to say, I arrived in time. They were only days away from..."

Darcy's voice broke. His fist tightened and the anger welled up inside him as if it were yesterday. Elizabeth gently stroked his other hand.

"I am sorry. It still must be very painful for you. I only hope he is not able to deceive Lydia to any greater degree than he has already deceived us."

"Do not worry yourself, Elizabeth." He turned to her and smiled. "There are enough officers there to keep Lydia's interest, more so than Wickham, and he should have no reason to focus his attention on her. Perhaps we ought to be worrying about the other officers." Darcy hoped his smile would convince Elizabeth of his words and ease her mind.

Darcy turned his head to look out the window. He did not want her to see the concern that was etched across his face. It was not so much Lydia's immature behaviour, her outspoken views of the desirability of the officers, or her tendency to do things without thinking that concerned him. It was the fact that *he* was now Lydia's brother, by reason of being married to Elizabeth, and he wondered what Wickham might do in response to that. That was what troubled him.

They rode the remainder of the way in silence; each consumed with thoughts and worries of their own.

When they arrived at Netherfield, Elizabeth could not bring herself out of the carriage quick enough. She wanted to see Jane, needed to talk to Jane; hoping she would have some encouraging words for her. Jane and Charles came rushing out of the house to greet them.

"Oh, Jane, how are you? It is so good to see you!"

"I am so glad to see you as well. Did you both have a wonderful wedding journey? I am sure Paris must have been beautiful!"

"Oh, it was!"

"You must tell us all about it. Come, let us go in."

Charles and Darcy greeted each other and the two couples walked toward the house.

As the sisters walked in arm in arm, a look of concern quickly passed Elizabeth's face. "Jane, you are aware that Lydia was allowed to go off to Brighton?" The two of them stopped as the subject was brought up.

"Yes, she has been gone about a week now."

Elizabeth waited until the men had joined them. "I wish I could have warned her about Wickham before she left."

Darcy then spoke. "We are both a little concerned about her being there, knowing how deceptive Wickham can be."

Jane looked at the two of them and took Elizabeth's hand in hers, and then looked at Darcy. "The day before she left, Georgiana and I paid a visit to our sisters. Georgiana wanted to get to know each of them a little better. When she found out about Lydia's plans, she had a little talk with her."

Darcy looked quite taken back by this. "Did she tell her about what happened with her and Wickham?"

"I believe she did, William. Georgiana told me as we returned to Netherfield that she felt she had to speak to Lydia, as she was completely unaware of his true character."

Darcy shook his head. "I cannot imagine how difficult that must have been for Georgiana."

Elizabeth looked up at him. "See, Will, I told you your sister is growing up." She turned back to Jane. "I feel a little more at ease now. Lydia should not be caught off guard by any lies he tells her now. Now there is only Lydia and all the *other* officers I need worry about!"

They all nervously laughed and proceeded into the house.

"Oh, speaking of Georgiana," Jane went over to a table and picked up a letter. "She wrote me, asking me to appeal to the two of you to bring Kitty back to Pemberley when you return. She has been quite lonely and knew Kitty was rather distressed at not being able to join Lydia in Brighton. She writes that she did not say anything about this in a letter she wrote to Kitty, in case it would not be agreeable to you.

Elizabeth looked over at her husband and raised her eyebrows questioningly at him. He shrugged. Elizabeth was not confident that this form of communication was the most accurate, but she determined that they both had agreed to it.

"I think it would be fine. We must send a message to Longbourn directly, though, so she can be ready to leave first thing in the morning."

Darcy looked surprised at Elizabeth's comment. "Lizbeth, do you not think we should wait and see if your parents give permission first, before we make plans that she is coming?"

Jane and Elizabeth looked and each other and laughed.

"What… what is so funny?"

"You do not know my family well enough, Will. She will definitely be allowed to go."

Elizabeth composed a note and promptly dispatched it to Longbourn. Within an hour a reply was received, and, as she had expected, Kitty would be joining them as they returned to Pemberley on the morrow.

The remainder of their stay with Charles and Jane was very enjoyable. They were able to share the highlights of their time in Paris without the nagging worry of what may be happening in Brighton. The four of them enjoyed each other's company -- the two long time friends and two favourite sisters -- well into the early hours of the morning.

The next morning, with the Pemberley carriage all packed with the Darcys' things, the couples said their farewells. The two sisters would have greatly loved to spend more time together and seemed inseparable in a hug that would have to last them until they saw each other again. They were not certain when that would be.

Darcy and Bingley looked on, waiting for them to draw away from each other.

As they stood off to the side, they sensed an even greater bond between them now, because of the sisters they had married, that went beyond the years of friendship they had experienced.

Bingley turned to Darcy. "Do me a favour, Darcy. Keep a lookout for a moderate estate in Derbyshire that might be had for my wife and I, either to let or to purchase. Jane and I have talked about whether to purchase Netherfield, but seeing how close she and Elizabeth are, I believe it would be most favourable for both of us to find a country estate closer to you. That is, if you would not mind having us living nearer to you."

"I think it is a wonderful idea, Bingley. I shall keep my eyes open for something."

"Thanks, Darce."

Elizabeth and Jane soon pulled themselves apart and, with tears in their eyes, said goodbye. They knew not when they would see each other again, but the ladies promised to write each other often. Darcy promised the same to Bingley, as he actually enjoyed the task of writing a letter. Bingley could only make the promise that Jane would write for the two of them. Settled in the carriage, Elizabeth drew near her husband, tears still filling her eyes. He pulled her even closer as the carriage pulled away. "Let me dry those tears, Elizabeth. You would not want Kitty to see them, would you?"

He leaned over and tenderly kissed her eyes, tasting the saltiness of her tears. She struggled to bring a smile to her face, when Darcy came up with an idea. He reached into his pocket and pulled out a handkerchief that was familiar to them both. Elizabeth smiled when she saw the embroidered handkerchief with "EB" in the corner. He brought it up to her face and gently wiped the tears.

"Where has that been?"

"I inadvertently left it at Netherfield when we departed for Paris. I found it last night in with some of my other things."

Elizabeth reached up and lightly fingered it. She thought of everything that handkerchief had gone through, in bringing the two of them together. Her tears were soon replaced by a very contented smile.

As Darcy saw her spirits improve, he could not help but congratulate himself on his idea to bring it out. It appeared to have worked.

She gave her husband back the handkerchief that they had both earlier agreed he would keep. She turned her attention to a small bag she had brought along with her. Reaching inside, she pulled out some embroidery thread and a pure white handkerchief. It was the one Darcy had given her to replace the one he now had. Darcy looked at her questioningly.

"Just as I embroidered that handkerchief on the ride to Pemberley with Jane four months ago, I thought I would embroider this one with my new initials on our ride to Pemberley today."

"And what were your thoughts on your ride to Pemberley those four months ago?"

Elizabeth smiled, thinking back on her reasons for agreeing to go. "My main reason for going to Pemberley, as you so accurately deduced when you awoke, was to reunite Jane and Charles. That was my main intent and my sole focus. My conviction that Jane and Charles were meant to be together was enough to overrule any trepidation I felt in you awakening from unconsciousness and finding me there."

"Thank goodness for your determination and conviction. If it were not for that, we might not be together right now."

"Perish the thought!" laughed Elizabeth.

The carriage pulled up to Longbourn and Kitty excitedly came out with Mr. and Mrs. Bennet. Darcy and Elizabeth stepped down to greet them while Winston secured her things on the carriage.

As they prepared to leave, Mrs. Bennet left them with some last minute instructions. "Now, Kitty, you behave yourself, and Lizzy, you make sure she listens to you." Mrs. Bennet gave out orders that she herself never enforced in her own home. "Goodbye, Kitty. Goodbye, Lizzy." She herself held a tattered handkerchief and waved it excitedly at them as she bade them farewell.

Elizabeth lightly kissed her mother's cheek and then turned and hugged her father. "Goodbye, Papa. Feel free to come to Pemberley any time to see us," she whispered in his ear. He felt admiration and appreciation that he was receiving this special invitation from his favourite daughter.

"Well if not sooner, I shall be there to retrieve Kitty in a few weeks' time. I am grateful she will be in such good company at Pemberley."

The three travellers made themselves comfortable in the carriage, anticipating a full day's journey. If they made good time, they should get there by late afternoon. Darcy looked forward to stepping back onto the grounds of Pemberley with his most beloved wife by his side. Elizabeth anticipated the role of the Mistress of Pemberley and what that would require, but relished more the idea of simply being Mrs. Fitzwilliam Darcy. And Kitty rode the whole way in awe of this man, wondering of his estate, and pondering whether she would ever be fortunate enough to meet someone as wealthy and handsome as he.

Chapter 9

Pemberley

As she awaited the return of her brother and his wife, each passing day slowly gave way to a new week. Georgiana fervently looked forward to their arrival, but found herself fighting increasing loneliness and boredom. She clung to the hope that when they did arrive, they would have Kitty with them, as she had requested in her letter to Jane.

She began to feel the need for a diversion beyond her daily studies with Mrs. Annesley, whose thoughts were now more focused on preparing to leave. As such, she simply encouraged Georgiana in her reading, needlework, and practicing on the pianoforte. Georgiana obliged her with a self-imposed willingness and voracity meant to keep her mind off her loneliness and from straying to musings of that someone who had unwillingly invaded her thoughts.

Since the day she had encountered him at the swing, each time she stepped outside the house, she could not stop herself from casting her eyes about the grounds hoping to catch a glimpse of David Bostwick. Each time she and Mrs. Annesley took the carriage out, she kept her eye open for him. Each time she saw the elder Mr. Bostwick, she yearned to inquire after his younger son.

She was certain that he was now occupied at the Lochlin estate and was only working occasionally with his father at Pemberley. That would mean she would not have the opportunity to see him as frequently, as they would seldom cross in social circles. She convinced herself that once her brother and Elizabeth returned, she would have more to keep herself occupied. But now, she felt lonely and she simply wished for someone else her own age to be a companion to her.

Georgiana, feeling a growing restlessness within her, poured her heart out into her journal, conveying to this silent listener all her fears and confusion, her thoughts and her questions. When she reread what she had written, however, it only increased her confusion. Elizabeth had conveyed to her that writing her thoughts down would help her to sort them out. This was not the case now.

She could not help but compare her attraction to Mr. Bostwick to what had transpired with Mr. Wickham. She was confident the character of each was completely different from the other. But as she contemplated it, she saw several similarities. She had known them both for most of her life. Because of that, she believed an attachment had formed somewhat easily on her part. They were both exceedingly attentive towards her and she felt flattered by it.

Wickham skewed his attention with excessive compliments and charm. She had been vulnerable and he knew how to take advantage of that. Her experience around men had been very limited. Here she was, a young girl on the verge of womanhood, and a charming gentleman had suddenly showered her with endless confessions of love and devotion, however empty they were. Little did she know that the only love he had was for her fortune, and his devotion was solely toward himself.

Could Mr. Bostwick, she wondered, be attentive towards her for the same reasons? She had been fooled before. How did she know whether she could now discern the difference? But then, there was another, quite different consideration that she needed remember in regard to Mr. Bostwick. He was not her equal, was very much beneath her in station, and therefore, it could never be.

How often had it been stressed over and over to her? It was not *who* she married, but *what* his situation in life was, that was important. It often came from her governesses and her father, and after his death, her brother and cousin. The only respite had been from Mrs. Annesley, who encouraged Georgiana not only in charitable acts toward those in inferior stations, but encouraged touching their lives personally. It was not until their talk in the carriage after encountering Mr. Bostwick that she heard her even speak of associating only with those of equal consequence.

Certainly there were eligible young men that would be more suitable for her; young men who had equal or almost equal fortune as herself, who were of the same prestigious rank in society as the Darcys, and who were of the highest connections and finest breeding. Georgiana sighed at the mere thought of it.

She felt great apprehension in the prospect of meeting new people, particularly young men. She would imagine herself at a ball, surrounded by society's finest people, and being introduced to a line of young men who would meet all the qualifications that her name required. They would be wealthy, some might be handsome, and there would be sons of earls and lords and who knows who else. But whenever she imagined herself meeting these young men, she could only see herself as she knew she would be -- quiet and shy, nervous about being able to carry on a conversation, fearful that she would do or say something wrong, or apprehensive that they simply would not like her. Her heart pounded in contemplation of this.

On this particular afternoon, later in the week, she decided that a walk out about the grounds was more preferable than staying indoors reading or playing the pianoforte. She repeatedly told herself that her walk was not for any reason other than a desire to get some fresh air. But deep down inside there was always that persistent hope…

She had been practicing on her pianoforte and Mrs. Annesley sat across from her in the music room doing some reading on her own.

"Mrs. Annesley," began Georgiana. "It is such a pleasant day outside. Would you mind if I walked about the grounds?"

"That would be fine with me, Miss Darcy. Please do not stay outside too long. I believe you still have some reading to do today."

"I should enjoy taking a book out with me and finding a nice place to sit and read."

"Certainly, dear."

Georgiana picked up a novel she was reading and moved toward the great front door. As she stepped outside and gave a glance out across the grounds, she breathed in the fresh air. She looked down at the gardenia bushes planted in the flowerbed by the door. The flowers were mostly gone now, but she smiled at the memory of them.

Turning her attention back to the grounds, she felt compelled to walk in the direction of the lake. It was one of her favourite places to go when she wanted to sit and think, second only to the swing. The prospect from there, looking back towards the house always gave her much pleasure. She could look across the lake to Pemberley and delight in its mirrored reflection in the still water.

She walked down to where the lake narrowed to a small stream that drew its water from the lake. Years ago, a bridge had been built across it, which enabled one to quickly traverse it to the other side. She stepped out upon it, and walked to the middle, pausing to look out at the water.

From this spot, the house was shielded from view by a hedgerow and she recalled the first time she came here by herself, quite unwillingly as a young girl. She had suddenly felt lost and frightened because she lost sight of the house.

Georgiana was ten at the time and had been outside when David and his brother Samuel came by. The two boys had been doing some simple gardening work with their father when Samuel found, in Georgiana's eyes, an excessively large bug. Because he loved to torment Georgiana, he picked it up and started chasing her with it. He had to have been fourteen and David about thirteen.

If there was anything Georgiana hated, it was bugs, especially big bugs. Samuel started coming after her with it and she took off running. She did not stop to look back, she did not know whether he was still coming after her, but she ran and ran and ran.

She was tall for her age, with long, skinny legs, and was able to outrun Samuel at first. It was fear that propelled her and she soon came to the bridge, crossing over it without looking back.

When she finally stopped running, it was not for lack of fear, but because she had become completely exhausted. When she looked around her, the house was nowhere in sight. The bridge looked vaguely familiar, but she could not recall how she arrived here. She was afraid at being unable to see the house, but even more alarmed that Samuel might suddenly emerge with that bug. She was too tired to go any further, and in a feeling of great despair and anguish, fell down upon the grass and began to cry.

She soon became aware through her tears that someone had come by and was standing over her. Her heart began pounding fiercely as she thought it was Samuel. As she turned her head to look up, she instinctively brought her hands up to protect herself from any bug he might dangle above her.

She was relieved to see it was David. He smiled nervously, not really sure what he should do to stop her from crying. He stood awkwardly by her side.

Finally he had said to her, "Come, Georgie, you best be getting home."

When Georgiana looked up at him, David's shirt and face were completely dirty, and his forehead was bleeding a bit.

For some reason, his presence calmed her and in a choked voice admitted to him, "I do not know how to get home and Samuel will come after me."

Rather than laugh at her silliness or make light of her fears, he kneeled down and took her hand. "Come, Georgiana, I will show you home. And Samuel will never hurt or scare you again."

As he helped her up, he pulled out a handkerchief and gave it to her. She wiped her eyes and her face. David wanted so much to remove the pain and terror from her and found the only thing he could do was to speak soothingly to her. "Do not worry yourself, Georgie, I will protect you. You know that. No one will ever hurt you."

Georgie looked up to him with her wide, tear filled eyes. "Do you promise?"

David took a deep breath and looked away. "If I can help it." As he pulled her up to her feet, they awkwardly stood facing each other and then David reached for her hand and led her back safely to the house.

She had been too young to understand it then, but looking back, she felt David had very likely intervened for her. She was certain he had stopped his brother from pursuing her and ended up fighting with him. She knew there were times when he came between her and Samuel and wondered how many more times she had never known when he acted as her protector. Samuel, at least, never bothered her again.

Georgiana walked from the bridge to a clearing beyond where she had collapsed those years earlier. From here she could see the house again. Its still reflection in the lake made it a most pleasant prospect. She sat down against a large oak tree, leaning back against its trunk.

As the years passed and she became more confident in venturing out, she often returned to this exact spot. She would arm herself with her books and needlework and lose herself in the characters of the novels as she read. She would become someone else in her daydreams as she worked on her samplers. On the swing she tended to analyse and frequently admonish herself because of who she was or what she did. Here, however, she would simply dream about being someone that she was not.

In her daydreams she was confident and pretty. She could speak with eloquence and grace. She had a joy that exhibited itself in an endless smile and a charming, engaging laugh. There were many young men who were most interested in her, ready to duel each other for the honour of asking for her hand.

How she had ever mistaken George Wickham for the man of her dreams, she was not quite certain. He was handsome and charming; that she knew for a surety. But how she allowed him to deceive her, she could not fathom.

Georgiana opened her book and began reading. Why was the heroine of every story able to speak so eloquently so as to capture the attention of her hero? Why was she always beautiful and confident? She wondered whether she would eventually grow out of her shyness and quiet disposition. She was lost in her thoughts and reverie when she heard someone approach. She turned and saw the subject of her earlier musings coming toward her.

"Miss Darcy," David bowed. "Are you enjoying this fine summer day?"

Georgiana's heart leapt so abruptly that, at first, she was unable to speak. "Yes... thank you."

He turned so that he was now looking out across the lake at the house. "It is a mighty fine prospect from here."

"I have always enjoyed coming over here." She was glad to finally have found her ability to speak in return.

"Do you mind if I sit?" David asked.

"No..." Georgiana awkwardly motioned her hand for him to do so.

As he sat down opposite her, he asked, "Are your brother and his wife returned yet?"

"No, but I expect them any day now."

He nodded his head and smiled. There was silence and he thought, *She has such a sweet voice and yet seems so afraid to use it in more than an answer to a question.*

He looked over at the bridge. "Do you remember when my brother chased you with that bug and you found yourself all the way over here? You did not know how to get home." He turned to look at Georgiana.

"Yes. It was the first time I had ever come so far alone."

He smiled and looked back toward the house. At least she was answering in complete sentences. In the past he had often tried to talk to her when she would answer with merely a nod of the head, or if he were fortunate, a 'yes' or a 'no.'

"Miss Darcy..." He thought to himself how odd that sounded, when all his life he had called her Georgie, and how much he wanted to now. "I understand that Mrs. Annesley is leaving."

"That is correct. She is waiting until my brother returns and she will then go up north to be with her son and his wife."

"I am sorry to hear that she is leaving. I believe she was a good companion to you that both you and your brother approved."

Georgiana looked down and felt a twinge of discomfort, thinking of Mrs. Younge. "Yes." She did not wish to elaborate on the subject. She feared where it might lead.

He sensed her sudden uneasiness and changed the subject.

"There is talk of your brother helping to start a school. I understand it is for the deaf where they learn to communicate using signs."

"Yes. They have lately been in France, where they visited such a school."

"I am sure that the Franks will appreciate it greatly."

"Yes, they have already begun using the signs to communicate with Eleanor, as William gave them some information on it."

"I should be interested in it when they get things started. One of Lochlin's tenants is deaf. It would certainly make it easier to communicate with him. I shall have to see about us both availing ourselves of the classes."

"I am sure that would be possible, Mr. Bostwick." Georgiana suddenly had the fleeting thought again about her heroine and being able to speak eloquently and she absently picked up her closed novel and looked down at it.

David saw her action and wondered if she desired his absence. "Miss Darcy, I will not keep you. I was passing by, on my way to see my father. I will not take up any more of your time."

He started to get up and then continued, "I hope that you do not think me impolite for intruding upon your privacy. I would not wish you to look unfavourably on me."

Georgiana slowly moved her eyes up to meet his as he rose. She felt her breath begin to slip away as their eyes locked together, but when the slightest smile tugged at the corners of his mouth, she suddenly felt all fear and nervousness disappear. She was able to smile back at him.

"Mr. Bostwick… you have always displayed the kindest behaviour towards me. I cannot think of you as anything but a gentleman."

With those words, David looked down. He drew his hand down the trunk of the tree she was leaning against. "I am thankful for that. My father always tried to raise us with the most proper manners. My eldest brother seemed to have a more difficult time learning them, as you well remember."

Georgiana laughed, "Yes, I do!"

David smiled at her burst of emotion. Suddenly he became contemplative. "I also have your brother to thank for that."

"Fitzwilliam? Why?"

"I would often watch him. I watched how he walked; how he talked. I watched to see how he handled himself when he was angry or sad, how he treated you, how he treated others, and his staff. I felt he was the most distinguished man of my acquaintance. I often thought if I could grow up and be like him… Well…" He turned and looked at Georgiana and shrugged. "Obviously I can never be like him; there is a great chasm between the likes of him and me." He sighed and looked back out towards the lake. Suddenly he was lost in thought and silence, battling in his mind a conflict of real regard for this young lady and rational reasoning of their different situations.

Georgiana was at a loss to know what to say. She was not even sure what he was trying to tell her. But she felt her affections growing steadily, without any effort on her part, in the moments since he had arrived.

David did not leave immediately as he had intended. They continued to talk and Georgiana began to respond with less anxiety and nervousness, and more elaboration and interest. Quite unexpectedly, Georgiana found herself losing some of her awkwardness and shyness. Both of them unknowingly lost track of time and neither noticed the carriage that pulled up in front of Pemberley.

Chapter 10

The Pemberley carriage pulled up in front of the estate and the door was quickly opened for Master Darcy, Mrs. Darcy, and Kitty. It had been a long day of travel for them and they were all anxious and relieved to finally be home.

As they had travelled through Derbyshire, Elizabeth took in the beauty that comprised this great place and pointed out scenic places of interest to Kitty. There was ruggedness in the rocky peaks and rock formed caves, which contrasted greatly with the green valleys below. Elizabeth already felt a great sense of contentment knowing this was to be her new home.

As they drew near the small village of Lambton, they entered thick woods interspersed with farm land and pastures. When they finally entered into the beautiful grounds that were Pemberley, Elizabeth could not help but look out and try to get her bearings, watching for the sudden appearance of the fine house. Darcy seemed preoccupied with a book he had brought along and Elizabeth wondered if she would ever grow as complacent about this place as he seemed to be. She could not imagine ever approaching Pemberley without having a surge of anxious anticipation.

When at length they turned into the drive that took them to the front of their home, Darcy finally looked up from his book, closed it, and put his hand upon Elizabeth's. He and Elizabeth looked upon the stately mansion with a variety of emotions.

Darcy breathed in a contented sigh, knowing that when he had last left here, his heart was in turmoil and he was languishing over whether Elizabeth would ever return his regard. And yet here she was by his side, now his wife.

Elizabeth recalled her emotions when she left, wondering whether she would ever have the privilege of seeing these excellent grounds again; still trying to sort out her feelings toward the master of this great estate. As she looked out at all that was Pemberley again, she could not help but smile, knowing she now lived in the very grounds she once only admired as a guest.

Kitty's mouth dropped and remained that way for an unusually long time when she saw the house. At long last she let out a soft, "My word!"

If she had ever been in awe of Mr. Darcy, now she had even more reason to be. She looked up and down the length of the edifice, completely surprised by its grandeur. Elizabeth, brought out of her musings by Kitty's response, smiled at her sister's reaction to it. *Her* first sight of it had been almost identical, although her arrival had been at nightfall and she had not been able to see it in all its splendour for the darkness.

As the carriage pulled up, a flurry of activity began and suddenly the servants were there to assist in unloading the luggage. The Darcys were besieged with questions about their wedding journey, and received excessive, endless greetings welcoming them back. After cordially answering everyone's inquiries, they made their way inside and introductions were made to Elizabeth's sister.

When they entered the house, Darcy looked around, feeling a great sense of pleasure at being home. Mrs. Reynolds greeted them warmly and took Elizabeth's hands in hers in a firm grasp. "Welcome back to Pemberley, Mrs. Darcy. It is so good to have you here again in the position you were meant to hold."

"Thank you, Mrs. Reynolds. You are too kind. May I present Miss Catherine Bennet, my sister? She is Kitty to us."

"It is a pleasure to meet you, Miss Bennet."

Darcy suddenly seemed preoccupied and Elizabeth noticed him anxiously looking around. Finally he asked Mrs. Reynolds, "Do you know where Georgiana is?"

"I believe she stepped out earlier to take a walk. I am sure she will return shortly. Perhaps you both need to freshen up. I am sure Miss Darcy will be back when you have finished. Miss Bennet, let me show you to your room."

"Thank you, Mrs. Reynolds." Kitty followed the housekeeper to her room.

Elizabeth suddenly realized that she had never been in the rooms that would be hers and her husband's. She had an idea where they were from what Darcy told her, but she waited for him to show her the way.

Darcy offered his arm to his wife and for the very first time, they walked through the halls of Pemberley as husband and wife. They continued up the stairs and Elizabeth found herself once more passing through the hallway that contained all the portraits of the Darcys from generations past. It suddenly occurred to her that her likeness would most likely be painted and would be placed up here alongside the others.

They passed the servants who were returning from taking their belongings to their rooms and came to a door where Darcy stopped. Elizabeth practically held her breath as he opened it. She stepped through and recognized immediately that it was his room. She walked in and gasped slightly as she took in the simple elegance of it.

The room had an overall masculine emphasis, although not unpleasing to Elizabeth's feminine tastes. The furniture was dark and heavy, but the fabrics of the draperies and bed coverings were made up of chiefly dark greens that seemed to mimic the very woods that surrounded Pemberley. It gave the room a very woodsy feel, which was especially appealing to Elizabeth and it very much suited her husband.

"This," he said as he stretched out his arms, "is the master's chambers. It became mine once my father died."

He walked over to one side of the room and opened a door. "This is your dressing room here; mine is over there. And then…" He walked through to the other side and opened another door. "This is your private bed chamber. There is another door that goes out to the hallway." Elizabeth walked in and looked at a very decidedly feminine room.

"It is quite nice." She looked around at the dresser, chair, and dressing table, and a small but elegantly made bed. She knew her mother used a separate room than that of her father, but had not really anticipated her doing the same. She looked at Darcy questioningly, wondering whether he was expecting her to use this room unless he requested her in his.

"I am glad you approve, but I do hope you will find it more to your liking to spend your nights with me in *our* room. That is where I would prefer you to be, *every* night, Lizbeth."

"I am glad to hear that," laughed Elizabeth. "I should prefer that myself."

"I thought you could use your room for times when you wish to be alone. It is quite a nice room to sit in and read. It gets a good amount of light."

Darcy had been very anxious to show her the rooms and glean her response of them. "Do you approve of our chambers, Lizbeth?"

"I do most heartedly. I very much approve."

"If there is anything you would like to change…"

"No, no, it is fine!"

They returned to their bed chamber and Elizabeth walked over to the window. She reached out and felt the fabric of the draperies. They were open and she saw that the prospect from their room, which was at the corner of the house, looked out over the front. The view from the other window looked out toward the courtyard. She noticed that this window faced east and had a small table directly in front of it.

"Will, this will be a perfect place for the crystal candelabrum."

"I thought it would be. During the summer months, the sun should hit it directly, making our own room glisten with rainbows on sunny mornings." He came over toward her, with all the love and admiration of a new husband. Darcy lifted his long arms and propped them across Elizabeth's shoulders, bringing his hands together behind her. Pulling her close and leaning over, he met her lips with his. It had been a long day and how pleasant, he thought, was her kiss to him. When they parted, Darcy kept his arms draped across her, admiring her face.

A movement outside caught Elizabeth's attention. She turned to look out the window that overlooked the front. As she did, she spotted Georgiana emerging from behind some trees at a bend in the front drive and walk toward the house.

"Look, Will. There is Georgiana now!"

Elizabeth spoke before she noticed a young man step out alongside her. Darcy turned to glance out, and Elizabeth sensed him tense up immediately when he realized she was walking with a young man.

"Who is that walking with Georgiana?" Darcy barked out the question.

Elizabeth could instantly determine from the abruptness of his words that he was not pleased.

She brought her hands up and gently wrapped her fingers around his arms that were still resting on her shoulders. She softly answered, "I would have no way of knowing."

Darcy removed her hands from his arms and brought himself to stand directly in front of the window, watching as they continued to walk toward the house.

At that moment Mrs. Reynolds came into the room after showing Kitty to hers. "Is there anything else I can do for either of you?"

"Mrs. Reynolds, would you come to the window, please, and tell me who is with Georgiana?"

She walked over slowly; fairly certain she knew who it was. The talk amid the Pemberley staff had been rampant about an occasional sighting of the younger Mr. Bostwick and the master's sister. There had been adamant arguments amongst them in favour of and against this kind of attachment. Most gave hearty approval of the young man himself, but could not fully endorse an affection between them due to the difference in their situation in life and mindful of what Master Darcy would say about it.

When Mrs. Reynolds came to the window, she saw the young man as she suspected. She was grateful that they were keeping a proper distance apart, but she knew the fact that they had been out on the grounds together would not please her master.

"It is Mr. David Bostwick, Sir."

"Bostwick's son?"

"Yes, Sir."

Elizabeth watched her husband's countenance darken as he brought his hand up and vigorously rubbed the back of his neck.

"Thank you, Mrs. Reynolds." He briskly walked toward the door. "Excuse me…"

"William!" Elizabeth said the words before she even knew what she wished to say.

He turned abruptly and met her impulsive look with an impatient one of his own. His shoulders rose with every breath he took, indicative of the inner turmoil he was experiencing.

In the pause that ensued, Mrs. Reynolds quickly excused herself and left the room.

"Yes, Elizabeth," he answered very slowly.

Elizabeth feared he might be reacting a little more harshly and hastily than he should. But suddenly the reality of who she now was, who she was married to, and her responsibilities as Mistress of Pemberley became a little clearer. In addition to that, she now had the welfare of this sixteen year old girl partly in her hands; this young girl who had even more demands on her that would greatly affect and influence her life. She decided to tread lightly and slowly.

She walked over to Darcy and gently put her hand upon her husband's arm. "Will, let me have a talk with Georgiana about this at some later time. We have only returned and Kitty is here, as well. Let us put off any discussion with her on the subject and try to simply show her how happy we are to see her now that we are returned."

Darcy turned to look at her. He slowly took in a deep breath to control his piqued emotions. He made a motion and sound as if he were about to say something, but stopped. After a small amount of deliberation, he finally spoke. "Perhaps you are right, for now. But this cannot be ignored." Darcy turned to leave the room. "I shall be downstairs."

Elizabeth suddenly felt that her life had altered considerably these past two days from their time abroad. She realized that they had spent a kind of fairy-tale life in Paris and now they had both been thrown into the real world.

Wedding journeys were nice, but they did not prepare you at all for what you would encounter when you began your life anew.

She turned and looked at the empty door frame that her husband passed through. She knew her husband was agitated and concerned about Georgiana and this young man. Was it because he did not approve of this young man and his character? Was it because of what happened with Wickham and he did not trust Georgiana to know better? Or was it that he, at the very core of him, would never allow an attachment between his sister and any young man who did not meet the strictest criterion?

~~*

When Georgiana entered the house through the courtyard door, Darcy was waiting for her and was the first to greet her. She was too elated to see him to even consider that he may have seen her with Mr. Bostwick, who had walked on. She had missed him too much to notice the rigid demeanour that permeated his body. She was too happy to notice the smile that was missing from his face. Noticing anything amiss was the last thing on her mind. She ran up to him and brought her arms around him in a very tight hug.

He brought his arms around her, all the while looking out the door she left open and watched as Mr. Bostwick quietly walked away. He brought his hand up and stroked her hair. "It is good to see you, Georgiana. It is good to be back."

"William, I have missed you so much! When did you return?"

"We arrived about a half hour ago."

"Hello, Georgiana."

Georgiana turned and saw Elizabeth walking toward her. They both quickly moved toward each other and hugged.

"Elizabeth, welcome to your new home!" Georgiana felt as though the past two weeks were the longest she had every lived.

"Georgiana, we have someone here to see you." Elizabeth turned and waved for Kitty to come in.

"Kitty! You came! I am so pleased!"

"Hello, Georgiana. I was so very happy to be invited. You have no idea how dull it has been at Longbourn!"

"It shall be so good to have your company here."

The three ladies accompanied Darcy directly into the dining room, as Mrs. Reynolds announced that their meal was ready. Elizabeth slipped her arm around her husband's, whose face was still etched with a look of concern. This gave Georgiana and Kitty a chance to walk together. Elizabeth outwardly smiled when she heard their giggles as they talked, but inwardly she felt the disquiet of her husband.

Seated around the table, Georgiana and Kitty continued to talk and giggle. Kitty seemed to have the natural ability to draw the young, shy girl out, and Elizabeth thought this could become a good friendship. She was confident that it could have a very positive effect on both of them.

The two girls asked all about their trip to Paris and Elizabeth answered with great detail and cheerfulness. But her husband remained silent for the most part and she noticed how he tapped his fingers repeatedly against the table. She made a mental note that he must do this when agitated, as opposed to rubbing his fingers together when nervous.

By the end of the meal, the girls had heard all about Paris, the deaf school, their driver Jacques, and all the sights they saw and experiences they had. Georgiana wanted to hear all about the deaf school and Kitty was most interested in knowing whether Jacques was handsome. Elizabeth hoped that being away from Lydia for a while would drive this sphere of fixation from her.

When they had finished dining, they continued to sit around the table and talk. Darcy allowed Elizabeth to relay most of their experiences to the girls. He found it difficult to engage in such a lively discussion with the feelings that were bearing down upon him. His thoughts were elsewhere. Elizabeth noticed an occasional creased brow and narrowed eyes as they fell upon his sister.

After dinner, Darcy excused himself and went to his study, while Elizabeth remained with the girls and visited with them. She acutely felt his absence as she attempted to display an attentive attitude toward the girls.

It was not until later that evening when Mrs. Annesley requested a discourse with the Darcys that she saw him again. Mrs. Annesley joined Darcy and Elizabeth in the study and it was then that she informed them that she would be required to leave her position to go be with her son and wife as they were having a baby.

"I am sorry that I shall not be able to stay much longer, Mr. Darcy. I have so enjoyed being Georgiana's companion. I do hope that I have lived up to all your expectations."

"You have been most superior, Mrs. Annesley."

"Mr. and Mrs. Darcy, allow me to say that Georgiana has been a delightful young lady to get to know and has grown tremendously over the past year. It took a while for her to open up to me, but she has been a pleasure to work with."

"I am glad to hear that," Darcy assured her. "I only hope we can find someone else as excellent as yourself."

"Sir, if I may, Georgiana has expressed to me her opinion that she no longer wishes to have a companion. She feels that she no longer has a need for one."

"And did she give her reasons for this?" asked Darcy.

"As a matter of fact, yes, she did." At this Mrs. Annesley turned to Elizabeth. "She believes that you, Mrs. Darcy, may be all that she needs now."

"My wife?" asked Darcy.

"Yes." She turned back to Darcy. "She feels that, if it is agreeable with you, she would prefer Mrs. Darcy to give her guidance and direction, as she already feels extremely comfortable around her and an openness to share with her. She has already completed the studies I intended to give her and whatever more she desires to learn, I believe Mrs. Darcy could simply encourage her in the right direction with books to read on her own."

"Georgiana appears to have it all figured out," Darcy commented.

"Will," Elizabeth joined in. "I would consider it an honour to take Georgiana under my wing, so to speak. I so enjoy her company and she does seem to be able to talk easily with me."

Darcy knew how long it took his sister to open up to new people. Yes, it did seem that she formed an almost instant bond with Elizabeth when they met here at Pemberley a few months back. It would certainly take away the stress of finding another woman they deemed suitable.

"I see no harm in seeing how it works out," Darcy consented. "Mrs. Annesley, let me know if there is anything I can do to help in your preparations to leave. I appreciate all you have done for Georgiana."

"Thank you, Sir. I am going to attempt to take my leave in a week, if that is acceptable."

"Well, as it appears we have no need to find a replacement for you, Mrs. Annesley, that would be fine. Feel free to take as much time as you need."

"Thank you, Sir. You do know that I shall miss Georgiana greatly. She is an extremely delightful girl."

"Thank you." Darcy paused.

"If that is all then…"

"Mrs. Annesley," Darcy broke in. "When my wife and I returned this afternoon, Georgiana was out on the grounds. We saw her return with a young man. Have you noticed, or are you aware of anything going on between my sister and Mr. Bostwick's younger son?"

Elizabeth quickly turned to Darcy and then back to Mrs. Annesley.

Mrs. Annesley thought in silence, contemplating what to say. "I cannot say that there is or is not a strong sentiment between them, Sir. I have seen them together but a few times. The first time, we were in the carriage, returning from Lambton. He was rescuing a lamb that was stuck in a fence. Mr. Lawson stopped the carriage to see if he could give assistance. Miss Darcy and I both exited the carriage and talked with him."

"Go on." Darcy encouraged her to continue, anxious to know more.

"She seemed a little bit uneasy. I would say she acted nervous in his presence. I attributed it partly to her naturally shy nature. But there was something else, Sir. I would have to say that the way he looked at her and talked to her… well, he was most attentive towards her. I believe she was quite flattered and yet obviously disconcerted by his attention."

"It does not take much for her to be flattered, I dare say," muttered Darcy to himself, although it was loud enough for the two ladies to hear.

"Mr. Darcy, we had a talk about him afterwards on the way home. I encouraged her to remember who she was and who he was."

"Well apparently she has forgotten it, as she was with him this afternoon."

Mrs. Annesley looked down. "Mr. Darcy, may I speak freely?"

"Certainly."

"Georgiana is a young lady with a generous fortune. She was born into a sphere of society that demands much, but... and I am sorry if this offends you... but gives little. She has the most compassionate heart towards even the lowest individual in society. All that she has seen of society in London... well, she has often confided in me that she does not feel as though that is where she belongs."

She paused, waiting for a response from Darcy. When he said nothing, she continued. "Mr. Darcy, you may not consider Mr. Bostwick to be of suitable class and connections for your sister. But of character, there is none finer."

Mrs. Annesley turned to look at Elizabeth. "I am grateful for you, Mrs. Darcy. I am confident that you will be a most exceptional companion and confidante to her. I trust that you will bring a dimension to her life that will give balance to her obligations and desires in life. Now, if you will excuse me..." She rose and left the two of them in the study.

Darcy was silent. He could have argued Mrs. Annesley's point, but knew that with her leaving soon, it would have been futile. Elizabeth could see that he was battling something in his mind. She walked over and placed her hand on his shoulder as Mrs. Annesley departed the room.

"You know, Elizabeth, that her argument is completely wrong."

"Excuse me?"

"It is not merely Georgiana's feelings about society. It has more to do with her fortune and ensuring that no one woos her into giving it up to them."

He reached up and placed his hand over hers. "I agree with Mrs. Annesley about you, however. I know that with the partiality Georgiana has toward you, you shall be able to guide her in the right direction here."

Elizabeth sighed deeply. "And what direction would that be?" she asked quietly.

"Is it not obvious to you?" Darcy suddenly seemed unsettled. "He is not... Elizabeth, you must realize he will never..." he stopped, fighting those same words that he had used during his first proposal that Elizabeth had found so offensive. "I cannot have Georgiana... her situation is very different than ours."

"Is it?"

"Elizabeth, there are some things you do not understand," Darcy barked back at her rather impatiently.

She paused, taken aback at his implication. "Yes, Will, I am sure that there *are* things I would not understand. I did not grow up in your society or with the fortune that Georgiana has. But I do understand that you feel it is wrong for a person of wealth, such as your sister, to marry anyone who does not have equal fortune or connections. It matters not what their character may be, or if there is genuine affection between them. To you it is simply black and white. If you will excuse me now, I shall retire for the night."

Elizabeth walked away, angry with herself for her outburst, knowing that it *was* different for Georgiana. She was young and vulnerable. She had much to learn in matters of the heart. She *did* have to be protected. But she was concerned that her husband was again inclined to prejudge this situation without first discovering if there was even a need. Perhaps there was nothing between them but a friendship; perhaps there was nothing with which to concern themselves.

Darcy put his head into his hands when Elizabeth walked out of the room. He knew she was comparing this situation to the two of them and would not understand his adamant position against affection between the two. But there were things of which she was not aware and he did not feel in command of his emotions enough to explain his actions to her. Now, the main thing on his mind was apologizing to his wife. He suddenly wondered whether she would take advantage of her private bed chambers this night.

~~*

Elizabeth readied herself for bed and sat up with a book, awaiting her husband. She wondered how long it would be before he left his study and came to their room. She finally heard him approaching and closed her book, turning toward the door to watch for him.

He walked in slowly, his eyes glancing up to her with a look of great regret, which softened with relief at finding her there. He came in and sat down on the edge of the bed. Without looking at her, he softly said, "I see you are in our room. I am glad." He rubbed his hands together and took a deep breath. "This was not how I anticipated our first night in our home, Lizbeth. I am sorry."

She reached out her hand and stroked his hair. She sat up and brought herself behind him, pulling her legs underneath her and, taking his shoulders in her hands, she began massaging them. He reached up and grabbed both her hands and pulled them down and crossed them across his chest.

"Forgive me, Lizbeth, for how I have behaved since arriving home. I fear this whole incident with Georgiana and this young man has me seriously troubled. It has brought back too many painful memories and I regret that my conduct tonight was not the most amiable."

"Will, part of it was my own fault. I am sorry for my behaviour and the words I said. I should never have walked out on you."

"Can we begin over, do you think?"

"I would certainly hope so, Will. But this is life; our life, *now*. What occurred today with Georgiana is really only the beginning of what we will have to learn to deal with *together* from now on. It occurred to me earlier, that our first days of married life, our time in Paris, was pretty much like a fairy-tale. Everything was perfect. Looking back, it is almost as if we were two different people there. It was wonderful, but it is not what we should expect our real life to be like."

He brought both of her hands up to his lips and kissed them. "I need you more than ever, Lizbeth. I cannot do this alone. Not again." He turned and wrapped his arms around Elizabeth. "Promise me you will always be there for me."

"You know I will. Whatever we go through, we shall go through together."

The love that they shared that night was one of firsts, of forgiveness, and of frustrations temporarily forgotten.

Chapter 11

When Elizabeth awoke the next morning, she discovered her husband was already up and gone. She looked around the room and smiled blissfully. As they had anticipated, there were small rainbows scattered about the room from the prisms on the candelabrum. She sat up in bed and yawned, stretched out her limbs, and wondered what her first full day as Mistress of Pemberley would bring.

She was about to bring herself out of bed when her husband walked in with a tray.

"I see that you are awake. I brought us something to eat."

He walked over to the bed and carefully sat down, bringing his legs up and stretching them out before him as he balanced the tray in his hands. Elizabeth pulled herself up to the head of the bed so she could sit with her back against the headboard.

She surveyed the array of foods that he had brought up. There were fruits and breads, fruit juice, and hot tea.

"I wanted our first morning to be reminiscent of Paris, when we ate in a roomful of rainbows. Thankfully the sun obliged, although I hope you are not disappointed that there are not as many rainbows. Perhaps if we start the day in this manner we can capture a little bit of what we had there. Our 'fairy-tale' life, as you called it." He tilted his head and looked at her with eyebrows raised, hoping for a delightful response.

Elizabeth obliged him with a warm smile and a good morning embrace and they enjoyed a leisurely breakfast. Darcy informed his wife the things he needed to do that day and asked if there was anything she wished to do. One of the first things she desired was to get to know the staff and see how Pemberley was run.

The return of Darcy with Elizabeth to Pemberley would change all that Pemberley had been for many years. There was now a mistress who was lively and vivacious, witty and personable. It had been many years since Pemberley had seen a mistress and most of the present staff had never known the late Mr. Darcy's wife.

Elizabeth knew that it would be best to tread lightly, as the staff kept a well-run household. They had been used to doing things a certain way for many years, probably with little or no interference from the master, and Elizabeth did not want to upset the order and rhythm that her husband and the staff had come to expect.

The staff, on the other hand, had been advised by Mrs. Reynolds to inquire of Mrs. Darcy about her preferences as to how things might be done or what she may want changed. Both sides inquired much but demanded little, not wanting to offend the other.

Georgiana enjoyed the company of Kitty and found that the camaraderie that she offered along with the warmth and affection that her brother and Elizabeth lavished upon her helped keep her mind occupied. Georgiana took great delight in giving Kitty some beginning lessons on the pianoforte. Kitty reciprocated by giving Georgiana a chance to practice the steps to a few different dances that Georgiana had only before been able to perform with a teacher, her brother, or Mrs. Annesley. Kitty, however, had enjoyed performing these dances for several years already with a genuine male partner.

In those first few days, Elizabeth would often hear them giggling and found herself tempted to eavesdrop. She joined them on a few of those occasions and enjoyed seeing Georgiana opening up to Kitty as well as noting how Kitty's manners and behaviour were much improved. She was grateful that the two of them seemed to be developing a strong friendship and felt that both the girls were having a positive effect on each other.

The subject of Mr. Bostwick seemed to have been forgotten, at least from her husband's discussions. Elizabeth hoped that if there was something Georgiana wished to discuss, she would come to her on her own initiative. She did not see anything in the young girl's demeanour to make her suspicious. She felt that what she and her husband witnessed from the window was, indeed, just a friendship, but she would keep her eyes and ears open.

Darcy quickly settled into a routine of work, going over with his steward the management of his properties, making visits and business contacts, and working with those who were involved in the development of the school for the deaf. The one thing that took up quite a bit of his time was spreading word of the school and getting additional funding toward it. That part he desired to do on his own.

With his energies focused in that direction and making preparations for the arrival of Mr. Fleming, Elizabeth was able to concentrate on spending time with Georgiana and Kitty. She knew that Kitty would only be with them for another few weeks and felt that if she could have any additional input into Kitty's life before she returned to Longbourn, the greater benefit it would be for her.

When Mrs. Annesley's departure was upon them, Georgiana and her companion exchanged a tearful farewell. As much as Mrs. Annesley was desirous to be with her family, she was saddened to leave Georgiana. Elizabeth was grateful that both she and Kitty were there to ease the pain in the farewells and were able to take Georgiana's mind off the loss.

The three ladies decided after Mrs. Annesley left, to spend the day together by going into Lambton. Elizabeth was anxious to take a look around this delightful village in which her Aunt Gardiner had lived as a young girl and to pay a visit to some of her aunt's long-time acquaintances, as Elizabeth had promised her. She invited the two girls to accompany her.

Darcy, on the other hand, had some free time before setting out to make a business contact. After the ladies departed, he took advantage of the solitude and decided to walk the grounds. He walked down the front path, deeply breathing in the fresh summer air. As much as he enjoyed Paris, it felt good to be home. The lawns were at their greenest. Obviously they had received enough rain so far this summer to keep them their deepest shade. He thought back to how long he had been away from home. It had been almost six weeks since he walked these grounds! How he had missed Pemberley!

He thoroughly enjoyed his walk, only wishing Elizabeth was at his side. He brought his hands together behind him as he slowly looked around, greatly admiring the natural beauty surrounding him. He was grateful for such capable workers and a most excellent head gardener.

Darcy saw a group of gardeners working up ahead and directed his steps toward them. When he came upon them, he immediately saw the elder Mr. Bostwick in their midst.

He walked up and called out to him. "Bostwick, how are you?" Darcy inquired.

"I am well, Mr. Darcy. It is good to have you back. Does everything appear satisfactory?"

"Most assuredly, Bostwick. You and your men are doing a superb job. Everything looks splendid and I am most pleased. But there is something I wish to talk with you about. May I have a moment of your time?"

Bostwick looked to his workers, "Carry on. I shall return shortly."

Darcy brought his hands together and rubbed his fist in the palm of his other hand. Bostwick had been working on the Pemberley estate since he was a young man and now, as head gardener, his duties were to oversee all the under gardeners that were on the Pemberley staff. Darcy could not have more respect for the man and consequently, he was not looking forward to this conversation.

Bostwick wiped the dirt off his hands as he walked over to join him. He could tell immediately that Darcy was not happy.

"What is it, Sir?"

"Bostwick, I do not wish to sound alarmed, I am only concerned about something I witnessed when my wife and I returned home the other day."

"Is something wrong with the grounds, Sir?"

"No, no, that is not it at all." Darcy took in a deep breath. "It is your son."

"My son? Samuel or David?"

"I believe it is your younger son, David."

"David? What has he done?"

"At this point I do not believe he has done anything wrong. I only wish to prevent something from happening that cannot be."

The two men locked eyes, Bostwick waiting uneasily for him to continue, and Darcy searching for the right words.

"It concerns him and Georgiana."

Bostwick's eyes shot open wide instantly. "What is it you are suggesting, Mr. Darcy?"

"I am not suggesting anything. I am only telling you what I observed. The afternoon we returned to Pemberley, we saw the two of them walking toward the house together from out on the grounds."

Bostwick rubbed his palms down the length of his pants, trying to grasp the degree of seriousness of this situation. "Was there anything improper in what you saw, Sir?"

"No, not as such, but it was the fact that they had been out on the grounds together without a chaperone."

"Sir, you know they have been friends since childhood. One does not suddenly ignore another simply because they are both grown up. Miss Darcy was never forbidden to have any contact with either of my sons when they were younger despite the difference in class. Georgiana has a most tender heart toward people. I believe she may have been displaying her natural, kind self toward a long time friend."

"Possibly. But what of your son? Can you speak for him and his designs?"

Bostwick realized he really could not say. The responsibilities he had as head gardener kept him away from his family a great deal this time of the year and he had had very little time recently to converse with his children on what was going on in their lives. But he did know his son and his character and he would vouch for it any day.

"Mr. Darcy, I am not aware of any *designs*, as you say, my son has on Georgiana, but I can guarantee that he would do nothing imprudent. I did not raise him in that manner and I am confident that he would never do anything to cause you alarm. You have my word on it."

"Bostwick I do not doubt that. But I also know how vulnerable my sister is and I am asking you to help me ensure that things go no further. I want to do everything in my power to ensure my sister does not get hurt."

"What are you suggesting, Sir?"

"This may sound harsh, but I must insist that, for the time being, your son no longer work at Pemberley. Perhaps he can work on the grounds at the school."

"That will not be necessary, sir. He is now working for Lochlin on his estate, managing his small property and tenants and doing whatever extra work is needed. In fact he shall be leaving tomorrow with Lochlin to go up north for about a week. He most likely will only rarely have any need to come by Pemberley anymore."

"Good, good. You understand, Bostwick, I have nothing against your son."

"Yes, Sir."

Darcy turned away. He was not looking forward to dealing with another situation with Georgiana, however different this one may be. He breathed in slowly to calm his erratically beating heart. How he disliked this! And how grateful he was that he had Elizabeth now who would be able to smooth things over on Georgiana's part.

~~*

As Elizabeth, Georgiana, and Kitty came into Lambton, people immediately noticed the carriage as it made its way through the streets. People seemed to strain to see inside, making every attempt to get even the slightest glimpse of the occupants. *Could the new Mrs. Darcy be in it?* they wondered.

Mr. Lawson drove the carriage through the main street of the village, and then brought it to a stop in front of a modest sized home. Following the directions Elizabeth had given him, he easily found the home of her aunt's childhood friend.

The three young ladies enjoyed their short visit with Mrs. Turnell. She shared stories with them about Elizabeth's and Kitty's aunt when she was younger, and they shared with her their memories of her as their aunt. It was a short visit, but they all enjoyed it. Elizabeth made a promise that when her aunt and uncle came to visit her, she would make a point of inviting Mrs. Turnell to Pemberley. Mrs. Turnell could not have been more pleased at that announcement.

Georgiana asked Lawson to take them to Lambton Inn so they could enjoy some light refreshment. When they arrived, Georgiana greeted a few people with whom she was acquainted and introduced Elizabeth and Kitty. Most of the townsfolk of Lambton were very interested in meeting the new Mrs. Darcy and those who were fortunate enough to make her acquaintance that day were quite pleasantly surprised by her lively and affable personality.

The three ladies enjoyed a light meal while giggling about sisters, one particular brother, and life in a house full of servants. Kitty kept prodding Georgiana to apprise them of all the funny things that had happened over the years at Pemberley with an army of servants running the place. Kitty and Elizabeth took great delight in sharing anecdotes of their unique family members and humorous things they had done throughout the years. By the end of the meal, the three ladies felt a very strong bond. Elizabeth could not recall a time when she felt closer to Kitty and continued to hope and pray that she would be able to return home a changed girl with improved behaviour.

As they gathered up their belongings and made their way to the door, Elizabeth stepped out first and almost collided with a young man hurriedly walking past.

"Oh, I am so sorry, I did not see you!" Elizabeth offered.

"No, pardon me, ma'am, it was my fault."

A slight gasp from behind her caused Elizabeth to turn toward Georgiana, who stood stricken in place. Elizabeth realized this was the young man with whom she had seen Georgiana walking that day she and Darcy returned.

"Good afternoon, Miss Darcy," he began, a broad smile appearing across his face.

Georgiana barely was able to answer him and make proper introductions.

"Good day, Mr. Bostwick… May I present my brother's wife, Mrs. Elizabeth Darcy… and this is her sister, Miss Kitty Bennet." She took in a deep breath before she continued. "This is Mr. David Bostwick."

"Miss Bennet, it is a pleasure to meet you and I am glad to finally make *your* acquaintance, Mrs. Darcy. I have heard much about you."

"I hope what you have heard has not been too unfavourable."

"Certainly not. In fact it has been notably favourable. You are highly esteemed around Pemberley."

"Thank you. I appreciate the compliment." Elizabeth intently observed everything about this young man as well as Georgiana's response. "Mr. Bostwick, do you live here in Lambton?"

"No, we live outside town, about two miles from here. My father is the head gardener at Pemberley. I have worked the grounds there for several years, but recently have been hired to work for a gentleman, Mr. Lochlin, who owns an estate south of Pemberley. I came in today to buy a few things needed there."

"Ahhh," Elizabeth responded.

There was a brief pause and Elizabeth stole a glance at Georgiana, noticing her still flushed cheeks. David looked at Georgiana as if he was about to say something, but was halted by Kitty.

"Mr. Bostwick, what kind of work do you do for Mr. Lochlin?"

"I help him manage his estate and properties. It is a small one, with a handful of tenant farmers and such. I do for him whatever he needs done. He is an older gentleman who is finding it a little more difficult to get around these days, as much as he hates to admit it. He has always been a most lively, energetic man." He then turned to Georgiana. "Would you describe him as such, Miss Darcy?"

She smiled and paused before answering. "He has always been… young at heart, yes."

"That would be a good way to describe him."

Elizabeth instantly saw the look of delight in Georgiana's eyes as Mr. Bostwick complimented her on her choice of words.

"How long are you to be at Pemberley, Miss Bennet?" He turned and asked Kitty.

"I think for only two more weeks, but I am hoping… I hope that my parents might allow me to stay longer."

Elizabeth looked at her in surprise. She had not mentioned anything about extending her stay, and now suddenly she was speaking about delaying her return. *How very interesting!* Elizabeth thought to herself. How very *complicating!*

Georgiana stood off to the back watching the interaction. She felt a twinge of jealousy when Kitty began to strike up a conversation with Mr. Bostwick and seemed to have no trouble at all saying what she thought. Georgiana wondered where *her own* ability to converse had disappeared to since the last time she had seen him. Her only consolation was that every now and then he would look over to her and smile.

His smiles did not go unnoticed on Elizabeth's part. She knew beyond a shadow of a doubt that he held a deep regard for Georgiana. But both she and Georgiana had been charmed and fooled before and would not take it at face value. She was determined to find out more about this young man and what, indeed, he felt about Georgiana. And, more importantly, what Georgiana's feelings towards him were. If things were as she suspected, a talk with Georgiana was not only necessary, it was needed *directly.*

They stood outside and talked but a little while longer and David finally excused himself after having expressed his pleasure at making the acquaintance of Elizabeth and Kitty. He then wished them all a good day. They ladies walked toward the carriage and Elizabeth sensed that Kitty was about to burst while Georgiana was struggling with something deep inside.

Once within the confines of the carriage, Kitty finally let out everything she was holding in.

"Is he not the most handsome man? And so polite! Georgiana, why did you not tell me about him? You were not planning on keeping him all to yourself now, were you?" Kitty laughed, craning her neck to catch a final glimpse of him through the window. Fortunately, she did not notice Georgiana's stricken face.

"But of course Georgiana, you must only fall in love with someone in the upper class of society. He would never do for you. But I, on the other hand, can fall in love with anybody." She looked out the window to see if she could still see him. "I think he shall do fine." Kitty continued to laugh and Georgiana looked to be on the verge of tears. "Do you think we shall see him again?"

"Kitty, please!" Elizabeth knew it was too late to prevent the damage already done and was disappointed to see ugly remnants of Lydia's influence come out at this most inopportune time.

Elizabeth contemplated these two younger girls in her company. Georgiana had come a long way since that first day she had met her, but she still struggled as she weighed each thought far too long before she spoke it. Kitty, on the other hand, thought very little about what she would say before she said it. Georgiana still harboured a tendency to guard her feelings and feared what others might think of her, while Kitty gave little consideration to the feelings of those around her. Elizabeth hoped her time with both of them and their companionship with each other would have a positive effect on them both.

Elizabeth could not censure Kitty for speaking that way of such a man -- he seemed most amiable -- but she could condemn her for the way she carried on about him without any concern for how Georgiana might be feeling. Elizabeth could see that Georgiana was suffering most grievously. She could not address this situation now; the only thing she could do would be to change the subject.

"Kitty, have you written home to Mama and Papa yet?"

Kitty turned to her, decidedly reluctant to change the subject, but obliged. "No. You know I am not good at writing letters."

"The only way you will improve on letter writing is to actually write one. I think they would be delighted to hear from you. Perhaps you could write a short letter, ask them if it would they would agree to your remaining here longer, and then I shall add a little to it before we have it sent off."

"If you insist."

Elizabeth looked to Georgiana. "Georgiana is a wonderful letter writer. Perhaps she could assist you. It is not that difficult. Would you be willing to do that, Georgiana?"

"Yes… certainly… I would be happy to oblige you."

Georgiana's countenance improved slightly, but Elizabeth was very well aware that the precise subject she needed to talk to Georgiana about *gently*, Kitty unknowingly just did very *heartlessly*.

When they finally returned to Pemberley, after being gone most of the day, Elizabeth was pleased to find her husband had returned also. The girls quickly disappeared once inside the house, and Elizabeth sought out Darcy. She was told he was in his study.

She tapped lightly at the door and entered at his, "Come in." She directly walked up to him as he stood up to greet her. He pulled her close and Elizabeth reached up to kiss him.

"How was your day, Will? Did you get some work accomplished?"

"I made one contact about the school which was very profitable."

"Good. Is it someone willing to invest in it?"

"Yes." He shifted his weight to his other foot. "I… uh… also talked with Bostwick about his son."

Elizabeth's eyes widened at this. "You did? What did you say?"

"I told him we saw Georgiana and David walking together and I asked him to help me ensure it does not go any further than this. He assured me his son will no longer be coming around here."

Elizabeth glanced down at his desk and ran her fingers along the edge of it. "We ran into him while in Lambton this afternoon."

"David Bostwick?"

"Yes."

"And?"

"He seems a very friendly, agreeable young man. Kitty seemed quite taken by him."

Darcy turned, walking to the window that was situated behind his desk and absently looked out. "Well, he may be fine for Kitty, but not for Georgiana!

"What?" Elizabeth instantly reacted, her jaw dropping and her eyes widening at his blunt statement. In her mind she knew Georgiana was of a different class than Kitty, but in her heart, she took offence to the fact that he still was inclined to view her family in such a condescending way."

At her outburst, Darcy turned back to Elizabeth and saw her eyes had darkened and realized immediately that what he had said greatly angered and offended her. He rushed over to her, not wanting her to walk out on him like she had the other night. "Lizbeth, I did not mean…"

"I know, I know." Elizabeth shook her head and put up her hand to stop him. "You are correct. He would actually be most a most suitable choice for Kitty."

Darcy cupped her face with his hands. "No, it was very wrong of me. I am sorry for what I just now said, Lizbeth. It was very insensitive and unkind, both to you and your sister. Will you forgive me?" He lifted her face up to his. "I do not know what comes over me when dealing with Georgiana in these situations. It is definitely not easy for me." He took in a deep breath. "Have you had the opportunity to talk with her yet?"

"No, Kitty, however, did it for me, although most heartlessly."

"What do you mean?"

"In very pointed and unthinking words, Kitty let your sister know that he was not good enough for Georgiana but would be fine for herself."

"What was Georgiana's reaction to that?"

"She was very quiet. I could see the pain in her eyes." She looked up at Darcy. "I do believe, in observing them both together this afternoon, that they indeed share an affection for each other. I do not know to what extent."

"Then you agree with me, Elizabeth, that one of us needs to talk with her."

Elizabeth took both of her hands and clasped them around one of Darcy's. She looked up at him with her beguiling eyes and began to plead her case. "I would like to wait, Will. I would prefer it if she came to me asking to talk. I do not want her to feel as though I have come into this household to wield a whip around."

"Would you prefer I talk to her?"

Elizabeth laughed a hearty laugh. "Oh, most definitely not! You are still so stung by what happened between her and Wickham and she is still so ashamed. I fear your manner with her would be dreadful and she would be simply devastated! Give me some time and let us wait and watch."

"Elizabeth, I will agree to it for a short time. But you know I have a responsibility for her that I take very seriously, and I must do what I believe is necessary to ensure that she and her fortune are not taken advantage of."

Chapter 12

On the following day, Darcy suggested that if the weather permitted, he would like to take them to visit the property upon which the school for the deaf would be built.

The day proved to be pleasantly warm, with a slight breeze. Darcy had previously given an eloquent description to Elizabeth of the plans for the school and she looked forward to being able to better visualize what it would look like after seeing the land upon which it would reside. She was very anxious to go out to the property and enjoy a pleasant outing with her husband and sisters.

After a satisfying breakfast, Darcy, Elizabeth, and the two young ladies set out for the property. It was about an hour's carriage ride and the ladies animatedly talked and laughed while Darcy read through some work he brought along. He seemed acutely proficient at being able to focus on the work in front of him and take no notice of everything else around him. Elizabeth passed the time enjoying the scenery and joining the conversations between the two girls.

Kitty brought up the subject of Elizabeth's first visit to Pemberley a few months back. The ladies laughed freely as Georgiana and Elizabeth apprised her of all the details about misunderstandings, a lost handkerchief, and discovering how very special the gardenia scent became to a certain someone. The three repeatedly turned to look upon Darcy, as he was often spoken of and laughed at, and only a slight twitch could be seen at the corner of his mouth.

Elizabeth could not believe that he heard not a word they said, and she wondered if he was indeed oblivious to it or steadfastly ignoring it. She was curious how much it would take to draw him out of the little world in which he found himself at present.

As Georgiana continued to tell the tale of the handkerchief, with Elizabeth's additional revelations, he barely registered an acknowledgement of their conversation. She cocked her head and looked up at him. He slowly turned the page of the papers he was reading keeping his eyes steadfastly glued to the pages before him.

When Georgiana told Kitty that she discovered her brother had been carrying around Elizabeth's handkerchief with no apparent inclination to return it to her,

Kitty burst out laughing. When the subject finally came up about the gardenia scented toilet water that he had purchased and kept hidden, using it to keep the handkerchief scented, all three ladies laughed mercilessly at him.

Kitty was awed by his evident ignorance to the conversation and giggles taking place in the carriage. Elizabeth was amused by it, and Georgiana appeared not at all surprised by it. Kitty turned to Georgiana and whispered, "Do you think he even *hears* what we are saying about him?"

"I would not be surprised if he has no idea. He has learned over the years to tune everything out when he wants to be focused on something else. And he can become *quite* focused!"

Elizabeth could not help but wonder, as well, whether he was so absorbed in his reading because he was indeed tuning every other thing out, or he was simply refusing to oblige the ladies with any type of response to their laughing at his expense. She thought of this same trait that her father had and how he so frequently and conveniently blocked everything, especially his wife, out. She did not want this in their relationship. But then again, she believed, as well as hoped, that her husband did not view her in the same light as her father viewed her mother.

Kitty again whispered to Georgiana with a conspiratorial look at Elizabeth, who was seated next to him. "What do you suppose it would take to get his attention?"

Elizabeth saw this as a challenge. She began to look upon it as a competition between his focused concentration and her creative persistence. Armed with her determination to avert his attention away from his reading and her ploy to show both girls that he could be attentive and affectionate towards her, she determined to pursue a pointed attack.

She began by casually bringing her arm through his, and with her other hand, brought it over and gently stroked up and down his arm. There was no response; no movement of any kind.

Moving from that failed attempt, she brought her arm up and around him, letting her fingers play with the curls on the back of his neck. She occasionally let them trail down into his collar. She remembered how delightfully he had responded to this on their carriage ride in France. But at the moment he seemed oblivious to it all.

Being defeated again, she decided to try a different manoeuvre. She moved her hand a little further around the side of his face and, continuing to sneak her fingers through his hair, soon found his ear. The two girls were busy talking and, although watching Elizabeth's curious behaviour, said nothing about it, except for some light giggles. As her fingers began to playfully tease his ear, he suddenly turned.

"Elizabeth!"

Elizabeth jumped back sharply and wondered if her persistent actions had finally stirred him. Perhaps, however, they stirred him to annoyance.

"Look! Out this side. We are here! "

Elizabeth was taken aback at this, wondering if he had even noticed anything she had done. The carriage stopped and suddenly he was back in their midst, pointing out where things would be, and eagerly telling them of all that was planned before they even exited the carriage. Elizabeth shook her head amusedly at this perplexing husband of hers.

When they stepped out of the carriage, they were looking out over a slight hill, with the peaks off in the distance. It was a beautiful setting. There was an area that was somewhat level, and this was where the school would be built. There was a small lake down an incline from the school and a wooded area off in the other direction. Other than that, there was a lot of natural rock.

"Some trees and brush will have to be removed," he told them, "but for the most part, the land is ready to be built on." After touring the site, they walked the short distance to where the houses would be situated. It was another flat area and the houses, although not large, would be generous for the occupants. The house for Mr. Fleming would be the largest.

Elizabeth caught the excitement again that she had had when they visited the school in Paris. Georgiana had no idea of what it would be like, but she was anxious for it to begin for the sake of little Eleanor. Darcy continued with his explanation of what they could expect. The elder Bostwick had already started making plans for the landscaping, although it was to be kept as natural as possible on the outer grounds. Surrounding the school there would be a fine lawn and the flower beds would boast the finest flowers grown in the area.

Upon Darcy's request, and with Bostwick's affirmation, young Mr. Wilcox was to be put in charge of the grounds. Although still under Bostwick's authority, he would have a group of men under him that would work solely at the school. Darcy had wanted to do something that would help out this young man and his wife, whose small home near Lambton was barely large enough for a growing family. One of the benefits as head gardener at the school would be to have a small home of his own on the school grounds. In addition to the schoolhouse itself, the plans included four or five dwellings, one of which would be for Mr. Fleming and his family and another for the young Wilcox couple.

From the first time Darcy had visited Wilcox in his parents' home, he had been determined to help him and his wife. Building this home for them would finally be a way to do that.

The drawings for the school were completed, but they awaited Fleming's approval. Darcy was confident there would not be any major changes, so he took the plans along to better explain what they were going to do and where things would be. He was anxious for Fleming to arrive from Paris so they could get things started as soon as possible.

When they had finished walking the site and seeing it all through Darcy's eyes, he turned and asked Elizabeth, "What do you think, my dearest? Do you approve?"

"I like it very much indeed!"

Darcy smiled and looked at the two girls who were standing on either side of them. Knowing what Elizabeth was trying to accomplish earlier while in the carriage, he unexpectedly put his arms around her back, catching her off guard as he pulled her close. "Good. I am glad to hear that."

Elizabeth found herself actually blushing, as this was the last thing she would have anticipated at this moment. She dared not discourage him, though, as he brought his head down and kissed her lips. Elizabeth heard a gasp and a giggle from either side of them as the girls knew not how else to respond to the sight before them.

Darcy pulled away, though, before Elizabeth had time to take her mind off the girls and what their reaction might be and simply enjoy the kiss. He acted as if there had been nothing unusual in what he did. It took her a few seconds to pull herself together and she could not believe that he had turned the tables on her. He smugly took Elizabeth's arm and in an irritatingly calm voice asked, "Shall we go?"

Elizabeth tried to attain some command to her countenance, as she struggled with a surprising response of discomfiture in the way he had kissed her and a slight provocation in that he seemed so self-satisfied with what he had done.

Darcy escorted Elizabeth toward the carriage, as the two girls grabbed each other's arms and continued to giggle. Elizabeth delicately rolled her eyes as she felt as though she had been duped by her husband. All that time he was resisting her efforts to distract him in the carriage, he was most likely plotting this.

As they gained some distance ahead of the girls, Elizabeth turned to him. "What was that, Mr. Darcy?"

"What could you possibly be referring to, Mrs. Darcy?"

"That kiss back there?"

"You mean my outward display of affection, which you thoroughly enjoyed, if I recall correctly, while we were in Paris?"

"You did that on purpose!"

"Of course I did it on purpose! You cannot presume that I will only kiss you by mischance! Or only when you *expect* it! Besides, you are not so innocent yourself, plotting to distract me while in the carriage. That was your intent, was it not?"

"I was only attempting to see what it would actually take to command your attention."

"Ah, I see. But the kiss, you did not enjoy it?"

"Of course I enjoyed it."

Darcy began to smirk. "Then what, may I ask, is the difficulty?"

"There is no difficulty. You took me by surprise, that is all."

"Ahhh, then you do not want me to be a husband who surprises his wife on occasion with a kiss."

"That is not what I said."

"Then you *do* want me to occasionally surprise you. Or, do you want me to warn you when I am about to surprise you? But then, it would not be a surprise if I did that, would it?"

Elizabeth could not help smiling and looked back at the girls who seemed very content to have distanced themselves from the pair, as they whispered between themselves. "Perhaps you surprised *them* more than you surprised me!"

He looked back at them and nodded. "Yes, perhaps I did. I cannot imagine what Georgiana must think!"

"Or Kitty!"

"Perhaps we can surprise them a bit more?"

Without waiting for an answer, he pulled Elizabeth into an embrace and kissed her for what seemed an eternity. The girls immediately stopped their talking and their walking as they gazed upon this couple. Georgiana had never seen her brother display any type of affection for any woman but herself. She thought it quite charming that he could be so unrestrained in his affections for his wife.

Kitty was awed that this kind of affection could be felt and shown by a husband and wife. She had never seen it from her parents and had always been of the opinion that they merely tolerated one another. She wondered whether her parents had ever had this kind of love, or whether the love between her sister and this man would someday diminish in intensity and become like that of her parents. Somehow she doubted either.

Both girls sighed as an impression came to them that they hoped to have this kind of love in a marriage of their own.

~~*

When they returned to Pemberley, after spending a very enjoyable day out at the site, the four of them gathered in the dining room to have some refreshments and tea. While they were visiting and looking back at their time together, Mrs. Reynolds brought in the mail, giving most of it to Darcy, but one letter she handed to Elizabeth.

Elizabeth looked at the letter and was startled at first by the return name. It was from Lydia. Her face whitened in response, unsure what, if anything, her sister would have to say that might be acceptable to read in front of Kitty and Georgiana. She hoped it would be short, sweet, and, she could only hope, very *un-Lydia-like!*

She could not lie about whom the letter was from, as inquiries poured forth from everyone. As all eyes were upon her, she told them it was from Lydia. Elizabeth immediately noticed Kitty tense up. She was feeling both a strong curiosity and an angry indifference to know all that Lydia had been doing since her arrival in Brighton.

Elizabeth slowly opened the letter and saw that it was written in a rather hurried way. It was short, and as her eyes quickly glanced over the missive, immediately saw Wickham's name. Her heart began beating nervously as she wondered what she should do. She knew she could not read the letter as is to either of these girls.

"What does she say, Elizabeth?" asked Georgiana.

"She does not say much... She... uh... says that she is having a good time." Elizabeth quickly scanned the letter to get the basic gist of it and find something to say. "She says that she is enjoying her stay with the Forsters... and she is doing plenty of sea bathing... and is meeting many new people. That is about all." With that, she quickly folded the letter and put it down on the table, placing her hand upon it.

"Lydia has never been the best writer," Kitty offered in somewhat a bitter tone.

Kitty felt the same sting of jealousy from not being able to go to Brighton that she had felt initially when Lydia had first been asked. A sudden irritation came upon her because of it that she had not felt since coming to Pemberley.

"Come, Georgiana," Kitty suddenly said. "Let us go outside. I feel the need for a walk."

The two girls stood up and excused themselves and Georgiana turned and looked back at Elizabeth before walking out. Elizabeth could have sworn she saw her blush.

Elizabeth was grateful when they left the room. She believed that Kitty had been eager to leave because she was still struggling with her feelings of envy toward their youngest sister. When they left the room, Darcy asked, "What did Lydia *really* say, Lizbeth. I can see you did not read what she actually wrote."

"It is not anything she says that is wrong, I did not feel that I should read it aloud, especially in front of Georgiana." She handed the letter to her husband.

Dear Lizzy,

You will not believe what the hero I am here in Brighton. Hah! When I came into town, the Forsters introduced me to all the new officers and acquainted me with all the latest news of the officers I knew from Meryton. And would you believe it? When I asked about Wickham, they informed me that he was engaged again, this time to a sixteen year old girl who lives here in Brighton. And I bet you won't be surprised when I tell you she has a sizeable fortune. Can you believe he did it again!!! Just like with Mary King! And Georgiana! Now, I bet you cannot guess what I did! I told the Forsters all about him; what Georgiana told me, all that he had done, and how he is not who everyone thinks he is. How he is only interested in the money. (Tell Georgiana not to worry, I didn't mention her name.)

Well! After that, this girl's father and Forster checked into him, and found out he had run up numerous gambling debts again and owed lots of money to the merchants in town that he had no way of repaying. And guess what! The girl's father forced him to call off the engagement. Imagine that! They were so thankful to me! LAAA! After that, Wickham disappeared and no one has seen him since. I am certainly the hero! This girl's father is eternally grateful to me and all the officers are upset that he seemed to deceive everyone, especially the ones who are out the money he owed them! Tell Georgiana thanks for telling me about him. I am having a wonderful time and there are so many more officers here, I shan't ever run out of anything to do. Mrs. Forster and I are having a grand time! The weather is great and the sea bathing beyond expectation. Say hello to Kitty, I understand she is there.

Hope you had a nice honeymoon.

Yours, Lydia

Elizabeth watched as concern was drawn across her husband's face. "What do you think, my dear?"

Darcy looked up at her. "Well, I suppose we shall not have to worry about Lydia and Wickham, at least. I actually feared in the beginning that she would do something rash or foolish with him. I would not have put it past him to try to get to me through her, now that we are family through marriage."

"Do you think we have any more reason to fear her association with him?"

"No, I think Lydia is probably too tempted by all the other soldiers to have any regard left for Wickham, especially with her knowing the truth about him.

"She seems quite pleased with herself that she is the hero, even at Wickham's expense."

"So it seems."

"But there is something else that concerns you, is there not?" she asked.

"I am only concerned about how much Lydia publicly said about him. Wickham has never had his character disclosed like this. He has always been able to keep one step ahead of the truth being found out. I may have made the wrong decision in keeping his character to myself in the past. I believed... hoped... that he would someday grow up and improve his lifestyle. Obviously he cannot or will not do that. Perhaps I should have disclosed it earlier, but in a way I feared his temper and what he might do. He is probably now very angry."

"Do you think he will do something to get back at her? Do we need to possibly warn her?"

Darcy's hand went up to his face, rubbing it anxiously. "I have no reason to suspect him capable of anything harmful." He took a deep breath and slowly let it out. "I really do not know."

He looked at Elizabeth. "I *am* concerned that he has disappeared and no one knows where he is. He has no money. I wonder what trickery and deceit he will employ to survive." Darcy took in a deep breath. "He had better not come here."

"Well, we shall have to hope that is not in his plans and we never hear of him again."

Darcy looked at her with concern etched deeply into his face. "Yes, for that we shall hope."

Chapter 13

Lochlin's Estate Leddesdale Manor, One week later

David Bostwick sat in the study going over the figures that he had accumulated from his recent trip up north, where he had visited with Mr. Lochlin's brother. They owned some joint property, and David was working out the division of dividends coming from it.

Leddesdale Manor was a large home in comparison to some, and for a man living alone, Lochlin felt it was more than plentiful for his needs. Although neither as large nor elegant as Pemberley, it had potential. Most of the rooms were never used and were therefore neglected. Lochlin kept a minimal staff to meet his daily needs.

He had only hired David because he had little desire to do the business required to keep up his property. He had always done it himself, but now he was not inclined to oversee it. His eyesight was fading, and he knew his mind was not as keen as it was in his youth. He knew he was in the winter years of his life, and wanted to spend his final years doing the things he wanted to do. He had never been a man of leisure to the degree that some were, but recently he had decided he wanted more freedom and not be tied down by work. So he hired David.

He had lost his wife several years earlier. They had three daughters, all who had married well. He had a total of seven grandchildren, but they all lived a considerable distance from Derbyshire. His free time would give him more of an opportunity to visit them. He had an older brother who had children and grandchildren, and that was the extent of his family.

Even though he was getting on in years, not a day went by that he would not have David laughing at something he said, or marvelling at what this man still attempted to do at his age. As Georgiana had said, "He was young at heart," and he daily lived up to that portrayal.

Mr. Lochlin came in this afternoon, late in the day, to pay David a visit while he was in the study. "Bostwick, I have something I need you to do for me."

"Yes, Sir. What is it?"

"I am going to give a ball here."

"Excuse me, Sir?"

"You heard me, a ball. I have not given a ball at Leddesdale in years, and I thought it was about time that I had one. Would you not agree?"

"If that is what you want, Sir."

"My brother and his family are coming for a visit. I thought it would be a good way to introduce them to my friends. Besides, my brother has two grandsons, my two great nephews, who are coming and I would like to introduce them to a few young ladies. I dare say they are two very eligible young men."

He handed David a roughly handwritten list of names. "Here is my guest list and the details about the ball. I want you to have some invitation cards made up, address them to the guest list, and then please deliver them."

"Yes, Sir."

David took the guest list and began to peruse it. It was a very impressive list. He was inviting most of the wealthy land owners and prominent people from the area. It was going to be an upper class affair. Suddenly his eyes found themselves on the names Mr. and Mrs. Fitzwilliam Darcy, Miss Georgiana Darcy and Guest.

His eyes rested on the words "and Guest" and his thoughts took him to a scene where he was escorting Miss Darcy onto the dance floor. He shook his head in reproach and soothed himself with the fact that her guest most likely would be Miss Bennet. He wondered whether they would even come. He knew it would be difficult for him as the time drew near watching the preparations being made for this lavish event. How much he would want to be here to see her. He pushed aside those thoughts and got to work on the invitation cards.

~~*

The next few days passed quickly, as Darcy spent a great deal of time getting the plans for the building of the school underway. He hired a long time friend to oversee the work that was being done so his time would not be consumed by this project.

Elizabeth began making calls with Georgiana -- with Kitty in tow -- to visit some of Pemberley's tenants. Elizabeth saw in Georgiana a very different young lady on these visits. She seemed to have a natural ability to reach out to those less fortunate. She was truly caring and compassionate and she seemed to lose some of that shyness that she so often exhibited. Elizabeth could see the bonds of friendships that the young girl had formed with these people. Elizabeth enjoyed meeting them also, and was pleased for Kitty to have this experience.

When they visited the Franks, something seemed to change in Kitty. She had never known anyone who was deaf, but when she met Eleanor, she followed Georgiana's lead and played with the child and treated her as if she was no different than other children. While Kitty and Georgiana played with Eleanor, Elizabeth talked with Mrs. Frank and was pleased to finally make her acquaintance. She told her of their visit to the deaf school in Paris and how wonderful it was.

That afternoon Mrs. Frank spent a little time teaching the three of them how to sign the letters of the alphabet. When they left the Franks' home that day, the three ladies spent the time in the carriage spelling out words and laughing when one of them got a letter or two wrong. They enjoyed taking turns spelling words using the signing alphabet, and then trying to decipher what the other was attempting to spell.

"What fun we could have with this!" Kitty whispered to Georgiana.

Elizabeth shook her head at the conspiratorial tone, "Yes, but remember, *I* am learning it as well, and you shall not be able to put something over on me!"

"No, but perhaps we could conspire against William!" Georgiana said mischievously. They all laughed at the thought.

Elizabeth saw that Kitty and Georgiana were good for each other, and she had added an appeal to Kitty's letter home asking whether she could remain at Pemberley longer. She could only conjecture how Mary was faring being the only Bennet daughter remaining at Longbourn, although she did have Jane close by. She knew Mary tended to keep to herself anyway. She was also not certain when Lydia would be returning home, but felt that when she did, she did not want Kitty there. Elizabeth did not want to give Lydia the opportunity to destroy all the improvements that had been cultivated in Kitty's behaviour and character.

The next day being Sunday, they attended church services for the first time since returning from Paris. Elizabeth was anxious to attend and meet the reverend and more of their neighbours.

When they arrived, the foursome walked in to heads turning and murmurs. A young man with a most genuine smile quickly came toward them and warmly greeted them.

"Good morning, Mr. Darcy, Miss Darcy. It is good to see you."

"Thank you, Reverend Kenton. May I present my wife, Elizabeth Darcy, and her sister, Kitty Bennet?"

Kenton extended his hand to both with a very fervent handshake. "It is a pleasure to meet you both. Mrs. Darcy, may I say I have only heard wonderful things about you."

"Thank you, Reverend, you are too kind."

He then turned to Kitty. "Miss Bennet, how long do you plan to stay in Derbyshire?"

"My visit was originally only to be two weeks, but I have written home asking permission to remain here a little longer."

"I do hope you receive that permission." His gaze lingered on Kitty for a moment and then returned to the rest of the party. "Please come in and sit down. I do hope you find our humble church to your liking."

"I am sure we will," assured Elizabeth. "I would like to thank you for allowing the deaf classes to be held at the church until the school is built. That was very thoughtful of you."

"It is a pleasure. The church building is not used on a daily basis, and except for an occasional wedding or funeral, it should be available. I cannot think of a better use for the church than this. Except, of course, Sunday services."

"I am so glad you think so," Elizabeth commented.

Darcy escorted the three ladies to their pew and they took a seat. Elizabeth thought to herself how much she liked the reverend. He was so unlike her cousin, she was sure she would find his sermons more interesting. But what was even more interesting to her was his manner around Kitty. The question crossed her mind whether he was married. If not, he would make a fine prospect for her.

Elizabeth did find herself enjoying the service and Reverend Kenton's sermon. He did not have the pompous air about him that her cousin Mr. Collins had. He seemed more sincere and caring, and made the sermon he preached and the scripture he used to base his sermon on, come alive and practical to one's life. He was unlike the older ministers at the Longbourn and Meryton churches who seemed to repeat the same sermons over and over again, only with the names and circumstances changed. No, she thought, she would like Reverend Kenton and looked forward to returning.

After services, Elizabeth had the opportunity to meet a few people that she did not know. Darcy seemed both eager to introduce her, yet eager to leave. Elizabeth easily struck up conversations with those she was privileged to meet and was bemused as her husband obligingly left the responsibility of the conversation up to her.

Reverend Kenton came up to them as they were getting into the carriage to leave. "I do hope you enjoyed today's service and will feel the freedom to join us at any time." He looked at Kitty, hoping to get a response, but Elizabeth answered instead.

"Thank you, Reverend Kenton. I believe we shall."

~~*

The next day Elizabeth received a letter from home with her mother's permission that Kitty could remain there as long as she was neither troublesome nor in the way. Elizabeth was greatly pleased. Having Kitty at Pemberley took care of two things. First, it gave Georgiana a companion more her age, and second, it gave Kitty an opprotunity to really blossom into the young lady she was meant to be. At home she often had to compete with Lydia, who always made her feel second best. Lydia was the one who attracted the attention of the officers, who looked better in the pretty dress and bonnet, and who got the most laughs from the crowd. Kitty was now able to be herself and Elizabeth could see that she began to feel better about herself as well.

When Elizabeth received the letter and was now assured of her staying, she decided to take Kitty to a local seamstress to have some clothes made that she would need for the cooler months. Georgiana decided to stay back, as she wanted some time alone to spend practicing on the pianoforte.

Georgiana walked into the music room, and feeling the warmth and stuffiness of it from the late summer day, walked over to the window and opened it slightly, allowing a refreshing breeze to swiftly fill the space. She put her face to the window to breathe in the fresh air that was more than anxious to give her some of its refreshment.

She walked back over to the instrument, and, sifting through the pages of music, looked for something inspiring and uplifting. Upon finding a piece that appealed to her, she opened it on the piano, and sat down to begin playing. She was content at first to simply play, letting her nimble fingers warm up as they moved agilely across the keys.

Whenever Georgiana played, as often as she could, she would close her eyes, opening them only occasionally to look ahead at the notes. She felt that by playing with her eyes closed, it helped draw her into the music and she was able to forget everything and everybody. She became the song, whether it was soft and romantic, dark and foreboding, lively and fun, or sad and melancholy. Today she picked out a soft and romantic piece.

At some point in the song she began to sing. Her voice was clear and sweet, and although soft, it was carried along on a gentle breeze to the courtyard below. Unbeknownst to her, a young man was leaning against the side of the house inside the courtyard, enjoying this private concert.

David Bostwick had come to Pemberley to deliver the invitation card to the Darcys. He had come into the courtyard looking for his father, hoping to pay him a visit. It was there that he first became aware of the sound of the music being played. He paused, listening; wondering whether it was Georgiana playing, although being fairly certain it was. When she began singing he was most assured it was.

He closed his eyes in remembrance of playing in the courtyard with his brother and hearing a very young Georgiana plunk out her lessons, over and over again. At the time he had thought how tedious it must be to have to practice the same thing repeatedly. But now, as he listened to her play, he felt it had been well worth it, for now she played so beautifully and he felt he could listen to her for hours.

He rarely had the privilege of hearing her sing. He wondered whether she ever performed for anyone, as shy as she was. As he was not one to socialize in the same class as the Darcys, he knew not how she fared in social settings. He could only surmise that she would feel reticent if she had to perform before even a small audience. He was convinced, however, that she would do it admirably. Her voice was as smooth and clear as a crystal bell.

Suddenly he wondered what she would be like at a ball. How she would be at Lochlin's ball... how she would be dressed... how she would dance.

He would probably never know. But for the present moment, even though he had a delivery for the Darcys, he indulged his desire to listen to her play and sing, resting his head upon the house and closing his eyes.

He was unaware of the presence of someone coming into the courtyard. It was not until he heard his name called out in a most severe tone by a very familiar voice that he opened his eyes and struggled to come to attention. Mr. Darcy had walked into the courtyard, and seeing him against the house, walked over to him to inquire what he was doing there.

"Bostwick!"

"Mr. Darcy... Sir... it is good to see you, Sir...Welcome back... Sir." He straightened himself up, pulling himself awkwardly away from the wall.

David was almost as tall as Darcy, so when he came up to him they were nearly eye to eye. "Did you have some reason for being in the courtyard young man, or were you holding up the wall?"

"No… Sir… I mean… yes, Sir." David inhaled deeply, attempting to calm his suddenly unsettled nerves. "That is, Sir, I came to bring an invitation from Mr. Lochlin for your family. He is giving a ball, Sir." He nervously held out the invitation to Darcy. Suddenly he felt like a fool. Why was this man causing him so much discomfort?

Darcy looked up to the window that was above where they were standing, listening to Georgiana's singing and playing. He narrowed his eyes as he looked back at the young man. "I believe cards and letters customarily get delivered to the front door. Perhaps you were unaware of that civility? Or did you happen to know I would be walking into the courtyard at this moment so you could present it to me?"

"Uh… no, Sir. I…" *Do I tell him the truth or make something up?* His mind struggled with what would be best to say. Finally, "I heard Miss Darcy playing, and thought I would come over and listen… Sir."

"And why would you want to do that?" Darcy demanded to know.

"Because she plays and sings so beautifully. She does play and sing beautifully, do you not think so?"

"Of course I think so!"

Both men took in deep breaths, staring at each other as two bulls ready to charge each other would.

Finally Darcy spoke. "Mr. Bostwick, would you come with me please?"

Darcy turned, not waiting for him to answer. They walked out of the courtyard toward the front, and Darcy turned toward the south, keeping a few strides ahead. When they came to the front steps of the house, Darcy stopped and faced the young man.

"Wait here, please." Darcy walked on past him, leaving him alone and bewildered at the steps. This was the exact place he had encountered Georgiana a few months back after not having seen her for a few years. He suspected that this time his encounter here would not be so pleasant.

Darcy knew that the elder Bostwick was working in a garden off to the south of the house and set out there. He found him and apprised him of the situation, asking him to have a talk with his son and request that he not come again onto the grounds of Pemberley. He returned to the house a different way.

Mr. Bostwick walked with apprehension to where his son waited. When his son looked up and saw him, he wondered what was in store for him.

Mr. Bostwick eyed his son with grave concern. "Hello, Son."

"Hello, Father."

There was silence; neither really knowing what to say. Finally his father said, "David, I am almost finished with work for the day. Would you wait for me and we can ride home together?"

"Yes, Sir."

"As a matter of fact, you can come along with me and help me out whilst I finish."

David joined his father as they returned to where he had been working, and finished by putting away gardening tools in the shed. His father was quiet as he did so, affirming to David his sneaking suspicion that his father was going to have a talk with him. He was not looking forward to it.

When Mr. Bostwick locked the shed, they both retrieved their horses, and they set out for home. They rode side by side in silence for a while. David knew his father was usually more talkative. He normally would ask about his day or tell him about his. David knew by his father's silence that he was formulating what to say.

Finally the elder Bostwick brought up the subject that was pressing on his mind, more so from the talk with Darcy than his own conviction.

"David, it has been brought to my attention that on occasion you have been seen in the company of Miss Darcy on the grounds of Pemberley. Is that true?"

David's throat seemed instantly dry, and he swallowed several times, hoping to alleviate the constriction he now felt. He took a deep breath and wondered whether he should play ignorant, or admit to his father that indeed, he had spent some time with her on a few occasions.

"I… uh… we have encountered each other a few times, yes."

"By accident or your design?"

David grimaced. He thought to himself how only one time had it been accidental. That was when she walked outside after her brother had recovered from his accident and he was standing right by the door planting gardenias. All the other times he had seen her from afar and purposely sought her out.

"Well?"

"Father, I had not seen Georgiana for a few years. You certainly must remember that we were childhood friends."

"And you certainly must remember that her brother is my employer! I cannot have you risking everything I have, the trust and confidence Mr. Darcy has in me, because you have some sort of fancy for his sister! This will not do! And it is not merely that, look at the difference in your stations in life!"

David glanced down at his hands tightly gripping his horse's reins. He had to calm down, he had to demonstrate to his father that first and foremost he was mature and level headed. He finally looked up and turned to his father.

"I am quite aware of the difference in our stations. It is something I think about constantly. I know that I would have nothing to offer her in life but the clothes on my back, when she has been used to so much." David sighed, the truth of the words stinging more severely as he spoke them aloud. "I have often thought… hoped… that if I could get into the university…"

"David, an education will still not be enough to put you in the same class as the Darcys. You are not a man of financial independence and never will be. Besides, you know we cannot afford an education like that. We put you through a trade school and that shall have to suffice. You are who you are and nothing else will ever change that."

"Yes, but perhaps I could find something in addition to my work at Lochlin's. If I could earn a little more, I could save up to attend university in a few years."

"By your lingering in the courtyard just now, it seems apparent that you have a little too much extra time on your hands that could be put to better use. I think I know of something for you if you do not mind the work."

"What is that?"

"I have been talking with the Reverend Kenton at the church, and he needs someone to care for the grounds. The present groundskeeper is too old to continue. He asked me if I knew of anyone who could use the work. You have learned all you need to know about gardening and landscaping from me, I think you could do this a few hours a week when Lochlin does not need you. That should be enough to help you earn a little more money. But I doubt it would be enough to pay for a college education."

David considered this. "I should like the position, if I may have it."

"I shall stop by and let the reverend know tomorrow you are interested. Perhaps you should come with me and talk with him about the wages." They rode in silence for a while longer. Finally his father gave him the message from Darcy that he was not eager to have to relay to him. "And Son…"

David looked over at his father. "Yes?"

"Mr. Darcy has made it very clear that he does not want to see you on the grounds of Pemberley again. I think it would be wise for you to put Miss Darcy out of your mind."

David looked at his father but remained silent, yet his thoughts resonated within him. *I can try to put her out of my mind, but not my heart. You do not realize that since I was fourteen, she has been the only girl I have wanted to marry.*

.~.~*

Darcy entered the house through a side door and as he closed it behind him, he leaned against it. He took his hand and raked it through his hair and told himself that as much as he did not like to do this, he had to. He knew David Bostwick to be a fine man. He had great respect for his father. If only there was some other way. But he was one of only three people who knew the specific details of the financial arrangements his father had drawn up for Georgiana before he died, and he had to look out for her interests. He took a deep breath. No, there was no other way. He had to do everything in his power to discourage any sort of alliance between David Bostwick and his sister!

Chapter 14

Darcy and Elizabeth anxiously awaited word from Fleming regarding the details of his arrival and, of course, whether they had secured Michelle's adoption. Word finally came, and they were thrilled to hear that they would all be coming to Pemberley in a few weeks; Fleming and his family, newly adopted Michelle, and Jacques, who had returned to Paris and contacted Fleming about coming over with them.

This news set Darcy into motion getting things finalized for their arrival, and sent Elizabeth into an excitement that invariably affected Georgiana and Kitty. As she talked to them about the day she and Darcy had spent in the school, all three of them could not help but think of little Eleanor and her family, and how much this would mean to them in addition to all the others who would benefit. Elizabeth took great delight in the interest Kitty displayed. Being away from Lydia was the best thing that ever happened to her. She wondered about Lydia's well being and whether she had returned home yet, since she received only that one letter from her. Elizabeth determined to set aside some time to write to Jane to inquire about her and her husband, and also whether she had any recent knowledge of how Lydia was faring.

Darcy had spoken with people throughout the area about the deaf school and was compiling a list of potential students for the classes. The list consisted of interested people, both deaf and hearing, who lived close enough to the school that they would be able to make the trip on a daily basis. Until the school facility was built, and while classes were being held in the church, only those who could come and go daily would attend.

Once the school was built, there would be those who would come from further distances and live at the school. Some might stay on a weekly basis and return on the weekends while others might choose to live there on a more permanent basis.

Darcy was encouraged by the interest of not only deaf people, but others as well who had the desire to communicate with the deaf, whether it was with a family member, friend, or business associate. When the school began, Mr.

Fleming would work with the adults and Mrs. Fleming would work with the children, which would include her daughter, Michelle, and Eleanor.

Darcy put off the ground breaking for the school until Fleming arrived, so he could look over the final plans and the property, in case he had any suggestions. Once he had given his approval, things would commence.

The other event that put the Darcy household in an excited uproar was the upcoming ball. Georgiana, Kitty, and Elizabeth had several fun outings selecting what they would wear to this grand affair. Elizabeth knew it would be significant for her, as it would be her first ball in Derbyshire as Mrs. Fitzwilliam Darcy.

Georgiana wondered silently whether David would attend the ball while Kitty wondered the same thought aloud. Due to Kitty's frequent outbursts about the subject, Elizabeth thought this would be a good opportunity to see for herself what Georgiana's feeling for this young man were.

Georgiana had gone into the music room to play, and Kitty was resting in her room. Elizabeth walked in to the music room and sat down, enjoying the fluid movement of Georgiana's hands and the beautiful sound they evoked from this instrument. When she had finished, Elizabeth complimented her on her playing.

"That was beautiful as usual, Georgiana."

"Thank you, Elizabeth. Would you like to hear something else?"

"Perhaps a little later. Right now there is something I would like to talk with you about."

Georgiana turned, folded her hands in her lap, and gave Elizabeth her full attention.

Elizabeth nervously smiled, and took a deep breath. "Georgiana, it has been apparent to me, and I imagine to yourself as well, that Kitty has developed something of an interest in, or perhaps more of an infatuation with Mr. Bostwick, the young man we met that day in Lambton."

Georgiana's eyes quickly averted, and then swiftly darted back. "It does appear that way," she whispered softly.

Elizabeth pursed her lips as she hoped her next words would open the doors for Georgiana to share her feelings. "Georgiana… I was wondering… are you aware of any reason that I should discourage Kitty from this fascination?" Elizabeth looked warmly upon Georgiana, who again looked away. This time she did not return her eyes to Elizabeth.

"He is a very well-mannered man, Elizabeth. He has always been very kind to me. I mean… he has always been very kind." She took a deep breath, and Elizabeth stared intently at her eyes, which were lowered. It appeared to her that the young girl's eyes were welling with tears.

Suddenly one tear escaped and rolled slowly down her cheek. She quickly removed the evidence with a wipe of her hand. Elizabeth got up from where she was sitting, and came to sit next to Georgiana on the piano bench, putting her arm around her.

"Is this the young man you talked with me about that day we took a walk up to Oakham Mount?"

Georgiana put her head in her hands and nodded, completely giving way to the tears that had pooled in her eyes and now freely rolled down her face.

Elizabeth gently spoke to the girl, and soothed her. "Would you care to talk about it?"

"I do not know what to do with my feelings for him. When I returned to Pemberley after your wedding, I kept encountering him, and each time that I did…" She again wiped at the tears that rolled down her cheek. "Each time I did, my feelings for him would grow stronger and stronger. Yet I know Fitzwilliam would never approve."

Elizabeth took in a deep breath. "Do you think Mr. Bostwick has the same regard for you?"

"Oh, Elizabeth, I am not certain. I only know that when I am with him, he makes me feel like I am the only one who matters. The more time I spend with him, the more I feel that I can talk with him, and I want to talk with him. I feel as though I am a different person around him… that he brings out something in me that is often hidden deep inside or too afraid to come out."

Elizabeth inwardly sighed. On Georgiana's part, this was serious indeed. "How much time have you spent with him since your return, Georgiana? And under what circumstances were they?"

Georgiana told her how they would encounter each other on the grounds and visit. She told her of their friendship as children, and how, during the times she visited with him, they had laughed over some of the things they used to do.

"How has he behaved in your presence, Georgiana? Has he been honourable toward you?"

"Oh, yes, Elizabeth. He has never done anything that Fitzwilliam would disapprove of… except perhaps being born into the situation in which he was born."

Elizabeth sighed again at the truth in Georgiana's assessment.

"I know in my head the disparity in our situations and what that means. But I seem to be unable to do anything about how I feel," she continued. Suddenly she looked to Elizabeth with much anguish on her face. "You are not going to say anything to Kitty about Mr. Bostwick, are you?"

"Of course not, Georgiana."

"Will you tell Fitzwilliam?"

Elizabeth patted Georgiana's shoulder. "Your brother already suspects. We saw the two of you walking together toward the house the day we returned to Pemberley."

Georgiana turned to look at Elizabeth. "He saw us? I cannot believe that he has not come to talk with me about it."

"He wanted to talk with you right then and there, but I asked him not to."

"Oh," she answered slowly. "Was he very angry?"

"Georgiana, I would say that he was considerably concerned."

"What Kitty said in the carriage… about me not being able to fall in love with just anyone…"

Elizabeth silently nodded, her heart aching for the dilemma this young girl was facing.

"I realized it was true. But I look at you and William and see how happy the two of you are, and wish that he could reconcile in my favour what he reconciled for himself when deciding to ask for your hand. He seems to have a different standard for me that I cannot see him abandoning."

"Georgiana, I know that it appears to you that your brother and I could be compared to you and Mr. Bostwick. But unfortunately, it is not altogether the same. It is expected for the man to support his wife. There was no problem with that in our coming together. In respect to Mr. Bostwick, he has very little. He would, in a sense, be supporting you with your fortune. A man can very easily lose respect for himself when he is not the main provider."

"But Elizabeth, I do not care for all my money. If I could be happy, to be married to a man I love deeply and who loved me, I would be content to live even in a pauper's cottage."

Elizabeth smiled at the girl, as she remembered how similar her own words to Jane were about Georgiana's idealistic dreams. "Oh, Georgiana, you say that now. But look at what you have been used to. It would not be easy to give it up."

Georgiana turned to Elizabeth. "So you would stand by my brother, then, in his views regarding Mr. Bostwick?"

Elizabeth swallowed hard, giving herself time to think. "Georgiana, as I said on our walk that day, you are still young, and there are many young men out there who would love to be introduced to you. Give a few of them a chance, and do not allow yourself to believe that he is the only one you could ever love. Will you do that for me?"

Georgiana looked up at her and gently nodded her head, but her heart seemed intent elsewhere.

~~*

Darcy was in his study reading when Mrs. Reynolds announced Mr. Lochlin, who requested some time with him. Darcy agreed, closed his book and waited for him to enter. He wondered what this could be about.

When Lochlin came to the door, Darcy rose and extended his hand. "Lochlin, it is good to see you. How have you been?"

"I am well, thank you. Older, but still able to get around."

"Good, would you like to sit down?"

"Yes, thank you." Lochlin breathed in deeply and looked around. "It has been quite a while since I have been here. You have a great place here, Darcy. It looks to be in excellent condition."

"Thank you. And how are things are Leddesdale?"

"Oh, with every year that goes by I swear it gets bigger and more useless. One of these days I shall like to sell it and buy something smaller. I do not need a place that big anymore."

"Lochlin, if you do decide to sell it, let me know. I have a friend who may be interested in it. He has asked me to be on the lookout for a place for him to either let or buy in the area."

"I will, but it probably will not be for some time. I heard that Kendleton is on the market."

"Is it? I will have to check into that, although I believe it may be too small for his tastes. Now, Lochlin, to what do I owe this visit?"

Lochlin brought his palms together and rubbed them briskly. "My brother's side of the family is coming for a visit and will be here for the ball I am giving. He has two grandsons that will be there… my great nephews. Are you and your family planning to attend?"

"Yes, I believe we are," Darcy said, feeling some apprehension begin to rise up.

"Would it be acceptable to you for me to introduce my two nephews to your sister? Perhaps secure a dance or two with each of them?"

Darcy took in a deep breath. It was bad enough that he was agitated over seeing her walking with a young man. Now he was expected to give his approval for an introduction of someone he had never met! He looked up at Lochlin who was anxiously waiting.

"Tell me about these young men, Lochlin."

"The eldest son is heir to Callesbury in Lancashire. He is a very fine young man and had a good education at Oxford. The younger one is eligible for a good living. He may not be as suitable for Georgiana in your eyes, but both are of excellent breeding and connections."

Darcy contemplated this man's words. Unfortunately, Lochlin's words did not give him the heart of these men. He also knew that Georgiana had not been presented at court yet, and he would prefer she wait for any introductions of the sort until after next season when she officially came out.

"I do not know, Lochlin. She is still quite young."

"Darcy, she is sixteen, is she not? Many a young lady is brought out when she is but fifteen. Besides, it is only an introduction; we are not making a marriage contract here." He smiled when he said this, to reassure him.

Darcy looked up at him. Suddenly he realized this might be a good way to turn her thoughts away from one very ineligible young man. "Fine, Lochlin. You have my permission. We shall also be bringing Elizabeth's younger sister who is almost eighteen. Do me a favour and include her in the introductions as well."

Lochlin stood up and reached out his hand. "I will, Darcy. I appreciate it." After shaking upon it, he turned, and left the room.

Darcy took in a deep breath as he watched the man leave. He tensed as he contemplated what his role as Georgiana's guardian had entailed in the past and what it would mean for him in the future. It was difficult for him to imagine any young man being good enough for Georgiana. He knew he would have the tendency to be suspicious and overly critical of them, one and all.

~~*

On the day before the ball, David was busier than ever. He had begun working occasionally on the church grounds, and found his work with Lochlin increasing at the same time, especially as the day of the ball grew near. He sat in Lochlin's study this day, looking at the numbers in the ledger in front of him, but not really comprehending a thing. All he could think about was the impending ball. He had seen the list of guests who had replied that they were coming, and the Darcys were on the list. All he could think of was Georgiana at this affair and how pretty she would probably look. He wondered if there was any way he could remain at Leddesdale and see her. If only he could be a mouse, and watch from a hidden corner of the room.

He sighed. Lochlin's brother and his whole family had arrived. He had met them all briefly, including the two great nephews. He was definitely not impressed with them. The older was about twenty-one, the younger one about nineteen. It was very apparent to him that they kept their distance from the likes of himself -- the hired help. So it surprised him this day when there was a knock on the door. He opened it to find the elder Andrew Lochlin asking for a moment of his time.

David invited him to come in and sit down.

Andrew surveyed the room while David surveyed him. He could not imagine what he wanted, but patiently waited for him to proceed.

"Bostwick, my great uncle informs me that you have spent a good amount of time at Pemberley."

David started at this, his eyes narrowing. "Yes, my father is the head gardener there."

"Then you are acquainted with Miss Darcy?" He lifted one eyebrow to look at him.

David felt his heart begin to pound fiercely as Lochlin so nonchalantly mentioned her name. "Uh, yes, we are acquainted."

Andrew gave a quick satisfied nod. He got up from his chair, and brought himself over to the desk, setting himself down on the corner of it. "My uncle has secured permission for my introduction to Miss Darcy at the ball. He seems to think she would make a most suitable match for me. So, tell me, Lochlin, what is she like? I mean, is she attractive? Does she have a pleasant figure?"

David's heart now began to race in anger, and he now knew for a certainty that he disliked this rake sitting before him. But he also knew he could jeopardize his job if he told this young man off as he so wanted. "She is sweet and kind, a quiet girl…"

"Good!" Lochlin interrupted. "I do not like the talkative type. I prefer a woman who knows her place and does not babble on incessantly. But then I do hope she is not so quiet that I have to force her to speak two words on her own. So… to the more important details, what does she look like?"

"She is… she is…" To him she was beautiful, but not in the classic sense that he would be used to. "She has a sweet face, and is pleasantly tall and slender."

"Well, I hope she is not too thin. I prefer women to be curvaceous, if you know what I mean. But I guess I shall have to judge for myself when I see her. Tell me, since you are an acquaintance, is there any advice you can give me that will win me her favour?"

David could barely think through his anger. "I do not think there is any…" Suddenly he looked up at Lochlin and inwardly grinned at his inspiration. "No, wait; there is something that she is truly impressed with." David paused for effect. "Let her know, in great detail and with much passion, of all your possessions, your great estate, how big it is; how many rooms there are and how lavish it is. You know she has been used to only the finest at Pemberley, and she most likely would only settle for something of equal distinction. You must call her attention to all your wealth and what you someday will inherit."

"Ahh, I think I can manage that without any problem whatsoever. Our estate is grand, and although I really do not need her fortune, it will supplement what I have nicely. Thirty thousand is what I believe I heard. One cannot be too particular when it comes to a woman with a fortune like that, can they?"

David slowly, most minutely shook his head. He gritted his teeth as he added one final suggestion. "Make sure you also talk about yourself in the most favourable way. She idolizes her brother, and he will only settle for someone who is as exceptional as he is.

Andrew continued to press David for details and advice, thanking him for each helpful suggestion. By the end of this questioning, David was satisfied that he had steered Andrew in a direction that would most definitely *not* win Georgiana's favour. Andrew was satisfied with the plan he had already set in motion for gaining her approval.

He stood up to take leave and turned to walk out of the room, but abruptly stopped. As he reached the door he turned back to David, "I understand her parents are both dead, but this elder brother she has is her guardian. He is most protective of her, from what I hear. Is that correct?"

David nodded slowly. "Very protective, indeed."

David looked down, not wishing Andrew to see the look on his face that betrayed the defeat he was feeling. Defeat that had originally begun with Darcy -- his *Goliath* -- just the other day. He gained some of his composure and looked up to the brash young man standing before him. "I imagine he only looks out for her best interests."

Andrew turned to walk away. "Well, I know how to charm even the most overbearing father. I am sure I can handle her brother." With that he walked out and closed the door.

David tightly gripped his hands into a fist and did not move for a several seconds. If it had been in his power at all, he would have run out there, shaken some sense into Lochlin's nephew and sent him packing. There was no way he was even remotely close to being suitable and good enough for Georgiana.

David continued to stare at the closed door. *So you think you can charm her brother. I really doubt it. But you will have to go through me as well.* He curled both hands tightly in a ball. *And I will ensure that she never returns you any regard!*

David leaned his forehead down into the palm of his hand, propped up by his elbow. Suddenly the realization of the truth of his words earlier penetrated him. *She has been used to only the finest... She will only settle for a lifestyle of equal distinction.* The very words he used to mislead Andrew about how to impress Georgiana were words that now convinced him of his unsuitability.

He could not fault Darcy for his interference. *He only looks out for her best interests.* If he were to view circumstances through Darcy's perspective, David would have to realistically agree that he was most unworthy to vie for Georgiana's affections. He slowly stood up, picking up some books from the desk and walking over to the bookshelves, sliding them in their place.

He thought of his deceitful advice to Lochlin. Would this be his only purpose in life with respect to Georgiana? To keep her from those men who would use and abuse her solely to gain her fortune? If he never could have her, did he really think he could ensure her happiness by being the one to weed out those that were most undeserving? He sadly shook his head. He knew that he would be inclined to view each potential suitor as unworthy of her, including himself first and foremost.

He sat back down and leaned back, stretching his long legs out in front of him, feeling greatly disconsolate. *And I thought I could not feel worse than the day Darcy ordered me to stay away from Pemberley. I guess I was wrong.*

Mr. Lochlin suddenly charged into the room. "Bostwick, I have a big problem! I have to ask you to do a big favour for me tomorrow night at the ball!"

Chapter 15

The Ball!

The sun seemed very anxious to peek up over the horizon on the morning of the ball. Georgiana and Kitty were so excited about it that they were like children awakening on Christmas morning. Their very first thought when they arose was to take a peek at the dresses they were to wear and anticipate how they would wear their hair and what accessories would go with it. They joined each other in their respective rooms and compared notes, shared feelings, and dreamed about their expectations for what it would be like.

For Kitty it was like a dream come true. She was aware that this ball would most likely be unlike any that she had ever attended, except perhaps the ball at Netherfield. But this would be a ball with only the finest guests and it thrilled Kitty to think that she had been included in the invitation. She greatly looked forward to seeing another elegant estate and comparing it to Pemberley. She also had come to imagine that the ball might provide her the opportunity to meet a variety of young men of generous standing.

Georgiana's eager expectancy came from the hope that Mr. Lochlin would have invited David Bostwick. She reasoned that, after all, he was a great help to him and was looked upon favourably by Lochlin. The thought of a chance to dance with him took precedence in her mind all day. She wondered if her brother would allow it. She did not care; she only longed to see him dressed in his finest and hopefully making a fine impression upon her stubborn brother.

The afternoon did not pass quickly enough for the girls, and eventually they decided it was time to begin the laborious process of getting themselves ready. Elizabeth smiled at the excitement of the girls, comparing it to the dispassionate repose on the part of her husband. She was convinced that if it were not for the fact that he wanted her to meet some of their acquaintances, he would most likely not have attended.

Kitty was extremely anxious to put on the dress that she had made especially for the ball. It was an exquisite dress, one of the finest she had ever owned. When she slipped it on over her head, and saw her reflection in the mirror, she gasped at the difference it made. She had never considered herself pretty, but somehow this dress made her feel and look like a princess. She waited patiently as Lillian, one of the maids, worked wonders with her hair, adding some ribbons and flowers for a special highlight. She was certain that once she was dressed and all ready to go, she would actually look prettier than Lydia ever did. It gave her a great sense of satisfaction.

Georgiana sat still as her personal maid, Alice, expertly worked on her hair. Alice was a year older than Georgiana, the daughter of one of the kitchen help who had a natural talent with hair styling. She and Georgiana had been long time friends and she now had the prime position of being her personal maid.

She tried to sit calmly, but knew she would not rest easy until she knew whether Mr. Bostwick would be at the ball. But if he asked her for a dance, what would her brother have to say? Georgiana firmly resolved that if he did seek a dance with her, she would definitely oblige him, brother or no.

As Alice was working on her hair, there was a knock on the door. "Come in."

Darcy walked in and commented immediately on how beautiful she looked. "I believe, my dear sister, that you shall be the belle of the ball tonight."

"Oh, William, I think not. There will be many ladies more beautiful than myself there tonight."

"None that I will find, save for Elizabeth, of course. And I could never choose between the two of you, who is more beautiful."

He sat down, and Georgiana smiled at his compliment. She could tell he desired to tell her something more than how beautiful she was. She turned and folded her hands, put them in her lap, and waited.

"Lochlin came by the other day with a request."

Georgiana's eyes gingerly met her brother's. She wondered to herself, *Could it have something to do with Mr. Bostwick?* She waited for him to continue.

"He has asked me to introduce you…" Darcy paused. "…to his two great nephews tonight."

Georgiana reacted by biting her lower lip and pinching her brows down over her eyes. This was not what she expected, nor what she wanted. She began to nervously rub her hands together. She looked down, and asked, "What did you tell him?"

"I gave him my permission. I told him that they could count on two dances from both you and Kitty."

Georgiana squirmed a little in her chair, but pulled from deep within to fabricate the mannerly response that was expected of her. "Yes, Sir. Thank you for telling me in advance."

Darcy tried to smile, but it lost something in the translation and became more of a grimace. He uncomfortably excused himself and left a bewildered Georgiana to deal with this news. *An introduction.* Why could she not attend a ball and dance with those she knew and with whom she was comfortable? Alice continued her handiwork with her hair as Georgiana attempted to cover up feelings of nervousness that were beginning to overwhelm her. She was grateful that her brother thought enough of her to warn her, but she wondered if it would have been better for her peace of mind to have told her when they arrived at the ball. At least she would have been spared all the anxiety she was now beginning to feel.

"Miss Georgiana," Alice began gently. "You will do fine tonight. You will look so beautiful, I am sure these young men will have no choice but to admire you."

Georgiana shook her head. "You know me too well, Alice. I *am* nervous. But I am not nervous about making a good impression on these men. I am nervous about everything that is required of me when I am introduced. Having to carry on a conversation with someone I do not know…" She took in a deep breath. "It is not easy for me."

Alice laughed. "So much like your brother. Two peas in a pod, I say." Alice walked around to the front of Georgiana and began working magic with curls that were framing her face. "Then I would recommend you do not worry about that, either. If they want to talk, let *them* talk. You be yourself. If they are worth the effort, I am sure you will be able to graciously perform the social civilities required of you." Alice wrinkled her nose at Georgiana and lifted her chin up with her fingers, admiring her handiwork. "If they do not appreciate what they see in front of them, they are not worth it!"

The two girls laughed, and Georgiana felt a bit more at ease.

As Darcy and Elizabeth, Georgiana, and Kitty each finished getting ready, they gathered downstairs. Georgiana looked upon her brother and Elizabeth and thought they made the most handsome couple she had ever seen. Kitty had undergone a transformation, her peach damask dress bringing out the natural colouring of her skin. The style of the dress accented her figure, her hair had been done up in a most flattering way. Being dressed in such an elegant manner actually seemed to subdue her personality a bit.

Georgiana looked elegantly sweet in her light blue dress. It was not excessively ornate, but had a refined beauty to it. The blue in the dress lit up the blue in her eyes. Darcy could see by the look on her face that she was still feeling somewhat strained. He was grateful when Elizabeth pulled her aside to give her some encouraging words. He had told Elizabeth of the forthcoming introduction, and although Elizabeth knew Georgiana most likely would not be thrilled with this prospect, she did not see any harm in it. She attempted to make light of the situation so Georgiana would feel less pressured by it. Kitty was told about the introductions and she could not have been happier to be assured of meeting at least two young men of prominent consequence this night.

As they were preparing to walk out the door to the waiting carriage, Kitty made a surprising announcement. "I would like to be introduced tonight as Miss Catherine Bennet."

Elizabeth looked at her with a surprised smile. "Kitty, are you sure?"

"Do you have any reason to object to me going by my given name?" she asked.

Elizabeth exchanged a glance with her husband and turned back to her sister. "Catherine, I believe you have made a very mature decision."

As one of the butlers opened the door, Darcy extended his arm out to allow the two young girls to exit before him. "Elizabeth, Georgiana, and *Catherine*, shall we go?"

Elizabeth smiled at her husband and took his arm, squeezing it in appreciation. She knew that by Kitty giving up that childhood nickname, she was declaring to everyone that she was growing up; *had* grown up.

The carriage ride over to Leddesdale Manor took about a half an hour. It was a very pleasant evening with a clear sky. The stars were becoming brighter and brighter as the late summer sun dipped down over the horizon and left in its wake a darkening sky.

By the time the carriage arrived at Leddesdale, darkness had settled around them. Torches lined the drive that led to the front of the estate. Every window appeared to be lit from within, and the impression it first gave was one of gaiety and celebration.

Carriages were lined up along the drive and as each one pulled up directly in front, its occupants were helped out. The manor was truly elegant, a decidedly different style than Pemberley, but nonetheless quite dramatic.

Darcy frequently looked over at his wife, admiring her beauty and envious of the inner calm and joy that seemed to permeate through her. She would be perfectly at ease in this situation even though she knew very few of the people here. He, however, would still struggle with small talk and simple conversation even though he would know most of the people here. He trusted that having his wife by his side would make this ball one of his most enjoyable. And he was very eager to introduce his wife to everyone.

They walked up the large stone steps that led up to the house. Kitty, now to be known as Catherine, tightly clutched Georgiana's arm as she glanced around her. She was quite impressed with the house, even though it was not as grand a home as Pemberley. Darcy and Georgiana walked in impervious to the grandeur, and Elizabeth simply appreciated its elegance.

When they entered the home, Mr. Lochlin himself greeted them. He was joined by his brother and his brother's son and daughter in law.

Darcy greeted him first and introduced his wife and sister-in-law.

"I am delighted you have come. Miss Darcy, you have grown into a most charming young lady. And Mrs. Darcy, Miss Bennet, it is a pleasure to make your acquaintance." He turned to introduce them to his family. "May I introduce my brother, Lawrence Lochlin, his son, Geoffrey Lochlin and his wife, Barbara. Their two sons are inside somewhere, most likely dancing. Give me some time greeting my guests, and then I shall bring them over for the introduction."

Catherine felt an increasing sense of awe as she contemplated actually meeting and dancing with someone of great fortune. Georgiana, on the other hand, felt uncomfortably anxious as she struggled with fear and nervousness building up inside her.

They all began to walk toward the ballroom, but Lochlin stopped Darcy, saying quite unexpectedly, "Darcy, feel free to have a look around. It may give you a good idea of whether your friend might be interested in purchasing Leddesdale if I ever decide to sell."

Darcy hoped Elizabeth did not hear, or that she would not inquire as to what he was talking about. Not that he was disinclined to tell her, but Bingley had asked that he not mention it to her until there was something definite and he could talk to Jane about it. But Elizabeth, being ever so attentive and curious, would not oblige her husband's inner hopes.

When they turned to leave the hosts, she quickly grabbed her husband's arm and asked what that was all about.

"What?" asked Darcy.

Elizabeth shook her head. "Selling Leddesdale, a friend who is interested?"

"Ah, yes. I have a friend interested in moving to Derbyshire."

"Who?"

Darcy had a sheepish grin and stalled, causing Elizabeth to grow quite impatient.

"Who, Will?"

He took a deep breath and took hold of her arm tightly. "Bingley."

"Charles and Jane want to move here?" she asked in a most decidedly excited voice. "Why did I not know?"

"Jane does not even know. Charles asked me to keep an eye open for something in the area he can let or buy."

"Oh, Will. That would be so wonderful!"

"Now, Elizabeth, do not get your hopes up. Lochlin is not even close to selling yet. It may be some time before he does and even then it may not work out. Charles did not want you or Jane to know until he is more certain that something is available. And at this point, there is nothing definite."

His last sentence seemed to find itself on deaf ears. Elizabeth suddenly was looking at every inch of the house as they walked through it, making mental notes of what she liked and did not like. The entry had been very grand. Now what did the outside look like? It was quite dark, but she remembered how impressive it looked all lit up. As they walked toward the ball room, she was suddenly curious as to what the rest of the house looked like.

The music, which was being played by a small orchestra in the ball room, echoed throughout the great hall. Catherine swayed to the music, feeling more anxious by the moment to join the dancers already out on the dance floor, but knowing she must simply wait to be asked. She could do nothing to secure herself a partner. The fleeting thought crossed her mind that if her outgoing sister Lydia were here, she would be securing partners for the two of them without any trouble. At this ball, she would have to be content to wait for introductions, as she knew not a soul in the room save for those with whom she arrived.

As they continued on, Darcy appeared to single out certain people and he made introductions to his wife and Catherine. When they finally entered the ballroom, they walked to an area where they could easily observe those who were currently on the dance floor and see those coming in.

A couple approached their party and Darcy readily introduced them. They lived on the far side of Leddesdale and were eager to meet Elizabeth. Darcy frequently went on hunting parties with this gentleman, and he hoped Elizabeth would like his wife.

Jacob and Miranda Adler very graciously welcomed Elizabeth to Derbyshire and offered her any assistance she might need in getting acquainted with the people in the area or finding her way around. Elizabeth took an instant liking to Miranda and was grateful to find someone whose company she enjoyed. She also noticed that her husband seemed notably at ease in the company of Jacob, and thought that this might be a couple they would enjoy doing things with.

Catherine and Georgiana stood together awkwardly looking out amongst the dancers while the two couples conversed. Georgiana was content to watch, feeling much apprehension about actually going out onto the dance floor, but knowing it was inevitable with the arrangement her brother had made. Catherine, having felt so grown up and pretty earlier in the evening, now began to feel a hint of uncertainty in herself. She had been living in the finest home with one of the finest families in Derbyshire, but now she felt her insignificance as she faced those around her. As much as she wanted to be different, be *Catherine*, she still felt very much like Kitty Bennet of Longbourn, the one who paled against five times prettier Jane, lively Elizabeth, and flirtatious Lydia.

Reverend Kenton came up to them when the Adlers had moved on and extended his hand to Darcy. "Good evening, Mr. Darcy. It is good to see you tonight."

"Thank you, Reverend Kenton."

"Mrs. Darcy, it is a pleasure to see you again."

"Thank you Reverend Kenton. You remember my sister, Miss Catherine Bennet."

Kenton noticed the change in name, but said nothing. He turned and bowed politely. "Miss Bennet."

"Good evening," Catherine politely replied.

"And Miss Darcy, how are you this evening?"

"I am quite well, Reverend."

"I am glad to hear it." He turned back to Catherine. "Miss Bennet, how are you finding Derbyshire?"

"I like it very much."

"It is a very fine place to live. I have lived here only two years and I do not think I should ever want to leave. Do you know yet how long you shall be staying?"

"My stay here has been extended, but a time of departure is not yet fixed."

"Good, good, I am glad to hear that." Kenton paused slightly and was about to say something when an older woman approached him.

"Reverend Kenton, we need your help again. My husband and Mr. Jenson are in another one of their discussions about the scriptures. Can you please come and set them straight?"

Elizabeth watched with humour as Kenton turned back to them with a look of great frustration. "Those two men… I fear discussion means argument. I have never in my life seen two men so intent on trying to better the other in their 'knowledge' of things. Now it is the scriptures." He shook his head. "These two need to let the scriptures travel the short distance from their brain to their heart, if you ask me. Please excuse me, the duties of a clergyman never cease."

Reverend Kenton walked away masking his disappointment with a smile. He knew that as a reverend he was to make himself available to one and all at any function he attended. But for some odd reason, that thought did not seem as palatable at the moment, and he felt as though he would have enjoyed remaining in the company of Miss Kitty… no, that was Miss *Catherine*… Bennet for the evening.

Elizabeth turned her attention to the two girls as they all watched the dancers finish up a set of dances. Elizabeth silently wondered if the two young men who had been promised an introduction and a dance were in this very room. Perhaps they were now out on the dance floor and would soon be coming over to meet the girls. As she was not familiar with most of the people at this affair, she would have no way to pick them out.

The dance was soon completed and Lochlin walked up to the foursome with two young men flanking either side of him. Darcy eyed them warily, Catherine smiled hopefully, Georgiana nervously looked down, and Elizabeth found herself amused at the variety of reactions. But they all had the same fleeting thought course through their mind, *Here it comes*!

The two men were dressed in the finest that money could buy, and as they walked over, Darcy could not help but notice a little too much of a confident bounce in their gait. He narrowed his eyes as he took in everything from the way they had their cravats tied to the direction their eyes were turned.

"Darcy," Lochlin's voice was laced with a laugh. "May I introduce to you my brother's grandsons? Andrew here, is the eldest, and Michael is the second eldest."

Darcy shook their hands, mentally noting that the elder son's grip was unnaturally forceful, and the younger son's was pathetically limp. Elizabeth could sense their eagerness to progress with the introductions, while at the same time perceiving that Georgiana would have done anything in her power if she could but delay them indefinitely. The young girl nervously clasped her hands together and seemed to look everywhere but at the young men.

Darcy made the introductions, and Andrew seemed quite intent on securing two dances with Georgiana at once, while Michael, in acquiescing to his elder brother, seemed to *settle* for Catherine. As it seemed the next dance was about to begin, the two young couples, along with Darcy and Elizabeth walked over to the dance floor and lined up across from their partners. Darcy situated himself between the two couples to better keep his eye upon them.

Elizabeth inwardly chuckled at the overbearing lion her husband became when Georgiana was involved. He was relentless and ruthless. As the first notes of the music began to play, she felt a sudden sympathy for any man who would attempt to woo this young girl. But she also felt sorry for Georgiana, who was very aware that any man would have to get past her brother's iron inquisition before being allowed to pursue her. In some ways, that could be beneficial, as in the case of Wickham. But in others it might not.

The dance began and Georgiana concentrated fully on getting the steps right. She need not have feared, as it was one of repetition, and one she readily knew, but she did not want to make any mistakes. Andrew Lochlin watched his partner with curiosity. Yes, Bostwick said she was quiet. As for her beauty… well… she was not a striking beauty, but she had potential. A little too thin, but then all he had to do was to dwell on her fortune and he could be very content.

He attempted to begin some conversation with her during the dance, but her look of dismay when he did, discouraged him from pursuing it further. He would wait until the dance was over. He laughed to himself as he thought she was young and inexperienced, and most likely not used to dancing and talking at the same time.

Catherine and her dance partner seemed to have an easier time making conversation. She found out that he had plans to attend Oxford, as his brother had. He found out that she was one of five sisters and lived in Longbourn in Hertfordshire. He expressed interest in that, but in reality had no idea where Longbourn was. He was the second eldest brother of three sons, and had one younger sister. His family's estate was Callesbury in Lancashire.

Elizabeth watched the two young ladies while Darcy kept his eyes on the two young men. When they came to a turn in the movement of the dance, he wanted to make sure their hands were in the proper place and not wandering where they should not be. He felt the exertion of keeping tabs on these two men was more than that of the dance itself.

When the dance finally came to an end, Georgiana was quite flushed. Andrew escorted her over to the side, grateful to escape the wary eyes of her brother who had been approached by others guests. He proudly reminded her that he had been promised a second dance. She told him that she preferred to sit the next one out if he did not mind.

"What do you think of Leddesdale Manor, Miss Darcy?"

She nervously looked at him, realization overwhelming her that he was intent on remaining by her side until he had claimed his second dance. "It is very nice. Mr. Lochlin has a very nice home." She glanced at him momentarily, and returned her eyes down when she found he was gazing intently on her.

"It is nothing compared to our Callesbury. I would venture that you would be quite awestruck by it. Our ballroom is close to being twice this size. The grounds are much more expansive as well. We have always referred to my uncle's place as his 'little' home." With that, he let out a laugh and Georgiana closed her eyes briefly in disgust.

There was an awkward silence and Georgiana searched her mind for something to say. But even when something came to her mind that would have been appropriate, she had no desire to say it. Alice had told her if the young man was worth it, she would be able to be graciously civil and charming. At this point she did not see that he was worth any extra effort and determined she would be simply civil.

When Georgiana did not seem inclined to continue the conversation herself, he continued on, praising his estate and all that he would someday come to inherit. When she garnered the courage to look up at him again, his gaze was no longer upon her, and he seemed quite in a world of his own.

She became quite amused that he seemed to not care if she was interested, let alone whether she was even listening to all he was saying. That was fine with her, as she did not feel pressured to participate in his conversation at all. Besides, he seemed very satisfied with the sound of his own voice and his magnificent estate and his own noble personage. Now all she had to look forward to was one more dance with him and her obligation would be fulfilled. But the thought of even one more dance with him began to cause her much anxiety.

After a lengthy pause in his one sided conversation, he seemed to suddenly think of her. "Would you care for some refreshment, Miss Darcy?"

She nodded and said she would greatly appreciate it since she was suddenly aware of how thirsty and hungry she was. He gently took her elbow, and they set off toward a young man holding a tray of drinks. She tensed at the touch of his hand taking her arm and began wondering if there was anything she could do to discourage him from remaining by her side, as well as relinquish the second dance with her. When they approached the servant carrying the tray, he was facing the other way serving someone. When he had finished, Andrew tapped him on the shoulder.

"May we have something to drink?" he asked.

The servant turned around, and Georgiana gasped as she saw that it was David. The look of panic that instantly swept across his face at seeing her standing there was as quickly masked by sheer determination and will. His dream of seeing Georgiana at the ball, and his nightmare of her seeing him in the ignoble position of servant both instantaneously came to pass.

"Miss Darcy," David meekly said, knowing to socially converse with her in his position tonight would be highly improper. Yesterday, Lochlin had been desperate and asked for his help in serving at the ball because many of his help had become ill. David knew it would give him a chance to see Georgiana and keep an eye on Andrew Lochlin. He only hoped he could remain out of her sight, as he had not wanted her to see him in this capacity. Obviously he had not been successful.

Georgiana barely smiled and lifted her eyes to him. She gave a discreet nod of her head and took the glass he offered her. "Thank you," she softly breathed and looked back to the ground.

"Bostwick," Andrew began. "Bring us a small plate of food. I believe my young lady here is hungry." He looked over at Georgiana, and drew his gaze up and down her figure. Under his breath to David he added, "I must say that dance with her has made me a little hungry as well." He eyes looked to David as if they had a hidden meaning. He understood all too well.

Bostwick sharply drew in a breath and felt his hands shaking angrily, the liquid in the glasses quaking on the tray. He put the tray down and left to gather a plate with an assortment of foods for them. As he walked away, he kept himself tall and erect, but inwardly he wanted to shrivel up and hide. She had looked beautiful. He knew she would. She was everything that he had imagined and more.

When he came to the table that had a wonderful spread of foods upon it, he picked up a plate and without thinking placed a variety of items upon it. He turned and steeled his resolve to return.

Georgiana kept her gaze glued to the floor, her feelings at odds with what here eyes took in before her. She had been hopeful to see David tonight, but this was not exactly the way she had envisioned it. In the instant she recognized him and saw him dressed and working as a common servant, the difference in their stations became painfully more apparent to her. It troubled her heart to know she could not even talk to him because of their respective station at this ball; she as an invited guest; his being a hired servant.

When David returned with the prepared plate, she barely overheard Andrew criticizing his selection of food and felt he was being rudely demanding. She felt herself growing somewhat unsteady. The pressures of the evening, her sense of discomfort with Andrew Lochlin, and this unexpected encounter with David Bostwick all contributed to bring on a sense of dizziness which slowly began to overtake her. The voices around her became unintelligible and the room began to spin when suddenly she felt some strong arms surround her as she collapsed.

David had seen her face grow white and watched in concern as she had begun to sway. In an instant he shoved the tray of food into Andrew Lochlin's hands and reached out and caught Georgiana as she started to fall. "Miss Darcy!" he called, while Lochlin only looked on, completely perturbed by this dreadful inconvenience and the very curious lady before him.

David brought Georgiana over to a chair and gently propped her up in it as she slowly began coming back around. Darcy and Elizabeth rushed over.

"Georgiana, what happened, are you all right?" Darcy pushed aside the young servant who had brought her over to the chair.

Georgiana's head rolled around aimlessly and her eyes looked upon her brother as if she were trying to comprehend the situation. "What happened?" she asked.

"You must have fainted." Darcy turned to the young man. "Bring us some…" He looked up at the young man's face and halted in his recognition. "Bostwick, bring us some water, please."

"Yes, Sir."

Darcy turned back to Georgiana. "Relax, honey. There is nothing to worry about."

Georgiana felt an extreme case of discomfiture as she noticed people had begun to gather around her. Catherine soon joined them, followed by Mr. Lochlin, very concerned over what happened at his ball.

"Darcy, is she all right? How did this happen?" he asked nervously.

"She is all right, Lochlin. She only needs a little air. Can you keep everyone away?"

"Definitely." He turned to those who had gathered near. "All right, everyone. She is well, she is well. Let us get back to dancing and having a good time. Miss Darcy merely needs a little air." Whether he was more nervous about what happened to Georgiana or whether the success of his ball would be hindered by this incident was hard to tell.

David returned with some water and Elizabeth reached out and took it, giving it to Darcy. He held the glass while Georgiana took small sips. Elizabeth turned back to David. "We are very fortunate that you were right there to catch her, Mr. Bostwick. Thank you."

Andrew, who berated himself for not being the one to catch Miss Darcy, did not fail to hear Elizabeth's words to him. He looked down at Georgiana and the fuss that was being made over her. Fortune or no, she was not worth the effort. He turned and left the crowd in a huff, intent on finding himself a more worthy partner for the evening.

Catherine stood back, concerned for Georgiana. She had to admit she had not even thought of her since they were first introduced to Mr. Lochlin's nephews. She danced twice with Michael and had begun to dance with Daniel Hargrave, a fashionable young man from the area to whom she had been introduced. She was dancing with him when she heard Georgiana had fainted. She excused herself from the dance and immediately rushed over.

She was followed by Reverend Kenton, who came by and stood across from Darcy.

"Darcy, how is she doing?"

Catherine turned to face the reverend. "I believe she is feeling a little better."

"Do you know what happened?"

"I am not sure. She simply fainted."

The two men watched over Georgiana as she slowly sat up on her own and they let her sit there and rest a while. Most everyone else resumed their activities in conversing or dancing.

Once the reverend had ascertained that Georgiana was improved, he slowly walked to Catherine's side. "It appears Miss Darcy will be all right."

"Yes," answered Catherine. "It was possibly too much excitement for her."

The reverend brought his hands behind his back and clasped them. *Too much excitement.* Catherine had been snatched up in the first three dances since he had earlier talked with her, and as much as he would have liked to, he had not been able to secure one dance with her. He was not confident that this was the right time or not to ask. But as she was standing right next to him at the moment, and without a dance partner, he decided to give it a try.

"Miss Bennet."

Catherine looked over at him. "Yes?"

"Would you do me the…"

At that moment Darcy stood up carrying Georgiana in his arms. "Come, I think it would be best if we took Georgiana home."

Elizabeth turned to those standing near. "Would you please excuse us?"

Catherine looked casually at the reverend. "I am sorry, it appears we must leave. But you were saying?"

"I…I was saying it would be an honour to have you visit services again."

"Oh. Thank you. I am sure we will."

Catherine turned to follow, feeling a great sense of disappointment for having to leave the ball, but grateful for the time she had. As they walked through the great house, Catherine suddenly had a sense that being here in Derbyshire with her sister's family was the key to meeting and marrying someone who would be able to give her everything and anything she ever wanted. And she would do it all without any help from Lydia!

As they made their way toward the front door, Darcy stopped and apologized to Lochlin for having to leave early.

"She will be all right, I hope."

"I think she overexerted herself. Thank you for inviting us, Lochlin."

"Yes, we had an enjoyable time," Elizabeth contributed and the parties said their goodnights.

The Darcys' carriage was summoned and they all climbed in. Georgiana felt a little guilty for not insisting she was all right and could stay. She actually did not want to stay. She did not think she could abide any more of Andrew Lochlin's boastful discourse and she certainly did not think she could look upon David all evening, being continually reminded of the disparity between them.

~~*

David stood where he was, disappointed that they were leaving. Watching Georgiana grow pale disturbed him. He wondered if it was something Andrew had done, or if it could have been her seeing him thus. He stood there for a moment after they had left the room, Georgiana in her brother's arms.

Reverend Kenton stood standing a few feet from David, looking at the door through which they all exited. He was feeling that same sense of disappointment. It seemed as though he was getting nowhere with Miss Bennet.

The two were lost in their own thoughts when they both turned and bumped into the other.

"Excuse me, Reverend. I was not watching where I was going," apologized David.

"No, it was my fault," corrected Reverend Kenton. "I suppose my mind was elsewhere."

There was the fleeting thought in Kenton's mind that at that moment, they were both feeling very much the same. He smiled at David, and then moved on to visit with others in the room.

~~*

When the Darcys and Catherine settled in the privacy of the carriage, Darcy inquired of Georgiana what happened.

"I really do not know. I suppose it was partly due to my nervousness and the exertion of the dance."

Elizabeth took her hand. "Perhaps you should have eaten something before going. I am sure all these little things added up."

Georgiana sighed as she considered all those little things, plus the one big surprise of seeing David there; not as a guest but as a servant. She closed her eyes and leaned her head back. She had thought… had hoped… that David would be at the ball. She had imagined him dressed up in his finest, and perhaps she would have had the pleasure of dancing at least one dance with him. She felt her closed eyes filling with tears as she began to grapple with the reality of what she had witnessed tonight. She and David Bostwick lived in two very different worlds and she could not see how those two worlds could ever merge.

Chapter 16

Darcy resolutely insisted upon rest for Georgiana on the ensuing days. Although she maintained that she was not likely to suffer from faintness again soon, her brother would not allow her to overtax herself. She reluctantly conceded to his wishes all the while declaring most firmly that she was in perfectly good health. Despite her words, however, her countenance betrayed a conflicting message. Physically she was in good health, but emotionally she was suffering. Elizabeth was the only one to realize it.

Out of curiosity and concern, Catherine went to Georgiana as she was resting in her room to inquire why she had fainted at the ball. Georgiana knew what had initiated the feelings that began to overwhelm her, or at least who. Andrew Lochlin!

Georgiana looked at Catherine and wondered whether she would understand. Catherine seemed to be able to remain composed in situations that caused Georgiana much consternation. But she and Catherine had grown quite close the past month, and knew she could confide in her new sister without fear of shame or ridicule.

"It was Andrew Lochlin. He seemed more interested in boasting about all his material wealth and wanting to impress me with it. I was growing quite uneasy by the minute around him. Catherine, I often wonder if a man is more interested in my fortune than me."

"You are definitely in a unique situation; one that I shall never have to worry about." Catherine secretly wished, though, that she had just a little bit of a fortune with which to tempt an eligible bachelor. "Is that what caused you to faint?"

Georgiana looked at Catherine with assessing eyes. Could she tell her about David Bostwick? "Partly." She paused for a moment and then added, "Catherine, I am so sorry we had to leave the ball early. Did you enjoy yourself for the short time we were there?"

"Oh, yes. I did enjoy the dancing. I was also able to meet some fine young men from the area, as well. Georgiana, I hope you do not mind my saying this, but… I do so want to marry well, and I am very grateful that I am having the opportunity to meet some fine, suitable men."

Georgiana knew now that Catherine no longer had an interest in Mr. Bostwick. "Catherine, there is one other reason that I believed caused me to faint. It was seeing Mr. Bostwick there… as a servant."

"Why should that make any difference? You know he is no higher than a servant in rank."

Georgiana sighed. "But he is much higher in my esteem than that." She looked up at Catherine, whose eyes had suddenly widened with great surprise. "I care a great deal for him."

Catherine suddenly began giggling. Georgiana looked at her in surprise, but began giggling herself. "What is so funny?" she asked as they both lost themselves uncontrollably to laughter.

"Your affections are leaning toward a man who literally has no right to ever return your love because of your great fortune, and I have a desire to fall in love with a man who probably would have no interest in me because of my lack of fortune. Are we not a pair?"

With that, both girls laughed so hard, tears fell down their faces. But Georgiana's tears were a mixture of mirth and melancholy, as she pondered her situation and her feelings.

~~*

Darcy had been formalizing all the last minute details in preparation for the Flemings, who were expected to arrive any day. They were expected to arrive any day. He made several trips to the church to talk with Reverend Kenton about beginning classes there, and then met with the company he had hired to begin building the school. Finally, he made more contacts to solicit additional funding and spread the word to people who might be interested in attending classes.

With joyous anticipation, Elizabeth worked with Mrs. Reynolds and the Pemberley staff getting rooms in the house ready for the Flemings, and a room in the staff quarters for Jacques. She warily kept an eye on Georgiana, however, knowing that some little glint of joy in her eyes had vanished, and she could not help but wonder if it had to do with the ball, her fainting, and perhaps Mr. Bostwick.

When the party from France finally arrived at Pemberley, it seemed immediately to enliven everyone's spirits. With their arrival, the situation changed considerably with three children now in the home. The Flemings had a son Michael, their daughter Melissa, and newly adopted daughter Michelle. Two adjoining rooms on an upper floor of the manor had been secured and readied for the family.

Upon seeing Pemberley for the first time, different emotions were evoked among the group. Jacques, who had already begun his duty as carriage driver and had conveyed the Flemings from London, had no idea the grandeur that was Pemberley. He came to the sudden realization that everything he had ever hoped to accomplish in his life had finally materialized. Never would he have to sleep in his carriage again. Never would he have to wonder where his next meal would come from. All because of a chance meeting with Mr. and Mrs. Darcy when they arrived in Paris a little over two months ago.

Mr. and Mrs. Fleming silently looked upon each other when they first saw Pemberley through the window of the carriage. Their gaze immediately turned to the three children. Mr. Fleming quickly got their attention and spoke, as well as signed, "When we get inside the house, do not touch a thing!" Judging by the outside of the house, the couple was convinced the inside would be furnished and decorated in a very exquisite and exceptional manner.

Elizabeth found great joy in seeing Michelle again. When the carriage first pulled up the long drive, Elizabeth hurried out to greet them with much anticipation. Her initial glimpse of the young girl was when she crawled down from the carriage after her parents. Their eyes met and Elizabeth watched in delight as Michelle very timidly spelled out her name with her fingers.

The thrill and joy at seeing this brought tears to her eyes. For several days, Elizabeth had practiced saying 'welcome' using sign language and was rewarded with a big smile when Michelle signed back 'thank you.' Elizabeth gently reached down and picked her up, giving her a big hug.

When the Flemings stepped inside, their previous suspicions were confirmed. Never had they seen such an elegant home. Their house in Paris had been very modest, and before leaving for Paris they had lived in a small cottage just outside London. When they were shown to their room, Mrs. Fleming secured permission to confiscate every precious and breakable accessory that was found in the children's room and within their reach. She requested that Mrs. Reynolds keep them stored safely and securely away for the duration of their stay.

Their first week at Pemberley was spent getting acquainted and reacquainted. The ladies visited while overseeing the children, the men arduously perused the particulars about the school, and Jacques spent much of his time with Winston, riding around the countryside getting familiar with the roads and the surrounding area.

The children quickly settled into their new 'home' and did a proficient job at entertaining themselves for hours. Georgiana found a box of old toys with which she had played long ago. Michael entertained himself with a set of blocks and the two girls each claimed a doll. Elizabeth, Georgiana, and Catherine watched in awe as they played in silence, but communicated with signs. Michael pretty much kept to himself, but when he spoke, he used words and signs.

As they watched the children, Mrs. Fleming agreed to work with the three ladies on signing. She was pleasantly surprised to see how much they already learned on their own, and when she offered to teach them more, they heartily agreed.

Elizabeth was very pleased with this woman, whose gentle demeanour and genuine laughter would be a delight to have around Pemberley. Darcy and Fleming often became engaged in very animated conversations about the building of the school and they eagerly tossed ideas back and forth. Elizabeth could see that these two men would work well together.

A few days after their arrival, Jacques drove Winston and Mr. and Mrs. Flemings out to the school property. Elizabeth, Georgiana, and Catherine remained back with the children. Michelle had her moments when she would simply cry out for attention and affection, and at other times would prefer to keep to herself. Melissa was an independent little girl and did not seem to be at all afraid of the new people or surroundings in her life. Michael was all boy, but was very protective of his sister. Of course, with the addition of Michelle, he now had double duty as protector.

Georgiana seemed to have a natural ability to draw the children to herself, and Elizabeth was grateful that a joyful serenity seemed to have returned. She was fairly confident that having the children around was allowing her to keep her mind off what had been disturbing her.

When the Flemings returned from the property, their excitement peaked. They were ecstatic with what they had seen and were envisioning what could be done with it. They had also visited the church where the classes would begin the very next Monday. Darcy invited Reverend Kenton to come the next evening for dinner so they could discuss things even further.

The following morning, Elizabeth arranged to take Mrs. Fleming and her two daughters to meet Mrs. Frank and little Eleanor. She thought if Eleanor could interact with them before classes began, it would be less traumatic for her. They had previously made the acquaintance of Mr. Frank while he was working on the grounds at Pemberley.

When they arrived, Mrs. Frank cheerfully welcomed them in. She showed them with great pride what they had been learning in sign language, and Mrs. Fleming was very impressed.

"Are you planning to attend the classes yourself, Mrs. Frank?"

"Oh, yes. My husband and I will try to come as often as we are able. I thought I would like to be there the first few days and stay with Eleanor so that she feels comfortable."

"You come as often as you like. My husband thought it would be good to have an evening class one night a week for anyone who cannot leave work during the day. You and your husband might consider that as well. We have found that the more practice you get, both in the classes and at home, the sooner you will become quite adept at it."

As the three ladies talked, the three girls played together quite compatibly side by side. While Eleanor could not communicate as well as Michelle and Melissa, she was certainly not shy about trying, and somehow the girls effortlessly adapted how they made one another understand what they wanted.

That evening they were joined by Reverend Kenton, who came for dinner and then remained afterwards to meet with the men and discuss the church's use for classes until the building was completed. During the course of the dinner, Elizabeth was amused to see the attention he directed toward Catherine. But her sister seemed completely oblivious to his attempts to draw her into conversation. She simply answered "yes" or "no" and did not seem inclined to elaborate. Elizabeth was quite confused by this as he was a fairly handsome man and certainly likeable, and it was quite apparent that he held an interest in her. She hoped that Catherine's earlier fancy for men in red coats was no longer a concern. At length, he seemed to get the hint that she did not return his regard and directed his conversation back to Darcy and the Flemings.

They talked about the logistics of the classes, and agreed that while the adult class could easily meet in the church, it would be best for the children to meet in the parsonage. It had a very nice sunroom that would be very comfortable during the warmer months. In the colder months they could move into the sitting room which would be smaller but warmer.

Initially the classes would meet only through the morning. Their idea was to teach new words each day, and then encourage the children to practice them when they went home. They concluded that anything more than a morning session would be too long for the younger children. Since some parents would attend the adult class while the children were in classes, it was more feasible to end all classes at mid-day until the school was built.

By the end of the evening, they had most of the anticipated details worked out, and Reverend Kenton asked if he could end the evening in prayer. He prayed that these classes would reach the deaf community in a way that had never been done before. Elizabeth appreciated the genuineness of his prayer, and in her heart prayed that Catherine would begin to appreciate him as well.

The week did not pass quickly enough for everyone, as their shared anticipation was very evident. On the first day of class, Elizabeth, Georgiana, and Catherine willingly accompanied the Flemings to the church to see how many would be there and to help out where they could.

The children's class had six children ranging in age from four to twelve in addition to Eleanor, Melissa, and Michelle. Michael attended class, as well, but he was looked upon as a helper. The morning was spent reinforcing simple words with signs until each child grasped the fact that each position of the hand represented a word. For some it was a long, tedious process, but others learned quickly. It was beneficial that at least one parent of each of the children came to the adult classes, as they would be able to work with the child at home.

The sunroom worked wonderfully. Toys had been collected and strategically placed around the room to make it very inviting to the children. Many of the words taught that day were in fact the very toys the children played with.

The children thoroughly enjoyed the class and their lessons that they did not want to leave when it was over. Georgiana took the hands of the children and escorted them over to the church to meet their parents.

Elizabeth and Catherine remained back with Mrs. Fleming to put away the toys and Reverend Kenton came in to offer his assistance.

"Did your class turn out well, ladies?"

Elizabeth brightened with his question. "Oh Reverend Kenton, Mrs. Fleming was wonderful! She works so well with the children and I am confident each of them went home having learned something!"

Mrs. Fleming shrugged off the compliment. "It was certainly not all my doing. I had much help! I could not have accomplished as much as I did today without you."

Reverend Kenton walked over to Catherine, who was placing some blocks into a wooden crate. "Did you enjoy your time with the children, Miss Bennet?"

She looked up at him and nodded. "Yes, they were a joy to work with." She then turned her attention back to the task before her.

"Are you ladies planning to come often with Mrs. Fleming?" His question was directed to anyone, but he kept his gaze upon Catherine.

Elizabeth gave Catherine a few moments, hoping she would answer. Finally Catherine looked back up to him, and replied, "I believe I shall like to come perhaps one or two days a week." She looked over to Elizabeth. "What about you, Lizzy?"

"It may not be possible for me to come as often, but I shall certainly come when I have the opportunity."

"I am glad to hear that. You are welcome any time." He stooped down to where Catherine was picking up blocks and he picked up a few. "Would you like some help with these, Miss Bennet?"

Catherine looked up at him to answer, and suddenly saw something in his expression that she had not noticed in her previous associations with him. His eyes had a gentle smile in them that seemed to convey something more than an offer to help. Her heart leapt with a burst of anxiety.

Realization that his attentions toward her were more than just civil and friendly surprised her. She had done nothing to encourage him, and faced the unfortunate situation of having to discreetly and politely discourage him from any further consideration. He was, after all, only a clergyman! This was not part of her plan!

"Thank you, Reverend Kenton, but no. I am nearly finished. Perhaps Elizabeth could use some help." She winced as he slowly brought himself up and walked toward her sister. She shook her head as she pondered this situation. She only hoped he would understand her hint without having to come right out and tell him she did not return his regard.

Over at the church, Georgiana reunited each child to his or her parent, and set out to return to the parsonage. As she walked past the back doors of the church, they unexpectedly opened and Mr. Fleming walked out with David Bostwick and another gentleman. She was so surprised by the unexpected appearance of Mr. Bostwick that it halted her in her tracks.

"Ah, Miss Darcy," Mr. Fleming began. "How were the children's classes today?"

"They went quite well, Mr. Fleming."

"Good! I am glad to hear that! Miss Darcy, are you acquainted with Mr. Bostwick and Mr. Carson, here?"

She looked over at David, and tentatively nodded her head. "I am acquainted with Mr. Bostwick, but I have not had the pleasure of being introduced to Mr. Carson." Her voice trembled as she tried to maintain her composure.

David remained silent while Fleming made the introduction. "Miss Darcy, this is Mr. Carson. He is one of Lochlin's tenants."

Georgiana watched as David turned to the other man, who watched intently as he said his name. Mr. Carson smiled and bowed, saying, "You are Miss Darcy of Pemberley? It is a pleasure to meet you. I know of you and your brother." His speech was intelligible, but Georgiana recognized that he was most likely deaf. Apparently he was able to read Mr. Bostwick's lips.

Fleming then motioned for Carson to come with him. "Excuse me, Miss Darcy, I would like to give Mr. Carson some additional leaflets to take home with him. He will only be able to come to classes once a week, but Mr. Bostwick has agreed to work with him at home."

Georgiana turned her head, watching the two men walk over to the carriage. She knew that if she turned back to David, she would be required to say something, and at this moment she knew not what to say. She had struggled the past week with her feelings toward him. She had grasped at the ball the disparity of their stations. Yet now she wondered if she had it within her to keep her resolution to put him out of her mind if she were to continually see him.

She was still looking toward the two men when David said, "I hope you have fully recovered from that night at the ball."

"Yes, thank you, I have." His reference to her fainting should have caused her a sense of embarrassment, but instead, she detected a sincerity of compassion in his voice and she could not help feeling a sense of warm regard for him that she feared nothing would shake.

"You must be working a great deal for Mr. Lochlin, as I have not seen you around Pemberley lately."

"Uh, no, I have not been around Pemberley for some time." He could not, and *would* not tell her why. He assumed she was not aware that her brother had ordered him to stay away.

"But did I understand Mr. Fleming to say that you are going to take the class yourself?"

"When I have the opportunity to attend. I believe I might be able to come one day a week, most likely Monday, and then again to the evening class. I work on the grounds here at the church just a few days a week, and Mr. Fleming has agreed to work with me an hour or two on those afternoons that I am here."

"And you are bringing Mr. Carson?" asked Georgiana.

"Yes. He and I can communicate fairly well. He knows how to read and write and can read lips, so we have managed to get by. He does feel the need to learn sign language so he in turn can teach it to others, or communicate with others who may only know that form of communication. I felt it would benefit me, as well." Georgiana could tell by just the tone of his voice that he was smiling.

Georgiana was finally able to turn her eyes to meet his. Could no one else see the goodness in this man and not just the station in which he was born? Even she, herself, had only seen the disparity in their stations at the ball, and presently she regretted having done that. She returned his smile through very accepting and admiring eyes. She softly took in a deep breath as she realized that all she had accomplished in putting him out of her mind since the ball had just become futile.

"Mr. Carson is very fortunate to have a friend such as yourself."

All she had to do was look at him and talk in that manner, and David was lost. Her brother may have ordered him to stay away from Pemberley, but he certainly could not order him to stay away from the church. At least he hoped Darcy's patronage in the church did not oblige him that.

David politely murmured a thank you, and Georgiana excused herself, aware that she had been gone some time and should return to help the others. She could not hide the smile that was firmly planted across her face as she came in. Elizabeth noticed that she was even humming when she walked across the threshold. But then, Elizabeth had also noticed, when she had left the parsonage earlier to look for her, that she was very much enjoying a conversation with David Bostwick at the front steps of the chapel.

That night as they ate, they each eagerly shared their own unique stories of what they had observed that day to a very attentive Darcy. Each had their own favourite moments that usually had to do with one of the children or an adult suddenly grasping what was trying to be conveyed. Elizabeth could not help but notice the difference in Georgiana and debated whether or not to tell her husband what she had witnessed.

She knew that if she told her husband, he would not be happy and would force the issue with Georgiana. She would not have even known he was there if she had not stepped out to look for her. She decided she would give her a few days of respite and say nothing. She did not intend to make a practice of keeping things from her husband, but she knew he would react most negatively in hearing about his sister and this young man in particular. She decided for now she would wait and watch.

The next day Elizabeth wrote a long overdue letter to Jane, describing in great detail the events of the first day of the school. It had been a while since she had written, and so she wrote also of the ball, how Kitty now wished to be called Catherine, Reverend Kenton -- his apparent interest in Catherine and her apparent indifference, the Flemings, Jacques, and finally she inquired after Lydia. She pondered whether to say anything to Jane in regard to Bingley's comment to Darcy about looking for a place to live near them. She decided against it, as there was still nothing definite. She sent the letter off immediately.

Georgiana and Catherine talked amongst themselves and decided, with Georgiana's ardent encouragement, to try and visit the classes at least one day a week, preferably on Monday.

Elizabeth noticed the girls usually visited the class only one day a week, so she felt Georgiana's feelings for Mr. Bostwick could not be so very ardent, as she would probably have made excuses to go more often. She felt she had been right in not saying anything to her husband, allowing it to be a mere friendship on Georgiana's part.

In the weeks that followed, Georgiana always made it a practice to visit the classes on Monday, and then to escort the children after class to the chapel before the adults left, if just to make eye contact with David. She admired him for what he was doing. It was not often they had a chance to converse as they had that first day, but just walking in and seeing him turn to look at her and acknowledge her was sufficient. She would more often than not stand in the back watching him talk with others, both in words and signs. He was apparently becoming more proficient in his use of sign language and feeling very comfortable using it.

After a while he began to walk to the parsonage whenever the adult class ended earlier. When he came, he usually conversed with the reverend. The two of them would stand together in the back of the room, waiting for class to end, each with their own train of thought and focus of attention keeping them secretly occupied and hopelessly forlorn.

It was one day almost a month later when Elizabeth unexpectedly visited the class that it became very apparent to her the truth of the situation.

Elizabeth decided to surprise the girls one Monday afternoon. Darcy was out of town and she had no obligations to fulfil so she joyously set out to meet them. After the class had ended, Georgiana remained behind to help Mrs. Fleming clean up. On this particular day, Mr. Bostwick walked over to the parsonage himself. He entered and saw Georgiana picking up some toys from the play area and went to offer her assistance.

Elizabeth came to the door soon thereafter. From her vantage point just inside the door, she could see Mr. Bostwick talking animatedly with Georgiana while he picked up toys with her. Elizabeth kept herself drawn back, not wanting either one to notice her, as she desired to observe them unnoticed. The fact that Georgiana was more intent on listening and conversing than finishing her task surprised Elizabeth. She had never before seen Georgiana so... animated!

It took but a moment to recognize the sparkle in Georgiana's eyes and the fact that she seemed very comfortable conversing with Mr. Bostwick. Elizabeth realized Georgiana must have been seeing him on a fairly regular basis these past few weeks. Elizabeth wished Georgiana had felt the freedom to come and talk with her about this and she now berated herself that she had only assumed they had a friendship. She knew from the look on both of their faces that this was not just a conversation between friends. It was a conversation between two people who greatly cared for one another.

She drew back, and while outside the door, tried to determine what to do. Darcy would not be home for several days, but she felt she must discuss this with him when he returned. She decided for now that she would walk over to the chapel and talk to the adults there, allowing her the chance to dwell on her options. She would not let Georgiana know she saw them together, at least for the time being.

When Georgiana finally walked over to the church, she was surprised to find Elizabeth there. David had departed and she was grateful that Elizabeth had not chosen to come over to the parsonage. She had nothing to hide in her actions with Mr. Bostwick, but she knew how her brother felt, and could only assume Elizabeth would inform him that she had seen them together.

That evening, as they were gathered for the evening meal, Darcy returned home, having finished his work early. He hurriedly went upstairs to freshen up, and then came back down and joined them. The conversation, as usual, centred on the school. Mrs. Fleming made an innocent comment, however, that caused three people very much consternation.

"I believe I have never seen a finer gentleman than Mr. Bostwick. The fact that he goes out of his way to bring Mr. Carson to class is so commendable, and he is always so willing to come to the parsonage and help us clean up afterwards."

Georgiana started at this and her eyes inadvertently went to her brother.

Elizabeth, who was sitting next to him, felt him tense, and ever so gently she reached over and placed her hand upon his and gave it a slight squeeze. His eyes narrowed as he looked back to Georgiana, whose guilt was evidenced by her blush.

"Mr. Bostwick is coming to the school? Is that Mr. *David* Bostwick?" Darcy asked as his eyes remained on his sister.

"Yes," Mrs. Fleming continued, unaware of the parade of emotions being felt by the three.

Darcy noticed Georgiana as she tried to conceal a flinch and turned her eyes away from him.

Mrs. Fleming continued, "He is only able to attend class on Mondays because of his work for Mr. Lochlin."

At this, Elizabeth turned in surprise to Georgiana, realizing that her only reason for going on Mondays was it was the only day he attended classes. She chided herself for not being aware of this.

Mr. Fleming picked up where his wife left off. "He also helps at the church working the grounds on Thursdays, so I have been working with him in the afternoon those days with private lessons. What a fine young man he is! And he is learning so quickly! He also has been helping me with some of the administration duties." He turned to Darcy. "I hope you do not mind."

Darcy turned his head to Fleming and answered in a detached manner, "No, not at all."

Darcy started to sit up straight as if he was about to speak again, and Elizabeth tightened her hold upon his hand. She did not want him to begin discussing this now in front of Catherine and the Flemings. "Would anyone care for some dessert," asked Elizabeth, trying desperately to change the subject.

"No," Darcy said, sliding his hand out from under hers. "I am no longer hungry and I shall go to my study. Georgiana, would you please join me there when you have finished? I am no longer hungry."

The look he gave Georgiana caused her to shrink back and close her eyes. The last thing she wanted to do was hurt her brother or disappoint him again. She recognized that same look from a year and a half ago. *But this time it is different!* She screamed to herself. *This time is so very different!*

As he stood up and excused himself, he then turned to Elizabeth. "Elizabeth, would you please see me after I have talked with Georgiana?"

He did not wait for an answer, and the two ladies who were just singled out for a meeting looked at each other. Georgiana's eyes pleaded with Elizabeth for mercy, and Elizabeth smiled at her, but her smile certainly did not have all the positive emotion behind it, rather it covered up a rather dim outlook.

When everyone had left the dining room, Elizabeth approached Georgiana. "Honey, do you wish for me to go in with you?"

"No, thank you, Elizabeth. I need to learn to face my brother on my own. I am aware of his feelings toward Mr. Bostwick and I even understand them. I think it is about time to get this out in the open between us."

Georgiana walked toward the study, and Elizabeth sank down in a chair in the sitting room across the hall that gave her a view of the door Georgiana just walked through. Her heart was probably just as torn as Georgiana's. She leaned back in the chair and closed her eyes. She suddenly began to pray, "O Lord, give her wisdom and strength in this. Give me a little as well. Help me to know what to say to my husband."

She sat still for a few minutes, and suddenly an idea came to her. She stood up, and quickly made her way down the hall and to their bedchamber where she walked over to the candelabrum and smiled.

When she came back into the sitting room, she was clasping something tightly in her hand. She returned to the chair, and after a while saw Georgiana fling the study door open and depart down the hall. Elizabeth could not see Georgiana's face, but she could easily tell that she was distressed.

She slowly walked to the study and knocked on the door and he beckoned her to come in. Instead of being seated at his desk, he was pacing the floor, his hands gripped tightly behind his back. The look of anger and pain was fully imprinted on his face.

Elizabeth walked over to him. "You know, Will, when you are angry, you get this little knot right here between your eyebrows." She reached up and touched the culprit lightly with her fingers. He reached up and took her fingers in his hand. She noticed a slight trembling come from him as he brought her fingers to his lips and kissed them.

"And your eyebrows, my dear, pinch together in the centre, here," pointing to her forehead, "when you know you have been caught trying to hide something." Neither moved as their eyes seemed intent on trying to read the other.

Finally Darcy was able to ask, "How long have you known they have been seeing each other?"

Elizabeth winced. "Will. They are two people who both have an interest in and an involvement with the deaf school. They have known each other a long time. They are friends. They talk."

"How long have you known?"

"I saw her talking with him the first day of school. I did not think there was anything to be concerned about as she only seemed intent on attending the school one day a week. I believed if she had strong feelings for him, she would be going more often."

"And that day was Monday, was it not?"

"Will, if you saw the two of them together…"

"Elizabeth there are things you do not understand."

"Then enlighten me, Will." Elizabeth pleaded with him with her eyes. "I know that his station in life is decidedly beneath Georgiana's, but he is not at all like Wickham. You cannot compare him to Wickham." She brought her hands up to his face and stroked his cheek. "If only you could see Georgiana when she is around him."

Darcy reached up and took Elizabeth's hand. He held on to it tightly. "Elizabeth there is more to this than his inferior station."

There was something he was not telling her, but Elizabeth needed to convey something to him first.

"Hold out your hand."

He looked at her suspiciously, but did as she said. She gently placed something in his hand. "Now, what is that?" she asked as she looked up at him.

He opened his hand and saw a prism. He picked it up with two fingers and began twirling it. "It is a prism from the candelabrum I gave you in Paris. What has this to do with Georgiana?"

She took a breath to help direct her thoughts. "What is the one thing this little prism creates that we enjoy so much?"

Darcy huffed impatiently, his eyebrows furrowing. "Rainbows," he answered curtly.

"And what is it that causes the rainbows?"

Darcy sighed impatiently. "The sun hitting the prism. Now what…"

"Will, imagine the prism is Georgiana, and the rainbows are the very special, very beautiful parts of her character that we get a glimpse of when her shyness does not get in the way. Now, imagine the sun is that person who so naturally brings them out; the person who can shine through her. The rainbows are the beautiful aspects of her character that, at present, only a certain *someone* brings out in her."

Darcy eyed her warily. "You are trying to tell me that Bostwick is the sun to Georgiana's prism.

"He does seem to make her shine!" Elizabeth cried.

Darcy sat down at his desk, watching the prism as he twirled it in his fingers. "Very good object lesson, my dear, but there is something of which you are not aware that has affected my whole perspective of this relationship."

Elizabeth sat down as well and turned her attention to him. "Then tell me."

"When my father met with his attorney to draw up the financial arrangements for Georgiana's fortune, he took the strictest care to make certain that no one would marry her solely for her money. At least, they would not be able to marry her and secure her fortune straight away."

"Go on."

"Georgiana has a grand fortune of 30,000 pounds. That is quite an enticement for any young man, particularly a man of little or no fortune. So what he did, and no one, not even myself, can make any alterations to it, was to ensure that the amount given over at marriage as a dowry would only be equal to the worth per annum of her intended. After that, half of whatever is remaining would be turned over after five years, and the remaining at ten." Darcy turned in his chair and looked at Elizabeth. "You see, my dear, if Georgiana and Bostwick were to marry, they would be living on his meagre income for at least five years before he received anything substantial from her fortune, and they would not receive the sum of it for ten years. They would have very little to live on!"

Elizabeth looked down, contemplating these words. "This is complicated, indeed. Does Georgiana know?"

"Previously no one knew of the arrangements but me, my cousin, and my father's attorney. I just informed Georgiana of it now."

"How did she take it?"

Darcy looked at her through pained eyes. "She took it hard, although she insists her fortune means nothing to her or to him. I knew immediately by this assertion that her feelings for Mr. Bostwick were great indeed."

Elizabeth turned, folding her arms in front of her, trying to make sense of this.

"When she almost eloped with Wickham I had that as an ace up my sleeve in case he did not back down solely on my insistence. He had very little financial worth, and therefore would have received very little upon their marriage. He would not have been able to pay off his debts from what he received. I never did have to inform him of those details. I believe he would have run, though, once he verified the truth of it."

"If she and Mr. Bostwick were to marry, and I am not saying they have even considered it, they could always live here at Pemberley," Elizabeth suggested.

"That is true, but do you really think that Bostwick is the type of young man who would live off someone else? Imagine what it would be like for him to live here while his father is out working the grounds. I think not. Besides, no matter what help I offered him, I fear he would refuse it. And knowing Georgiana, she would as well. In fact, she basically told me that now. I do not want to see my sister living in poverty. This is why I have been so against it. It is not so much his station in life. I concur with you that he is a man of exceptional character, but regarding his ability to support Georgiana, unfortunately he does not have the means."

Darcy reached out and placed the prism back in Elizabeth's hand. He closed her fingers over it, holding on to her hand. "Lizbeth, I have done everything I can think of to prevent an alliance between them before things went too far. In addition to his inability to support my sister, there is also the fact that she needs the experience of being out in society. She has a great need to learn to socialize more… particularly with people she has not known all her life. You gave her a journal to help her with her shyness around people. I am just asking that we encourage her to put some of these things into practice, meet new people, and improve her social skills. Do you not think that she needs to learn these things as well?"

Elizabeth sighed. "As *you* had to learn."

Darcy nodded slowly. "Yes, as I had to learn. I had to learn many things before I was ready to marry."

"So what do we do now?"

"There is only one thing we must do."

"What is that?" she asked.

Darcy brought his eyes up to Elizabeth. "Next week we will leave for London for the season. Georgiana has asked about being presented at court and being brought out in society. She shall have her wish, and I shall endeavour to put her in as many situations as I can to expose her to society. In addition, much to my consternation, and possibly hers, I shall seek out introductions for her of the most eligible young men in London."

Chapter 17

Elizabeth left the study with a better understanding of her husband's reaction to Georgiana and Mr. Bostwick, but with a greater concern for his sister. She immediately went up to Georgiana's room, and as she briskly climbed the stairs, she contemplated just how similar her feelings were to that day a half year before. That day she had also hurried to Georgiana's side, knowing she would most likely find a grief stricken young lady, since Georgiana had just discovered that Elizabeth and her brother were not engaged as she had wrongly assumed all along.

Elizabeth once again approached the closed door and gently knocked. But instead of resistance, as happened before, she was welcomed in by the young lady. Elizabeth slowly opened the door and found a pensive Georgiana lying upon her bed, her pillow tucked beneath her chin and her arms crossed tightly around it.

Elizabeth silently sat down on the side of the bed and took Georgiana's hand in her own. Just as she was about to offer some soothing words to her, Georgiana spoke. "William just told me about the arrangements our father made for me. Were you aware of them?"

"No, Georgiana, I had not been. He just now informed me as well."

Georgiana knitted her eyebrows together as she pondered the situation. "I am not so terribly upset that my father made those arrangements. I can understand his reasoning, I suppose."

"He was only looking out for you because he loved you so dearly."

Elizabeth waited for her to continue. When she did not, Elizabeth helped her along. "It does change the way you might look at things, does it not?"

Georgiana sighed deeply and pulled the pillow in tighter. She looked at Elizabeth as if to assess whether her next words would reach receptive ears. Elizabeth, almost sensing her contemplation, gently smiled, and Georgiana continued. "Elizabeth, I love David Bostwick and I believe he loves me. This arrangement does not alter my regard for him. I have never loved him based on what my fortune would do for him -- or us."

Elizabeth was surprised by the intensity and honesty of Georgiana's confessed emotion. "Georgiana, have you and Mr. Bostwick openly shared your feelings for one another?" Elizabeth held her breath as she waited for the girl to answer.

"No, we have not. Mr. Bostwick, I believe, holds that he has no right to express any such affection because of our difference in class. But in the way he speaks to me… the manner in which way he treats me… I do believe he returns my regard."

Now it was Elizabeth's turn to let out a deep sigh. "Oh, Georgiana, life can sometimes be so complicated."

"I told William that my fortune means nothing to me."

Elizabeth patted the hand she held. "But you must consider what this would mean for you and Mr. Bostwick if you should ever marry."

Georgiana dipped her head into the pillow in front of her. "I doubt that William would ever allow it anyway." Suddenly the tears filled her eyes again. "He is quite intent on introducing me to men of the highest connections and significant consequence. Did he tell you we are leaving for London?"

Elizabeth nodded.

"He told me quite adamantly that it is his design to introduce me to men who are more equal to the standing of our name while we are there this season. And he firmly insists that I make a concerted effort to be the ever polite, ever charming, and ever amiable young lady that our name demands."

Elizabeth reached up and smoothed some strands of hair that had escaped down Georgiana's face. "Georgiana, you must realize that the obligations you owe to your name are inherent to who you are."

"But I do not want to marry out of obligation, Elizabeth. I want to marry for love. Just as you and my brother did."

Georgiana suddenly swung her legs off the other side of the bed and stood up. Folding her arms across her chest, she faced away from Elizabeth. "I have, however, agreed to do what my brother says. I have agreed that we shall go to London, that I shall be presented at court and brought out into society, and meet all those fine, eligible men that are just waiting to sweep me off my feet. I will do this for him." She turned around slowly and faced Elizabeth. "But I cannot promise him that I will find any man who is better, finer, and more suited for me than Mr. Bostwick."

~~*

The next week passed with hurried preparations and a mixture of varied emotions concerning the imminent departure. Catherine was terribly agitated about this whole prospect. It was not about going to London that had her nerves completely tied up in knots, but the possibility that her parents would not allow her to go. On their way to town they would stop at Longbourn and Catherine wondered whether her parents would allow her to continue on with them. How wonderful it would be, she thought, to go into town with the Darcys, be presented at court with Georgiana, and be the first Bennet sister to be properly brought out into society. Then, of course, there would be all the balls that would follow. She inwardly hoped that Lydia would hear of this and be outrageously jealous of her!

The Flemings were sad to see them all go, but were obligated to remain and continue the classes. They actually preferred doing that to going to town, but felt awkward remaining at Pemberley. Darcy assured them that this was most acceptable to him, and implored them to feel free to ask Mrs. Reynolds if there was anything they needed while they were away.

The subject of David Bostwick was not discussed again between Georgiana and her brother. She knew that to even suggest that she and Catherine visit the school one last time would be out of the question. As Monday came and went, and the day of their departure grew nearer, she felt an even greater sense of urgency in seeing David one last time before they set out for London for the season.

On Thursday afternoon of that week, the Flemings finished morning classes and decided they wanted to visit the school property and see how things were progressing. Mr. Fleming took his family in a small Pemberley curricle, driving it himself.

Over the midday meal, Darcy mentioned that he wanted to take a drive out to Manor to see it before leaving.

"It is the only estate around here that is for sale until Lochlin decides to sell his. I thought we could look at it and give Bingley a good description when we see them on the way to London. From what I recall, though," he began, "it is considerably smaller than Netherfield, but I should like to see it just the same."

He inquired whether Elizabeth wanted to see it with him, and she was most eager. Catherine, ever willing to see a grand estate, no matter what size, was willing to visit as well.

Darcy looked at Georgiana. "Georgiana, will you be joining us?"

"I think not, William. I should like to practice on the pianoforte for a while. But I do remember the place years ago when the Swifts let it and I would go over and play with their daughter. It had the most beautiful sitting room, and the sun room had a lovely view. I do agree it is not quite as big as Netherfield, but it is quite nice; quite homey."

Darcy, Elizabeth, and Catherine set out in the carriage, driven by Winston. Georgiana watched them leave and then set off for the music room. As she turned to leave, she saw Jacques return from Lambton, and suddenly had an idea. She stepped outside, and came up to him.

"Jacques, I am so glad you have returned. Everyone is gone, and I must get over to the church one last time before we leave for town. Do you think you can take me?"

Jacques nodded, stating that he needed to take some things in first, and would return in a moment. Georgiana hoped no one would notice her leaving, and that no one would return before she did.

When they finally departed for the church, Georgiana sat in the carriage with flutters of anticipation consuming her. Perhaps it was mixed with twinges of guilt. She had never been one to cause anyone concern. She had always been the most agreeable, compliant child. But now she knew what she had to do, and it was something that her brother would be greatly upset about if he knew.

She recalled David saying he worked on the church grounds on Thursdays. She hoped he would be there today.

When they arrived at the church, she told Jacques to wait at the carriage for her. She was not sure how long she would be.

As she began walking towards the church, she kept her eyes open, searching the grounds for any glimpse of David. She did not see him, and, finding herself at the door of the church, opened it and let herself in. As she walked in, the emptiness of it created an even more sacred feeling than it normally did. She looked around at the beautiful stained glass windows that allowed the sun to pour into the church in a myriad of colours. The smell of the wooden pews made her think back to her childhood, coming into this place holding her father's hand and sitting close beside him, feeling safe and secure.

She sat down in a pew in the darkened church and bowed her head and closed her eyes. After a few moments of sitting there in silence, and wondering if she should venture out on the grounds to look for David, she heard the door open behind her. She slowly turned her head and saw that it was David who had entered, adjusting his eyes to the darkness as he walked towards the front. He must have been working in the grounds, as he was covered quite excessively with dirt.

As he came upon the pew in which Georgiana quietly sat, her voice startled him.

"Good day, Mr. Bostwick."

He stopped, halted by her voice and turned in surprise to see her. Self consciously he looked down at himself and brushed himself off. "What are you doing here, Miss Darcy? I was not aware anyone was still here."

"I asked Jacques to bring me here one last time before we leave."

"You are leaving?"

"Yes. To London for the season. We leave on the morrow."

"I see."

David looked upon her face and forced a smile. He turned, taking a deep breath to calm himself and then turned back to her. He wanted to say something, but seemed to be having difficulty forming the words. Georgiana simply watched in silence.

Finally he came directly in front of her. "You will be presented at court this season?"

"Yes."

"Hmmm." He slowly nodded his head. "I do believe you will make a beautiful addition to the ladies at court… and to all of society, for that matter."

"Thank you."

Georgiana was all too aware of their solitude in the confines of this place of worship and as she stood up and met his eyes, she could not pull one rational thought from her mind.

Finally, with an intensity that radiated from his eyes, David stepped toward her and said, "I believe this means numerous parties and balls and introductions."

Georgiana nodded.

David pursed his lips together. "Would you promise me something Miss Darcy, when you are brought out into society?"

Georgiana met his eyes with hers, marvelling at how she had just in recent months moved from so easily blushing around him to being so at ease and comfortable in his presence.

"What would you have me promise?"

"When you are brought out in society, and are introduced to all the gentlemen lining up to make your acquaintance, and you begin making choices as to which ones you would wish to make a call on you and get to know better…"

Georgiana looked down and took in a nervous, ragged breath. David reached his fingers under her chin and lifted it up so she was again looking up to him. "Promise me, Georgiana, do not settle for second best."

She did not know if it was due to their being within a church, but as he spoke those words to her, a voice inside of her told her that anyone other than David Bostwick himself would be second best. Was it simply her own wishes, or was it the voice of the Almighty? Her response was to knit her brows together, and she quickly closed her eyes, not wanting him to read her thoughts. She was startled by the touch of his hands coming upon her shoulders. When she opened her eyes, he had stepped in a little closer.

"Promise me, Georgiana. You know you deserve only the best," he whispered.

They stood still as statues, their eyes betraying to the other their deep feelings. David fought for some sense of control, wanting nothing more than to hold and kiss her. When Georgiana did not turn or back away, he took a step closer. Georgiana, in a sudden realization of the holy place in which they were standing alone, suddenly turned.

"Perhaps we ought to go outside and walk."

She briskly walked toward the door and he followed close behind. As they came to the door, he stepped ahead of her to reach out and open it for her. "Where do you wish to walk?"

"I do not know. Where were you working today?"

"I dug out a stump of an old tree that had fallen."

"Show me where it was."

He pointed the way as he broke into a bemused smile, and they walked away from the church and the parsonage. He offered her his arm and she gratefully took it, allowing them to walk as close as propriety would allow.

They came to a grove of trees and David gestured to the large stump he had dug out and the wood he had cut up from the fallen tree. He laughed when he told her, "It may not look like it, but this chore took me almost all day."

He walked over to a neighbouring large tree and leaned against it, while Georgiana sat on the stump. She looked around, enjoying the beauty of the grove and the fact that she was alone with David. "It must have been a great deal of work."

"I admit I am tired. My work for Lochlin is definitely less strenuous." He looked down at himself and acknowledged his appearance. "And I come away from there looking a little better than I do working the grounds here." He sounded apologetic for his dirty clothes.

Georgiana was silent, knowing she wanted to tell him something, but not knowing where to begin.

"Miss Darcy, you seem to have something on your mind. Is anything amiss?"

Georgiana looked at him, and softly smiled. "You know me too well."

"What is it?"

"My brother shared some information with me recently of which I was not aware, and I do not know what to make of it."

A look of concern swept across his face. "What was it he told you?"

Georgiana did not answer for a few moments as she formulated her words in such a way to allow her to gauge his reaction.

"Apparently my father made some particular arrangements for how my fortune would be distributed once I am married. At the time of my marriage, as a precaution against marrying someone solely interested in my fortune, only the amount of money that my intended receives per annum would be turned over. Then half of the remainder would be turned over at five years, and the remainder at ten years."

"I believe he must have been looking out for you when he did that."

"Yes, but what if I fall in love with someone who then finds out about this arrangement and it alters how he feels about me?"

David pushed himself away from the tree and came toward her. "Miss Darcy, if someone truly loved you, this should not affect how he feels for you." He wanted so much to say it did not affect how he felt for her, but was held back by uncertainty for her feelings for him. "Perhaps, though, it would affect how you felt for someone if you were counting on your fortune to help you out once you were married."

"Oh, no! It has not... it would not affect how I felt for someone in that situation."

Their eyes locked and Georgiana slowly stood up. David walked toward her, perceiving that the words left unspoken were clearer than the words they actually spoke. "Georgiana." How he had longed to speak her name, "I have no right to own the feelings I have for you, but what you just told me has not made an iota of difference in my regard for you."

Georgiana smiled and closed her eyes. When she opened them, David had bridged the distance between them. Her heart resonated within her as she quietly spoke, "You asked me, back in the church, to promise not to settle for second best."

David reached out and took her hand in his again. As she looked down and watched him cradle it in his, she barely whispered, "I promise you, I will not." David tenderly stroked her hand, and then slowly brought it up to his lips, placing a tender kiss upon the back of it. She marvelled at how right it felt. He allowed the kiss to linger just long enough for him to command his senses, pulling himself away and dropping her hand. "Please forgive me, Georgiana, for overstepping my bounds. I had no right..."

"Please, it is up to me to determine whether you have a right or not, and I have allowed it."

David smiled at her. "I shall miss you these next few months. I shall most likely come to class each Monday and still look for your sweet, smiling face."

"I shall miss you as well." Georgiana absently brushed off some dirt that was caked on David's shirt. As she did this, he brought her hand up and captured it against his heart. He then brought it up to his lips and left an imprint of a kiss in her palm.

Georgiana smiled and said in a barely audible whisper, "I must go."

David kept hold of her hand and their arms stretched out as far as they could go as Georgiana slowly backed away. Before their fingers finally broke apart, Georgiana unexpectedly drew back to him. David lost no time in wrapping his arms around her, and Georgiana rested her cheek against his chest as he held her in an embrace.

David dropped his head, kissing the top of her head.

She slowly looked up and David gazed into Georgiana's face. His eyes betrayed the yearning he felt to lean down that small distance and kiss her lips. He took several deep breaths before finally releasing her. "You best go before I lose all semblance of being a well-mannered man.

Georgiana gave him a tender smile. "Yes, I suppose I must." A trembling sigh escaped. "Good bye, David. I shall see you in the spring."

"Goodbye, Georgiana. I shall count on that."

Georgiana walked away, her thoughts solely on the young man she just left. When she came upon the carriage, Jacques was not there, but she did not have to wait long for his return. He was silent as he helped her into the carriage, and his glance at her made her wonder if he had seen her with David. But as he did not say anything to her, she decided not to worry about it.

As the carriage pulled away, she compared her feelings for David to Wickham. The two men were like night and day, and her feelings toward the two of them were even more dissimilar. She believed now that she had not been in love with Wickham, but had looked upon him strictly as a brother figure, misconstruing that as love. David had said she deserved only the best. A sudden wave of fear swept through her and she hoped that David would never find out how senseless and immature she had been in almost eloping with Wickham.

~.~.*

David walked slowly back to the church. He knew it was going to be a long winter without Georgiana, but he felt that what had just transpired between them would enable him to get through the coldest of winters and an eternity of time. He held hope in his heart that Georgiana returned his love, and she would return from town with that love still intact. He pushed away thoughts about her brother and how determined he would most likely be in disallowing it.

His mind thus engaged, he did not notice the figure standing before him in the path that led to the parsonage.

"Bostwick," came the gentle, yet firm voice.

David looked up and found himself looking into the eyes of Reverend Kenton. "Reverend, how are you?"

"I am somewhat confused."

"Oh?"

"You and Miss Darcy...?"

David flinched. "Sir, you saw us?"

"Yes, I did. Actually Jacques and I both came to the clearing and saw the two of you just before Miss Darcy walked away.

David lowered his head and shook it, knowing what that meant.

"There is no need to worry yet, as I explained I wanted to have a talk with you to find out some things before anything was said to Mr. Darcy." He turned and faced Bostwick. "I was not aware that you and Miss Darcy had an understanding."

David tensed nervously. "I must confess that the only understanding she and I have is that our regard for each other... our love... will be frowned upon by almost everyone and will most likely never be tolerated."

Kenton looked at him and softly murmured, "Particularly her brother. I do not necessarily approve of your actions out there, however I can sympathize with you, my friend. I also know what it is to love and not be considered good enough."

David looked at him startled. "Reverend Kenton, you have feelings for Georgiana, as well?"

Kenton laughed. "No, Bostwick, not Miss Darcy. But I confess I do for Miss Catherine Bennet. Only in *our* situation, I believe we would be a most *suitable* match. Unfortunately *she* does consider me worthy enough for her. I believe that the time she has spent with the Darcys in their great estate amidst all their finery has made her set her sights on an alignment with someone of a much higher class than me."

David sympathetically chuckled. "We are a fine pair, are we not?"

"We are indeed." The reverend sighed. "But we can make it a threesome and also include Jacques. That is why he came to talk to me. He has become exceedingly fond of one of the Pemberley maids, and he wanted to know what is right and wrong in that regard."

"Of the three of us, *he* will most likely be the only one who gets the desire of his heart."

Kenton laughed. "You may be right there."

The two men walked aimlessly toward the parsonage, but David suddenly stopped. "Do *you* think it wrong?" David looked at him, desiring an honest answer.

"I assume you are speaking of Miss Darcy and yourself?"

David nodded.

"Within the dictates of society, I would agree that it will be frowned upon and I even understand why. But within the dictates of the scriptures, which I would place as a higher authority, although not everyone else would, I would have to say it is not wrong... as long as the motive is pure." Kenton looked at him. "Is your motive pure, in that it is based on a love for Miss Darcy and not her fortune?"

David looked down at the ground and shook her head. "It would *have* to be,

Reverend Kenton, from what Georgiana just told me."

David explained to him the circumstances surrounding her fortune.

Kenton interpreted the situation back to him. "Basically, if you were to ever marry her, her dowry would be based on your wealth, and being the second son of a head gardener with no assets and little formal education, initially it would not be much."

David nodded. "But that is of no consequence to me other than I could not offer Georgiana what she has been used to."

"Or what she is entitled to, as others will say. I believe that Miss Darcy is a young lady who has never been impressed by all that she has, and she definitely has a heart toward those less fortunate than she. I can understand her loving you instead of a wealthy suitor whose only interest is in all his wealth. She has grown much under the influence of Mrs. Annesley and now Mrs. Darcy. She has developed a keen ability to see the heart of a person and has placed a greater importance on that than any fortune or position in society could offer."

Kenton stopped and turned to David. "I will not say that an alignment between the two of you is right or wrong. I will insist, however, that you guard your actions so that you do not behave unwisely and without proper decorum toward her. That I must insist!"

"So what do I do?" asked David. "I do not believe I can stop loving her."

"The same thing I am going to do right now," laughed Kenton. "Shall we go in and drown our sorrows and try to put the two ladies leaving for town tomorrow out of our minds?"

"That does sound like a very good idea," agreed David.

"Unfortunately the strongest thing I have is a billiard table. Does a good, all consuming game of billiards appeal to you?"

"Yes it does," assured David. "Yes it does."

As they came into the billiard room and Kenton racked the balls, David sighed. "I have often considered Mr. Darcy my Goliath in life. It seems as though he is the one obstacle, and a big one at that, blocking my way to Miss Darcy. Apart from, of course, her family, my family, and all the rest of society. But I have always felt that if only Mr. Darcy would accept me, it would pave the way for everyone else. I just do not seem to be able to make any progress with him, and yet David in the Bible was able to conquer his Goliath in one attempt. It seems all I end up doing is being pushed farther away by him."

Kenton looked at him thoughtfully. "Perhaps, Bostwick, Mr. Darcy is not your Goliath at all."

"What do you mean?"

"David had another enemy that gave him much more grief than Goliath ever did. That was Saul. And if you know your biblical stories at all, you know that David had to endure Saul's harassment and even attempts to kill him for years. David was to be king, and Saul would not readily give up his throne to him. He pursued him relentlessly, trying to keep David from getting what was truly his. Yes, I believe that instead of Goliath, Mr. Darcy can be compared more to Saul, whom you may have to face as your antagonist for a very long time."

"That is not highly encouraging," sighed David.

"Bostwick, there is another possibility you must consider. He may *never* change his opinion of you because your station in life is so decidedly beneath Miss Darcy's. You must face that reality as well."

David moaned. "I often have."

"Come, let us try to turn our mind to the game before us, shall we?" He turned to the billiard table gesturing to the racked balls. "Do you want to break or should I?"

David sighed. "I will break." He laid his cue stick down, aimed carefully, and hit a shot scattering the balls across the table. He knew it would be a long winter for him.

Chapter 18

The late fall morning broke with all the signs of an impending winter crouching at the door. The weather had recently been surprisingly mild for fall, but on the morning that the Darcys and Catherine Bennet left for Hertfordshire before continuing on to London, it turned cold and windy. The skies were clear, but the wind whipped about as if it had just been released from years of captivity. The temperature dropped and made one wonder if the north wind had packed its bag and come down to England for an extended stay.

They were dressed in their warmest clothes in the predawn light as they waited inside for the carriage to be loaded, the warming bricks to be heated, and the horses to be hitched. Both carriages were being taken, as Darcy always had Winston at his disposal with his carriage, and Georgiana had hers. There was no reason to change the way they did things now. With four of them going to town, there was an even greater probability that they would have need for the second carriage.

When all things were readied, the four of them boarded one carriage. They felt it would help the time to pass more quickly as well as keep them warmer if they rode together. The ride from Pemberley to Hertfordshire would take most of the day.

As they settled in for the ride, Georgiana and Catherine made themselves comfortable with blankets and pillows and promptly leaned their heads back and closed their eyes. They had been awakened early that morning and now looked forward to catching up on some of their sleep.

Elizabeth took advantage of the quiet of the early morning to watch the scenery pass by. As the sun slowly began to make its way above the horizon, it shone on the Derbyshire peaks that rose in the distance. The colours from the early morning sky were reflected against them and it was too beautiful a sight to miss.

"Girls, wake up! Look at how beautiful the peaks are!"

"Hmm?" Georgiana let out a yawn.

"I am too tired," complained Catherine.

Darcy looked over at his wife. "I fear they do not appreciate the beauty of nature as much as you do, my dear, especially at this time of the morning."

"But it is beautiful, do you not think so?"

As Darcy ducked his head a bit to get a better glimpse of the peaks outside the window on Elizabeth's side of the carriage, he nodded. "Very beautiful, indeed, Lizbeth."

"The colour on the peaks from the morning sun is simply breathtaking."

"Ahh, but you should see how breathtaking you are, my dear, enjoying the scenery. You simply take my breath away."

Elizabeth smiled. "Now Will, talk like that will get you anywhere. But remember we have two young ladies with us."

"Mmm. Unfortunate. We do have that other carriage…"

"I will not even attempt to reply to that, my dear."

Elizabeth enjoyed watching the country pass by as the sun became bolder and bolder in the sky. The wind, however, was insistent and persistent in bringing the cold down with it, so there was little chance of warming up.

At length, the girls stirred from their sleep and Elizabeth opened a basket of food that had been prepared for them. As they enjoyed a mid morning snack, they talked of Longbourn, London, and how to talk Mr. and Mrs. Bennet into allowing Catherine to accompany them into town.

"Elizabeth, you must help us convince Mother and Father to give their consent for me to remain on with you. You and Jane were so often able to go to town to visit Aunt and Uncle Gardiner, and I have seldom gone. And besides, Georgiana needs me there with her!"

Darcy looked up from his book and joined Elizabeth in looking from Catherine to Georgiana and back again.

"She needs you?" he asked.

"Yes!" Catherine nudged Georgiana with her elbow. "Tell them, Georgiana."

"We have been talking… Catherine and I… and I feel that she would be a great help for me when I am presented at court, if she can be there with me as well. I feel that I would not be nearly so nervous making a curtsy in front of the queen herself if I have Catherine by my side."

"Is that so?" asked Darcy sceptically.

"Please, Elizabeth. I could represent all the Bennet daughters who have never been presented at court, and I would do Georgiana a service as well."

"It appears as though these girls have figured it all out, Lizbeth." Darcy turned back to his reading.

"Yes, it would seem they do," she agreed. "Catherine, I see no harm in talking to Mother and Father and encouraging them to allow you to go. But remember it is their decision and not ours to make."

Georgiana and Catherine looked at each other and gave one another a hearty grin. Catherine felt a little more confident that her parents would allow her to go if William and Elizabeth were strongly in favour of it. Georgiana truly felt that she would need someone by her side at the presentation, as the thought of going before all of those in the court, especially the queen herself, would be enough to make her faint!

The carriage arrived at Netherfield in late afternoon. Jane had invited her parents and Mary to dine with them, and they were already there when the party from Derbyshire arrived.

Elizabeth could not bring herself out the carriage quick enough when she saw Jane and Charles coming toward them from the house. Behind them came Mr. and Mrs. Bennet and Mary.

"They are here! They are here!" they could hear Mrs. Bennet wail.

Elizabeth took in a deep breath and girded herself so as not to become impatient, embarrassed, or allow her mother's behaviour to spoil her visit.

As each of them stepped down from the carriage, they were warmly greeted with fervent hugs. Mary appeared to be very happy to see them, and Elizabeth sensed something different about her; perhaps she had grown up and changed for the better. It seemed to Elizabeth that her countenance displayed a little more joy and a little less censure.

"It is so good to see everyone," Elizabeth said.

"How is my favourite daughter?" asked Mr. Bennet into Elizabeth's ear as he hugged her. "It has been far too long."

"I am doing quite well, Father."

He reached out his hand and shook his son-in-law's hand. "Has my daughter completely turned your life upside down at Pemberley, Son?"

Darcy laughed. "My life and everyone else's there, Sir. But fortunately she is loved by all."

"Good, good!" he laughed.

"Shall we go inside?" asked Bingley. "It is far too cold to be greeting each other out here when we can be doing it just as well inside."

Elizabeth took Jane's arm as they walked in. "It is so good to be here!" she said to her. "By they way, are Charles' sisters here?"

"No," replied Jane with a mischievous smile. "Something prompted them to leave for town this week. I cannot recall what it was. Perhaps you shall pass them coming back on your way down."

Elizabeth laughed. "I shall most certainly look out for them!"

Chattering noisily, they all made their way up the steps of Netherfield, and congregated in the warmth of the sitting room.

"Lizzy, there is so much to tell!" began her mother, clasping her hands together.

Elizabeth swallowed hard, hoping they were not in for an update on all the latest gossip from Meryton.

"First of all, there is news from Lydia."

"Lydia? What does she have to say? I have only received one letter from her and it has been some time."

"She is married!"

"Lydia? Married? How can this be?" asked Elizabeth.

Darcy had been conversing with Bingley, but suddenly his attention was pricked when he heard this. "To whom is she married?" he asked abruptly.

"Yes, Mama, who did she marry?" Elizabeth's eyes reflected her fear in what her mother's answer would reveal.

"Well, I suppose we can be grateful he is an officer. An officer she had come to know quite well in Brighton."

Suddenly her father broke in. "If you ask me, this whole thing sounds peculiar. I knew we should have demanded she come home at the end of summer."

"Mama, who is he?"

"Oh, his name is Carter. Matthew Carter."

Darcy and Elizabeth both let out a very audible sigh of relief when they did not hear the name they both were dreading.

"What do we know about him, Mama? Papa? Why did she marry so suddenly? And without inviting the family?" Elizabeth's eyes reflected the concern and suspicion she was feeling.

"Oh I am sure she was so in love with him that she felt it was something she had to do." Mrs. Bennet offered. "The company is leaving Brighton, and I suppose she felt that in order to go with him, she would need to marry him immediately. Just think, Lizzy, an officer! How well they must look together!"

Elizabeth's brows furrowed. She did not like discussing this in front of Georgiana and Catherine, although they were both adult enough to hear it. As much as Elizabeth did not like the sound of it and was concerned about how it might reflect on her family, she had to find out.

"I am only vexed that she is not to have a real wedding here with her family," lamented Mrs. Bennet. "Oh how much she must be disappointed!"

"Oh, yes," chuckled her father. "I am sure coming back and having a wedding with her family was first and foremost on her mind!"

"Do not be so silly, Mr. Bennet. Surely she misses us. Now I have three of my daughters married! And to think Mrs. Lucas still only has one!"

Elizabeth let the subject drop as her mother suddenly felt inclined to do the same, although her thoughts continued to roll it about in her mind.

Mrs. Bennet turned to Catherine. "Kitty, how did you enjoy your stay at Pemberley? Did the Darcys introduce you to any eligible young men of good…"

"I go by Catherine, now Mama. I have enjoyed my stay at Pemberley very much." Catherine told her of all that she had done since her arrival over two months ago.

Elizabeth took this opportunity and looked at Jane who was sitting silently beside her. "What do you think about Lydia's getting married so abruptly?" Elizabeth asked in a whisper.

"We know how much Lydia desired to marry an officer. She was so fond of a man in a redcoat. I believe she simply accepted a proposal of marriage and saw no reason to wait to come home and marry."

Elizabeth shook her head. "Oh, Jane. Do you not see? I would not be surprised that in a month we will hear the news that she is with child, and then in six months we will have news of a baby who has miraculously been born two months premature!"

"Lizzy, you must not think that way!"

"All right, Jane. You continue to give her the benefit of the doubt. I hope for Lydia's sake that you are right and I am wrong."

Elizabeth was suddenly drawn back into the conversation between her mother and Catherine when she heard, "London! Now you want to go to London?" It was her father, who seemed a little exasperated with his daughters going off in all directions. "Was not Pemberley enough?"

"Now, Mr. Bennet," his wife pleaded. "Perhaps we should consider this request. Think of all the opportunities she will have being with the Darcys. I imagine it would be highly beneficial for her." Mrs. Bennet continued to smile, thinking of all the young men in the highest class of society who she would have the opportunity to meet. "Think of all the cultural activities there would be for her to partake of. No, I think it is an excellent idea."

This conversation was fortunately the only real discomforting display Elizabeth had to endure. The rest of the evening passed smoothly enough and the Bennets eventually gave permission for Catherine to accompany the Darcys to London for the season. It actually seemed agreeable to Mary, as well, who would, by this account, continue to remain at Longbourn alone. But to Elizabeth's delight it was soon discovered that this was not such a fretful thought to her, as she had met a very eligible gentleman who surprisingly enough seemed to return her regard. Elizabeth was certain that nothing could entice her away from home right now.

They settled that for the Christmas season they would all gather in London; celebrating together with the Gardiners.

After dinner the men set off for the study to talk. Darcy enjoyed his time with Mr. Bennet, who had a keen knowledge of literature, an extensive interest in history, and enjoyed talking about his Lizzy. Darcy was willing to oblige him.

Elizabeth could not bear to be away from Jane, and was grateful that Mary and her mother seemed content to talk with Catherine and Georgiana. She hoped, for Georgiana's sake, that her mother did not get carried away about some inane subject and put Georgiana ill at ease. Jane and Elizabeth spent the evening talking and laughing, comparing notes about their husbands, and getting caught up on both of their lives.

When the men came out, the remainder of the evening was spent pleasantly. Catherine returned home with her parents and Mary. Darcy, Elizabeth, and Georgiana remained at Netherfield. There they stayed for four days, before heading down to London.

~~*

London in winter is the place to be. People have boarded up their country homes and have come to town to enjoy all that it has to offer. In the cold winter months, there is not much one can do while in the country, but in town there are concerts, the theatre, ballet, parties and balls that are never ending. The air may be stale and grimy, but there is an excitement that overtakes you as soon as you come into its limits.

This, of course, would be in the more fashionable part of town. In Cheapside, where Elizabeth's aunt and uncle lived with their family, one would have more of a tendency to dwell on the struggle to work hard to keep food on the table. Fortunately her uncle had no need to worry about that, as he owned a successful business. He did have to work, however, and that was the big difference between himself and Darcy; between one who owned a home in Cheapside and one who owned a home in the fashionable part of town as well as land in the country.

There would be few who lived in Cheapside who could boast of having acquaintances in the fashionable part of town with whom they were socially intimate. This was not the case between the Darcys and the Gardiners. Even though they lived in Cheapside, Darcy regarded them as fashionable enough for him and pleasant enough for his company. Simply put, he enjoyed their company. Elizabeth was most grateful that they were usually his first choice when looking for someone to share a box seat at the theatre or concert. In reality, he was grateful that he was no longer required to make compulsory and obligatory appearances at social events with the town's elite.

Almost from the beginning, the Darcys and Gardiners, along with Georgiana and Catherine, took advantage of the many offerings of concerts and the theatre, and Elizabeth and Catherine both attended their first ballet. Darcy felt greatly content as he escorted his wife to these events. As he sat in the box seat at an opera, he could not help but think back to even a year ago, as he would try to enjoy any one of London's offerings, all the while a woman -- either one that he had escorted or one he met while there -- would continually try to impress him with what she thought he wanted to hear and how he wanted her to behave. Instead, she usually ended up trying his nerves.

How ironic that the woman who was to win his heart enjoyed countering his opinions, had no wish to impress him, and had never even been presented at court. She would never be accepted into his society on her own.

Her visits to London consisted of living and socializing for the most part in Cheapside, yet to him she was the most fashionable lady in substance, nature, character and intelligence that he had ever met. No, she had never been considered part of the ton, yet to him she was worth much more than everyone in the ton put together.

He would frequently watch Georgiana. When he had turned around and was not looking, Georgiana had grown up. When had she become a woman? She was still shy. He watched as their small, intimate group talked, and she rarely asserted herself, although she did participate in the conversation more than she used to. His heart was gripped, as he thought of her being brought out into society and how easily she could be devoured by those who were so calculating and manipulative to raise their own social status at the expense of others.

He thought about all he had learned this past year; all that he had learned about himself because of Elizabeth. He had finally been able to view society, *his* society, and what it demanded through her eyes. He had never been enamoured by it and thought himself above the rules, but in reality he acquiesced to them. It was only when he met Elizabeth that he realized how closely tied he was to a system of rules that he never really thought he held to.

Georgiana faced the same dilemma; only to her it seemed to not be a dilemma at all. To her the answer was simple. She seemed not inclined to struggle with the disparity between herself and Bostwick as he had with Elizabeth. Elizabeth had told her husband of her talk with the young girl and her strong affirmation of love for Mr. Bostwick. Darcy had to be very guarded in responding to Elizabeth about this, so as not to offend her in stating his opinion that Bostwick was not good enough for his sister. But did he really believe that?

The truth of the matter was he did not want to have to be the one to put an end to it. He hoped that in bringing Georgiana out this season, she would have the opportunity to meet many young men who would be a more suitable match because of fortune and connections. She was still young, he reasoned, and there was plenty of time for her to come to the realization on her own that she could love, and *should* love, someone more suitable. That was his hope, but in the back of his mind he warred with the thought that he was again acquiescing to the rules set down by society, and not his heart.

Their frequent cultural excursions were temporarily put on hold for the holiday season. Jane and Bingley arrived with Mr. and Mrs. Bennet and Mary. The Bennets had received an invitation to stay with the Gardiners, but as Elizabeth had also extended an invitation, that was the one they accepted.

When they arrived, Elizabeth and Darcy were quickly apprised of the latest news. Mrs. Bennet was quick to let Elizabeth know that Lydia was going to have a baby. As she joyously raved about this wonderful prospect, Elizabeth looked to Jane, who was silently looking down. When she finally looked up, she sadly smiled, acknowledging that Elizabeth had unfortunately been correct in her assumption.

Elizabeth thought the impropriety of Lydia was most disgraceful and humiliating to her family, and saw that her father recognized the truth of the situation. If her mother did, she did not let it affect her feelings about it.

Later, when they were alone, Jane approached Elizabeth, "You were right again, Lizzy."

"Believe me, Jane, I wish I had not been."

"Mother seems completely ignorant of the situation," sighed Jane.

"Or she is choosing to be ignorant," countered Elizabeth.

Jane sighed.

"What is it, Jane?"

Just before we received news of Lydia's condition, I had suspicions that I was with child."

"Oh, Jane, that is wonderful!"

"No, Lizzy, I lost the child." Jane looked down as her eyes filled with tears.

"Oh, Jane, I am so sorry!"

"I have not told Mother or Father. It happened so quickly."

"What a burden that must have been for you to carry."

"I have accepted it and moved on. But please do not tell them."

"If you do not wish it, you know I will not."

As the days with her family passed, Elizabeth was most grateful for the very excellent staff that helped to make everyone's stay comfortable. She need not have worried, as her mother was too much in awe to even think of any complaint, and bestowed praises on the meals, the furnishings, the servants, and even the perfect way the house was situated so that the sun shone in just the right windows.

Darcy endured Mrs. Bennet's effusive praises, and was grateful for Mr. Bennet's preference for the library; consequently he spent a great deal of time with him in there. He was also grateful for Mrs. Gardiner, who willingly took Mrs. Bennet out shopping, much more than she needed.

Their first Christmas was thusly spent in a small gathering of family and friends.

As they joyously entered the New Year, they eagerly began focusing on presenting the two young ladies at court. Elizabeth escorted Georgiana and Catherine on numerous shopping expeditions looking for the right materials to make up the perfect dress for each of them. They looked at silks and satins, velvets and laces, and an array of trimmings. They conferred with each other about colours and styles and ultimately both girls talked with expert seamstresses about their desires and the orders were placed for the gowns they would wear.

As the day for the presentation drew nearer, they began discussing the details of the ball that would be held in their honour. Catherine truly felt that the ball was for Georgiana and she yielded all major decisions to her. Georgiana, having quite an aversion to being the centre of attention, especially among people she did not know, requested that her coming out ball be a small and intimate affair. She desired to only invite the closest of friends and relatives. Now small is a relative term, and to Georgiana it would seem small meant no more than twenty, whereas Catherine believed the number would lean more toward at least a hundred.

A guest list was drawn up, and after much agonizing, it was pared down to about forty people of only the closest family and friends. The one looming question that stood out in everyone's mind was their aunt, Lady Catherine de Bourgh, who had been ordered out of Pemberley by Darcy last year and from whom they had not heard since that fateful day. She had refused the invitation to his and Elizabeth's wedding, although that had not surprised him.

Elizabeth gave her opinion on the matter. "I am inclined to extend her the invitation, Will. We can at least do that much and leave the decision to her."

Georgiana agreed. "Fitzwilliam, I should like her to at least know she is welcome and I would very much like to see my cousin Anne, as well."

Darcy was not convinced. "We know how she can be, and this is one of Georgiana's most important events of her life. I should be most displeased if she did anything to ruin it."

Elizabeth took her husband's arm. "Will, I would be willing to bet that she would behave most properly in such an important affair as this. She would have to look upon this event in Georgiana's life with much approval."

Darcy looked at Georgiana. "Are you truly in favour of this?"

Georgiana nodded.

"Then we shall send her an invitation and leave it to her bidding whether she accepts."

~~*

Weeks passed quickly and the day of the girls' presentation at court drew near. Georgiana reluctantly acknowledged that coming to London had been good for her. She loved the variety of things to do and reunited with several close acquaintances, introducing them to Catherine.

Elizabeth worked closely with the servants in making the preparations for the ball. She was grateful that this first ball they were hosting as husband and wife would be a smaller affair, although the details seemed to grow and grow. Decisions about refreshment, decorations, music, and musicians sometimes seemed endless. She was pleased that her aunt graciously guided her along with advice on the best places and people who offered these services.

Elizabeth was confident that the servants at their London townhome were most capable of carrying out this type of affair, but she had also gleaned information that a ball had not been held here for some time. There had not been a formal affair hosted since before the elder Mr. Darcy died. For that reason, several of the Pemberley staff were brought to London to help.

Invitations were sent out and final fittings were made for Georgiana's and Catherine's dresses. An announcement was drawn up for the *Morning Post* for each of the ladies, and then they had very little to do but sit and wait; some more nervously than others.

~~*

The anticipated day finally arrived. Georgiana and Catherine spent much of the morning having their hair meticulously washed and curled, drawn up and embellished with flowers and ribbons. They eyed their respective gowns with much anticipation, waiting for that moment when they would finally slip it on.

Family began arriving. The Fitzwilliams arrived in London, staying at their own townhome. Everyone enjoyed seeing them again.

To say that Mrs. Bennet was excited about this opportunity for her daughter would be an understatement. From the moment she and Mr. Bennet, along with Mary, had arrived until the time they set out for court, her lavish praises and exultations could be heard through the whole house. Mr. Bennet actually displayed an uncommonly similar response, as he was thrilled for one of his daughters to actually be presented at court.

As family and friends gathered downstairs at the Darcy townhome, the two young ladies made their grand entrance for the family. They came out together, grasping each other's arm, and slowly walked down the staircase to the oohs and ahhhs of everyone below. Both girls had chosen velvet with silk trims. Georgiana was in burgundy and Catherine in deep midnight blue. Many a comment was spoken that one would be hard pressed to find a prettier pair of girls in all of England.

As they set out for the Queen's Court, it was particularly noticeable that Lady Catherine had chosen not to come. The two girls kept together, as much for Georgiana's peace of mind as Catherine's. As they came to the court, they were escorted into the Queen's drawing room with all the other young ladies being presented, their name announced, and each quickly curtseyed. It was over before you could blink, but it was a monumental moment for each.

The ball which followed was a triumphal success. Georgiana was grateful that this was not the type of ball where dozens of eligible bachelors would be lined up to make her acquaintance. She was surrounded by those she knew well and loved. She had received numerous invitations to other balls, however, and knew they were compelled to attend some at a later date. On this day, *her* day, however, she was comfortable enough to sing and play for those in attendance.

Just after Georgiana had finished playing a set on the pianoforte, a guest was announced. "Lady Catherine de Bourgh and Miss Anne de Bourgh."

Everyone turned to see the stately lady walk in with her daughter. Darcy held his breath as he watched her approach his sister. He started to intercede, but Elizabeth gently held him back. "Give her a chance, Will."

Lady Catherine walked over to the young lady, who looked so grown up in her gown and fashionable hairstyle.

"Georgiana, what a pleasure it was to see you presented at court today."

"You were there, Aunt?"

"You did not think I would miss it, did you?" She looked over at her nephew, and turned back to Georgiana. "Thank you for inviting me."

Lady Catherine behaved herself admirably. Nothing was mentioned or even hinted at regarding the incident the last time they had seen her. She was tolerably cordial to Elizabeth, and even enjoyed some conversation with her.

Elizabeth crawled into bed later that night, grateful that the evening was over, but having enjoyed it thoroughly, and she snuggled up to her husband. "You have a very lovely sister, Will. You must be very proud of her."

"She is who she is not by my account, I must admit, but I am extremely proud of her."

"Oh, I think that a lot of who she is can be attributed to you." She smiled and leaned her head against him. "And I am not the only one with that opinion."

"And just who else shares this opinion?"

"Your Aunt Catherine."

"My aunt? She told me to my face just last year that I was not the best guardian; that I lacked what she called prudent wisdom in raising her!"

"Well, she extolled your praises tonight, Will, and not only to me."

"Did she? I believe you and Georgiana were correct in inviting her, Lizbeth, even though that woman can behave in an extremely ill manner. She is family, however, and it appears she has completely forgotten about what had her so violently upset with me previously. That is good."

He pulled Elizabeth closer to him. "Thank you, Lizbeth." He kissed the top of her head.

"For what?" she asked.

"For being everything I have ever wanted and needed, and even more so, in a wife, and also being the same to Georgiana as a sister, a confidant, and a friend; her being brought out this season, all that has transpired with her and Bostwick, and even handling my aunt. Lizbeth, I could not have done it without you."

Chapter 19

Spring

Georgiana was feeling the effects of returning to the country after spending a very busy four months in town. The four months seemed to pass in a whirl as she reflected back on all she had done, all she had learned, and how many people she had met. That she felt considerably more grown up pleased her, and when she found herself in situations that had previously caused her to shrink away, she was now able to face confidently.

She knowingly faced an adjustment being back at Pemberley that would be great. Ever since her brother and Elizabeth had returned from their wedding journey, Catherine had been her constant companion. Now Catherine was back at Longbourn and she would be greatly missed. She felt a loneliness in her solitude at Pemberley that was quite foreign to her. Even the enjoyment of playing the pianoforte seemed to be missing something, as Catherine was not there to listen to her play, comment, and intersperse her practices with giggling.

Although the school building was not completed, the Flemings' home was, and they just recently had moved into it. Darcy and Elizabeth found themselves constantly engaged, having been away from Pemberley for such an extended time. Darcy had much work to catch up on and Elizabeth found that her position as Mistress of Pemberley had some obligations that she needed to tend to as well. She was aware of the loneliness that Georgiana struggled through and often offered to spend time with her as the opportunity arose. She was well aware of how much the young lady missed the companionship of Catherine.

As much as she was grateful to be back at Pemberley, Georgiana looked back with fondness upon her time in London. She had been introduced to many fine young men, and she was even able to admit to herself that she was grateful for the introductions, although it was questionable whether she would become enamoured with any of them. There were very few that she willingly conceded to a second calling. And to those she did, none of them were given an opportunity for a third.

But she had done, most diligently, what her brother requested. She had made every effort to be polite and civil, and endeavoured to engage herself in conversation with any young man who sought out and was given an introduction. She had chuckled at that directive from him, as she had so many times witnessed her brother standing off to the side when he felt uncomfortable, disengaged from any conversation. Perhaps that was why she was as shy as she was. She never saw him animated when he was around strangers, and she thusly behaved in a similar fashion. It was only around those with whom he had a close familiarity that he felt comfortable enough to engage in any sort of extended conversation, and it was only since his marriage to Elizabeth that he ever showed any sort of liveliness himself.

The balls had been magical; the dancing superb. Perhaps her season in town had had the effect on her that her brother had so desired. It had drawn her out, provided her with introductions to several eligible young men, and perhaps shown her what she would miss if she were ever to marry someone like Mr. Bostwick. There was also the possible objective that she would forget what her feelings toward him had been entirely.

Mr. Bostwick. Being away from him all these months made it seem as though everything that had passed between them had been a dream. Had she really felt so strongly for him? Had he really kissed her and made her feel as he did? They had been home a month now and she had not seen him. She had even gone out to the church with Elizabeth to visit the deaf classes and did not see him there. She began to wonder if he had solely been a figment of her imagination!

She finally saw his father working out on the grounds one day, and walked up to him.

"Good day, Mr. Bostwick."

"Why, hello, Miss Darcy. How was your time in town?"

"It was very enjoyable, thank you, Sir."

"I understand that you were presented at court."

"Yes, I was."

"Did you attend all the compulsory balls after that, then? There were probably quite a few."

"I cannot say that I attended all I could have, but there were several." Georgiana paused. "I hope that your family is well, Mr. Bostwick."

The elder Bostwick met her eyes. He nodded and stated, "They are all fine, Miss Darcy. Thank you for inquiring of them."

Georgiana was hoping for more, but nothing else was forthcoming. "I am glad to hear that. Please excuse me."

Georgiana turned to leave, feeling disappointed, and somewhat akin to being in the middle of a conspiracy. She felt from the glance he had given her that he was aware of her feelings toward his son and possibly his for her. If he felt it was wrong as strongly as her brother did, she was convinced that she would most likely never see him again!

Georgiana went back into the house and walked to her room. She picked up her journal that she had faithfully been writing in during their time in London.

She had found it most helpful while she was there, especially when she was in situations where she had the tendency to pull into herself. When she was pressed to have to come up with conversation, she recalled things she had written in it. She had begun a page, which had actually become several pages, entitled, "Things That I Feel Comfortable Talking About." She began making lists of anything and everything in which she had at least a small degree of knowledge. It had almost become a game for her, to try and bring up at least one of those subjects in every conversation in which she found herself. It had actually worked for her!

She looked further into her journal to the pages she entitled, "Men I Met in London" and reread her descriptions of some of the young men who had sought out introductions with her.

Mr. John Holcomb -- tall and blonde, laughs a little too frequently and does not seem interested in what I am saying. Very much like Andrew Lochlin. Claims to like music, but when pressed about composers, had very little to confirm his claim.

Mr. Joseph Parker -- not very tall, not very handsome. I believe he is quieter than I am; impossible as that sounds. Terribly difficult to carry on a conversation with him. Cannot recall one thing that interests him as he did not speak enough to inform me.

Mr. Theodore Shilling -- I must confess he was handsome. He was a gentleman and a cheerful conversationalist. I gave consent for a second calling. Brother seemed pleased with him. He knows his family well and would consider him a highly suitable match for me. So what did I find about him that did not meet my expectations? I do not know. I cannot say, but something was missing. It is for the better, because I believe he felt something was missing as well.

Mr. Richard Bleakly -- do not like the name. Looks much like his name. Seemed to me to be a little too desperate. His prospects for a second calling are bleak.

Georgiana giggled at that entry. It was not kind of her, but she had been in a peculiar mood that day and he received the brunt of her peculiar musings.

The names went on and on. She picked up her journal and decided to take it outside to read and make some entries for the day. William and Elizabeth had gone to a neighbouring estate to visit some friends who were passing through and staying with family there. She walked over to the swing, and sat down, opening her journal again and reading through the entries she had written.

She was not really swinging, but swaying, as she read about her and Catherine's presentation at court, their ball which followed, and all the other balls they subsequently attended. Her coming out season had proved to be all that she had ever hoped it to be. It had been a delightful time, but there had been no special connection between her and any of the men she was introduced to.

Catherine had seemed to enjoy every introduction, every dance, and every gentleman that called. But she, too, had come away disappointed. Whereas she sought and welcomed the attentions of the gentlemen, once it was discovered that she was only related to the Darcys through marriage, that her family was not of a very high breeding, and there was little wealth associated with her family, the calls dwindled, and then ceased.

She made light of it by saying that she knew all along there would not be a man good enough for her. She rationalized away her disappointment by saying it would be best for her to return to Longbourn and accept who she really was. Georgiana knew that Catherine had set her hopes upon meeting someone of high standing, and she was certain that if they had attended all the balls they had been invited to, she may have eventually met someone willing to love her despite who her family was and what they were worth. But as it was, she went home with only fond memories of a very enjoyable season in town, being presented before the queen, and able to make the claim that she was the first and most likely only, Bennet daughter to do so.

Catherine had to admit a disappointment that she never felt herself truly accepted as one of the fashionable ladies of good breeding, connections and fortune. She could not help but realize that most likely it was because she was not.

Georgiana's mind was thus engaged when she felt the swing suddenly pushed from behind. Her heart leapt as she smiled at the thought that David was behind her like he had been so many months before. This time, however, when the swing went back, the hands did not push the swing, but rested on her back as she was pushed. Instead of welcoming this unexpected touch, it made her feel most uncomfortable. She was quite ready to turn around and speak her mind to David when she saw that it was not David! It was George Wickham!

Georgiana gasped as he quickly came around and wrapped one of his hands around her wrist, bringing the swing to a stop. "Hello, my sweet Georgiana." His eyes held a sinister gleam in them.

"Mister Wickham! What are you doing here?" Georgiana could not prevent the flush from overspreading her face.

Wickham eyed her with a feigned look of disappointment. "What is this *Mister* Wickham? What happened to George? You used to call me George," he whispered as he leaned it toward her. "Do you not remember how well we thought George and Georgiana sounded?"

Georgiana trembled and tried to remove her hand from his grasp, but was not able to. "What is it you want, Mr. Wickham?"

He shook his head, "Georgiana, I have only come for what was supposed to have been mine!"

Fear coursed through Georgiana as the look he gave her suddenly made her fear his presence. "I do not know what you mean." Georgiana pulled harder this time, causing Wickham to grab her with his other hand, forcing her to drop her journal.

"Come Georgiana, I know you are not that naïve. You must know that you are the only woman I have ever wanted."

At that, Georgiana was pulled from the swing and as she tried to scream, his hand went across her mouth. With one hand free now, Georgiana tried pounding him, but it appeared to have little effect. With very little effort he was able to drag her away from the swing, and into the direction of the trees that bordered the children's play area.

Georgiana's heart pounded. If only she could scream, perhaps one of the gardeners would hear her. She had to escape from his grasp, but he was too powerful, and it seemed the more she struggled, the tighter his grip on her became.

He forcefully brought her into the wooded area behind Pemberley. No one would be there; no one would hear her this far away from the house and the gardens. There would be no gardeners around, as this part of the woods was left as natural as possible. They came upon a horse he had secured earlier, and he brought her over to it.

"Now, Georgiana, I am going to release my hand from your mouth, and I would not scream if I were you. I have a knife and I am not afraid to use it. Besides, no one will hear you this far away from the house." With that, he removed his hand from her mouth and pulled a knife from the saddle bag, just to show her he was not lying.

With tears filling her eyes, and her body shaking, she asked, "Why are you doing this?"

"Why? Why you ask?" Wickham sneered. "Because it is your family's fault, particularly your brother's fault for the ruin of my life!" He began pulling out rope from the saddle bag on the horse with his free hand. "Your father promised me a living and your brother denied giving it to me. You promised yourself to me and your brother interfered and stopped it. And just recently, I was to be married to a very fine, well bred lady, whose wealth would have been all I ever needed to live a most comfortable life, and your sister-in-law began spreading some vicious rumours about me that brought that to an end!"

"My sister-in-law?"

"Yes, your sister-in-law Lydia! And the stories she began telling were stories I understand *you* told her!" Wickham took out the rope and he began to tie Georgiana's hands behind her.

She looked down at the ground, and felt herself beginning to feel faint. A wave of dizziness swept through her causing her to lose ability to think rationally. She felt she would faint any minute. But by sheer force and determination she forced herself to think of something to do... something to say... to change Wickham's mind as to whatever his plans were for her. She had to try to calm him down and get him to think about what he was doing.

The ropes hurt her wrists, and she winced. She watched him get out a cloth and come toward her mouth.

"What are you going to do?" she asked, her voice broken, revealing the panic beginning to overtake her. "I am sure my brother will pay you... anything you need... anything you ask for."

Wickham looked at her with astonishment. "My dearest Georgiana, do not worry, I shall ask your brother for money. And he shall pay me more than he ever has in the past. But dipping into his fortune will not cause him the same pain that he has caused me. That is far too easy for him." He wrapped the cloth around her mouth and tied it behind her head. "He must pay for what he has done to me, for the ruin he has inflicted on me, but not with just money." He then traced a finger down her cheek. "He needs to know what it is to hurt...to *really* hurt. What I want, I will take, and he will regret ever denying me what I deserved."

Georgiana could say no more with the cloth tightly wrapped around her mouth, but she had heard enough to know Wickham was angry and she was going to pay the price one way or another. As he picked her up and placed her on the horse, her eyes were too blurred with tears to determine where they were going. But there was one thing she was sure of. Wickham knew the territory and the lay of the land as well as anyone, having grown up and explored the woods and peaks that made up this county. She had no doubt he had made plans as to where they were going and she was sure it would not be nearby nor where any people would be close by.

It was late in the afternoon, so she knew they could not go far before stopping for the night. She was certain he would not try to travel at night. She could only hope that someone would see them and stop them. But if no one did, what would happen tomorrow? If he did intend to keep travelling, certainly she would be seen and people would be out looking for her by then. Her mind assaulted her with thoughts of what his intentions were, hopes that they would be discovered, and despair that they would not.

As her mind reeled, Wickham brought himself up on the horse and sat behind her. She felt something go over her, and realized it was a large hooded cloak. Although it may still look suspicious, she knew he might get away with this if he encountered anyone, as there was very little chance that anyone at present knew she was missing, let alone kidnapped. She had to come up with a plan before they got to wherever it was they were going. She never believed Wickham could be so heartless, revengeful, and evil! But at the moment, all she could do was pray.

~~*

Darcy and Elizabeth rushed into their house, with Durnham and Winston following quickly behind them. Mrs. Reynolds, in trying to greet them, was quickly interrupted.

"Where is Georgiana?" asked Darcy.

"Why I believe she is outside…"

"Durnham, Winston, see if you can find her and get her in! Elizabeth, would you please check her room and all the rooms upstairs where she might be?"

Elizabeth left immediately and rushed up the stairs, a look of concern sweeping across her face.

Mrs. Reynolds began to fear for the safety of the young lady, but could not fathom why. "What is it, Mr. Darcy? What is wrong?"

Darcy frantically walked the floor of the house, Mrs. Reynolds following behind him. "We just returned from Lambton. While we were there, we were told that Mr. Wickham had stayed at the inn last night." Darcy continued looking in the rooms Georgiana would most likely be in, and took in a ragged breath as he answered. "He has no business there. There can only be one reason he is here."

"Sir, certainly you do not think Miss Georgiana is in any kind of danger from him?"

"On the contrary, Mrs. Reynolds, I am *greatly* convinced of her danger from him. He feels betrayed by me and possibly even Georgiana. I have been witness to many malicious and revengeful actions on his part, and I will not rest easy until we know where she is and where *he* is!"

They soon ascertained that she was not on the main floor, and Elizabeth came down, shaking her head. "I cannot find her upstairs, Will."

They both quickly walked toward the door, to assist the two men who had been sent outside. Just as they reached the door, Winston came walking in, carrying something.

"What is it? asked Darcy.

"Sir, this was by the swing, in the dirt. I do believe it is Miss Darcy's journal."

Elizabeth gasped and her hand flew to her mouth. The journal looked like it had been dropped carelessly on the ground, very unlike the way Georgiana would have treated it. They all immediately ran outside, in the direction of the swing where it was found.

Durnham had set off walking towards to woods. Winston pointed to the swing. "This is where I found it, Sir."

"She must have been sitting on the swing writing in it or reading it, and something made her drop it." Elizabeth spoke the words but did not want to believe what they led her to believe.

Durnham came back from the wooded area. "Sir, I am afraid there is something up here you might want to see."

They hurried behind Durnham as he led the way. There were definitely signs that someone had been here. They found some signs of food that had been eaten and discarded recently. They walked further in, and saw the signs that a horse had been there.

Both of these things convinced Darcy of two things. First that someone had definitely been there. And secondly, that they had been there for some time just watching and waiting.

"Get the horses saddled, and round up whatever men you can!" Darcy barked the orders at Winston and Durnham. His breathing was harsh and Elizabeth could see the flames of anger burning within him.

Elizabeth came up to him and wrapped her fingers desperately around his arm. "You think it was him? You think Wickham was here and has taken Georgiana?" Tears began to swell up in her eyes, and her mind did not want to accept what they were now being forced to accept.

"I have no reason to doubt it, Lizbeth. He *was* here; I feel it in my bones."

The look etched on his face frightened Elizabeth almost more than the fact that Georgiana could not be found.

"Will, you do not think he will do anything?"

"I will not put anything past him." They walked swiftly toward the front of the house. "Lizbeth, you remain here. If there is any news, send someone out for us. But you must remain here."

There was something he was not telling her and it frightened her. "Will, he has only done this as a malicious way of extorting money from you, has he not?"

Darcy turned to her with great pain etched on his face. "This time, I fear, it is not just for the money."

"What do you mean?"

"He wants to hurt me more than I have ever been hurt before, and I believe he intends to do it with Georgiana."

Chapter 20

The once tranquil haven that was Pemberley was suddenly chaotic and turned upside down. Darcy gathered whatever men could be found to help in the search. He kept one back to remain with Elizabeth for fear that Wickham might come back for her. The decision whether to leave Elizabeth or go after Georgiana produced an inner battle within him, but in his heart he felt that Wickham would not return. Darcy was fairly confident that he was putting as much distance as he could between himself and his former home.

As to the direction they had gone he did not know, but Darcy felt that he would most likely keep to the woods where there would be less chance to be seen. That presented a problem in that the woods were extensive and they could have set off in any number of directions. The woods were too dense to give any indication of a trail that was left, so it was solely up to their speculation which route to take. Along the way they broke up and spread out, trying to cover as much terrain as possible.

Impatient and fretting back at Pemberley, Elizabeth could not rationally fathom how anyone could do something like this. It was painful to think about, difficult to imagine, and impossible to comprehend. She hated remaining back and doing nothing, but she was under the watchful eye of Smythe, one of the stable hands and was given resolute orders by her husband not to leave his presence or venture out.

Being so closely guarded to protect her from Wickham, and being able to do nothing while she waited for word on Georgiana, served solely to cause her reflection on that man's despicable behaviour. She had been so deceptively misled when she had first met him. To imagine she once thought of him as a gentleman -- a poor abused gentleman. She was overwhelmed with self rebuke and censure to think she had been so horribly wrong in deciding his character and regret that she had never made it public when she discovered the truth!

Her thoughts were of worry for her husband as well. What was Wickham capable of doing to him? What was her husband capable of doing in his present frame of mind? Her heart raced as she thought of Will's anger as he was leaving. Would he do something irrational, impulsive, or life threatening? It was all too much to bear.

Pacing anxiously back and forth, she approached the window several times and prayed that she would look out and see Georgiana walking back toward the house. She glanced at the sun which was slowly making its way toward the horizon, and shuddered to think that darkness and cold would soon sweep over the land. It was going to be terribly difficult to just wait. She was painfully aware that every moment they did not discover them could have devastating results.

Most of the female servants had congregated in the kitchen, holding a vigil of sorts. Georgiana was admired by each one of them, and they could not bear to think any harm could befall her. They talked in low, hushed voices, wondering what, if anything they could do. Alice, Georgiana's personal maid, began praying, and the others soon followed suit bowing their heads, folding their hands, as she offered up fervent requests for her protection and discovery.

When Alice finished praying, one of them suggested they begin preparing some food. In doing so, when the men returned and were hungry, they could offer them something to eat. In addition, it would give them something to do to help keep their minds off the dread and fear they all felt. Soon they were busy preparing a feast, and encouraged one another with words about how Georgiana would certainly need to eat when she returned.

Elizabeth's heart continued to pound with fear and dread as her feet pounded the ground in restless pacing. At the sound of a carriage pulling up out front, she hastened to the front door and opened it, without thinking that any danger might be on the other side. Smythe was there with her, ready to risk life and limb to protect her in the chance it was Wickham. It was Jacques, however, returning from an errand.

"Oh, Jacques! It is terrible!" Elizabeth collapsed in tears as the strain of waiting was taking its toll on her.

Jacques shook his head trying to comprehend what she was saying. "What do you mean? What is it?"

"We believe Georgiana has been kidnapped!"

"Kidnapped? By whom?" Shock swept through Jacques and spread across his face.

"Mr. Wickham. A former acquaintance who once lived here at Pemberley… the son of the elder Mr. Darcy's steward. The men have gone off to look for them!"

Jacques began immediately to unhitch the horse from the carriage. "What can I do?"

Elizabeth was not sure what to tell him. He would not be familiar with the terrain. "Spread the word! Go to the nearby houses and notify them. The men that are able can go out and help search. Just make sure they all know to be on the lookout for Wickham!"

Jacques soon had the horse ready to ride, and he hopped on. "Do not worry, Mrs. Darcy, she will be found!"

Jacques immediately set out, trying to determine which direction to go. Suddenly a thought occurred to him that there were some people who needed to know about this, and he determined to go there first. He headed directly over to the Bostwicks' home, knowing that although it would be difficult to hear, David Bostwick would wish to be told. From there he would go to the parsonage and inform Reverend Kenton.

He rode swiftly, and although he felt as if it took him forever to get there, it actually took no more than about ten minutes to get to the modest Bostwick home. He dropped down from the horse and ran up to the door and knocked loudly and quickly.

The door opened and the elder Mr. Bostwick greeted him. "Good afternoon, Jacques. What brings you here so…"

"It is Georgiana, Sir! She is missing!"

"Jacques, calm down. What happened?" He put his hand upon the young man's shoulder to help settle his nerves and bring him in; calling at the same time to his son. "David! Come in here at once!" He turned back to Jacques. "Now, tell me, son, what is this all about?"

"Georgiana… she has been kidnapped!"

"Kidnapped?" came a painful cry from the other side of the room. David had just walked in, and grabbed the wall, as if helping steady him.

Jacques looked to David, and nodded. "They think it was someone who once lived at Pemberley… the son of a steward."

David looked at his father. "Wickham!"

His father nodded, as well as Jacques. "Yes, that is his name!"

David turned to grab a coat. "Son, what are you going to do?" asked his father.

"I believe I know where he may have taken her and I am heading there at once!"

"How could you know where they went?"

"I do not have time to explain, Father, but you must find Samuel. Have him direct you and some men to the cave we once followed Wickham to when we were younger. I am sure he will remember." He then turned to Jacques. "May I use your horse, and Father will ready another one for you?"

"Absolutely!"

"David! You cannot go alone! Wait for one of us!"

"There is no time. Just go find Samuel and get there as soon as you are able!"

"Come with me, Jacques," Mr. Bostwick said. "Let's get those other horses and find Samuel at once!"

David rushed outside, adrenalin and anger adding impetus to the effort he exerted to move as quickly as he could. He jumped upon the horse, grabbing the reins in the process and digging his heels into the horse's flanks. He could not come up with one other thought than getting to Georgiana before anything happened to her.

The trees lining the road sped past him in a blur as he calculated in his mind the best way to get to this destination. If Wickham had indeed kidnapped her, he would certainly not take her any place, such as to Lambton, where there was a chance people might see him. Most everyone in Lambton still remembered Wickham, and they were certainly well acquainted with Georgiana. He was fairly certain Georgiana would not have gone with him on her own volition… he hoped not. That meant she was most likely in danger. He could only hope that he or any of the other men out looking for them would find them. He was not sure Wickham would be at the cave, but he knew there was a great possibility.

He recalled that day years ago, when he and Samuel thought they were being so clever in following George Wickham to the secret hiding place he had been boasting to them about. He claimed to have found a secluded place that one could get to from Pemberley without crossing any road but one, travelling through the dense woods, and one would be hard pressed to discover him.

That was a challenge enough for the two boys, who were often the brunt of Wickham's mean practical jokes and teasing. One day, when he was upset over something his father had asked him to do, believing he was above doing such a thing, Wickham angrily walked away. In front of the boys, he said he was going to his secret hiding place and no one, not even his father, would be able to find him.

Wickham may have been good at exploring the surrounding areas and finding obscure places to hide in, but he was ill equipped at detecting that he was being followed. It was true that the woods provided a constant cover for him on his way to this secluded sight, and it was not until they were in sight of the peaks that they finally came out from the woods. There had been only one country road he had to cross to get there. They watched as Wickham rode up to a rocky area, and sure enough, after he dismounted his horse, saw him walk into a small opening at the edge of the peaks.

They never let him know they followed him, and neither of them ever returned to explore the cave but once, years later. David was sure that he would be able to find it, and was just as certain his brother would remember its general location as well. He did not like Wickham; he never had. He never understood the elder Mr. Darcy's partiality to him, and certainly knew for a fact that he had not been a good influence on Miss Darcy.

Miss Darcy! Georgiana! What would she suffer at his hands? He kicked the horse again, desperately trying to spur him into a faster gallop. He knew in reality, however, that the horse was exerting all the effort he could, and kicking the horse was more out of anger and frustration than anything else.

He had one thing in his favour. If Wickham was on a horse with Georgiana, he would not be able to move as quickly. The horse would be weighted down more, so he would not be able to travel as quickly. The only question was how long ago had he kidnapped her? And of course, was this where he was taking her?

~~*

Wickham found his planned hideaway just as he remembered it. He dismounted, and pulled Georgiana off the horse after him. He removed the cloak that had covered her, and brought her towards the cave. He brought her in and mercilessly pushed her to the ground. She looked up at him briefly with disbelief in her eyes. He reached down and removed the cloth that had covered her mouth, but he did not untie her hands, which were tied together in front of her. She turned away from him, unable to fathom the hatred she saw in his face, unable to meet his eyes for the way he had handled her on the ride to this secluded place.

"I should imagine that at this moment your brother is a little concerned. His sweet, little, innocent sister gone. Do you suppose he knows you are safe in my care?"

Georgiana did not turn to him as she said in disgust, "I am not safe in your care!"

"What is this? You were once planning to marry me!" He squatted down in front of her and forcefully turned her face toward his. "You should have, you know!" She closed her eyes, for the sneer that crossed Wickham's face sent frightful chills through her body.|

~~*

With his mind set on one thing, David eventually made his way through the heavily wooded area, and came out on the other side in view of the peaks. The sun was just setting, and he knew he had to move quickly. But he also had to keep his eyes open so that if they were in the area, he would see them before Wickham saw him.

He slowed the horse down, and looked out across at the peaks. He was fairly certain the cave was south of where he now was, but watched out for any sign of them as he led the horse in that direction. He kept his horse to the edge of the woods, hoping that would give him some concealment.

At length he saw a horse tied to a tree, but somewhat hidden from view. It was directly across from where David remembered the cave to be situated. David's heart began pounding as he offered a prayer of thanks for finding them, as well as a prayer of protection for Georgiana as he now had to make an attempt to retrieve her from Wickham's clutches.

He rode slowly and quietly toward the lone horse, the sound of his erratically beating heart drowning out even the sound of the horse's hoof beats. When he finally reached the horse, he quickly dismounted. He ran his hand along the other horse, and he had no doubt that it had not been here long. It was still panting and sweating from a hard run. He looked toward the peaks and saw the cave immediately in front of him. He brought his horse and tethered it so it would be readily seen, as he would want the others to easily find them. He half walked, half ran toward the cave, working a plan in his mind, but really not knowing what he would do until he looked in the cave and appraised the situation.

It was questionable whether Wickham was armed with some sort of weapon or whether he was capable of violence. But he knew that if he was capable of kidnapping Georgiana, he had to assume he was capable of anything. He came to the edge of the cave and pressed himself quietly against the rock, listening for any voices. It was silent at first and he slowly began inching his face toward the opening.

Suddenly he heard a voice he recognized oh so well. "It will do you no good to fight me, Georgiana. I intend to get what I came for."

David knew he had to act fast and leaned his head further in. Georgiana was crouched in a corner of the small cave. Wickham's back was to him, bending down to Georgiana. He had no time to lose. He was about to charge into the cave when Georgiana caught sight of him, jerking her head his way, and crying out.

Wickham took no time in reaching down and grabbing her, and at the same time putting his knife to Georgiana's throat. He turned to face the young man at the entrance of the cave. "Stay right there. I have no qualms in using this!"

David put his hands up, showing that he had no weapon, and wanting nothing more than to keep Wickham calm and not push him over the edge, risking injury to Georgiana. "I have no weapons. Just let the girl go."

"No! She and her fortune belong to me and no one will take them from me this time." He held Georgiana tighter and took a few steps back.

David noticed the pale colouring and the fear spreading across her face, realizing he needed to do something quickly. He looked around the cave, trying to formulate some plan. In the meantime he would try to work on Wickham.

"Think about what you are doing… Sir. The girl has done nothing to you. Others will be here soon. You have no choice but to give yourself up."

"Others are coming, huh? And why are they not here with you?" Wickham sneered. "I think not. You just happened upon me by chance. No one will find us here!"

David slowly took small steps toward him. He knew that at any moment Georgiana might faint. He had seen similar colouring and expression on her just before she fainted at the ball. His mind frantically searched for something to do; something to say to appease this explosive situation.

Suddenly Wickham looked at him oddly, one eyebrow rising in speculation. His expression changed, and David was not sure why. Very slowly and suspiciously he said, "Wait just a moment. I know you! Where do I know you from?"

David started at this, grateful for the opportunity to stall any further thought of Wickham hurting Georgiana and quickly replied, "From Pemberley. I grew up around the grounds as you did."

"No, no! I have not been to Pemberley in five years! I know you from somewhere else, grown up as you are now, not some kid!"

David glanced over at Georgiana and saw that she was even more pale than the last time he looked. She was going to go down at any moment.

Suddenly Wickham blurted out, "Ramsgate!"

David turned back to Wickham in shock and suddenly Georgiana was pulled out of her near fainting state, the name 'Ramsgate' causing her to feel a panic surge within her.

David, however, said nothing, looking from Georgiana, ascertaining her condition and back to Wickham.

"You were at Ramsgate!" Wickham hurled at him again.

Georgiana now looked upon David with a different kind of fear. What could he be talking about, David being at Ramsgate? She could not help but notice the expression that changed on David's face.

He tried to dissuade Wickham from continuing on about his assumptions.

"Sir, I do not know what you mean. Now, hand the girl over to me before someone gets hurt."

"No, you were at Ramsgate! You were the one who so willingly provided me with drink all the while prodding me for details about my engagement! I thought you were a little too interested. Now I know why!" Wickham suddenly taunted David with, "I suppose you wanted to secure Georgiana for yourself! Now you are here thinking you can claim her for your own!"

Georgiana's eyes opened wide, feeling shame and regret sweep over her. Did he know about her and Wickham?

Wickham continued on, insisting he had no doubt it was him. As she kept her eyes on David, she suddenly realized he was making repetitive movements with his hands. At once it occurred to her that he was signing out a word.

She did everything she could to concentrate on what he was spelling out. "I...N...T...F...A...I...N...T..."

Faint! He wants me to faint! She moved her eyes up to his and slightly nodded, letting him know she understood. He gave her a reassuring look with his eyes and took another step forward. Georgiana knew she had to do this right, as her falling to the ground would hopefully distract Wickham enough to allow David to overpower him.

She closed her eyes, and then, when she felt she was ready, she looked back up to him and gave a single nod of her head. She purposely allowed her body to go completely limp and Wickham found her unexpectedly slipping through his grasp. As Wickham reacted by going down to try and catch her, David lurched forward, grabbing the wrist of his hand that held the knife, and pushing him away from Georgiana.

The three went down, and for a few moments David had the advantage. He manoeuvred Wickham's hands so that he no longer had a hold on Georgiana. "Get out of here, Georgiana! My horse is tied up outside! Get on the horse and get out of here!"

Georgiana paused, as she saw the two men struggle for possession of the knife. Fear kept her glued to where she was; not wanting to leave David alone in the grips of Wickham. David struggled to turn his head and saw that she was still there. "Please, get out of here! Get on the horse and see if you can find the others who are searching for you!"

Georgiana finally realized that was the best thing she could do for him, to bring him help. She could do nothing to assist David with her hands tied as they were. She ran outside, saw the horse and mounted it, grateful that her hands were not tied behind her back. Her heart beat wildly as she kicked the horse, hoping and praying fervently that she would find some of the others soon, to bring help for David.

David continued to keep his grip on Wickham, but the two were fairly equally matched in strength. Wickham still had the knife, and in that, he had the advantage. With a sudden, unexpected lunge, Wickham lashed out at David with the knife, catching him across his shoulder. David winced, but was able to push his hand back down. He knew that the knife had cut deeply, and could feel the warmth of the blood running down his arm. He knew his strength would soon begin to wane.

David had to keep Wickham down at least until Georgiana had a good enough head start to get herself to safety. That was his only goal. He knew that as his strength faded, Wickham would have no scruples that would prevent him from finishing him with the knife. At least he could know in his heart that Georgiana would be safe if he held on long enough.

The two men had not changed position since David had first leapt upon him. They were both exerting all their effort; David trying to keep Wickham down, and Wickham making every effort to push him off. David began feeling weak and knew he only had a few more seconds in which he would be able to continue his hold.

Wickham realized he would soon be able to push off this foolish upstart and make him pay for his interference. He let off a little, conserving some strength, and just when he felt David's strength begin to give out…

David was suddenly pulled off of him, and his weakening body was replaced by three or four men who came down on Wickham. David was brought over to the side, relief sweeping over him, and he looked into the face of Reverend Kenton and his father. His hand immediately went to his wound, pressing in tightly to help diminish the blood flow.

"You came just in time…" David said weakly. "I do not think I could have held him off any longer."

"You did well, Bostwick. Now take it easy. Let me look at that wound." Kenton began looking at the wound and found the cloth that had bound Georgiana's mouth and wrapped it tightly around his arm. "You need to get that cleaned out as soon as you get back."

David looked over at the men who had brought Wickham up and bound his hands. Samuel was one of them, and he met his brother's eyes and nodded with gratitude. Samuel helped the men take Wickham out, and then returned to his brother. "Were you seriously injured, David?"

"I shall be fine. Just a flesh wound."

"Good, we were worried we would not get here in time."

"Did you see Miss Darcy?" asked David with genuine concern.

His father answered. "We encountered her on the horse and she brought us back to you. Her brother is outside with her now. On our way here we found him, as well. We thought it best they not come near. Some of the men are shielding Georgiana so she does not have to see Wickham. They are holding her brother back because of his anger towards Wickham."

David nodded. He could hear the men mounting their horses, and assumed they were taking Wickham away. Kenton, his father, and brother remained with him while he tried to gain a little of his strength back.

The four sat quietly, letting David rest as long as he needed to. He took in deep breaths, and his father gave him a flask filled with water to drink. He closed his eyes and felt he could fall asleep right there.

"It was good you remembered this place, David," said his brother. "I do not think I would have, on my own."

David only nodded. His only concern now was that Georgiana was safe. But in the back of his mind he longed to give her the comfort she would require after having to endure such an incident. But he would have to relegate that to her brother.

Suddenly a figure appeared in the door. The sun had just set, and because of the darkness, he could not determine who it was. David strained his eyes to make out the figure who stood at the entrance of the cave, but did not enter.

"I wanted to personally thank you, Bostwick, for your quick thinking and being responsible for my sister's safety. Were you injured? Georgiana wanted to… we both wanted to make sure Wickham did not hurt you."

"I am hurt, but it is not serious."

'I am glad to hear that. I cannot thank you enough, Bostwick. She owes her life to you, and we are all greatly indebted to you and your quick thinking."

David nodded and Darcy turned away. The words were simple and few, but they meant a lot. He did not want anything from Darcy but respect, and these were the first words of respect he had spoken to him in quite a long time!

Chapter 21

Elizabeth, having endured the ever increasing alarm and fear of waiting for word to come about Georgiana, rushed anxiously to the door when she heard the sound of horses approach the house. She hurriedly stepped outside and felt both relief and concern sweep over her when she saw her husband coming toward the house carrying Georgiana in his arms.

"How is she?" Elizabeth cried.

Darcy seemed unable to answer in complete sentences. "Unhurt… scared… get her to her room."

Georgiana buried her face against her brother's shoulder, her arms wrapped tightly around his neck. She did not move, as Darcy took the stairs in long, determined strides. Elizabeth followed close behind.

The Pemberley servants, who had been waiting as anxiously as Elizabeth, huddled around Winston and Durnham peppering the two men with questions. The imperative question they wanted answered was "how is she?" and then they wanted to know everything that happened.

Darcy and Elizabeth continued in silence up to Georgiana's room. As they entered it, Elizabeth watched as Darcy laid her on her bed, her eyes searching his with questions. When he released her, Georgiana instantly turned away and curled up, releasing an onslaught of tears. Elizabeth decided the answers would have to wait, and walked over and sat down on the bed next to the young lady. She began lightly stroking Georgiana's untidy hair and soiled face, whispering assurances that she was now safe, in loving hands, and promising her that this would never happen again.

She kept her eyes on the face of her husband, noticing the exhaustion, grief, and anger visible in every feature. She felt he needed her comforting touch and words as well. She extended her hand towards him, and he took the single step needed to reach for it. She gently gave it a squeeze and he returned to her an appreciative smile.

After a few moments had passed and Georgiana's tears had somewhat subsided, Darcy motioned for Elizabeth to come with him. She joined him by the door of the room. "Lizbeth, stay with her awhile and see if you can get her to talk. She would not say a word to me all the way back. I shall be in my study. When you feel as though you can leave her, come down and we will talk."

Elizabeth glanced back with overwhelming compassion to the figure lying on the bed. "I will see what I can do, Will."

She walked back over to Georgiana as Darcy left the room and sat down again and stroked her face, removing several strands of hair that had fallen across it. She noticed that Georgiana's eyes were wide open, staring straight ahead, red from crying, but now were dry. Elizabeth wondered if the fear of the images that might appear prevented her from closing them.

Darcy returned downstairs to a solemn group of servants. "How is she? Is Miss Darcy going to be all right?" they asked.

Darcy raked his fingers soberly through his hair. "Physically she is well. Emotionally, I fear, she is in a lot of pain. She went through a dreadful time out there."

There was a collective sigh as they considered what their favoured young lady had to endure. "And how are *you*, Sir?" asked Winston.

Darcy looked at him with eyes that seemed to look right past him. "Angry, scared, relieved, confused." He shook his head. "I really do not know how I am!"

Darcy turned and slowly began to walk away. "I shall be in my study if anyone has need of me."

He walked into his study, feeling dangerously close to lashing out at anything or anyone. When he closed the door behind him, he tightened his hand into a fist and pounded once against the wall. He had always prided himself for his steadfast self control, and now berated himself for his lack of it. He was certain that if he had happened upon Wickham first, he would have had no qualms in dealing with him in a way he felt he deserved and would have left Wickham unable to get up and walk away when it was over. But it distressed him to realize that very reaction made him an equal to Wickham in desiring revenge!

Darcy poured himself some port to help relax his overly taxed nerves. He felt that every muscle in his body was taut, due to the strain of the last several hours. He absently sipped at his drink, desirous for its calming effect to overtake him quickly, but his mind would not release the very thing that was causing him so much disquiet.

For the past few hours he had been running solely on fear and anger, and now, as he sat at his desk and faced the solitude of his study, the reality of the day's events began to sink in. He had come very close to losing Georgiana, or at the very least losing the innocence that was hers. As his mind contemplated that truth, he dropped his head onto his arms, closed his eyes, and allowed a few tears to escape.

Some of those tears were out of self-censure, for not being there to protect his sister, for not taking the time with her two years ago so Wickham would not have even had the chance to form designs on her.

His tears also fell out of grief for what Georgiana had to suffer at Wickham's hands. First it was a love denied and ultimately discovered to not be love at all, but a deception motivated by her fortune. This time it was her very life that had been threatened by him.

He sat up, taking a deep breath to restore his faculties and took another sip of his port. The tears had stopped, not because his grief had ended, but because he was a man who did not cry often, and when he did, it was very little. He saw more benefit in putting his emotional energy into deliberate action. He resolutely determined that he would have to be strong for Georgiana and Elizabeth. They would both need him to be.

Darcy stood up from his desk and paced, and then angrily sat down again, reviewing the past few hours. He wondered how Elizabeth was doing with his sister, and hoped she was able to provide the comfort that he doubted he would be able to give Georgiana in his present frame of mind.

Finally, in the early morning hours of the new day, Elizabeth came to his study. Darcy quickly stood up as she came in the door and went to her, putting his arms around her. Her eyes were red from tears, her face was drawn with fatigue, and a look of concern covered her face.

"She is asleep," she began. "But I fear it will be a fitful night. I should like to sleep in the room next to hers in case she wakes up."

"Of course," Darcy had taken her hand and brought her to a chair. He sat down next to her, continuing to hold her hand, to give her strength as well as draw strength from her. "Did she say anything?"

Elizabeth nodded gravely. "It was very difficult for her to talk about it. She said Wickham made some accusations that his present difficulties were the result of your infliction, threats that this time you would feel as much pain as he had felt… and that he would take what should have been his all along."

Darcy's jaw tightened and his face reddened in anger again. "Elizabeth, did we get there in time… is she… did he…?"

Elizabeth looked up at her husband. "Fortunately, we may comfort ourselves with the knowledge that Mr. Bostwick did get there in time. She is unharmed in that way." She breathed in deeply before continuing. "But he did handle her in an exceedingly improper and rough way while on the horse." Darcy's grip on her hand tightened involuntarily and he trembled in anger as he heard this. "Of course she feels much betrayed."

Darcy stood up and turned away, not wanting Elizabeth to see the anger building up inside of him. His heart throbbed erratically and he struggled for composure before allowing himself to say anything. He slammed his fist into the palm of his other hand, digging and twisting it mercilessly. Words would not come, as his anger had so overtaken him.

Elizabeth walked over to him and stood behind him. "She told me what happened when Mr. Bostwick arrived. Are you aware of the particulars?"

Elizabeth felt as well as saw the tenseness begin to loosen as he turned around. He brought up his arm and wrapped it around her shoulders, "No, tell me."

Elizabeth told him of David's arrival at the cave and Georgiana reacting to seeing him, causing Wickham to grab her and hold her at knife point. "She said he was trying to get Wickham to put the knife down and not hurt anyone, when she noticed he was signing a word. It took her a while to realize what he was doing, and then she had to struggle to figure out what it was he was spelling out."

"What was he signing?"

"He was signing the word 'faint.' He *wanted* her to faint. When she realized it, she nodded to him that she understood, and when she went down, Wickham reacted by reaching for her. Mr. Bostwick lunged at him and grabbed for the hand with the knife."

"Clever thinking on his part."

"Yes," nodded Elizabeth. "She went on to say that once Mr. Bostwick had Wickham pinned, he yelled at her to get out of there and take his horse and ride. She was fearful to leave, afraid what Wickham might do to him, but he demanded she get out of there. So she rode out, found your party which had met up with the party of men with Samuel Bostwick who were headed to the cave as well."

Darcy went to his chair and fell back into it. "It appears we should be grateful they both had taken sign language classes."

Elizabeth nodded. "Yes, and possibly grateful as well that Georgiana fainted as she did in front of Mr. Bostwick at the ball. He may not have thought of having her do that, had she not."

Darcy let a slight smile grace his face.

"There was *one* thing, though, that seemed to distress Georgiana almost as much as anything else Wickham did," Elizabeth added in a most serious tone.

"What was that?"

"Wickham began making some claims that he had seen Mr. Bostwick in Ramsgate. He was saying something about him being the one prying for information about his engagement to Georgiana."

Darcy met her contemplative expression with one of surprise. "What could he have meant by that?"

"That is exactly what Georgiana wanted to know. She wonders, with great dismay, whether Mr. Bostwick is aware of what she did... what she *almost* did at Ramsgate two years ago. If he knows, she would feel so humiliated."

Elizabeth walked over to her husband and kissed the top of his head. "I think I shall go back up now, in case she awakens. Will you be able to sleep?"

"I fear none of us will sleep as well as we should. I shall be up for a while longer. You try to get a good night's sleep, Lizbeth. Come get me if you need me."

"I shall. Good night, Will. I love you."

Darcy stood up and wrapped his arms tightly around her, pulling her close as much for his expression of love as for the comfort it offered him. "I love you, too." His voice broke as all the pain and love he was feeling was evoked in those four simple words.

~~*

That night more than the Darcys were unable to sleep well. David Bostwick struggled with sleep most of the night. Fear had both gripped him when he first heard of Georgiana's kidnapping and had spurred him on when he really had no assurance he would find them.

He was grateful that he had found them and she had escaped Wickham's evil clutches. But he would do anything in his power to erase this night from her memory. He knew the pain and fear she had suffered would likely affect her emotionally for a long time.

He worried and wondered how she was faring. He felt he had earned the right to know and express his concern for her. He decided he would continue to honour Darcy's command to stay off the property, but he would write a note, not to Georgiana, but to Darcy, inquiring how she was doing and offering whatever comfort he could express in words.

While sleep eluded him, he began penning the missive he would dispatch to Pemberley first thing in the morning. He agonized over each word as he wrote, somehow hoping Darcy would see the genuine care and concern he had for Georgiana. He wrote:

Mr. and Mrs. Darcy,

Last night was a night all of us would wish had never happened. Why it had to happen one cannot fathom. And why it had to happen to Miss Darcy, God only knows. I would only wish that I could have taken her place and spared her the whole frightful nightmare.

I do hope and pray that this morning will bestow on her a freedom from the fear and terror that she had to endure at the hands of Wickham. I hope she can put this behind her and not allow it to continually grieve her. I am genuinely concerned for her and do hope that you will see fit to express my concern to her.

Your humble servant,
David Bostwick

~~*

The next morning Georgiana elected to remain in her room, seeking its solace and refuge, not desiring to come down and face anyone. She did allow Alice, her maid, to dress her, and for Elizabeth to come to visit with her as often as she wished.

Elizabeth had checked in on her several times during the night when she cried out. Neither slept well, and Elizabeth felt that emotionally Georgiana had a long way to go to recover. She felt that staying in her room this morning was what she most needed.

When Elizabeth finally descended the stairs and entered the dining room that morning, she saw that her husband was already there. When she looked at him, she felt his looks mirrored hers. It was painfully apparent that he did not sleep well either.

"Good morning, Will."

"Good morning, Lizbeth. How are you this morning? How is Georgiana?"

"Tired!" Elizabeth chuckled lightly. "She awoke several times in the night. She remains in her room by choice, as she does not want to come downstairs yet."

Darcy nodded. "Perhaps I should go to her." He started to get up, but Elizabeth stopped him by putting her hand upon his arm.

"Take care with her, Will. She is hurting a great deal."

He nodded and flew up the stairs to his sister's room. Elizabeth went to the sideboard and selected from a small drawer a stash of special ingredients for her favourite tea; camomile, honey and peppermint. If ever she was in need of its soothing effect, it was now. She let it brew as she carried it back to the table where she sat down and began to sip it.

It was quite a few minutes before Darcy returned. His manner seemed stiff, and he sat down beside Elizabeth, taking her hand.

"Something is wrong, Elizabeth."

"What is it?"

"I may not be the best comforter in the world, but I always have been able to somewhat soothe Georgiana's spirits by holding her. She has always welcomed a comforting hug from me when she is hurting. This morning she wanted nothing to do with me. She pushed me away."

Elizabeth reached over and took his hand. "Georgiana is feeling much distress about the way Wickham handled her, and the thought of a man, any man, touching her in even the most innocent way, might be causing her much anxiety. Even a loving hug from you right now would not be received by her in the way you would wish."

"How dare that Wickham!" Darcy spewed out.

"It will pass, Will. It will take some time. It may require you to be sensitive to her. When she is ready to receive your comfort and affections again, she will let you know."

Darcy closed his eyes as he realized the pain his sister was experiencing.

Mrs. Reynolds appeared cautiously at the door of the dining room. "Excuse me, please, but a letter from Mr. Bostwick was delivered." She handed it to Darcy as he stole a sly glance at Elizabeth. He looked down and began reading it to himself.

"What does he say?" she asked.

Darcy read the letter aloud. When he had finished reading it to her, Elizabeth commented, "That was very kind of him."

Darcy did not respond. His eyes remained fixed on the letter, his features becoming more and more clouded. He abruptly pushed his chair out from the table and said, "Excuse me," in a short, curt tone of voice.

Elizabeth sat in complete shock. That he would still harbour that kind of reaction to Mr. Bostwick after all he had done was beyond her. Could he not even appreciate the young man's concern for Georgiana and everything he had done last night? Or was this an example of her husband's resentful temper? Was his good opinion of David Bostwick lost forever? Had his opinion not even improved one degree in his mind?

She was too angry at that moment to follow him into the study and give him a piece of her mind. She sat at the table finishing her tea, not knowing how she would get through to him that his behaviour and attitude toward David Bostwick was most inexcusable.

When at last she finished her tea, she set out for his study. The door was closed when she came upon it, but she did not feel inclined at all to knock, so she burst forth through the door.

"Fitzwilliam Darcy. I have had enough of your unyielding behaviour and implacable resentment toward Mr. Bostwick. I know you do not consider him good enough for your sister, but apart from that, he is a good man, deserving your respect -- especially now! And you treat him with disdain and contempt when his only crime is concern for Georgiana!"

Darcy looked at her through pained eyes. "It was not my intention, Elizabeth, to view him with disdain and contempt..."

"But the way you looked at the letter... and then you seemed so upset when you got up to leave after reading what he had written!"

"I am sorry," Darcy sounded distracted. "I noticed something about the letter... I had to come in and check something."

Suddenly Elizabeth noticed that his countenance was not a man angered, but reflective and resigned, and was at a lost to know what he was alluding to. She inquired of him, "What do you mean?"

He brought over Bostwick's letter and handed it to her. "His handwriting -- it is very unique, do you not think so?"

Elizabeth looked at it and nodded, "Yes it is. But there is something more than just his unique handwriting, is there not? What is it, Will?"

"I recollected seeing it before."

"Where?"

"At first I could not recall, but suddenly I remembered reading another letter, and having the same thought about the handwriting."

Darcy reached over and picked up a letter that was lying on his desk. "I have kept this letter for two years in the bottom of one of my files."

"What is it?"

"Do you remember I told you that I had received an anonymous letter from Ramsgate advising me that Mrs. Younge was putting Georgiana in very inappropriate situations with Wickham?"

Elizabeth nodded mutely. He handed her that letter. When she looked at it, she knew immediately. The handwriting was the same. "It was obviously written by Mr. Bostwick!" She looked up at her husband. "Wickham was correct, then, and he *had* been there!"

"Yes. He not only had been there, but in talking to Wickham as he must have done, he became intimately aware of all the details of their intended elopement!"

Darcy walked back around his desk and sat down. "If what Wickham claims is true, I would imagine Bostwick must have seen them together, and later, upon encountering Wickham alone, bribed him with drink to get him to spill out all the wretched details. When he discovered what Wickham's intentions were, he wrote for me to come immediately."

"Why do you suppose he did not sign the letter?"

"Only he can answer that for certain."

"But you have an idea why," Elizabeth said.

Darcy's look of conflicted emotions echoed his pause in answering.

"I assume it may be due to him not wishing Georgiana to know he knew of the situation, being the indiscretion that it was. He would not want her to feel ill at ease around him because he knew."

"And after all this time, he has never once claimed credit for being the one responsible for getting you to Ramsgate in time to stop them." She said it quietly, but the truth of her words pained Darcy to the depths.

"Heavens!" he exclaimed. "I have treated him abominably this past year!"

"Will, whereas I am sure he expected your censure of a relationship between himself and Georgiana, he was probably never aware of how strong your feelings against him were."

Darcy turned to Elizabeth with impenetrable regret. "On the contrary, my love. I am ashamed to say he was very much aware of my feelings. I gave him orders last fall to stay away from Pemberley all together!"

"Will, say you did not!"

"I did."

He turned to Elizabeth. "I believe I have some apologizing to do. I must send for him directly!"

Chapter 22

Later that next day, after giving his testimony to the authorities who had arrested Wickham, David Bostwick sombrely made his way to Leddesdale to make an attempt at the work he knew he must attend to. It was hopelessly futile. He found himself miserably inept at concentrating on the figures and percentages before him, and was making very little progress on the work spread out upon the desk at which he sat. He had dropped his head into his hands when Lochlin came in.

"Bostwick, I must ask you to put aside what you are doing and get over to Pemberley right away."

He stood up anxiously and asked, "Pemberley?"

Lochlin nodded, "Yes, Pemberley."

A wave of discomfort carried his eyes down to the floor. "I cannot go to Pemberley, Sir."

"You cannot go to Pemberley? What do you mean by this?"

"I… I have been ordered by Mr. Darcy to stay off the grounds there."

"After what you did last night? This makes no sense at all! Why would he issue such an order?"

"It was last year, Sir."

Lochlin eyed him doubtfully, and was too intrigued at this unusual bit of news to give away the contents of the message he had just received. Instead, he asked, "What sort of indiscretion was it, Bostwick, that brought this about? I cannot imagine such a thing! Did you kill some gladiolas when you were an under gardener there? Or perhaps you trimmed a tree too severely for Darcy's taste?" He laughed, but when he noticed the solemn look on Bostwick's face, he changed his tone.

"Tell me, son, whatever did you do to receive his censure?"

David felt an uncomfortable blush pass across his face. "I… he… discovered I had feelings of regard for his sister, and she, I believe, returned those feelings."

Lochlin began laughing and was obviously enjoying some aspect of his admission, but David did not see the humour in this situation.

He turned and clasped one hand fervently into the other. "So our esteemed Fitzwilliam Darcy, who takes a wife from a common family in a common country village, a woman with no fortune, no connections, nor anything to recommend her, prohibits his sister from entertaining similar notions."

David attempted to interject. "Sir, it is different in our case. Mr. Darcy, I believe, is only looking out for his sister."

"Oh, Bostwick, your generosity and forgiveness toward Darcy is most admirable, but I, for one, find it completely unmerited. Nevertheless, you must get over to Pemberley! You do not seem to be making much progress with your work in the state you are in anyway. You can start up again when you return."

"I cannot, Sir. I have been ordered."

Lochlin met Bostwick's look of resignation with one of determination "And I have orders for you, as well, Bostwick," he said to him, holding out a short piece of stationary. "Darcy is the one asking for you to come."

~~*

Elizabeth was in with Georgiana when the young Bostwick arrived. Although he had every reason to believe this meeting should unfold in a most civil and even pleasant manner -- due to what he had done last night -- his feelings directed him otherwise. With nervous deportment, he applied to the housekeeper to see Mr. Darcy.

Darcy was sitting in his study when David was announced by Mrs. Reynolds. He stood up to greet the young man whom he had previously regarded as an unfit suitor to his sister, and now had to regard as a guardian angel of sorts. He reached for his hand and shook it with a decidedly firm grip.

"Come in, Bostwick. Thank you for coming so quickly. Have a seat. I hope I have not taken you away from anything too important."

"No, Sir. In fact, I was having difficulty concentrating on my work." As David nervously sat down in the chair Darcy offered, he furtively cast a glance at Darcy as he walked back around his desk to his chair. "May I inquire after Georgiana, Sir?"

"She is as might be expected. She slept little last night, the fear she experienced those few hours has not yet dissipated. We are grateful she was not harmed physically, however her emotional recovery most likely will take some time."

"I do hope and pray she will have a speedy recovery, Sir. Emotional hurt can oftentimes require a longer recovery and there is very little specific remedy that can be applied."

"Very true, Bostwick. And emotionally, she has been through a lot."

Darcy looked down at his desk and saw the letter Bostwick had delivered that morning. He picked it up and fingered it in both hands. "That was most kind of you to send word of your care and concern for Georgiana this morning. Did you pen the letter yourself?"

David looked at him, feeling somewhat perplexed and insulted, his eyes narrowing at the implied assumption and a wave of defensiveness rising within him. "Of course I wrote it, Sir. I may not have received a formal gentleman's education as yourself, but I am able to read and write! But neither am I of the privileged class that can afford to pay someone to do it for me! Nor would I want to!"

Darcy looked up apologetically. "I am sorry, Bostwick. I did not mean to infer either of those things by my question. I simply meant that your handwriting is... shall we say... distinctive."

David nervously shifted in his chair, at once regretting that he had lashed out at Darcy with his erroneous assumption. "Forgive me, Sir, for assuming that was your intent." He looked down, feeling foolish and angry at himself for his reaction. He looked back up at the man that he had always held in such respect, and wondered how he could rid himself of the uneasiness that now dominated his feelings. "Yes, Sir, I have often been told it is unique."

Darcy nodded and suddenly seemed intent on changing the subject, putting the letter down. "Georgiana was able to give us a brief account of what happened yesterday. Do you mind giving me your version to perhaps fill in the details?"

David began by recounting how Jacques had ridden to their home with the news of her kidnapping. "I remembered at once the cave that Samuel and I had followed Wickham to years before. My only thought was that he would not take Georgiana anywhere near a village or town, for fear of running into someone."

Darcy asked, "So you were quite certain Wickham would take her there?"

"Mr. Darcy, I only hoped and prayed that wherever he had taken her, someone would discover them quickly. I did not necessarily wish it to be myself that found them; I only knew it could be a possibility."

"Go on."

"I rode as fast as I could. When I arrived at the peaks and headed in the direction of the cave, I soon saw a horse tethered to a tree a short distance from where I remembered the cave to be. I was fairly certain they were there. My only concern was getting to them before Wickham did anything to harm her. I had no idea how long ago she had been taken, how long they had been there, nor what he was intending to do."

Darcy could see the emotional toll Bostwick suffered reliving his fears and his anger at Wickham as he recounted his story. He was silent for a moment, as he recollected his thoughts. Then he continued.

"I walked quickly but quietly to the entrance of the cave and looked in. I was greatly relieved to see Miss Darcy was unharmed, but knew I had to get in there directly. Unfortunately her reaction to seeing me alerted Wickham of my presence and he grabbed her, along with a knife and threatened us, claiming that he had no qualms in using it."

Darcy shook his head in disbelief at the extent of Wickham's ruthlessness. "Then what happened?"

David brought his hand up and brusquely drew it across his chin. "I tried convincing him to give up, or at least give up thoughts of using the knife. I warned him that others were coming. I *hoped* that others were coming. I was afraid to agitate him because I did not know what might agitate him."

Darcy's face grew grave as he listened to the account. "That was wise, not knowing what Wickham was capable of doing. I am grateful for how you handled the situation. Then what did you do?"

David looked down, somewhat sheepishly. "I saw that she... that Miss Darcy was growing quite pale and I thought she would most certainly faint, much like she did at the ball. But she suddenly pulled herself out of it. I thought that if Miss Darcy *did* faint, it might be what was needed to catch Wickham off guard and distract him enough so I could grab him and the knife and she could get away."

"She said that you began signing the letters for the word *faint*."

"Yes, Sir. I hoped that she would realize what I was doing and be able to read my signing. She had been away from the sign language class so many months, I was not sure if she would understand what I was trying to get her to do."

"But she did understand."

"Yes, Sir. I am most thankful that she did. When she went down, Wickham reached for her and I went after him."

Darcy nodded. "That was very clever and clear thinking on your part, Bostwick. We owe you a debt of gratitude for all you did."

"I did nothing out of the ordinary, Sir. Anyone would have done what I did for your sister."

Darcy suddenly looked upon him with a guarded look. "There is another part of the story, however, that you seem to have left out."

"Sir?"

"Georgiana told my wife that Wickham began making some claims..." Darcy watched the young man intently, "about seeing you at Ramsgate two years ago."

David suddenly straightened up, looked away, and took in a nervous breath. "That is true. He did make those claims. I have been to Ramsgate, but I do not know to what he was alluding."

David spoke too quickly, Darcy observed, *and suddenly appeared more than a little disconcerted.*

"You do not?" Darcy reached over and picked up another letter from his desk, stood up, and began walking around the desk to where David was seated.

"You are quite sure you do not know what he was talking about?" Darcy stood in front of him, and leaned against the desk.

"No, Sir, I..." David stopped short as Darcy held the letter in front of his face. As he instantly recognized his own handwriting, and then the words he had written two years ago, the colour faded from his face.

He slowly moved his eyes up from the letter to meet Darcy's. "Sir, I did not wish for her to know that I was there."

"Would you be so kind as to tell me about it?"

David looked up to the man who was waiting patiently for an explanation. He closed his eyes for a moment to gather his thoughts, and then began. "I had gone to Ramsgate to visit an aunt and uncle who own a small inn there. Wickham happened to be staying at the inn. I recognized him at once. I knew he would not know me, as he rarely paid me any attention at Pemberley other than to harass me, and I had grown quite a bit in the years since I had seen him last. While he was there, he left during the day, but returned in the evening. One evening when he returned, he was drinking and getting quite drunk, and he began boasting about his clever scheme... how he had secured the love of a young lady with an unbelievable fortune. I thought to myself, 'I wonder who this poor girl is, and does she really know what she is getting into?'"

David stopped and anxiously pushed his hair from his forehead, more out of uneasiness than necessity. "The next day I saw him… with Miss Darcy on his arm. I could not believe it, and at first I did not know what to do. When he came back that night to the inn, I struck up a conversation with him, hoping he would tell me more. He is a man who willingly takes drink when offered it, and the more drink he has, the more willing he is to divulge what he may not have been so willing to do when sober. When he had revealed the extent of his plan, I knew it had to be stopped."

"What did he tell you?"

David looked up at him pained. "He said that a very young naïve girl he had known all his life believed his declaration of love and that she believed herself to be in love with him. He had persuaded her to elope with him, and that the fortune he would receive in marriage with her would set up him nicely. There was more, but…" David did not go on, and the two sat in silence for a few moments.

Finally Darcy said, "So you wrote the letter."

"Yes, Sir. I knew Wickham could not be doing such a thing with your knowledge, let alone your approval. I knew that I could do nothing to stop him from succeeding in his scheme. I only hoped you would be available to receive the letter and make your way to Ramsgate in time to prevent this from happening."

"You sent it without your signature. Why did you do that?"

David looked down. "There were actually two reasons. Mainly, I did not want Miss Darcy to find out that I was there and knew. She had not seen me at all. I felt there was no reason to draw attention to myself. I believed she would have two reactions to having her upcoming marriage broken up with Wickham. At first she likely would be hurt and angry. I did not want her to blame me and resent me for being the one who sent for you."

"And the second reason?"

"I knew Miss Darcy to be rational and wise and that she would ultimately respect your feelings. I felt she would eventually see Wickham for who he really was and would feel much shame and regret after her initial pain had subsided. I did not want her to feel any sort of embarrassment around me because I knew."

"As I thought." Darcy softly muttered.

"Mr. Darcy, I would appreciate it if you did not tell her of our conversation and my knowledge of what happened at Ramsgate. I do not think she needs to know."

"That may not be so easy, Bostwick. She suspects something already of your presence there because of Wickham's claims to that effect last night."

"I was hoping she was not paying close attention to what he was saying."

"Apparently she was, but I will keep this information from her as long as possible."

"Thank you, Sir."

Darcy stood. "Thank you, Bostwick." They shook hands and David turned to leave. "Bostwick, there is one more thing."

He turned back. "Yes?"

I wish to apologize for my words and behaviour toward you of late. You did not deserve them, and I am sorry."

"Yes, Sir."

"And Bostwick..."

"Yes?"

"Last year I asked you to stay off the grounds of Pemberley. Be advised that from now on you are welcome here any time."

"Thank you, Sir."

"Thank *you*, Bostwick."

David walked toward the door. As he reached for the handle, he suddenly stopped and turned around. "Sir, would it be acceptable to you if I pay a visit with Miss Darcy when she is more recovered?"

Darcy hesitated in answering and David waited, his heart pounding, as he wondered whether he had overstepped his bounds.

"In time, Bostwick. I fear presently she desires to see no one. She even prefers that I do not go to her. She still requires a great deal of healing. I will advise you when she is ready."

Thank you, Sir. Good day."

"Good day, Bostwick."

After David had left, Darcy went in search of Elizabeth. He was about to proceed to Georgiana's room when he saw that she was coming down the stairs.

"How did your meeting with Mr. Bostwick go?"

"Well, I think."

"How is he doing?"

"I can see that he is still shaken up about what happened. His story is pretty much the same as Georgiana's.

"What did he say about being at Ramsgate?"

"He was there. His aunt and uncle owned the inn in which Wickham was staying, and he overheard him one night boasting about his clever scheme and the young lady with a great fortune he was to marry. The next day he saw him walking around the town with Georgiana on his arm. When Wickham came back that night to the inn, he bought him some drinks and got him to talk. From the things he was saying, he realized he needed to notify me."

"Anonymously?"

"Yes. He did not want Georgiana to know that it was him that sent for me."

Elizabeth tucked her hand into her husband's arm. "What do we tell Georgiana if she asks about it?"

Darcy looked down at her. "I do not want to lie to her, but he has asked that we keep it from her as long as possible." Darcy drew in a slow breath. "She has been through enough emotional trauma, I do not think I want to add to it."

"So if she asks, we do not tell her Mr. Bostwick was there?"

"For now, until she is stronger, we can say we are not aware of what Wickham meant. Even though Wickham does not know it, I do not want to give him the satisfaction of knowing he succeeded in hurting Georgiana even more than he did, by what he said."

They walked together into the sitting room. Elizabeth took a seat in her favourite chair, and Darcy stood at the window. He stared out absently for some time. Elizabeth knew it was time for her to remain silent, as she could tell he was feeling greatly overwhelmed.

He turned his head and walked over to a table, picking up a book that had been forgotten the night before. Its pages of neatly written thoughts and feelings were bent from being carelessly dropped, and were soiled from the dirt it had landed upon. "Her journal," he said softly. "If she had not dropped this, we may not have known as soon as we did that Wickham had taken her." He began running through the pages with his hands, not looking at the contents, but thinking what this journal had meant to his sister, and now what it meant to them.

Elizabeth quickly stood up to take it from her husband's hands. "Let me take it back up to her."

Darcy let out a breathy chuckle. "You do not trust me, do you, Elizabeth? You are thinking I am going to read through this!"

Elizabeth only smiled. "Perhaps I only want to remove the temptation, dear."

"I have a right to read it. I am her brother and her guardian."

"That you are, and yes, maybe you do have the right. But perhaps for Georgiana's peace of mind and trust in your respect for her privacy, you will not."

Darcy reached for Elizabeth's hand and placed the book in it, smiling at her perception. "Go on, take it back to her."

Elizabeth carried the battered journal upstairs, while Darcy returned to his study. While he had been at the window in the sitting room, he pondered an idea that had been formulating in his mind for some time. He decided that now it was time to set things in motion. He sat down at his desk and pulled out a piece of parchment paper, taking a pen and dipping it in the ink, he began...

My friend Hamlin,

It has been almost a year since I visited with you...

Elizabeth came into Georgiana's room and found her sitting in a chair, facing a window that looked out over the lake in front of the house. Even though the spring day was fair, she was wrapped in a blanket. She looked up when Elizabeth entered.

"I brought something for you, Georgiana."

Georgiana looked at her journal. "It looks pretty bad."

"It is only a little dirt," smiled Elizabeth. "If we smooth out the pages and press them down, it should be as good as new."

Georgiana stared at it blankly. She then turned to Elizabeth. "I have no need for a journal, anymore."

"Georgiana, why would you say that? You know how much it helped you before."

"I am not certain I will ever want to write in it again."

Elizabeth sat down on the bed, opposite her. "Right now you might not feel like it, but you will. Right now nothing is the same; you feel as though it will never again be the same. But it will be, Georgiana. Believe me, someday it will."

Georgiana closed her eyes. She found that she had been doing that often this morning. She closed them, wanting to escape from the pain and hurt that her memories of the previous day assaulted her with. She wanted to close them from the overwhelming sense of gratitude and regard she still held for David Bostwick, but that was now tarnished by fear that he knew her deepest, most shameful secret. And if he had not known previously, if he had not been at Ramsgate, he certainly was now acquainted with the distressing facts by Wickham's words last night.

When Elizabeth stepped out of her room earlier, Georgiana walked over to her large, overstuffed chair and turned it toward the window. The sun shining though it seemed to give her a physical strength that made up for her lack of emotional strength. When she looked out over the peaceful grounds of Pemberley, wondering when she would ever feel a sense of peace within her again, she had seen David leave the house. She knew he must have been there talking with her brother. She knew there was the possibility that both her brother and Elizabeth knew exactly what Wickham's claims of his presence at Ramsgate were about. But right now she would not ask Elizabeth about it. Due to the emotional pain she was feeling, she did not think she could handle knowing the truth yet. No, she could not ask yet.

Chapter 23

Two weeks had passed since the harrowing incident. Georgiana, still feeling all the painful effects of it, ventured a little more out of her room, but she still preferred solitude, unwilling to see anyone or receive callers. Elizabeth thought it would be in her best interest to join the signing classes at the church again, or simply go out to the property to see how far along the school was in being built. But Georgiana declined.

Much to Darcy's and Elizabeth's consternation, she had reverted to being the same very quiet, self-conscious young girl Elizabeth had first met when she came to Pemberley. Elizabeth knew that there were many thoughts going through Georgiana's mind, but she was not yet ready to openly share what those things were.

Darcy was impatient for her to recover. He did not know how to handle her emotionally pushing him away, when she had always been so affectionate towards him.

"When will she ever let me near her again?" he would ask Elizabeth. "I wish there was something I could do!"

"All you can do is wait. Let her come back to you on her own terms in her own time."

"But she sits all day, does nothing, and sees no one. Is this normal?"

"Who can say whether this is normal? None of it is normal. We cannot force on her what we want, what we expect, and what we think is best for her. We did not go through what she did."

"There must be something we can do!"

Elizabeth looked up at him. "I have been thinking as much myself. I would like to ask Reverend Kenton to come and speak with her. Do you think she would be open to that?"

"Anything is worth a try!" Darcy answered in frustration.

Elizabeth talked with Georgiana about having the reverend come to talk with her and she agreed to it. They sent for him and he came immediately.

Georgiana was waiting in the sitting room when he arrived. Darcy and

Elizabeth showed him to the room and he walked slowly in. He knew that emotionally Georgiana was in pain, and hoped she would feel comfortable enough with him to talk about it.

"Good afternoon, Miss Darcy."

She looked up at him with a weak smile. "Hello, Reverend Kenton."

He sat opposite of her and clasped his hands together, resting his arms on his knees. "I hope you do not mind my coming to see you. Your brother and his wife are very concerned for you."

"I know." Georgiana looked like she was far away, and Kenton wondered how he would bring her back.

"Do you want to talk about what happened, Georgiana? I have been told I am a good listener."

They sat a few moments in silence. Georgiana knew she could trust the reverend, and had always been able to talk to him. She knew he would be willing to pray for her, which in her heart she knew would help bring healing. It was summoning the strength... and the courage... to verbalize her feelings that she found so difficult.

He did not want to rush her nor did he want to discourage her, so he remained silent while Georgiana struggled. Tears began to form in her eyes, and she reached into her pocked for a well used handkerchief.

Finally she said, "I feel so alone."

Kenton looked at her surprised, but let her continue.

"I know my brother and Elizabeth love me and want me better, but they did not go through what I went through, and I feel no one understands."

"I cannot say that even I understand precisely how you feel, Georgiana, but I think I understand what you are saying."

"William has always seemed to me to be so perfect; it often caused me to fear him more than love him. When I made a mistake in judgment two years ago involving Wickham, I was more devastated by my brother's disappointment in me than finding out Wickham loved not me, but my fortune."

Kenton listened patiently and silently, nodding occasionally.

"What Wickham did two weeks ago frightened me greatly, but it also brought it all back. It even reinforced my shame in realizing how great an error in judgment I made regarding him." Georgiana's breathing was heavy and her words were now interspersed with short sobs. "And now I find out that it is not only my brother who knew, but David Bostwick, as well."

Kenton shot her a startled look. "Bostwick?"

Georgiana nodded. "That night Wickham remembered that Mr. Bostwick was there... at Ramsgate... and that he had even talked to Wickham about his plans to elope with me."

Kenton leaned toward her. "Georgiana, what happened is all in the past. You have grown and matured and have nothing of which to be ashamed. If Bostwick knows, it certainly has not affected the deep regard he has for you."

Georgiana looked at him through tear stained eyes. "But how can I ever face him again?"

Kenton remembered the conversation he had previously had with Bostwick and how the young man seemed to care a great deal for Georgiana. "Georgiana, do not assume he has ever let that interfere with his regard for you."

They were silent again, and finally Georgiana said, "I will try, Reverend."

"Is there anything I can do for you, Georgiana? You said you were lonely. What can we do about that?"

~~*

When Reverend Kenton returned to Darcy and Elizabeth, he found them both anxious to hear how his time with Georgiana had gone. They were eager for his opinion of how Georgiana was faring.

After sharing the particulars of their conversation, he added. "She needs time. She still strongly feels the shame of what happened two years ago with Wickham. She did not go into details, but I was able to put together what may have happened. Wickham's recent actions reinforced to her the poor judgment she used in making those decisions. I believe she is feeling mostly shame, and part of it in light of the recent knowledge that David Bostwick is aware of the whole situation."

He looked at them waiting for some sort of acknowledgement. Darcy nodded. "He does know. He was there at Ramsgate. In fact, he was the one who notified me of the situation, although anonymously, and I was not aware of that fact until I talked with him the day after Wickham abducted Georgiana."

"That is something she greatly needs to work through."

Elizabeth looked at him pleadingly. "Reverend, is there anything we can do for her. Can you think of anything?"

"There are two things, actually. First, I think it would help to bring Miss Catherine back."

"My sister?"

"Yes."

Elizabeth smiled. "They did grow to be fond of one another. I know that Catherine would love to return, but would Georgiana be willing to receive her?"

"I suggested it and she seemed open to the idea. She says that she is very lonely. I think Miss Catherine would help take her mind off what happened."

Elizabeth slowly nodded. "They *were* good for each other. Catherine may be exactly the person to give Georgiana the companionship and encouragement she needs. Yes, I believe that might be a good idea!"

"Reverend, you said two things. What is the other?" asked Darcy.

"I believe she needs to talk with David Bostwick." He looked at Darcy. "I know what your opinion of the young man has been. But all things considered, Mr. Darcy, his character, his constant care and concern for Georgiana, and all that he has done, speak for themselves. They speak much louder than his station in life."

Darcy took in a deep breath and let it out slowly. "I do have a greater appreciation for him now, Reverend, and it is not due to him rescuing Georgiana. He is altogether a good man."

"I am glad to hear you feel that way." Kenton extended his hand to Darcy and bowed at Elizabeth. "I shall be going, then."

"Thank you, Reverend."

Darcy shook hands with Kenton. "Thank you. We appreciate your coming."

"I will come anytime. We need to keep praying for that young lady. She needs time. Time and our prayers."

~~*

Time and prayers appeared to begin healing Georgiana's spirits and each day brought a little more improvement.

Darcy and Elizabeth made plans to send for Catherine, and it was to Elizabeth's great joy that her husband suggested she invite Charles and Jane to accompany her. Elizabeth quickly sent off letters to both her sisters, feeling a sense of joyful anticipation that she had not felt for the past two weeks.

About three days after the reverend's visit, a letter came for Darcy. Mrs. Reynolds brought it to him. "Mr. Darcy, a letter to you from a Mr. Hamlin."

"Thank you, Mrs. Reynolds." He took the letter and turned to Elizabeth. "Come join me in my study."

The two walked in as Darcy quickly tore open the letter.

"What is it? Who is Mr. Hamlin?"

"Hamlin is an acquaintance from Cambridge. He works in the offices there. I visited him after my accident last year. It was then that I did some research on communicating with the deaf and read up on the deaf school in Paris. I wrote him a letter a few weeks back with an idea I had, and this is his reply." His eyes quickly scanned the letter as he spoke.

Putting down the letter, he looked at Elizabeth with a very contented grin on his face. Elizabeth did not ask with words, but her eyes and the tilt of her head asked for her. *What is this all about?*

"I wrote Hamlin asking him about getting David Bostwick into Cambridge this next year. I thought…"

"Cambridge! William! Are you saying what I think you are saying?"

"I would make an attempt to answer that, but you know how often you think I am saying one thing while in truth I am saying something else. Now, what do you think I am saying?"

Elizabeth smiled. "Are you going to provide Mr. Bostwick with an education at Cambridge?"

"So it would seem. He has been accepted."

~~*

Darcy sent a message to David Bostwick asking him to come by later that afternoon. Darcy asked Elizabeth to entertain his sister in the sitting room while the two men visited. He would send David to see Georgiana when they were finished talking, hoping it would have the positive effect on her that Kenton believed it would. Before he was due to arrive, Darcy joined them. Georgiana turned and smiled at him, and he walked over to her.

Darcy gently reached down and picked up her hand, lightly kissing it. When she did not pull it away, he tenderly stroked it for a moment and let it go. He was pleased that she was now allowing him at least this much.

When Darcy left the two ladies, Elizabeth felt both excitement and concern for Georgiana. She did not know how she would receive Mr. Bostwick. She had spoken very little about him since she relayed to Elizabeth all that had happened that night. It was as if she wanted to forget about him, which made little sense to her at all, after all he had done.

Elizabeth and Georgiana remained in the sitting room working on some needlework when she heard someone at the front door. She watched Georgiana, who showed little response other than to crouch deeper into the chair in which she was sitting. Elizabeth took in a silent breath and hoped and prayed that she would be up to facing David Bostwick in a little while.

David had received the message to come by Pemberley that afternoon at around three o'clock. He wondered if Darcy was summoning him so he could see Georgiana. His heart pounded as he considered that he might see her again. Except for those few minutes in the cave, when both of them were extremely upset and fearful, he had not really seen her, had any interaction with her, for almost six months.

He came to the door, this time not fearing Darcy's wrath or censure, but with nervous anticipation of seeing Georgiana. He was again brought to the study and welcomed by Darcy, who stood up when he came in.

"Good day, Bostwick. Come in."

"Good day, Sir."

"You are well, I hope?"

"Yes, Sir. And you... and your family... they are well?"

"Yes, thank you, Bostwick. Have a seat."

David sat down, placing the hat he had worn onto his lap and watched as Darcy rubbed his hands together, as if trying to formulate what he was about to say. He picked up some papers, and put them down again. Finally he turned his eyes to David's and looked intently at him.

"Bostwick, I have been doing a lot of thinking lately... about what you did for Georgiana two weeks ago as well as two years ago. I know you must think me a tyrant for the way I treated you, ordering you from Pemberley and not allowing you on the grounds."

"No, Sir, I have the greatest respect for you."

Darcy again reached for some papers that were sitting on his desk. "Yes, well, I... have an offer to make to you this time instead of an ultimatum." He looked at the young man sitting before him, knowing he had the full approval and support of his father and his employer, whom he had already discussed this with, but now wondered what David's response would be. "I have a good friend at Cambridge University who works in the admissions office there. I inquired of him, and already received approval, for you to attend Cambridge this coming year, if you accept it."

David looked at him in stunned silence.

"Son, do you understand what I said."

"You are offering me an education at Cambridge, Sir?"

"Yes, that is correct."

David leaned back in his chair, and then immediately straightened up again.

"Forgive me, Sir, but I find this hard to believe!"

"Bostwick, my father did this for someone years ago, who was very unworthy and unappreciative of it. I am only following in his footsteps, doing it for someone whom I deem has great potential, more admirable character, and one whom I want to give a chance at a better life. That was my father's intent, however little it was esteemed."

David could still barely utter a word. His heart throbbed with the anticipation of receiving something he had often yearned for, but never believed it possible to attain.

"Is this acceptable to you?"

"Yes! Of course!"

The effect of Darcy's offer was exactly what Darcy hoped it would be. He appeared highly pleased with the prospect of attending Cambridge. But the look of joyful anticipation quickly changed to concern as he asked, "Sir, if I may ask, what are the terms of this arrangement?

"Terms?"

"Yes, I would assume you would have me agree to certain terms if I accept this."

"Ahh, yes. The terms. And what do you suppose I should ask in return for you acceptance, Mr. Bostwick?"

The two men eyed each other, and Bostwick jaw tightened as he contemplated what accepting this might mean.

Darcy slowly continued. "You would not consider it exceptionally harsh if I insisted that you give up all thought of my sister, of entertaining any hopes of pursuing an alliance with Georgiana, would you?"

The elation that David felt at the prospect of obtaining a university education suddenly dissipated.

"That is a fair condition, is it not? For the chance of a good education at the university? That *is* something you have always wanted, is it not?" Darcy waited for the young man to answer.

"Yes, Sir. It has been a lifelong desire. It was really my only hope to improve my station in life." He turned away from Darcy so he would not be able to see the pain on his face as he weighed his options. He knew that without an education he would never be able to offer Georgiana what she deserved. The only way he could improve his life was to accept this education, yet doing that now meant giving up all thoughts of Georgiana. He knew, however, that for *her* to have the very best in life, he would have to give up all thoughts of her. That would be the selfless thing to do. "I have come to realize and appreciate the difference in our stations in life, Sir. It would be wrong for me to try to secure her affections without any means to support her well." He turned back to Darcy. "Accepting the education you are offering me would, I believe, ultimately be best for each of us."

Darcy smiled and nodded. "So you do agree, then, to give up all thought of Georgiana by accepting my support of you at Cambridge?"

David swallowed hard as actually getting to the point of agreeing to put thoughts of her out of his mind was very distressing, if not impossible to imagine, and he wondered if he could really say the words. In reality he knew she would always hold a place in his heart.

Finally, slowly, he answered, as all energy seemed to be drained from him, disappointment raging within him believing that Darcy still considered him unsuitable. "Yes, Sir, I agree."

"Good," Darcy stated. "For the next year, when the term begins, you are not to have any contact with my sister. If you come home from university for holiday during the year you are not to seek her out."

David sullenly nodded.

Darcy continued, "Then, after your first year has completed, if your grades are commendable, and if you and my sister still feel the same toward each other, those terms will be dropped."

David looked at him startled. "You mean that these terms are solely for the first year, Sir?"

"I believe that is what I said."

Suddenly David felt that he could breathe again and his heart began beating in a most joyous way. He appeared to be quite speechless, as he fully comprehended what Darcy said.

"Bostwick, one reason I want you and Georgiana to have this year apart is because she is still young. She has had a tendency to let herself be drawn into a relationship that is *easy* for her. She finds it difficult to meet new people."

"I know that, Sir."

"When she thought herself in love with Wickham, she was, I believe, settling for an easy way out. She had grown up with him, knew him well, or so she thought."

"Sir, are you comparing me to Wickham?"

"Only in regards to Georgiana. Like Wickham, she had also grown up with you, felt comfortable around you, and found herself easily drawn to you because of that. In character, however, you and Wickham are complete opposites."

"I thank you for realizing that, Sir."

"There is one more thing that is going to require time on her part. She has lost a bit of trust in men because of the way Wickham handled her. She needs time to develop that trust again."

David looked down, angry at Wickham for the abominable way he treated Georgiana, and angry with himself for not being there to prevent it from happening altogether. "I understand, Sir."

"Good. This is for your benefit as well, Bostwick. Your first year at university will be difficult enough and you do not need any distractions. I want you to fully concentrate on your studies. It will be best."

"Yes, Sir."

Darcy joined the young man, and put his arm around him as they walked toward the door to the study. "Now, Georgiana is in the sitting room. She does not know you are here, but if you wish, you may go in and talk with her. It will be up to you whether you tell her about Ramsgate. You may tell her about my sending you to Cambridge, even the conditions, if you wish. But remember, once the term begins, there is to be nothing between you until the year is completed.

Do I have your word?"

David stopped, turned to him and agreed. "Yes, Sir."

They shook on it, and Darcy escorted him to the sitting room.

~~*

Elizabeth looked up from where she was sitting when she heard footsteps coming down the hall. She cast a glance over to Georgiana who was now deeply engrossed in reading. Elizabeth stood up and spoke in a warm voice, "Good afternoon, Mr. Bostwick."

At her words, Georgiana turned her head abruptly toward the door. The first thought that crossed her mind when she looked up and saw him standing next to her brother, was that here were her two favourite men in her life. But that thought was soon pulled from her mind as she suddenly recalled that both these men were aware of a most wretched and shameful decision she had once made.

David's words in reply to Elizabeth seemed muddled in her mind. "Good afternoon, Mrs. Darcy." He looked over at Georgiana. "Hello, Miss Darcy."

Georgiana could only mutely nod a reply. He stepped into the room, and Elizabeth walked over to join her husband. Darcy looked at his sister and said, "I believe Mr. Bostwick would like some words with you Georgiana. We shall be outside."

Darcy and Elizabeth stepped out of the room, as David walked further into it. Georgiana felt tears swell up in her eyes as she contemplated all he had done for her, all he knew about her past, and yet, all the regard he still seemed to hold for her.

She was finally able to muster the courage and the strength to say, "It is good to see you, Mr. Bostwick. Please have a seat," all the while summoning every ounce of strength she would need to have this conversation with him.

Chapter 24

David took a seat across from Georgiana, nervously fingering the hat he had worn and that was now clutched in his hands. He looked at the young lady, who seemed intent to keep her gaze averted from him and glued to the floor. Her face was flushed and he watched as she closed her eyes a few times, in an apparent attempt to diminish the tears that were beginning to pool in them.

He felt an overpowering urge to breach the short distance between them and hold her in a comforting embrace; one that he had so long desired to give her since that horrendous night. Yet he could now clearly hear the stern admonition by Darcy on the terms of this education he was bestowing on him. He knew that to begin something now would make the next year that much more difficult to endure without her.

He did not even know where to begin this conversation with her, even having had two weeks to imagine what he would say to her when he saw her again. He felt akin to a man stepping out on thin ice, knowing that one wrong step, or in his case, one wrong word, could plunge them both into exceedingly uncomfortable conditions.

Georgiana felt a strong compulsion to find out the truth of what David knew about her and Wickham. Fearing that the mere mention of it would subject her to his disdain, she knew not how to go about it. The enduring silence between them seemed to irrationally overwhelm her with the thought that what happened with Wickham must be foremost on his mind as well.

The silence to David Bostwick, however, was a means to approach this subject with the right words, at the right time. He knew she was distraught and did not want to make things any worse. He had many things to tell her and he wanted to make sure she understood exactly what he was saying.

He finally broke the silence. "Miss Darcy, I have been waiting, most anxiously at that, for an opportunity to see you and talk with you." He watched her to see if she would look up, hoping she would so he could give her a reassuring smile. When she kept her eyes drawn toward the floor, he continued. "I have thought of nothing but you for the past few weeks, wondering how you are doing, hoping you can forget what happened, and praying you would be able to move on. I have wished that there was something I could do to take away your pain. Needless to say my work has suffered for my distraction, as Mr. Lochlin is always so willing to remind me."

He watched as a slight smile touched Georgiana's mouth. She still did not meet his eyes, but this was enough encouragement to spur him on. "Miss Darcy," he looked toward the open door of the room, wondering where Mr. and Mrs. Darcy were keeping themselves, but certain they were close by. How much he wanted to call her Georgiana, but did not dare. "I was so terribly afraid for you when I heard you had been kidnapped. But I cannot imagine the fear you must have felt."

With this, Georgiana looked up. When her eyes lifted up to meet his, and she saw care and concern written on every feature, a single tear ran down her cheek. David gripped his hat even more as he fought the urge to walk over to her and wipe it away.

Georgiana's heart pounded furiously as she contemplated the words she needed to say, and the courage she needed to utter them. She felt as though she was not getting enough air, and she took deep breaths to quiet her anxious thoughts. "I am… exceedingly grateful… for all you did that night to help me. I… am sorry that I have not… thanked you sooner."

He stood up and walked over to a small sofa and sat next to Georgiana's chair. "Please do not concern yourself with thanking me. There were many people out looking for you. I was fortunate to have had an idea where he had taken you. I rode out there not knowing whether that was indeed where Wickham was taking you. I was grateful I found you in time…"

Georgiana looked up and saw the intensity in his eyes. She had questions, but did not yet feel ready to ask them.

They sat in silence again and David watched the young girl struggle for composure. He decided to take the path now of least discomfort.

"Miss Darcy, has your good brother told you of the offer he made me?"

Curiosity brought her eyes up to meet his. "No."

"He has offered to provide me with an education at Cambridge University."

Georgiana's eyes opened wide in surprise at what she heard. "Cambridge? An education at Cambridge?"

David nodded. The look of apprehension and timidity temporarily left her face as her thoughts were now off Wickham, off herself, and now were on a most astonishing disclosure. Her brother was offering an education at Cambridge to David Bostwick!

She discerned from the smile on his face that he had accepted his offer. "I had no idea he would consider such a thing." Georgiana was as surprised as David was ecstatic. She knew the strong feelings her brother had harboured against David, although under the circumstances she knew they must have softened somewhat.

"I shall be leaving at the end of summer. I will probably take a trip out there in the next few weeks to talk to Mr. Darcy's friend, Mr. Hamlin, about my courses and what I want to study."

"Do you know what you want to study?"

He smiled, thankful that she was now focused on this and not her situation. "I should like business administration." He leaned in closer. "I have been helping Mr. Fleming out at the school with some of the administration details. As it grows larger, they should need an administrator. I would like doing that very much."

Georgiana took in a few short breaths as she caught a hint of his enthusiasm over this. "I think you would be very good at it."

David smiled softly. "It is not much, but it would be fulfilling. Mr. Fleming and I have talked about the need for someone in that position in the future as the school grows in size, but it has been apparent he thinks the position needed someone with more schooling than I had."

"Is this why my brother decided to provide this for you?"

"No, I do not think Mr. Fleming ever mentioned it to him, and I never did. He told me he is doing this because his father once provided an education for someone, and he wanted to follow in his footsteps."

"Wickham," Georgiana said softly.

David looked up at her and saw her pain return. "I thought as much."

Georgiana nodded. Her voice trembled as she told him, "He literally squandered my father's gift to him, and then betrayed me, when I always considered him a friend.

Georgiana's heart began nervously pounding as she knew it was now or never. With hands shaking and clasped tightly together, she drew every ounce of strength within her and finally asked, "What did Wickham mean when he said you were at Ramsgate?"

She took in a breath and held it as she waited for him to answer. Her furrowed brows conveyed to David the pain she was anticipating in awaiting his explanation.

With the gentlest and kindest voice, he replied, "It is true. I was there." He watched as she bit her lip and tightly closed her eyes. Her shoulders raised with every deep breath she took, in an effort to curb the sobbing that threatened to overtake her.

"Miss Darcy, please, do not let this distress you."

"What do you know?"

"It does not matter what I know."

"Please, Mr. Bostwick. Wickham said he talked to you. What did he tell you?"

David let out a frustrated sigh, desiring not to dwell on this, but knowing Georgiana would not let it drop until she knew all. "He spoke liberally one night after having had too much to drink that he had secured the acceptance of a young girl of enormous fortune to elope with him and become his wife."

Georgiana disconsolately looked down and shook her head. "And did he boast more of securing my affections or my fortune?"

David drew in a slow breath. "Miss Darcy… I do not think it matters now…"

"It matters to me. Please, Mr. Bostwick. I would like to know it all."

"What he said that first night that I overheard him was that he had secured the hand of a young girl of enormous fortune that would set him up for life. At that point I did not know he was talking of you."

Georgiana timidly looked up at him, her mouth completely dry. She tried to swallow, but found it difficult. "Go on."

David leaned closer to her as he softly spoke. "The next day I saw the two of you walking arm in arm around the town. When he returned that night, I bought him drink at the inn, to try and get him to tell me even more. I knew after our conversation that I needed to notify your brother."

Georgiana reacted to this revelation with a startled look at him. "You are the one who wrote the letter to my brother?"

David reached out to take her hand. "I hope you are not upset that I did."

Georgiana sank back in the chair. As much to herself as to him she replied, "From the time I was a little girl, you have always been there to rescue me." Her mind was reeling now, with thoughts of how discerning he must have been to Wickham's true character and how little she had been. "Usually your rescue attempts were due to someone else. That time, though, you rescued me from my own naivety and foolishness."

"Georgiana... there was no way for you to know his true character. All he had ever exhibited around you was a caring and generous gentleman. He even had your father fooled!"

Georgiana swallowed and looked up, meeting his eyes that were intently focused on her. "Georgiana, please do not let yourself feel disgraced by what happened two years ago. He is the one who has done wrong, not you."

"But I made such a poor decision in agreeing to his whole scheme."

"Perhaps, but you have always been a trusting, caring person. How were you to know what this man had become? Miss Darcy, now you are grown and mature. Let the past remain in the past. I do not think any less of you for it. I would hope that you would realize I never have."

The battle going on inside Georgiana was reflected on her face. She heard his simple words of admiration, but could she really believe them? He seemed to be able to forget what she had done, but could she? As she contemplated this, she suddenly felt as though a weight was lifted from her as she realized she could put this behind her. If he could, so could she.

Her gaze upon him now was one that was free from the past. David could see immediately that she no longer was bound by the chains of guilt and shame. She returned a smile to him.

"Thank you," she whispered to him.

He tightly squeezed the hand he had been holding. "Miss Darcy," he whispered. "There is something else I must tell you."

She looked down at her hand in his and began to pull away, fearing what he might have to say next. But he held on tightly and she left it within his grasp.

"Your brother made me agree to certain terms in accepting his offer to go to the university."

"Terms? What were they?" Her face pinched in uncertainty.

"He has asked me to not have any contact with you..."

Georgiana raised her shoulders in response and angrily stamped her foot before he was able to finish what he was saying. "He is sending you away to remove you from my presence. I knew there had to be an ulterior motive! He repays you for your kindness by providing you with an education, but all the while his real object is to separate us!"

"Wait, Georgiana." David gently put his other hand over the hand that he was holding. "He said if after the first year my grades are acceptable and we still feel the same way toward each other, he will drop those terms." He gently squeezed Georgiana's hand.

"He said that?"

David nodded.

Georgiana stood up and David followed suit. She took in a few deep breaths and suddenly the tears she had been holding fell freely.

"Miss Darcy..."

He took a step toward her, and suddenly she fell against him, as though the pain she had been carrying these weeks... these years... was finally ready to be relinquished. As her head fell against his shoulder, his eyes instinctively went to the door and his arms protectively went around her. He knew he could not push her away, but knew that if Darcy saw them he would not be pleased.

Georgiana's sobs became deeper, and he ceased worrying about her brother and focused back on consoling her. He held her close and spoke gently to her. "Everything is all right. If you need to cry, let it all out."

He tried to turn in an attempt to bring her back over to the chair and get her to sit down. She clung to him in mindless desperation and his attempts to move met with little success. He knew she was not thinking of how this would look if anyone saw them, and he hoped no one would pass by the door at that moment.

But at that moment someone did pass by. Darcy and Elizabeth, who had been standing close by, not close enough to listen, but close enough to keep things proper, heard her sobs. They both stood up and walked quickly to the door to see what happened. When Darcy saw his sister in Bostwick's arms he immediately reacted, taking a most definitive step in that direction to stop it. But instead, Elizabeth put out her hand and stopped him.

He turned and looked at her as if she was not in her right mind. Elizabeth gently pulled him away from the door where they could talk.

"What are you doing, Elizabeth? Did you not see him in there? I have given him my conditions for providing him with an education at the university, and he already defies them!"

"Will," Elizabeth said slowly, taking a deep breath to organize her thoughts. "Two things happened in there. First, it is apparent Georgiana has forgiven herself and no longer has the shame and embarrassment over what Mr. Bostwick thinks of her and what happened at Ramsgate."

"Still, that does not give him the right..."

Elizabeth put a finger up to his lips. "Think of what you saw in there."

"I know what I saw. You saw it as well!"

"Yes, and that is the second thing that happened. Georgiana is on her way to recovery in dealing with the way Wickham handled her. If she can receive Mr. Bostwick's comfort, I believe this is an indication that she will now accept your efforts of affection. I can almost guarantee it."

Darcy turned his head toward the room the two were in. "But still…"

"Fitzwilliam Darcy. He is merely comforting her, that is all. She is obviously distressed, but I think she is releasing everything she has held within her these past weeks as well as the past few years."

As they stood together, Darcy contemplated what he saw and what his wife said. With some misgivings, Georgiana and David came out of the room. When Georgiana saw her brother, she ran over to him and threw her arms around him, burying her head in his shoulder.

His arms immediately came up around her, and he lowered his head and kissed the top of her head.

"Thank you, so much, William." She looked up through tear stained eyes. "What you have done for Mr. Bostwick is wonderful."

She clung tightly to him for several moments. It was as if she was making up for those weeks of not letting him near her. Darcy sheepishly looked up at Elizabeth, and then to David. Elizabeth was most pleased with herself as she saw her husband smile at the young man and extend his hand to him in a handshake.

~~*

The following week Charles, Jane, and Catherine arrived. They all greeted each other as if it had been years since they had seen one another. The ladies gathered together and the men went inside.

Elizabeth noticed that her elder sister looked as much like an angel as she ever had, and Catherine had a look of ladylike maturity that only a year away from Lydia could have produced. "Tell me the news of home," Elizabeth pleaded. "How are Mama and Papa?"

Jane answered. "They are well."

Catherine interrupted. "But Mama is completely undone, again!" She laughed.

Jane explained. "Mary has accepted a proposal and is to be married in November."

Catherine continued. "I do not think I could have taken six more months of her nervous energy exploding at a moment's notice. I am so glad you had asked me to come back to Pemberley! Poor Mary! She shall have to deal with her alone for now, but she is in such a state of euphoria, I do not think she notices."

"Yes," Jane laughed. "We were talking on the way here about whether Mama will survive in that house with all of her girls married and gone. I am sure Catherine will find a man in no time."

Elizabeth thought to herself, *She already has one interested if she will take the time to realize it*, but instead she said, "I wonder how Papa will survive!" They all laughed.

Georgiana took Catherine's hand. "You have come at a wonderful time. We have such a treat for you! The school is nearly finished, and in two weeks we are having a grand picnic out at the property and everyone is invited!"

Catherine squeezed Georgiana's arm. "How delightful that will be! I am so excited to go back and see how everyone is doing! You must know so much more sign language than I do!"

"I have not been to the classes since we returned from London. Up until now I have not felt like it, and then I thought I would wait for you to arrive." Georgiana followed Catherine up to her room, and Jane joined Elizabeth in the sitting room.

When they were alone, Elizabeth grasped Jane's hands. "You look simply wonderful, Jane. Happiness is written all across your face."

"I am happy, Lizzy. I am with child again."

Elizabeth let out a squeal and gave her a smothering hug.

"You are the first person I have told. I wanted to make sure I did not lose the baby again before I told anyone. I think this time all will be well!"

"Oh, Jane, that makes me so happy!"

"Any news of that sort on your end, Lizzy?"

"Not yet, but it is just as well. William has been so busy lately with the school so close to being completed, and with what happened to Georgiana, there has been a lot of stress. I think it probably is best."

"What you both probably need is to get away. That is what Charles and I did."

"That would be nice, but I fear even now he would still be reluctant to leave Georgiana." Elizabeth sighed. "Is there any news from Lydia?"

"Very little and far between. The regiment has been moved a little farther north, so she and her husband have yet to come down."

Elizabeth looked at her with suspicions drawn all across her face.

"What is it, Lizzy?"

"Oh, nothing, Jane."

"Yes there is something. I can see that look in your eyes."

"Jane, no one has ever met him. Do we really know if she actually is married?"

"Lizzy! How can you think that of our sister?"

"I can think far worse! How can it be that he has not found even a few days to come down and meet his wife's family? If she does have a husband, of what is he afraid? Or what is he trying to hide?"

"I will not even entertain such notions!" Jane insisted.

"I knew you would not. That is why you have me for a sister!" They both let out half-hearted laughs that were suddenly drenched with unconfirmed suspicions.

"How is Georgiana doing?" asked Jane.

"Much better. There is a young man…" Elizabeth proceeded to tell Jane all the details about Mr. David Bostwick and how favoured he was by Georgiana, and how he came to be raised in favour in the eyes of her husband.

Meanwhile, the girls were sitting in Catherine's room giggling together, much as if no time had ever passed in their being separated.

"Georgiana, I must hear everything about what Mr. Bostwick did! Now do not leave out a thing!"

Georgiana was more than happy to fill Catherine in with all the details, and knew that having her around again would greatly improve her sense of well being.

Darcy had pulled Charles into his study and closed the door. The two of them, as well, discussed everything that had happened and what he was doing for Bostwick.

"So, Darcy, you would be in favour of a match between them?"

"What can I do? It would be hypocritical of me to try and stop it further. I chose a woman from beneath my station as my wife because I found her to be the only one I wanted to spend my life with; the only one I have ever loved so deeply. How can I allow less for my sister?" He looked at Bingley. "However I know that if they do marry, I shall have several family members to contend with."

"You are willing to do that for her and this young man?"

"He is a good man, Bingley. I cannot find fault in him other than his birth. His father has worked here all my life. He is a good man, as well. I know people will talk. I know that those in society in London will cast me from their midst for allowing such a thing."

"And Georgiana will never be accepted into society."

"She has never cared for that. Her heart is more inclined toward the lesser person and always has been. I should have seen that in her, but I have always been bound more by obligation than the better good."

"How many mamas of sons will be disappointed if they do marry!"

"Georgiana's happiness is more important."

"They will be set up for quite some time, with Georgiana's dowry and all."

Darcy looked up at him and shook his head. "No, it will be quite a while before they will be set up with any fortune of hers."

"What do you mean Darce?"

Darcy explained the terms of her financial settlement that her father had set up.

Bingley looked at him astonished. "So he will only receive the amount of money he is worth per annum at their marriage and receive portions of the remainder over the next ten years?"

"Yes. Even with the education at the university, his income is not likely to amount to much for quite a while. But Georgiana is willing to forgo all she has for him."

"Sounds like you have a strong regard for him, as well, Darcy."

"I have not always had one, mainly due to my suspicions of his mercenary motives as well as my expectations for Georgiana's duty to marry from the highest class."

"You have come a long way, friend! First it was you, now it is your sister! I do not know when our child comes of age and wants to marry, that I will be able to see things as clearly and objectively as you."

"You speak as if there is something definite in the works."

"Yes!" Charles smile was as wide as his voice booming. "Jane is with child. This time we are both anticipating no problems."

"I am very happy for you both. Now that makes an even better reason to find a place for you two nearby, and soon. Come, look at what I have found."

Darcy brought out some papers with descriptions of estates he had discovered for sale or to let. "Lochlin's estate, Leddesdale, is the closest. He is willing to let you come and look at it; however he is not even sure when he wants to sell. It is nice, but for reasons of immediacy, it may not work out. He pulled out a second sheet and put it aside.

"What is that one?" asked Charles.

"Kittridge Manor. It was on the market for some time but it has been pulled off for some reason. Elizabeth and I did go look at it, but thought it a little too small for your purposes."

Darcy pulled out two more. "These two are not in Derbyshire, but in the next county. One is about an hour ride from here, the other about a two hour ride. I think they are worth looking at."

"Good! We will go at your convenience!"

They later joined their wives in the sitting room, and soon Georgiana and Catherine came down as well. Their conversation was spirited and joyful, and as Elizabeth looked over at Georgiana and saw the light in her eyes again, she was so grateful. Jane had the look of a very glowing angel, and Elizabeth secretly envied her for the baby that was to come. She looked over at her husband, and for the first time in weeks, he seemed relaxed, unencumbered, able to enjoy himself, and altogether irresistible. Maybe tonight…

Chapter 25

The familial and friendly bond that the Bingleys shared with the Darcys, as well as that of Catherine and Georgiana, allowed for a very pleasant few weeks to pass. Charles was an enormous help to Darcy as the school was completed and plans finalized for the elaborate picnic that was to be held there. Jane helped Elizabeth, to the best of her abilities in her present condition, as she worked with the Pemberley staff in making plans for food and decorating, while Catherine and Georgiana were of great help to the Flemings who were taking the building that had been built and transforming it into a warm, friendly, and welcoming school. Mr. Fleming also worked on what he was going to say to acquaint everyone with the purpose and vision of the school.

The Pemberley household was kept busy with all the preparations, but it did not prevent the girls from attending the last few signing classes that were to be held in the parsonage. The first day they joined Mrs. Fleming there, Catherine explained away the nervous flutterings of anticipation as simply looking forward to seeing the children again. But why did her heart feel as though it was lodged in her throat?

As the two girls approached the parsonage, they saw Mrs. Fleming bringing some things in and walked over to help her.

"May we be of some assistance, Mrs. Fleming?"

"Oh, yes, thank you." She gave one bundle to Catherine and another to Georgiana. "I thought I could manage by myself, but it has become a little more cumbersome than I anticipated."

Catherine deftly managed to open the door, cradling her package in one hand, and as she held it open for the other two, she asked, "Do you think the children will remember me?"

As soon as she finished asking that question, a voice behind her answered. "I do not think that they would forget you, Miss Bennet."

She turned and faced Reverend Kenton, who had now grabbed the door and removed the bundle from her arms. "Let me take that for you."

If Catherine had not recognized the source of her anticipation earlier, she was convinced of it now. Unable to mutter much more than a shaky, "Thank you," she turned, and feeling unexpectedly flushed, walked into the room behind the other ladies.

"Miss Darcy, are you feeling improved?" he asked.

"Yes, Reverend. Thank you so much for asking."

"And you, Miss Bennet. It is good to see you again. I trust that you and Miss Darcy are enjoying each other's company?"

She stared at him as he spoke. Why had she never noticed the warmth in his eyes; the smile that always touched his lips? "It is very good to be back, Reverend Kenton."

"I am pleased to hear that." She was drawn into his gaze as his meaning was clearly reinforced in his eyes. "How pleasant it will be to have you both here today!"

Georgiana could not help but smile at what she perceived to be a very contented man before her. He obviously was pleased that Catherine had returned, but had Catherine returned with a willingness to share his regard?

When the children arrived, both young ladies were delighted when they eagerly came up to them, wanting to be hugged and held, to look through picture books, and show them how well they could sign the words in the books.

Reverend Kenton was eagerly disposed to remain this day as well, and Mrs. Fleming had not had such an easy day with the children as the ratio of teacher with child was two to one. As she had spent many an afternoon at the parsonage speaking with the reverend for the past six months, she knew his heart, and knew he felt as strongly for Catherine now as he did when she left last November. Back then, Catherine had dreams of marrying a man of great wealth and had not paid any particular attention to the reverend. Mrs. Fleming sincerely hoped that now Catherine was willing to see him with all his noble qualities, as well as realize he loved her.

That same day, the Darcys and Bingleys rode out to see the two properties that were available. The first one they went through, about an hour's ride away, was a strong possibility, well liked by all. Although not as grand as Pemberley, it was on a good amount of land, was in very good condition, and both Charles and Jane thought it suited them very well.

After walking through the house, and knowing that the other one they were to look at was another hour ride away, they made the decision to make an offer on this one and forego seeing the other. Once that decision was made, Jane and Elizabeth walked through on their own, eagerly sharing with each other about all they could do with it. Of particular interest was which room would be the nursery, and how they would decorate it.

Darcy and Bingley returned to the study and library, the two rooms the men were most interested in. Bingley valued Darcy's comments that there was adequate room for Bingley to work and relax in the study, and that the library was sizable enough to build up a modest collection of books.

On the ride home, they talked about the timing of their move, how they would tell the Bennets of their decision, all the times they would be able to get together now living more reasonably close, and all the fun they would have raising their families together. Elizabeth felt a fleeting inner alarm that perhaps she would not be able to have children. After all, it was approaching a year since they had been married, and there was not even a glimpse of hope that she had ever conceived. She smiled as they talked about how their children would be the closest of cousins, all the while wondering, even doubting, whether this would ever happen on her end.

That night at dinner, conversation was lively. They talked of the new home, the progress the children had been making in class, and, of course, the picnic. Elizabeth's thoughts, however, were, *Will I ever have any children?* and for Catherine, *What is this I am feeling for Reverend Kenton? I have never imagined myself being a clergyman's wife before*!

~~*

Classes ceased that last week before the picnic, as all materials that the school had used had to be moved from the church and there was too much to do to ensure that the picnic was a success. Darcy had sent out invitations to everyone in the surrounding area, as well as dignitaries, nobles, and those from around the country he had contacted who had expressed some sort of interest in the school.

On the morning of the picnic, Pemberley was quiet, as all the staff had left early for the property. The kitchen staff had prepared most of the food at Pemberley, as the kitchen at the school, although large, was not quite as nice as Pemberley's. All the gardeners had been working at both places, readying the grounds for a many people, planting flower beds and a few additional trees, but keeping the landscape as natural as they could.

Georgiana and Catherine were getting last minute touch ups with their hair and dresses by Alice, Georgiana's maid, as their conversation turned, as it usually did, to a particular gentleman. Catherine enjoyed teasing Georgiana about Mr. Bostwick, as she enjoyed watching her blush. Her comments usually centred about the year he would be away and under orders not to have any contact with her.

"I think, Georgiana, that if you look at your brother's orders, they are only inclined to go one way. Your brother has not ordered you to not contact Mr. Bostwick. Perhaps he would enjoy a letter from you now and then."

Georgiana blushed. "I could not do that!" she cried. "It would not be proper!"

Georgiana decided to turn the tables this afternoon and bluntly asked her about Reverend Kenton.

"And may I ask *you*, Catherine, how you will like being a clergyman's wife?"

Caught completely off guard, it was now Catherine's turn to blush. "Whoever said anything about me being such a thing?"

Georgiana laughed. "It is very apparent he has much regard for you, and I believe I have been noticing a hint of interest on your part!"

Catherine shook her head. "He is very nice, and very nice looking, I guess."

Georgiana looked at her surprised. "You guess? Whatever do you mean?"

"It is... it is... his collar!"

"His collar?" both Georgiana and Alice asked at the same time.

Catherine looked down. "I see his collar and I see our cousin, Mr. Collins. I know he is nice. I know he is attractive. But I cannot get past his clerical collar!"

Georgiana sighed. "How unfortunate that experience has led you to relate the collar with ridicule, when all my life I have associated the man of the cloth with trust, good principles, and respect."

Catherine sighed. "Perhaps in time."

It was silent for a while, when suddenly Alice nervously burst out, "What do you think of Jacques?"

"Jacques?" they both asked at once.

She slowly nodded.

"Why Alice, do not tell me you have a particular regard for Jacques?"

"He pays me considerable attention. I do not know if he is simply being friendly, or if he is singling me out. All I know is that when he talks with that French accent, no matter what he is saying, it makes me swoon."

Both girls burst out laughing. "Swoon?"

She blushed and looked down. "That is the only way I can describe it."

Georgiana turned to face her. "Alice, if my brother and Elizabeth brought him over here from France to work for them, they must have a high opinion of him. He is a good worker, very friendly." She suddenly began nodding her head. "I think you two would make a lovely couple!" The look on Alice's face reflected considerable reassurance and delight at hearing these words.

The party from Pemberley arrived early at the school property to ensure everything was in order. The three carriage drivers, Winston, Lawson, and Jacques, were sent out to the surrounding villages to pick up those who needed conveyance.

Small row boats had been brought out and put in the lake for guests to enjoy for the day. A children's play area had been constructed, croquet and badminton sets made available, and tables and chairs set up for the meal itself. The rooms of the school had been transformed from bare walls to lively, warm, and welcoming classrooms. The children's rooms were very colourful and filled with an assortment of toys. The adult classrooms were very simple, yet functional.

Although Elizabeth had seen the school in its final stages of completion, she had not visited since the classrooms were actually set up and decorated. For her it was like stepping back into those classrooms in France, and she had to shake herself to realize this dream they both had was finally coming to pass.

Georgiana and Catherine helped Mrs. Fleming with some last minute additions to the children's rooms, and Elizabeth walked around with Jane, giving her a tour of the school and comparing it to the one in France. Darcy was meeting with Mr. Fleming and going over with him all that needed to be communicated with those who would be there. Although Mrs. Fleming would be signing everything he said, he knew most people in attendance would not need, nor be able to understand, all she signed. But it would be a way to demonstrate the usefulness of not only the deaf learning to sign, but those who hear, as well.

Charles stood back, amazed at his friend's undertaking. This last year had definitely changed him. Whether the change began at Rosings when Darcy's proposal was refused, or after his accident and coming so close to dying, Charles did not know. But the respect and admiration he had always held for his friend had now grown enormously. He was markedly proud of his best friend, grateful that he was married to his wife's sister, and thrilled that soon they would practically be neighbours. He hoped that they would soon be blessed with a child, as well.

As people began to arrive, they were given the opportunity to walk the grounds, tour the school, and participate in some recreational activity. The most popular was the rowboats, as it was a beautiful day, the lake was clear and blue, and it practically called out to everyone there.

Georgiana and Catherine enjoyed having the children from their classes hanging on them, wanting them to push them in the swings, play ball with them, or simply hold them. As Georgiana and Catherine each pushed a child in a swing, out of the corner of her eye, Georgiana noticed two men standing off to one side. She knew she could not acknowledge them yet. She could tell who they were though, even though she was not looking directly at them. It was the way David Bostwick often stood, putting his weight on one foot and cocking his head the other way.

Catherine caught sight of them as well, and whispered to Georgiana, "We are being watched."

Her words caused Georgiana to blush, and now she knew she could not turn. Her eyes widened as she could see them begin to walk toward them. It was not so much that she was afraid to see David again. It was that her feelings for him were so overwhelming that they often caused her to behave curiously.

She finally turned to face them, and thought David looked very striking in his crisp shirt and neck cloth, great coat and hat. The reverend, although a fine looking man, had the distinction of wearing his clerical collar, and Georgiana thought how sad it was the Catherine had that unpleasant association. Could she only associate his collar to Collins and not see him as he was -- a good, decent, and attractive man?

"What a fine day for the picnic! You two young ladies seem to have your hands full!" Reverend Kenton laughed.

"The children are having a wonderful time!" Catherine replied. "I have no doubt they will love the school here." She looked up at Kenton and then added, "Although the parsonage was certainly a wonderful place to have the classes in the meantime."

He nodded, and wondered if she thought the parsonage would also be a wonderful place *to live*.

David and Georgiana simply stared at each other. He was soaking in every feature of her face, knowing that he would not have that opportunity once he left for the university. Finally he said, "Do you think the children would enjoy a boat ride?"

He signed "boat ride" as he said this, and the children squealed. Georgiana and Catherine had been pushing Michelle and Eleanor on the swing, and Georgiana was holding a younger child, Norene.

"Now you have done it, Mr. Bostwick. You are obligated to take the children out on one of the boats."

David reached down and picked up little Eleanor. "Let us go down to the lake, then."

They all turned to go to the lake, David allowing the ladies to walk before them. Kenton shot him a look, and wondered what he was up to. As Georgiana and Catherine walked ahead and the distance between them grew, Kenton looked at Bostwick squarely.

"What are you planning, Bostwick? Do you have some dastardly plan to get Miss Darcy in a boat with yourself, and myself in a boat with Catherine as well?"

David looked at him sheepishly. "Along with a few children, good Reverend. You do not need fear for your reputation."

"What about your promise to Mr. Darcy about Miss Darcy?"

"Technically it begins when the school year begins." He looked over at him and smiled. "Do not worry, Reverend Kenton. I simply want some time with her as a friend. I do not plan to overstep my bounds."

"Just reinforcing them?"

David raised his eyebrows. "I just want to create some moments that will make it hard for her to forget me this next year. Is that so wrong?"

Kenton shook his head. "I cannot say. I am not her brother. By the way, where is Mr. Darcy?"

"The last I saw, he was inside."

"Convenient."

"I am not worried if he sees us. We are actually on good terms now."

"Please do not ruin it, then."

Georgiana and Catherine were at the edge of the lake, and having a hard time keeping the two children they had, out of the boats. David put Eleanor down, and she ran immediately to one boat, climbing in. She pointed to Georgiana and then to David, and then signed, "Come here." David helped Georgiana into the boat.

"It appears we have our orders." Georgiana smiled as his touch caused her to give a faint sigh as a feeling of warmth flooded her body.

Reverend Kenton walked over to the boat into which the other two children had climbed. "May I help you in, Miss Bennet?"

"Thank you."

He took her hand and helped her into the boat. She settled down with Michelle in her lap, and Norene, who was a little older, sitting on her own. Kenton pushed the boat away from the shore, and climbed in, then used the oar to push away even further.

The two boats stayed close by, and Georgiana and Catherine often cast glances at each other. Catherine sent her looks of playful censure, as if she were doing something wrong. Georgiana sent her looks of encouragement, playfully suggesting she was not doing enough, having this opportunity with Reverend Kenton.

Catherine turned back to look at him, and thought, *If it were not for the collar, I think I could easily find him attractive. He is a fine looking man, very kind and considerate.* Definitely not grave, pompous, and preachy like her cousin Mr. Collins.

David and Georgiana avoided talking about their circumstances. He kept the conversation safe, at least for him. He knew that to broach the subject of their possible future together would not be right. He wanted to enjoy his time with her now, at this moment. Georgiana knew what terms he was abiding by, and respected him for it. In a way she enjoyed this time with him more than any other. They simply were able to enjoy each other's company.

Kenton felt nervous being "somewhat" alone with Catherine. He wished he could make his feelings known to her, and although the two children with him would not be able to hear any declarations of love, he still felt the timing was not right. She seemed somewhat more attentive, but he could not discern any evidence of regard on her part.

When they pulled the boats back up to the shore, the children were disappointed and they tried to convey to them that there were others waiting for a ride. The two girls took them back to the play area, and the two men excused themselves and went to visit with others.

As the meal was about to be served, everyone was called over to the tables. Although not everyone could hear, Kenton asked the blessing for the meal and a special prayer for the school, that it would be a blessing to everyone who would be involved with it, either as a student, teacher, or family member.

Georgiana spotted David in the crowd. He was sitting with a few of the adults that had been taking the signing classes, including Mr. Carson, who he had been bringing to the class since the beginning. She watched as he eagerly involved them in communication using signs they had learned. They would all end up laughing as they often failed miserably to know how to sign what they wanted to say, or the others failed to understand. She smiled a most contented smile as she thought back to his statement that he would like to be the administrator of the school. His heart was there. And so was hers.

The meal was received with great praise. The Pemberley staff did an exceptional job, and everyone heartily enjoyed the feast prepared for them. As the meal was being finished, Darcy stood up and shared his initial dream and vision for the school, how he visited the school in France, and talked with Fleming about coming over and starting one here.

Fleming then spoke, all the while his wife signing for him, sharing how this form of communication could bridge a gap for those born without the ability to hear, but who definitely had the ability to communicate with others. He shared his experience with his daughter, and then his adopted daughter Michelle. It was a very moving testimony.

When he finished, Darcy got up again. This was not planned, and Fleming wondered what he was now going to share. Darcy seemed somewhat emotional, a bit overwhelmed. "Right now I am a little astonished by something that has happened." He held up a piece of paper. "I was given a gift for the school…" He paused, taking a deep breath, before continuing. "Apparently a fund has been set up for the school, of quite a substantial amount. The school will receive the interest from this fund, which amounts to a yearly sum of over 5,000 pounds."

He looked up into the crowd and saw Elizabeth, whose look of astonishment mirrored his. "I do not know who set this up, but if this person is here, I wish to publicly thank them. It is…" he looked down and blinked his eyes a few times.

"It is most generous and I thank you."

When the meal was over, Catherine and Georgiana found Melissa and Eleanor again at their side, and this time Alice, Georgiana's maid joined them. Her responsibilities for the day, helping in the kitchen prepare the meal, were over. People were still mingling around and the carriage drivers were preparing to leave.

As they were talking and playing with the children, a Mrs. Webber came over. She and her family owned a grand estate south of there, and she had not seen Georgiana in some time. "Miss Darcy, you should be very proud of your brother. What he has accomplished here is quite remarkable."

They continued to talk and when Mrs. Webber left, Georgiana looked for little Eleanor. "Do you know where Eleanor slipped off to?"

The girls looked around, toward the playground, over to her parents, and did not see her. Georgiana walked away from the tables to where she could see the lake. She screamed at what she saw and started running.

"Eleanor! Eleanor! No!" But, of course, the girl could not hear her.

Catherine and Alice turned and saw the sight that Georgiana had seen. Little Eleanor was precariously climbing into one of the row boats and her movement within it was causing it to drift away from the shore.

They both screamed and started to run as well. As they approached the lake, the three young ladies were suddenly passed by three men who were shedding their great coats, neck cloths, and hats, and when they came to the water, thought nothing of diving in and swimming out to the craft.

When they reached it, one held up his hand and began signing for her to remain seated, and the other two gently guided the boat back to shore. As they reached the shallow shore, they stood up, bringing the boat in. Eleanor started to cry, not so much out of fear, but disappointment that her boat ride had ended so abruptly.

Georgiana, Catherine, and Alice watched in relieved amusement as David, Reverend Kenton, and Jacques produced a very upset, but dry, Eleanor to her parents. The sight before the three ladies was not anything they had ever beheld. Georgiana could not help but let her eyes fall upon the young man of her fancy, whose shirt was now clinging to his chest, his blond wavy hair dripping droplets of water, and a look of mirth in his eyes as he joked with the other two men about how the three had reacted.

Catherine's eyes went to the reverend. Without his collar, and a very transparent shirt clinging to him, there was suddenly an appeal that she had not before noticed. He looked over at her, and when noticing her gaze upon him, suddenly felt awkward and exposed. He should not be in such a condition while in her presence, and she should not be gazing upon him in the manner she was, but he surprisingly enjoyed it.

Alice looked upon Jacques with unrestrained admiration. That they both held a regard for each other was apparent. He looked at her and smiled, shrugging his shoulders at his appearance. She returned his gesture with a wide grin.

The Franks took Eleanor, much to her dismay, away from the lake. Now that the potential disaster had been averted, people began taking leave. Jacques could not stay and speak with Alice, as he had to get to his carriage. He would have to drive his patrons home soaking wet.

As they began walking back toward the school, Georgiana whispered to David.

"So it is David Bostwick to the rescue again!"

He looked at her and smiled. "Hardly. She was not in danger as long as she did not do anything to overturn the boat."

"You are too modest, Sir! If she had been left out there alone for any length of time, capsizing the boat would have been inevitable, especially if she tried to stand up."

"We were fortunate that the three of us were standing off to the side admiring our three favourite ladies when we heard you scream."

Georgiana blushed at his words, and he instantly realized with a slight tinge of guilt that he had gone against how he had resolved to deal with Georgiana before going off to the university. They walked back in silence and both noticed the animated conversation Catherine was having with Kenton.

He subtly pointed to the two. "This may have been the best thing to have happened in Reverend Kenton's favour. I do believe Miss Bennet is seeing a side of him that she had never before seen."

Georgiana laughed. "And Jacques?"

"Oh, he and Alice have both admired each other for some time. I have a wager that they will be married before the summer is over."

Georgiana smiled and suddenly wished she did not have to wait a year for David. She turned back to Kenton and Catherine, and a thought occurred to her that a marriage between them might happen before the year was out.

Darcy and Elizabeth had heard what happened, and were now coming toward the lake and met them. "Is everyone all right?" Darcy asked.

"Yes. Eleanor was a little anxious to have another boat ride, albeit by herself," David informed him.

Elizabeth took in the two men and the look of admiration in both Georgiana's and Catherine's eyes. She thought back to that night in the infirmary when Darcy was sweating. His night shirt was wet and she had to cool him down by applying cool cloths to his chest, nervously unbuttoning his night shirt to pull it back. *Yes,* she thought, *I suddenly found myself attracted to him that night, unexpectedly having a glimpse at his chest unencumbered by layers of dress. I do believe that Catherine and Georgiana had the same eye opening revelation!*

"So the boats were a success?" Darcy asked.

"They were very much a success," Kenton answered. "In fact, I believe the two of you could use some time together. Why do you not take yourselves on a nice, romantic boat ride?"

Elizabeth cocked her head and looked at Darcy. "That sounds very appealing to me, Will."

Darcy looked back up at the school. "But there are so many things still that need to be done."

Kenton took Darcy's arms and turned him toward the lake, giving him a little nudge. "Nothing that we cannot handle. You deserve this. I am giving you some very strong, spiritual advice, Mr. Darcy. I believe you need to heed it."

Darcy looked at his wife with feigned resignation. "It appears, my love, that we have our orders." He took her arm, and they proceeded to the boats while the other couples retreated back to the school.

As Darcy and Elizabeth rowed out onto the lake, sitting across from each other, he smiled. "It went well, today, Lizbeth. Do you not think so?"

"It went *very* well!" she smiled back at him. "You ought to be proud of yourself."

"I did not think it was in your disposition to like a man to be proud."

Elizabeth laughed. "There are *some* things we can take pride in. Our accomplishments are one of them."

Darcy took in a deep breath. "Good, because I have to say I *am* proud. Not so much of me, but of the Flemings, of Georgiana, of you. You all helped immensely."

"Yes, but you had the idea, the determination, and the wherewithal to proceed with it. Not everyone would have."

"I must admit I had my doubts along the way." He put the oars down, as they were now in the middle of the lake.

"Come here, Lizbeth."

She looked at him suspiciously. "Over there?"

He scooted toward the centre of the boat and patted the spot in front of him, and she carefully slid over, placing herself in front of him and leaning back. He gently drew his hands up and down her arms as he leaned down and kissed her head as they aimlessly floated.

She lifted up her head, unable to see him, but so that he could hear her. "Do you think we could get away somewhere… just the two of us?"

"Would you like that?"

"I should like it very much!"

"Where would you like to go?"

"I have always wanted to visit the Lake District. Perhaps we could get away on our anniversary."

"I do know of someone who owns an establishment at Ambleside. Would you like me to check into it?"

"Yes, that sounds delightful!"

They both closed their eyes as the small waves rocked the boat ever so slightly.

"This is nice, Lizbeth. I must tell the reverend that his spiritual advice was very much needed and enjoyed."

"You know he is fond of Catherine?"

"I had my suspicions. Does she return his sentiment?"

"I had my doubts. When she was here last, she developed such a strong determination to marry someone of wealth. I believe that has changed. I had not picked up any particular regard for him since she returned, but I think that now, with his wet and *collarless* shirt, she appeared to be looking at him differently. I believe her interest has suddenly grown."

"I do not think I would advocate such a practice… jumping into a lake to secure the attention of a lady. But I do believe that neither of those ladies could take their eyes off of those men in their wet shirts."

"You are not angry at Mr. Bostwick for the time he spent with Georgiana today? Did he not go against the terms you set for him?"

"Not really. My terms to him actually begin when the school year starts. I have been watching him. He is treading cautiously. You may want to have a talk with Georgiana about the wet shirt incident, however."

Elizabeth cocked her head. "In regard to what?"

"Well… that… she should not have looked at him in the way… that she was… looking at him."

Elizabeth smiled, glad that she was leaning against him and he could not see her amused expression.

He continued. "At least *I* did not have to resort to that sort of thing to entrap your affections."

Elizabeth laughed to herself, thinking of him in his clinging nightshirt. *If you only knew!*

Chapter 26

Darcy and Elizabeth walked arm in arm around the lake at Ambleside in the Lake District. She could barely believe that she had been able to whisk him away from his responsibilities at Pemberley and the deaf school and was now enjoying this hamlet in northern England.

Darcy had contacted an acquaintance of his and arranged for them to stay at an inviting inn with a room that overlooked the lake. As they walked out and enjoyed the beauty of the rolling green hills surrounding it, Elizabeth felt a peace and contentment that she had not known in months.

They ventured off the well worn path that wound its way around the lake and explored a stream that was insistently making its way to the larger body of water. At length they came to a small waterfall, and they sat down beside it, enjoying its playful sound and feeling refreshed by the droplets of water that occasionally sprayed them.

Darcy leaned all the way back and folded his hands behind his head, closing his eyes and basking in the warmth of the sun and in the love of his wife. Elizabeth leaned over as well, letting her head rest upon her husband's chest, content to listen to the sound of his breathing and the beating of his heart.

It was hard to believe that one year had passed since they were married. She reflected on the love she had for him, that, surprisingly enough, was stronger now than it had been then. She smiled as she pondered the man who would occasionally surprise her, constantly challenge her, and passionately love her. That she could be so happy was overwhelming to her.

Jane and Charles had moved into their estate a month ago, and in that short time, the two couples had eased into a routine of seeing each other frequently. Jane's pregnancy was progressing nicely, and with each visit it became exceedingly obvious the state Jane was in, both physically and emotionally. Physically she was getting larger by the day; emotionally she could not be happier.

There was still no sign of an impending child for Elizabeth, and she silently harboured fears that something might be amiss. She had not mentioned her suspicions to her husband and wondered whether he had ever considered that possibility on his own. But then she doubted whether he thought anything about it. That was probably something only a woman would do.

She listened as her husband's breathing changed and she smiled, realizing he had fallen asleep. Their getting away had been intended to allow the two of them some time together alone. They had not had that opportunity since returning from France. She realized it was good for him, as well, to force him to relax and get the needed rest he rarely allowed himself to enjoy.

At length she closed her eyes, but in what seemed like a few moments, she awakened, startled by the sound of grass rustling near by. She slowly lifted up her head and gasped. Standing a few feet away from them were three large sheep, all in a row, looking down at the couple as if they were intruding on their very own piece of land.

Darcy was awakened by Elizabeth's gasp and followed Elizabeth's gaze to the sheep. The three sheep seemed intent on fixing their stares upon Elizabeth and Darcy, until finally he muttered a "Get along now!" and the three sheep slowly turned and walked away.

"I do believe those sheep were not happy with us!" Elizabeth exclaimed. "I had no idea what they would do!"

"Oh, they probably enjoy sneaking up on unsuspecting travellers." Darcy stood up and brushed off his clothes and then reached for Elizabeth's hand to pull her up. "Besides, it is just as well they came by and awakened us. I am famished! How does getting something to eat sound to you?"

"Simply wonderful!" laughed Elizabeth.

Later, when they walked back to the inn, the proprietor handed them a letter which had arrived for them. As they walked into the dining room to get something to eat, Elizabeth opened it. There, on the outside of a folded piece of paper, was written,

I thought I would pass this letter from Lydia along to you. Catherine.

Elizabeth opened it and read the letter.

Dear Lizzy,

This past month I had the baby. It is a little boy and he is named Michael. We are doing fine, however I am still unable to make a visit home to see everyone. My husband has numerous responsibilities that keep him here. If I can, when the baby is a little older, I might try to come home on my own. I understand that Jane is going to have one. I hope she knows what she is getting into! They can keep you frightfully busy. I have not attended one ball in months! But then, Jane would probably prefer taking care of a baby to attending a ball. What about you, Lizzy? Any baby Darcy in sight for you? Well I must be off. Michael is dreadfully upset and will not stop crying. Say hello to Kitty, for me.

Your loving sister, Lydia

Elizabeth looked at the letter in shock. Darcy put his hand over hers as he could detect her agitation.

"I knew it! I just knew it!"

"Knew what?" he gently asked.

Elizabeth looked up at him from the letter. "She was pregnant before she married."

"You do not know that, Lizbeth."

Elizabeth took a deep breath. "But I do know Lydia. The baby came earlier than nine months from her wedding, if there really even was one!"

Darcy shook his head. "Whatever her situation, our concern should be for her and the baby."

Elizabeth shook her head. "That poor little baby boy, being raised by immature Lydia in who knows what conditions." Elizabeth was visibly shaken.

Darcy grasped the hand that his had been resting on. "Elizabeth, is part of this anger because you are not yet with child?"

She looked up at him, shocked. Tears formed in her eyes and Darcy had his answer. He pulled out his handkerchief and gently wiped a tear that rolled down her face. "There is still plenty of time, my love."

"But…" Elizabeth took the handkerchief from his fingers and wiped both her eyes. "I wonder if there is something wrong. It has been a full year! Certainly something should have happened by now."

"It is probably not our time, yet. Try not to despair. These past few months put us both under a great deal of stress. That may have something to do with it. Now…" He picked up the hand he was holding and brought it to his lips, placing a soft kiss on it. "As soon as we finish our meal…" He looked around to ensure no one was close by, and whispered, "I believe we have entertained ourselves outdoors quite sufficiently today. Let us go up to our room and see if we can find some agreeably engaging activity to treat ourselves to. Hmmm?"

She looked at him and smiled. "I should like that very much."

The rest of the week was spent exploring the country on foot and riding out to some of the other lakes. But what they enjoyed most was their refreshing and revitalizing times alone. To Elizabeth it was almost as if they were once again on their honeymoon.

~~*

The long days of summer soon gave way to cooler September ones. Each month Elizabeth awaited the signs that she might be with child; each time she was disappointed, but trusting it would happen sooner or later. Her husband was very attentive to each initial wave of disappointment and encouraged her to be patient.

Jacques and Alice were married in a small, very simple ceremony. The couple remained at Pemberley so Alice could continue on as Georgiana's personal maid, and Jacques made the drive out each day to the school, as that became his main source of responsibility.

That was also the month that David left for Cambridge. Upon leaving, he stopped by Pemberley to again thank Darcy for his generosity, and to hopefully say goodbye to Georgiana. When he arrived, he was brought into the sitting room where Darcy, Elizabeth, and Georgiana joined him.

They talked of simple things, while the bigger things of the heart were left unsaid. Darcy had been told of his desire to work toward being the school administrator, and suggested that when he returned home for summer holidays next year, they would put him to work there helping Fleming out with some of the administrative duties.

He was most grateful and thanked him. After a bit more small talk, he stood up, knowing it was time to leave, and everyone followed suit.

As they walked toward the door, Darcy turned to him. "Mr. Bostwick, there is something we would like to give you. Come with me, Elizabeth." She took his arm and they walked out of the room.

David stood staring at the empty door for a few moments, and then quickly turned to Georgiana. "You know I will miss you, and I will think of you everyday!"

She nodded slowly and whispered, "As I will."

He inhaled deeply and let it out through his teeth. "It will be a long year for me. I hope and pray it passes quickly."

"I will write to you every day."

"You cannot do that! It will displease your brother, and it will only make it harder for me."

"Ah, but I shall… in my journal. I shall write to you each day in my journal, and then when you return, I shall read to you each letter that I wrote."

David smiled. "Then I shall do that as well." They stood in silence, simply content to soak in each other's presence, knowing this would be the last time for a while.

Elizabeth and Darcy returned, with Darcy carrying a leather satchel. "This was very useful to me when I was at Cambridge. It may be several years old, but it is still in excellent condition."

"Thank you, Sir. I appreciate that very much!"

Darcy smiled, and the foursome walked out toward the front door. Elizabeth smiled at the thought that her husband, who did not really need her help to retrieve the satchel, purposely arranged it for the two of them to leave, allowing Georgiana and David a short time together alone.

They walked out, and Darcy, Elizabeth, and Georgiana stopped as David continued on a few steps. He turned back around, looking squarely at Georgiana. "I shall see you next summer, then?"

They all nodded and tears began to form in Georgiana's eyes. David rubbed his hands together, willing himself to remain where he was and not breach the short distance to Georgiana's side and embrace her in a consoling hug. Instead, he reached out his hand and took Darcy's in a firm shake, bowed to the ladies, and taking one last glance at Georgiana, he turned to leave.

~~*

The next few months brought anticipation of a baby for the Bingleys and a wedding for Mary. About a month before Charles and Jane were to set out for Hertfordshire, a baby girl was born to the jubilant couple. Hannah Elizabeth, they were most certain, was the sweetest, most beautiful baby they had ever seen. Charles' smile, which was, on any normal day, ready to burst forth for no apparent reason, now was firmly implanted upon his face. Elizabeth spent much of that first month with Jane, helping her out. Jane was actually very happy that her own mother was busy with wedding plans for Mary and therefore unable to come assist her, as Elizabeth's company was much more preferable.

As the departure drew near to return to Hertfordshire for Mary's wedding, the Darcys and the Bingleys decided they would set out together a week ahead of time. That would allow Elizabeth to help Mary and her mother with all the final preparations. With the baby being barely a month old, extra consideration was taken for their comfort. They all gave Jane strict orders that when they arrived at Longbourn, she was to rest and enjoy the baby, and not feel pressured by anyone to exert herself.

As pleased as everyone was that Mary was getting married, the prospect of this trip caused Catherine to be unusually disheartened, as she and Reverend Kenton had been getting along so well. She was not sure how she would endure the few weeks without him.

The evening before they were to leave, he came by Pemberley, appearing much more nervous than usual. With some finagling done ahead of time between Kenton and the Darcys, he was left alone with Catherine for a short while when they all conveniently left to see to some tasks that needed attending. Coming over to her, and feeling all the nervousness of a young lad asking a young lady for his very first dance, he got down on one knee and asked for her hand in marriage.

Catherine was quite overtaken by this; she had not expected it at all! But despite her surprise, she gladly accepted him. She then discovered, much to her joy, that he planned to ride out to Longbourn in a few days to speak with her father. He would remain the week, attending Mary's wedding, and then return immediately after. The two of them talked of a spring wedding, and both of them agreed that they would want to get married in his church.

The trip to Longbourn was uneventful, yet the anxiety all felt coming toward it was heavy. Netherfield had been let to someone else, and Mrs. Bennet had insisted that the girls and their husbands stay at Longbourn in their old rooms. Georgiana could stay in Lydia's old room, and of course, Catherine had her own.

Elizabeth knew this was not the ideal situation her husband would wish, but she also knew how hurt and irrational her mother would be if they declined. The small lodge at Meryton, and an even smaller inn nearby, were not of the highest quality, so they agreed to the arrangements. Elizabeth hoped she could keep her mother as much out of her husband's way as possible, even though he had previously proven that he could remain cordial in her presence.

When Reverend Kenton arrived, he was pleased to find Mr. Bennet quite accommodating and generous. His meeting with him proved to be agreeable and he was surprised how easily his approval for the marriage was given. Elizabeth made certain her husband was out of the house when Mrs. Bennet was told of her last daughter's engagement and her behaviour was as expected.

Mary's wedding was simple, but very nice. Since meeting Mr. Cardell she had been taking more time with her hair and dress, and along with a countenance that hinted of joy and contentment rather than judgment and censure, she was actually quite pleasant in appearance.

In the week that they resided at Longbourn, Elizabeth could not help but think how draining this must be for her husband, who had to put up with a crowded, noisy household, sleep in a much smaller bed, and be exposed to all the peculiarities of her mother without any chance of getting away... except on their walks. Any chance of intimacy between them was very slim, and it was not until the night after the wedding, when everyone seemed exhausted and desired to turn in early, did Darcy unexpectedly turn on the charm. Elizabeth was quite taken back with his insistence that he could be quiet as a mouse if need be, and, although she felt utterly suspicious that every person in the house could hear the creaking of the bed and would know what activity was taking place, she had no defences against his insistent persuasion. It had been too long!

After the wedding, they remained a few more days. Jane tired very easily, Bingley was eager to return to his home, Darcy was impatient, and Elizabeth could take no more of her mother's incoherent flutterings. In the days after the wedding it increased in intensity, and Elizabeth suddenly realized her mother was likely struggling with the fact that once they left, her house would be empty, except, of course, for her husband. Mrs. Bennet had a difficult time facing that she would, in a sense, be alone.

Mr. Bennet, who religiously sequestered himself in his study and kept to himself, saw little reason to change his behaviour, other than possibly to remain in there for longer spells since his wife would have no one but him to unload her sufferings upon. That made him extremely unsettled, as well.

When it was time to leave, Mrs. Bennet gave an urgent plea for Catherine to remain there.

"Why can you not get married here? It is not right for you to marry in Derbyshire!"

It was a useless point, however. Everyone had pulled together to argue in defence of it, and soon they were on the road, again, bound for Derbyshire.

~~*

Winter was cold and wet, allowing few opportunities to enjoy the grounds of Pemberley. Catherine was mired knee deep with her wedding plans, and Georgiana spent many a quiet, rainy afternoon writing in her special journal designated for her letters to David. Her pages were now filled with all her thoughts and feelings that she would read to him once he returned. Her heart ached for the sight of him, but the hope of seeing him again with her brother's approval allowed for her to endure anything.

As the days of winter slowly lengthened, and spring was teasing them with its coming, Catherine and Reverend Kenton began diligently finalizing plans for the wedding. Catherine wanted Georgiana to stand up for her, and Kenton wanted David Bostwick. That presented a rather complicated predicament, as he was not to see her during this year.

An appeal was made to Darcy, and when all attempts at making some other arrangement failed, Darcy consented to allow it, on the consideration that the only times they were to see each other were in some wedding activity. News of this gave Georgiana much happiness, and as the days drew nearer, she wrote more and more. As the wedding was only a few days away, and knowledge that

David had returned to Derbyshire, she finished writing one complete journal of letters. She decided she would slip it to him to take back with him to Cambridge.

The simple, but sweet wedding went smoothly, and from Darcy's vantage point in the second pew behind Mr. and Mrs. Bennet, he watched as Bostwick's eyes very rarely turned from Georgiana. He seemed a little too eager to extend his arm to her as he walked down the aisle with her when the ceremony was over. But Darcy did not concern himself. He knew that his sister and this young man were very much in love, and although he did not look forward to announcing any forthcoming nuptials to certain members of his family, he knew that now he could accept it.

When the ceremony was over, Georgiana slipped her journal into a coat which she carried on her arm, and before she went to leave, she handed it to him.

He looked at her in amazement. "What is this, Miss Darcy?" he whispered.

"My journal of letters to you."

David's sharp intake of a breath was most noticeable. He looked with deep affection into Georgiana's eyes. "You have no idea how much this means to me. When I am feeling lonely, as I often have this past year, I will open it and read some of your letters."

The leaning of his heart toward Georgiana was clearly reflected in his eyes, and she smiled softly, watching him clutch the journal to his chest.

She looked down, and then looked back up at him. "I am so glad I was able to see you again."

He smiled down at her and whispered. "Me, too, Georgiana, Me, too."

~~*

Now that Catherine was married and gone from Pemberley, Georgiana felt very much alone again. She often visited her in the parsonage, and enjoyed seeing the difference that married life had wrought in her. She was able to support her husband in all his clerical duties and visitations, added the right amount of a woman's touch to the parsonage, and be the loving wife she always wanted to be. She did not have a grand home or fine furnishings that Pemberley had, but she felt she had something more important. She was very grateful she had not allowed herself to be so taken in by her desire for a wealthy husband that it blinded her to the love and goodness that her own husband brought to their marriage.

About two months later, on a day that seemed like any other day, Elizabeth had gone out on an errand, and when she returned, she eagerly sought out her husband. He was in his study, and when she appeared at his door he was entranced by the look upon her face. The joy that exuded from it was almost contagious.

"What is it, dearest Lizbeth?"

"I have something to tell you."

He began to walk toward her, but was interrupted by Mrs. Reynolds. "Mr. Darcy, there is a gentleman here to see Mr. Bostwick. He says it is urgent and it concerns his son, David."

Darcy looked at Elizabeth and said, "Wait here, Elizabeth."

He rushed to the door and met the gentleman. "I am Fitzwilliam Darcy. You need to see Mr. Bostwick?"

"Yes, Sir, it is of a rather urgent nature. Do you know where I can find him?"

Darcy stepped outside and had the man follow him. "I believe they have been working down by the lake." For some reason, Darcy's heart was pounding, and the only thing he could think was that if anything had happened to David, he was sure his sister would not be able to bear up underneath it.

Elizabeth waited in his study, feeling that the news she was about to give her husband was the best news she could ever fathom. She paced the floor as she waited for him to return. She looked out the window, but could not see where he went. Finally, after what seemed an eternity, Darcy walked into the room.

The expression and pallor of his face hinted at some distressing news. He walked to his desk and sat down. She studied him with nervous apprehension, wondering whether she would need to sit down, as well.

"Will, you look as if someone has died! Tell me please, what has happened?"

He looked slowly up to her. "Someone has died."

Elizabeth's heart caught in her throat and felt a sudden burst of dread run through her. "Who?"

"Mr. Carson, the gentleman David Bostwick had been taking to deaf classes."

Elizabeth thought she would faint. She wanted to laugh in relief, but knew that would be highly inappropriate considering the circumstances. If only he knew how close her heart had come to stop beating, thinking he was about to tell her it was David who died.

"Will, I am so sorry to hear that, but you look as though you are in shock. Is there something else?"

Darcy rested his elbows on the table and brought up his hand to rub his chin. "It seems that quite a few years ago, Mr. Carson inherited Kittridge Manor from a distant uncle."

"Is that not the small estate we looked at that was for sale?"

"The very one. Carson was very settled and happy in his small home, and never had any intention of picking up and moving to what he considered would be a menagerie of unused rooms. So all these years he has let it out, putting away the profits from its rent."

Elizabeth listened attentively. "Apparently, David Bostwick, in his association with Mr. Carson, told him of his regard for Georgiana, and the barrier that existed partly because of me and the difference in their stations in life." Darcy paused, and looked up to his wife. "Carson originally had intended to try to sell Kittridge, but as a result of hearing about Bostwick and Georgiana, Carson made the decision to keep it and bequeath it to Bostwick in his will because of the care and concern he always showed him."

Elizabeth's eyes widened as she heard this news. "Mr. Bostwick is to inherit Kittridge Manor?"

"Yes. And I believe, as well, that it was Mr. Carson who contributed most of the funds given for the deaf school. All these years Carson has lived as a man with little or no money, and he actually was one of the wealthiest around."

Now Elizabeth knew she must sit down and Darcy continued.

"Recently Mr. Carson has been ill. The doctors told him he would probably not live out the year. He never told anyone. It was nothing that affected him physically. But he has lived this past year most grateful to Bostwick for his genuine concern for him. Carson had no immediate family and decided this was what he wanted to do for him."

"My word!" Elizabeth was speechless.

Darcy looked at Elizabeth. "In the matter of a few moments, Mr. Bostwick goes from being practically penniless to now being worth about six thousand a year!"

"My word!" Elizabeth repeated louder.

Darcy turned to Elizabeth. "Now, my dear. When you came in here earlier, you had something to tell me?"

Elizabeth shook her head in surprise that she had completely forgotten. "It seems as though this is a day of bearing surprising news." Her eyes sparkled like they never had before. "We are going to have a baby!"

~~*

When Georgiana was told about Mr. Carson and David's inheritance of Kittridge Manor, she was hesitant in fully comprehending it. Her feelings within first demanded that she grieve for Mr. Carson. She felt heartbroken that none of them knew the extent of his illness, and overwhelmed at his generosity and selflessness in the midst of his illness. Tears began to fall freely down her face, as she thought of how he must have gone through this all alone, never telling a soul.

Elizabeth listened in awe as this young lady's concern was more toward the gentleman who had died, than on what his gift would mean for her and David Bostwick.

While in class the next day, David Bostwick was summoned to the offices. When he arrived, he saw his father sitting there, and at once, knew there must be something wrong. A look of dread passed over his face, and his father raised his hand to assure him. "My boy, everyone in the family is fine, Miss Darcy is fine. But I do have some news to pass along to you."

When his father told him about Mr. Carson's death and his bequeath, he was rendered incoherent. To think that he had just received an unthinkable gift from a man he had not even known was sick. He berated himself for his lack of discernment. If he had truly been a good friend, he would certainly have realized it.

His father assured him that Mr. Carson considered him one of his closest friends, and appreciated all he had done for him.

"But certainly I could have done more!"

"David, Mr. Carson believed you did more than anyone else ever did!" As David took this all in, he leaned back into the chair in which he was sitting and could not utter a word. To have such devastating news followed by unbelievably agreeable news was taking its toll on him.

That night, after his father had left, David sat in his room, contemplating all he had been told. He read through Georgiana's journal, as he had several times already. Lately he had been reading her letters with the conviction that it would be years before he could offer her anything substantial, and he wondered how she would truly like living in a small home, having few or no servants, and a husband who needed to be away at work all day to help put food on the table.

Now he was faced with the humbling fact that a man whom he had always assumed had very little, had just changed his life around, and he could not even thank him! It was hard for him to calculate what it actually would mean, although he was determined not to let it change him. He was going to school with the hopes of being the administrator of the deaf school, and that was something he resolved he would not give up.

Epilogue

Georgiana, being the naturally shy young lady that she was, would not necessarily want all the details of her courtship with David Bostwick, every kiss, every embrace, and every affectionate touch to be recorded for all eyes to see. Suffice it to say, that when the school term ended, and David's performance at Cambridge passed Darcy's strict scrutiny, David approached his former adversary with his intentions, seeking to court his younger sister.

When Darcy gave him his ardent approval, David was overjoyed. He wondered whether it would have been as easy as it had been if it were not for his suddenly being the Master of Kittridge Manor. The magnitude of that still seemed foreign to him.

When he returned from school he walked through the great house, hardly believing it was his. He had never visited Kittridge Manor before, so he had not been able to fathom exactly what it was that now belonged to him.

In addition to the home, there were some properties along with it that would provide him with a consistent income. As soon as he had secured permission to court Georgiana, the two of them began talking of marriage. As he wanted to continue his education, they determined it would be best to put off marriage until the following summer, after the next school year ended.

David went off to school again in the fall, but this time with eager expectations of receiving letters from Georgiana, and looking forward to an occasional visit to see her.

Elizabeth's baby was due in November. Georgiana and Elizabeth spent much time getting ready for this event, and finally, when the time came, Darcy and Elizabeth were blessed with a little baby boy, whom they named Thomas Fitzwilliam Darcy. He was a little over a year younger than his cousin Hannah Bingley, who enjoyed her new baby cousin immensely.

Soon after the baby was born, a letter was received from Lydia, stating that her husband had died, and that she planned to return to Longbourn with her little boy. Elizabeth was quite distressed with the prospect that little boy was being raised by a very immature mother, and a senseless and often irresponsible grandmother. Elizabeth felt she was too far away to be able to do anything about it, and kept her anger and her suspicions to herself that Lydia had really never been married. She hoped Lydia's return home with the baby would give her mother a renewed sense of purpose.

The year at Cambridge passed much more quickly, and before they knew it, summer was approaching. When David returned home, he went to Darcy again, this time with the intent to ask for Georgiana's hand. He was given strong approval. Darcy even assured him that if he had come without any prospect of fortune, he would have received the same answer.

Darcy and Elizabeth both agreed that the past year had done wonders for Georgiana, as she had matured that much more to make her a little more prepared to be a wife. The wedding was settled upon to be at the end of summer, and David would return with Georgiana for his last year at Cambridge.

In no time, wedding plans were being finalized and announcements were sent out. Lady Catherine was greatly pleased that her niece was marrying the Master of Kittridge Manor. It sounded so grand, and she gave her blessing heartily, even though he did not seem to be someone that anyone from the "ton" knew anything about.

The wedding took place on a lovely summer day. The bride looked radiantly beautiful, and everyone commented on what a nice looking couple they made, and how fortunate it was that Mr. Bostwick had come into possession of such an unexpected gift. Many reasoned that Darcy would have never allowed the wedding if that had not happened, but a few wise, knowing people believed otherwise. Acquiring Kittridge Manor was a little piece of good fortune that made it easier to deal with all the ramifications of such an unequal marriage.

After the wedding they moved into the moderate estate and began making it their own. Both David and Georgiana had simple tastes, and decorated it without any lavish expenditure.

His interest in the deaf school remained and he continued doing the administrative duties even though his finances now eliminated the necessity to continue. Georgiana continued to help out in the classes as well.

Darcy and Elizabeth were typical parents who were very proud of their little boy and becoming a father actually brought out some rather humorous traits in the man. To see him on the floor with their son making funny noises and playing peek-a-boo was quite entertaining to Elizabeth and little Thomas, as well.

At length, Mr. Bennet became more and more concerned about the welfare of Lydia's son. When the boy was old enough, Mr. Bennet made frequent trips to Pemberley with his grandson, and from what Elizabeth could determine, he made every effort to be the main source of love, care, and discipline he needed.

Mrs. Bennet did not have to worry about Mr. Collins ever taking Longbourn from her. She died before Mr. Bennet, and by that time, Lydia was away from the house so often, leaving Michael with her father, that Mr. Bennet gave up Longbourn and moved to Pemberley permanently with the little boy. Elizabeth saw the amount of stress that taking care of him was on her father, and they began making arrangements for her and Darcy to become guardians of him.

Elizabeth had two more children, and they enjoyed growing up so closely with their six Bingley cousins, their three Kenton cousins, and after a while, their three Bostwick cousins. Mary and her husband had eight children, and they eventually moved to the county of Derbyshire, as well. Lady Catherine never discovered the truth about her niece's husband and how he acquired his wealth, and she died before it was ever made known to her.

David and Georgiana were looked upon by everyone that knew them in Derbyshire as a very caring couple. Coming into the wealth as he did never changed David, and the couple took an active interest in those around them who were not as well off as they were. Their home was generously opened to anyone needing it, and they treated the few servants they employed with a great deal of respect. They would quietly go into London, and when they did, they stayed at Darcy's townhome. They enjoyed the concerts and theatre, but declined any invitations from those in the first circles of society. Their hearts were so very tied to Kittridge Manor in Derbyshire and the school for the deaf and they spent most of their time there.

Georgiana loved her home, even though it was considerably smaller than Pemberley. She especially loved the sunroom that had brought her much enjoyment when visiting there as a child. Another special adornment in their home, which they put in their bedroom, was the wedding gift Darcy and Elizabeth had given them.

The day before the wedding, Darcy and Elizabeth had some time alone with David and Georgiana, and presented them with a nicely wrapped box. They opened it to find a crystal candelabrum with eight prisms hanging from the sides.

"Why this is almost like the one you have!" exclaimed Georgiana.

"We sent for it from Paris, from the same shop we bought ours," explained Elizabeth.

Georgiana turned to David. "When the sun comes up in the morning and hits the prisms, the room is filled with tiny rainbows! When we wake up in the morning, that is what will greet us!"

Suddenly, the thought of what Georgiana spoke caused a little embarrassment on her part, and she looked down, blushing. David smiled at the image that came to his mind.

Elizabeth explained the significance of the prism. "At the hotel we stayed at in Paris, there was a very large chandelier which had hundreds of prisms hanging from it. When the sun came up in the morning, rainbows were reflected all around us. Will surprised me and bought me the small candelabrum as a gift to remember that by."

She looked up at Darcy, and then back to the couple. "When I realized how the two of you felt for one another, I took one of the prisms to Will and told him that I thought the prism was like you, Georgiana, and that the rainbows that were reflected from it were the special traits of your personality that only Mr. Bostwick brought out. I told Will that he was the sunshine to your prism."

David and Georgiana looked at each other and smiled. "It is very true, Elizabeth," said Georgiana. "When in his presence, I felt different; I acted differently. I did not know how to make everyone realize that no matter how little his fortune, no matter his station in life, he was the one who brought out the very best in me."

And the very best man for her he proved himself to be. That a mere under-gardener could win the heart of Miss Georgiana Darcy and indeed be the best man for her is something that many likely found difficult to grasp. But earning the respect and acceptance of Fitzwilliam Darcy had been an even greater obstacle for him to overcome. He did it, however, most admirably, not owing any of it to fortune, connections, or standing in society. He did it all of his own merit and whole-hearted devotion to the young lady who had captured his heart when they were mere children.

The End

Kara Louise lives in Kansas with her husband.
They share their 10 acres with
an ever changing menagerie of animals.
They have one married son who also likes to write.

Other published books by Kara Louise

"Drive and Determination"

"Pemberley's Promise"

"Master Under Good Regulation"

and

"Assumed Engagement"

Visit her website, www.ahhhs.net

where you will find a variety of stories

written by her and Australian author, Sharni.